## Special thanks to the following people for breathing life into the Godsverse when I thought its light had been blown out:

Katrina Roets, Pat Shand, Starr, Ernie Sawyer, I'm a Ninja, Logan Waterman, Matthew Johnson, Gary Phillips, Ramsey Church, Phil, Melissa Hooper, Jean Lau, Eric P. Kurniawan, Peter Anders, Collin David, Nikres. Joshua Bowers, Jeff Lewis, Emerson Kasak, Linda Robinson, Susan Faw, Talinda Willard, Courtney Cannon, Dave Baxter, old_fogey@yahoo com, Nick Smith, Charlotte Organ, Chad Bowden, Jason Crase, John L Vogt, Philip R. Burns. Bloodfists, Death's Head Studio, LLC, Daniel Groves, Rodney Bonner. JF weber, Walter Weiss, Mitch Fittler, Stacey Henline. Stephanie, Kathy Ash, Charlotte Ulla Pleym, Ray, Jason Schroeder, Chris Call, Maximilian Lippl, Andrew Rees, Tawnly Pranger, Minarkhaios, Vincent Fung, Dave Kochbeck, and Bob Jacobs.

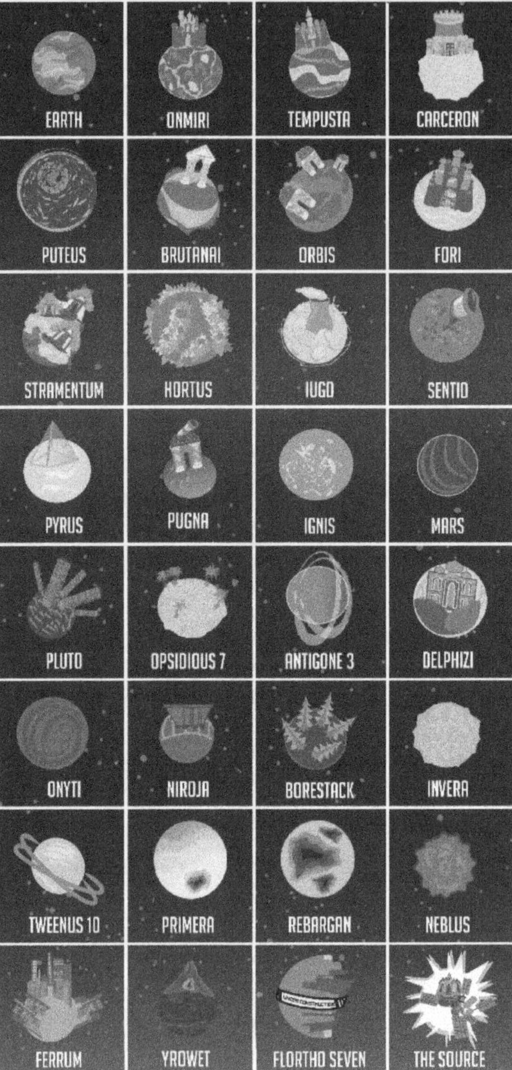

GODSVERSE PLANETS
EARTH
ONMIRI
TEMPUSTA
CARCERON
PUTEUS
BRUTANAI
ORBIS
FORI
STRAMENTUM
HORTUS
IUGO
SENTIO
PYRUS
PUGNA
IGNIS
MARS
PLUTO
OPSIDIOUS 7
ANTIGONE 3
DELPHIZI
ONYTI
NIROJA
BORESTACK
INVERA
TWEENUS 10
PRIMERA
REBARGAN
NEBLUS
FERRUM
YROWET
FLORTHO SEVEN
THE SOURCE

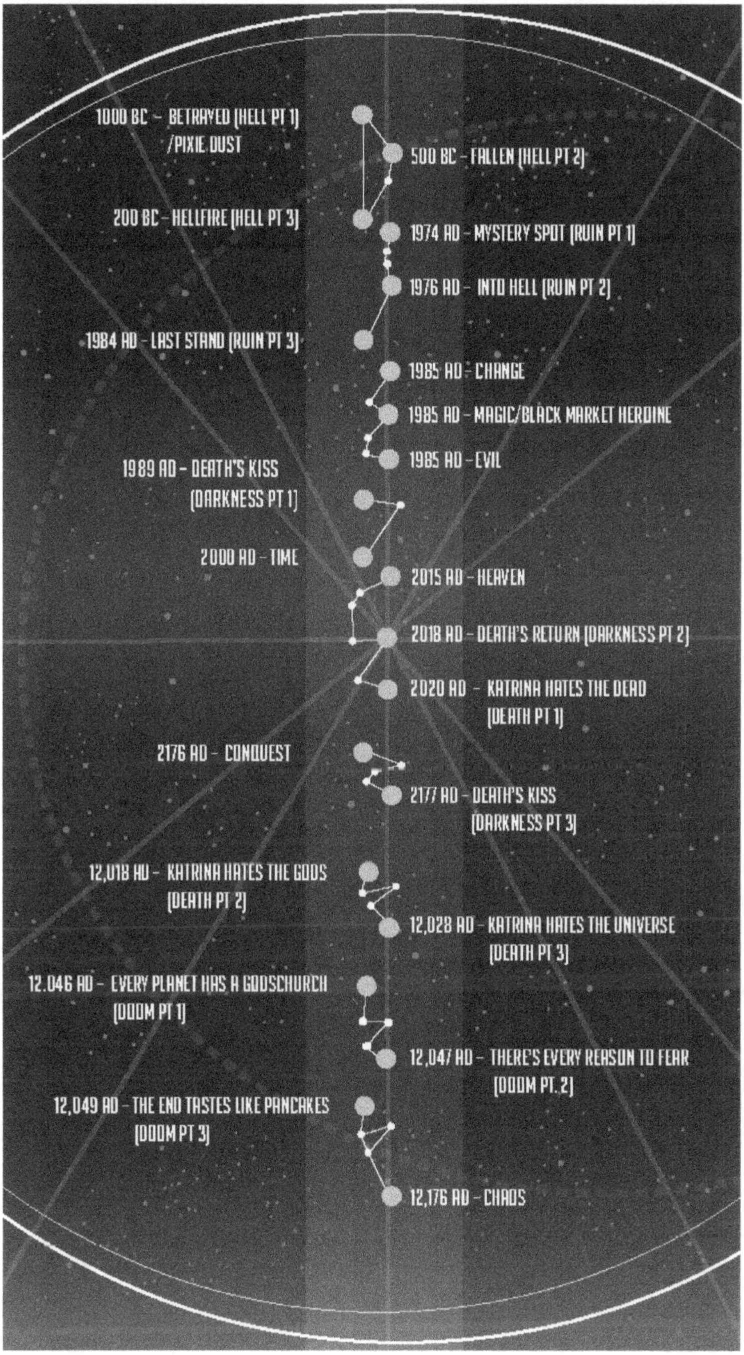

1000 BC – BETRAYED (HELL PT 1) /PIXIE DUST
500 BC – FALLEN (HELL PT 2)
200 BC – HELLFIRE (HELL PT 3)
1974 AD – MYSTERY SPOT (RUIN PT 1)
1976 AD – INTO HELL (RUIN PT 2)
1984 AD – LAST STAND (RUIN PT 3)
1985 AD – CHANGE
1985 AD – MAGIC/BLACK MARKET HEROINE
1985 AD – EVIL
1989 AD – DEATH'S KISS (DARKNESS PT 1)
2000 AD – TIME
2015 AD – HEAVEN
2018 AD – DEATH'S RETURN (DARKNESS PT 2)
2020 AD – KATRINA HATES THE DEAD (DEATH PT 1)
2176 AD – CONQUEST
2177 AD – DEATH'S KISS (DARKNESS PT 3)
12,018 AD – KATRINA HATES THE GODS (DEATH PT 2)
12,028 AD – KATRINA HATES THE UNIVERSE (DEATH PT 3)
12,046 AD – EVERY PLANET HAS A GODSCHURCH (DOOM PT 1)
12,047 AD – THERE'S EVERY REASON TO FEAR (DOOM PT 2)
12,049 AD – THE END TASTES LIKE PANCAKES (DOOM PT 3)
12,176 AD – CHAOS

# ALSO BY RUSSELL NOHELTY

**NOVELS**
My Father Didn't Kill Himself
Sorry for Existing
Gumshoes: The Case of Madison's Father
Invasion
The Vessel
The Void Calls Us Home
Worst Thing in the Universe
Anna and the Dark Place
The Marked Ones
The Dragon Scourge
The Dragon Champion
The Dragon Goddess
The Obsidian Spindle Saga

**COMICS and OTHER ILLUSTRATED WORK**
The Little Bird and the Little Worm
Ichabod Jones: Monster Hunter
Gherkin Boy
How NOT to Invade Earth

**www.russellnohelty.com**

# HELL

*Book 7 of The Godsverse Chronicles*

By:
Russell Nohelty

Edited by:
Leah Lederman

Proofread by:
Katrina Roets & Toni Cox

Cover by:
Paramita Bhattacharjee

Planet chart and timeline design by:
Andrea Rosales

# BOOK 1

*"Betrayed"*

# CHAPTER 1

"Then I ripped his leg off and beat him to death with it!" A fat, square-jawed ogre shouted to his monstrous friends.

They were all drinking ale inside the tavern they had occupied for the last ten days and nights. The innkeeper paced back and forth, a tall, lanky man with dark bags under his eyes. His body twitched with every word from the horde's mouth.

I had been eyeing them closely the whole of the night. Over the past few months, King Odgeir had sent a dozen of his best men to deal with Bjarngimur's monsters and expel them from the tavern, and twelve times all that made it back to the king were the heads of his soldiers, eyes cut from their skulls.

That would not happen a thirteenth time. The people of Odgeir's kingdom would not have to endure the tyranny of this menace for one more night. That was why the king's herald summoned me in the dark of night to deal with them. I never failed.

"Ha! That's a great story!" an orc shouted back. It was green-skinned and sported a mohawk down its lumpy head. I enjoyed killing all manner of vile beasts that strayed beyond the Veil, but orcs were my absolute favorite.

An orc was responsible for killing my father before I was born, so I had no love lost for them. I was only a few days old when a troll killed my mother. I had never met either of my parents, yet the memory of their deaths haunted me every day of my life. It was the reason I became the best monster hunter in King Odgeir's kingdom.

"Human!" a fiery-haired goblin shouted. "More ale! And be quick about it!"

The knock-kneed innkeeper shot straight up to full attention before spinning on his heels and hurrying to the spigot. He poured the ale into thick, metal steins and placed them on a wooden tray.

I counted twenty of Bjarngimur's men lining the wooden tables that stretched from one end of the tavern to the other. Bjarngimur and his monsters had menaced the countryside for years, but they usually disappeared into the trees before anyone could catch them. This was their boldest attack yet, and it would be their last after I was done with them.

Before Bjarngimur's monsters invaded, the tavern was quaint, sleepy even. I often drank there on my way through the deep forest. It was not so sleepy today, though, not with ogres, orcs, and goblins running amok. I would return it that way, in short measure.

"Don't be so scared, human," the fiery-haired goblin said with a fiendish grin. "I won't hurt you or your family unless you spill my ale, of course. Do that, and I'll cut off your kid's pretty, little face and feed it to you!"

The tavern burst with laughter. That kind of heartless cruelty was to be expected from monster kind, and it was what I was hired to stop. And I was a pixie, one of the fairy folk, which meant I was a monster, just like them. I might not look like a monster, but people lumped us into the same category. If you weren't a human, you were a monster. It was my greatest advantage and greatest burden all at once.

To catch a monster, you need a monster.

That's what King Odgeir had said to me ever since I started hunting monsters for his kingdom, back when he was just a prince, and his father, King Odgeir I, sat on the throne. Technically, my brother was King Odgeir II, but he hated to be called that. He never liked not being the first in anything.

After monsters slayed my parents when I was a baby, the royal family took me in. They should have left me for the wolves. They should have burned me at the stake, but they didn't. They kept me and raised me. I had been repaying that debt – gladly – ever since I could fend for myself.

The innkeeper stepped carefully to avoid spilling a single drop of the beer. I could tell by the fear in his eyes he fully understood the goblin would cut off his child's face. From the timbre of the monster's voice, I knew he meant it as well. That was the kind of thing monsters did, after all. They were callous, cruel, and mean.

"Hurry up!" the goblin shouted.

A visible shiver went up the man's spine, but he didn't spill a drop. He took another deliberate step forward and let out a deep sigh. In front of him, a short, fat orc with a pocked face chuckled to himself and stuck out his leg as the innkeeper went past.

The beers flew into the air and rained down on the monsters in the hall. Several of them stood from their seats and grabbed their weapons, but the goblin hopped onto a long bench and held up his arms.

"Wait!" the goblin shouted. "Don't be so hasty. I claimed this one fair and square. Go back to your drinks, boys."

The monsters grumbled and wiped themselves off before returning to their beers, annoyed and soggy. There was honor amongst thieves and monsters as well—though the code of ethics monsters followed was not one I'd call based on honor.

"That wasn't very nice," the goblin said, sauntering toward the innkeeper. I had been crouched in the bushes, waiting for the right time to strike, but I feared I didn't have time to wait any longer. "I thought I asked you not to spill my drink."

"Well…I…" the innkeeper stammered, turning back to see his wife and child huddled in the far end of the room. His wife had big, round, beautiful brown eyes. She ran her rough hands through their child's curly hair. "Please, don't hurt them."

"I warned you!" The goblin lunged forward. "But since you asked so nicely, I won't hurt your kid. I'll just kill you instead."

Another goblin piped up, "I want the kid, then!"

"Be my guest," the red-haired goblin said with a smile. He held a knife against the innkeeper's face. "I'll take care of you once you watch your kid get gutted."

"Please don't," the innkeeper sobbed, struggling to break free. He couldn't. Monsters were much stronger than humans, which gave them an unfair advantage in any fight. The only advantage that humans had was me, their secret weapon.

I couldn't hide in the bushes any longer. I wanted to wait until the crowd of monsters thinned out, but I would have to take my chances fighting against all of them. I would gain nothing from stealth. Frankly, I preferred a clean fight out in the open to hiding in the bushes. Most rangers didn't and relied instead on their bow, but I enjoyed watching the life drain from a monster's eyes. Up close.

"Don't squirm, human!" the goblin shouted as I sprinted toward the door. "Just enjoy the show!"

"Remember," the second goblin said, inching toward the little boy and his mother. "Your father's failure is what brought this on, not—"

I kicked open the door and flung a throwing dagger through the air. It whizzed past the monsters with deadly precision, borne from decades of practice, and embedded into the back of the encroaching goblin, who fell to the ground at the feet of the mother and her child.

"You're beyond the Veil, monsters." I lowered my voice as I stood at the front door of the tavern.

An ogre turned to me, and its eyes narrowed. "It's the pixie!"

I might have been as much a monster as they were, but I was nothing like them. They lived in the muck and the mire. They killed for fun, pillaged for sport. Unlike them, I chose the side of righteousness and defended humanity from their hatred.

"Ylfingur has a price on your head, pixie," a goblin with a protruding forehead growled at me.

"There is one on yours as well," I replied. "The king does not take kindly to monsters in his kingdom. Take me to Bjarngimur, and I won't collect on them, as long as you leave this place and return beyond the Veil, never to return."

King Odgeir's father, King Odgeir I, had established the Veil as a safe haven for monsters, where they could live their miserable lives for as long as they were able, without being hunted by humans. It was a magnanimous offer from the king, whose ancestors had battled with monster hordes for generations.

King Odgeir I could have wiped monsters from the world for good but instead chose to end the bloodshed and come to peace with them, as long as they left us alone. It worked for a while, but lately, more and more monsters were emboldened to cross the Veil and attack humans.

"You're outnumbered twenty to one," a pudgy orc said.

"Yes," I replied. "And I have beaten worse odds than that. In fact, I hardly think it a fair fight. You don't stand a chance."

"You won't beat those odds today!" An orc with a spiked, leather pauldron raised its club and shouted, "Get her, boys!"

The key to fighting a group of monsters was knowing that they were impulsive and irrational. They did not coordinate with each other, and their movements were sloppy. They'd knock into each other like stooges. It was just a matter of biding your time and letting them do your work for you.

However, I didn't have a lot of time, so I pulled out two ivory-handled daggers and threw them through the eyes of the closest attacking monsters. They fell to the ground in a heap as one of their orc brethren ran at me with a knife. I sprinted forward, dodging his swipe, and stuck him in the gut with one of my daggers.

I spun around to face the monsters creeping toward me. "Where is Bjarngimur?" I shouted. "This is your last chance."

The monsters laughed. They would have had the upper hand in any other situation, but they had never met me before or seen me use my pixie dust. Most monsters who have met me fell under my blade; few lived to tell the tale. Maybe they'd heard of the golden-winged fairy who could disappear in a puff of purple smoke, but I had never met a monster who believed the whispers about me. Much to their detriment, of course. The stories were all true.

I took off my cloak and tossed it across the room. I unfurled my hidden wings, which lit up my face with a faint glow.

"What're you gonna do?" A yellow-skinned orc with rotten teeth chuckled. "Fly away?"

"No."

Without another word, I reached into a blue pouch with stars on it that I kept held tightly around my waist. I pulled out a pinch of what looked like pink, shimmering, rock salt, the fine crystals just big enough to not fall through my fingers. This was my pixie dust, the magical powder that let me disappear in a puff of smoke.

Clenching a fistful of the dust, I raised my hand high in the air, then hurled the dust onto the ground. With a puff of purple smoke, I disappeared from the bar and reappeared in the middle of the monster pack, stabbing two of them through the throat before I dropped another handful of dust and disappeared again. This time I reappeared by the front door, where I ripped the sword from a goblin's hand and used it to cut him in half.

"Where is Bjarngimur?"

A massive ogre with rippling muscles swung a two-handed broadsword at me. I leaped backward into the air to avoid it. When the ogre swung again, I dodged it easily, then wheeled on him and cut him from navel to sternum with my dagger. I kicked him back into his friends.

"Tell me now!" I vanished again and reappeared to slit the neck of an encroaching orc. "And I will end you quickly!"

I disappeared to dodge the club of another ogre. When I rematerialized, I roundhouse kicked him into the wall and stuck two daggers through his chest.

"Refuse, and you will suffer greatly." I landed on the top of the bar. "Now, where is Bjarngimur?"

The ground rumbled beneath me. Something was approaching, and it was massive. In another moment, a hulking figure smashed through the door. A behemoth Cyclops towered over me and roared, his great, red eye staring at me with fury and rage. Smoke billowed from his nose, where a bull ring dangled. Two huge fangs protruded from his bottom lip, and when he opened his mouth to growl at me, I saw three rows of spiky teeth.

"I am Bjarngimur!" The Cyclops raised his massive, spiked club, the size of an oak tree, into the air. "And you will die, pixie!"

The huge lug must have expected me to be intimidated by his huge frame and deep, booming voice, but I had vanquished worse than him dozens of times in my life.

"Tell your men to leave, and I will spare them," I replied, floating down from the bar. "My quarrel is with you."

"Never!" Bjarngimur glared at me. "Attack!"

Half a dozen of his men still lived, and they ran toward me at his command. I dropped a pinch of pixie dust and disappeared behind their ranks, stabbing one in the brain before taking its sword and using it to stab another one in the gut.

Bjarngimur was strong, but he was lumbering. He didn't have a good turning radius. When I disappeared again, he couldn't stop himself or recalibrate his position, which sent him crashing into the wall of the tavern.

I reappeared between two orcs and stabbed them both through the ears with my ivory-handled daggers. They fell on either side of me. All that was left was the red-headed goblin, cowering before me, as frightened as he had made the innkeeper just a few minutes before.

"Leave this place," I said. "Tell everyone what you saw here. Never step beyond the Veil again."

The goblin didn't hesitate. He sprinted out of the hole Bjarngimur made in the wall and disappeared into the woods behind the tavern. He would not be back, at least not for a long time. Maybe I should have killed him, but I needed enough tales of my deeds to spread through the monster realm that they would never dream of stepping beyond the Veil again.

"Akta of the Forest," Bjarngimur shouted. "We have unfinished business."

I turned to see Bjarngimur smashing his hands together, growling. The great Cyclops lunged and swiped at me with his club, and I flew backward to avoid him.

"You are slow and dumb," I said to him. "Just like all the others."

His anger bubbled over into rage, and he swung his club wildly at me. The biggest ones were always the sloppiest, relying on their great strength to save them. It never does, at least not when I was involved. If I weren't so quick on my feet, I would have likely succumbed to one of Bjarngimur's blows. However, his brute force could never match my skill and determination.

I waited for Bjarngimur to lift his club over his head, so I could get a clear shot at his eye. The small tavern could not take much more abuse before it collapsed upon itself, and I couldn't let that happen.

Finally, the Cyclops lifted his arm. His club slammed down upon the ground with a great, thunderous crash, and I floated back again to avoid it. There was only an instant before Bjarngimur picked up his club again, and I had to capitalize on it. I only had one shot at his eye, the only place on a Cyclops that wasn't covered in a hardened, impenetrable skin.

I flung my dagger through the air just as Bjarngimur looked up. He didn't even have time to flinch before the dagger lodged into his eye, and he collapsed on the ground, dead.

"The biggest always fall the hardest," I said, walking up to Bjarngimur's dead body. The king demanded proof of my success in the form of the Cyclops' head. It was a messy business but using a broadsword I pulled from an orc's belly, I severed Bjarngimur's head after several chops.

When it was all over, I made my way toward the door, dragging the head behind me. I looked through the debris for my cloak along the way, and that's when I saw the innkeeper and his family huddled in the corner, shaking with fear.

"It's okay," I said. "They will never bother you again."

"Th-th-thank you," he stuttered. "How can we ever repay you?"

"The king is very kind to me." I picked up my cloak from where I'd flung it on the floor. "I apologize for the mess. The gold, weapons, and armor should be more than enough to cover the damages and live the rest of your life in peace."

# CHAPTER 2

Hogarth's caravan rolled through the woods every evening, carrying food and water from the countryside into the city. It was a favorite target of bandits, especially monstrous ones, so half a dozen guards protected the caravan at all times. Hogarth was kind and gave me a ride whenever I needed it.

"It's a nice evening," he said from the front of the caravan. He pulled the reins of his horse slightly to make her slow down. Cherry liked to strain ahead, even in her old age, but Hogarth was happy to ride leisurely through the woods, ensuring that everything made it safely to its destination.

"It is at that," I replied, pulling my cloak hood up over my head. "A bit cold, though."

Hogarth nodded. "It's getting to be fall soon, then winter after that."

"That is how the seasons go, my friend."

"Predictable," he said. "Just how I like it."

I could have transported myself to town in an instant using my pixie dust, but I enjoyed the slow, plodding progress of a horse-drawn carriage. It yoked me to the earth and reminded me how privileged I was to vanish in an instant and reappear a thousand miles away.

That was not the only reason, though. I started traveling by horseback long ago, even though I could easily fly because me being a pixie scared a whole lot of people. In the end, I was a monster, even though I looked human, and seeing me fly around and then disappear without a trace…it frightened folks. King Odgeir thought it would be better if I blended in as much as possible to avoid terrifying his wards, to avoid reminding them that their greatest savior was a monster.

The citizens of Odgeir's kingdom were nice, but they were fearful as well. They didn't like things that were different from them. My skin was already darker than theirs, and my ears longer. Flying over them would push them past their breaking point.

I mostly liked to travel by foot or horseback, so people could see I was on their side and not a monster like the others. Odgeir called it "public relations", but I just wanted people not to hate me. Most of my life was about convincing people not to hate or fear me.

It would have been so easy for them to hate me like they hated the other monsters, but they were all so kind and let me into their lives. I like to think that was because I made sure to meet and greet them as much as possible. I walked among them. I bought from their shops. People saw me more than they saw the king. Despite the fact that I lived in the castle with him, I wanted people to know I was one of them, even if I looked different.

So, I decided not to show my wings unless it was essential. I still wasn't sure exactly how they worked, even after all these years, but my wings could appear like magic when needed and disappear just as quickly when I didn't want to cause a scene.

That was usually the case—I didn't like to draw attention to myself. Even though I had killed over a hundred monsters in my twenty-six years, most of my life was filled with the banality of everyday existence, just like everyone else. On those days, it was nice to blend into the scenery to avoid being gawked at, or worse, threatened.

Yes, sometimes a new monster hunter, trying to make a name for themselves, would threaten me. The people of King Odgeir's kingdom loved me, and they kept me safe from those attacks.

"Did he put up much of a fight?" Hogarth asked.

"Excuse me?"

"The head, sitting next to you, oozing on my wagon. Did he put up much of a fight?"

"Oh," I replied. I had been lost in thought and forgotten that Bjarngimur's head sat next to me. "No more than usual."

"How is the king these days?" Hogarth asked.

"Regal," I replied curtly.

I didn't like speaking about my brother's business, as it was his own and not mine. At one time, we walked the streets of the capital together, cavorting with the townsfolks. He was the first to introduce me to his people, and I owed him a great debt. That seemed like a lifetime ago, now.

On the day of his coronation, he stopped being my adopted brother and started his life as the king of his people. On that day, we stopped spending time together. He stopped laughing. He didn't call on me unless it was to give me a mission. The only other time I saw him was when I returned with news of my conquest.

I wasn't sure why King Odgeir I adopted me when I was a baby. I liked to think it was because I was so young, and he was kind. However, it's hard to believe that he didn't see the potential in my pixie lineage for something greater, something he could mold to a higher purpose, just as he had his son. His son would become a great king under his guidance, and I would become a great monster hunter under the tutelage of his greatest knight, Sir Cleybourne. The two of us, working together, could offer his people lasting peace.

His whole life, my father was consumed by his pursuit of peace. He had only known war, and he worked relentlessly to end it. I wished my brother felt the same way, but our troops had fought six wars since he took over and always seemed on the go. He was never satiated with the size of his land or the scope of his power.

"I didn't mean to pry," Hogarth said.

"No," I replied. "I'm sorry. It has been a very long day, and you are very kind to offer me a ride."

"It's my pleasure, my lady. Having you in my caravan means I don't have to worry about marauders or monsters, at least for a night."

"Well, I appreciate it," I said. "The truth is, I'm not sure how my brother fares these days. He spends most of his days locked in the tower and most of his nights huddled away with his generals. I haven't had a chance to see him in weeks."

"Planning something, is he?"

"I'm not sure," I said, smiling. "I don't really care about any of that. I am excited to bring this home to him, though, because it guarantees me an audience with his majesty. This Cyclops terrorized his countryside for far too long."

"He sure did," Hogarth said. "I look forward to the peace…while it lasts."

"It will last as long as I draw breath."

"We both know that's not true," Hogarth said. "Soon, another will band together the monsters from the Veil, and they will be back."

"Then I will be ready for them, friend. We all will be ready for them."

*

By the time the sun crested over the horizon, Hogarth's caravan was nearly at the walls of Odgeir's castle fortress. A one-hundred-foot-high wall spanned the outer perimeter of the city, which could keep out most any monster. Once, an ice giant nearly destroyed the town. It was only at the last moments that I was able to send it to the depths of Hell. After I defeated the massive beast, King Odgeir demanded that his best mages construct an impenetrable wall around the city that not even a giant could destroy.

Of course, that didn't apply to me. I could still come and go as I pleased through the wall, as could any who used pixie dust, but there were so few of us anymore that it was almost as if pixies no longer existed. I had never met another fairy in my whole life, no matter how far my travels took me. I have heard rumblings of another pixie in the woods, one with a scar on his face and a patch over one eye, but I have never seen it myself, no matter how many hours I wandered there.

"Hope the ride was okay," Hogarth said to me as he stopped his horse and leaped down from the caravan.

"It was excellent." I hopped down from the back of the caravan and pulled Bjarngimur's head from the bed of the trunk, noticing the thick goo it left behind on the wood. "I'm sorry about that."

"It's fine, Akta," Hogarth replied. "Seeing that thing, well, it makes me feel safer going into the woods. You did a great service to me and my kin by killing it."

"Still," I replied, "go to the stables and have Paget wash it off and give your horse a nice meal for your troubles."

Hogarth replied. "Thanks. I'll say high to Magpie while I'm there, too. She and Cherry always get along like old friends."

I smiled. "That's kind of you. I plan to take her for a run myself soon when I'm able."

I wished that my pleasantness was because of my innate goodness, but it was truly a survival mechanism. I needed these people to like me, to love me even, and they would only do that if I were kind to them. I suppose I could have chosen to be ruthless to the point of cruelty and forced their respect, but I had no interest in fighting a violent coup or ruling with an iron fist over villagers who hated me.

Besides, the truth was that I loved this kingdom and all its citizens. They took me in as a child, and they treated me like their equal. They chose to let me walk among them and smiled when I did.

"Oh, my gods!" I heard as I dragged the head of Bjarngimur through the town. "Is that—"

"It's the head of Bjarngimur, the terrible," one of the fruit vendors shouted out.

"He's dead!" a priest said, covering his mouth in shock.

Dragging a giant cyclops's head through town wasn't a daily occurrence, even if the townsfolk in Odgeir's capital had seen plenty of monster violence. People stared, mouths agape, as I passed. For my part, I wanted to show them that I was once again victorious. If I could show my worth, they would see the value I brought to their lives and know their king would protect them.

A little, freckle-faced boy ran up to me with his little red-headed sister. "Can we touch it?"

"Quickly," I said, chuckling to myself.

"It's squishy," the boy said. "Ewww!"

"It's cool," the little girl said. "I can't wait to hunt monsters like Akta when I grow up."

I sighed a deep, contented sigh. I was an idol to somebody, to many people in this village, at a time when my kind was seen as evil throughout the land. The effort I put into earning and keeping their respect was paying off.

"Bucket!" a shrill voice cut through the air. "Hope! Let's go!"

"Mom!" the little girl shouted. "You'll never guess what we just did!"

The little boy and girl ran off to their mother, who smiled and gave me a slight nod of approval. I had made her children's day. Most every day was the same around the village, and they would surely talk about the head of Bjarngimur for weeks to come.

"That's unsanitary, you know," an old man said as I turned back toward the castle. His name was Edwin, and he was a widower who ran a small tavern in town.

"I know, but how else will people know how great I am?"

He grinned. "You could just tell them."

"Words are my brother's business. I prefer actions."

"It's very gross," he replied.

"Luckily, you just have to watch it pass by. I had to cut it off from between two very ugly shoulders, then travel with it from deep in the woods."

"Yes," he said, eyeing the blood on my shirt. "Well, you can't see the king looking like that. Let's fix you up with a meal and some clean clothes, so you don't drag blood into the castle."

*

While the castle made delicious feasts the likes of which were beyond compare, I preferred to eat in the town, among the people I protected. The castle was majestic and enormous, but it was also lonely. Besides my brother-king, whom I never saw, the castle was filled with servants, guards, and nobles. None of them had any time for stories of adventure.

Most days in the castle were filled with loneliness and solitary contemplation. I did not like being alone with my thoughts or hearing my footsteps echo off the stone walls. I wanted to be amongst the people, listening to the hustle and bustle of city life.

Perhaps it was because I was surrounded by silence during the long months of a mission that I longed for human contact when I returned. Often, I'd live in the wilderness for days on end, hunting and tracking my targets without coming across another living soul—and when I did, it was only to kill them. It didn't make for very good company.

"Tell us about the great dragon Aziolith again, Akta," the little boy pleaded. We were seated at the table eating his father's stew, which oozed off my spoon and down my gullet in a rather pleasant manner. It wasn't like any other soup I have ever had, and I wouldn't call it good, but I still enjoyed its interesting texture.

"I don't think your father wants to hear that again, Michael. He's heard that story since before you were born."

"It's fine," Edwin said, shoveling a spoonful of soup into his mouth. "I've heard all your stories a hundred times, except maybe this last one." He pointed to the head of Bjarngimur, sitting on the stoop outside his tavern. "That, though, might be a little close for you to tell."

I nodded. "In time, I will regale you with the story." I stood up. "But for now, I must be going. I owe the king a bounty. Thank you for the lovely meal, the lovely company, and the clean clothes. I appreciate them all."

*

I had taken most of the morning and much of the afternoon wandering through the city, meeting many old friends along the way. Each of them wanted a bit of my time, which meant I made it through the gates of the castle just as the sun fell over the horizon.

"You're late," Tilda scolded as we walked through the high-ceilinged halls. She was made up in white powder and held together with a tight corset, as was the style among noblewomen in the capital. I thought it garish and foolish to wear something that restricted your movement, but not having to worry about such things was one of the benefits of being rich. While the citizens of the town accepted me as one of their own, the nobility eyed me with much suspicion, and Tilda was no different. "He has been waiting all afternoon for you."

"I'm sorry," I replied. "I got carried away and a little nervous. I haven't seen my brother in—"

"The king. You haven't seen the king. He hates when you call him your brother."

"Don't you mean *you* hate it?"

The nobility resented the fact that their king and I were related by law, and they worked to downplay it at every turn.

"I am here at the behest of my king, not your brother, and we both expect you to treat your meeting with the reverence it deserves."

"Of course," I replied, tired of fighting. "That is what I meant. I haven't seen the king in many weeks."

"Yes, well, he has been busy running an empire while you were off galivanting around…" Her voice trailed off as her eyes landed on the rotting head I was carrying behind me.

"Protecting his kingdom." I followed her eyes and gave her a cold smile. "I think those are the words you are looking for."

"Yes, quite." She snapped her fingers at two palace guards standing on either side of the door. "Let her in."

"Nice seeing you again." I pulled Bjarngimur's head behind me, making sure to drag it over her opulent, white lace dress as I passed her. The goop would take days to wash off, and she would likely never rid herself of the smell.

No doubt, I had ruined her day. The thought of it brought me endless joy.

# CHAPTER 3

My feet echoed through the throne room on my way across the grand expanse toward my adopted brother. He sat regally on the throne, stroking the long, brown beard which hid his youth under thick tufts of hair. I hated that room, even back when our father sat on the throne. Everything about it was meant to make you feel small and insignificant.

The fifty-foot high ceilings almost audibly screamed that you didn't matter. Stained glass windows, showing images of the great kings of the past, shone down on the room with their disapproving countenance. But their expressions were fickle, and so their images glided across the room throughout the day as the sun moved. The entire room was meant to make the king look like the most important figure in the universe, like the sun revolved around him. It was the pompous arrogance of such an idea that made me hate it even more. It wasn't hard for somebody to lct all that go to his head, which is what I fear happened to my brother.

"What ho, good King Odgeir!" I said. "I return from my quest."

"I have been waiting for you all afternoon," the king replied from his throne, ten steps above the floor, another measure to make visitors feel small and insignificant in the presence of their king.

There was no joy in his voice or happiness when King Odgeir spoke. There hadn't been for some time. The weight of the crown weighed heavily on his head. Our father had been able to enjoy the trappings of his office and even find comfort in them. However, when the crown passed to my brother, so too did the burden. None of my father's joy transferred over to him with it.

"I'm sorry, my king," I replied. Like the nobles, he didn't like me addressing him as my brother in mixed company, as if being a king and being my brother couldn't happen at the same time. "I was held up."

"Yes," King Odgeir replied. "Held up with hero worship from your adoring fans."

"From my friends," I said. "They all asked about your majesty and told me how much they adored you."

That part was a lie, of course; a white lie designed to make my brother feel better and perhaps make him smile. He had not smiled in so long.

"Hrm," King Odgeir said, squinting his eyes. "Flattery will get you nowhere, pixie. What news do you bring me?"

I stepped up the stairwell toward the throne, dragging Bjarngimur's head behind me. "Your will be done, my king. The usurper Bjarngimur has been vanquished."

King Odgeir had been convinced that Bjarngimur was after his throne. He believed everyone was after his throne, especially if they were monsters. Often, I thought the crown had poisoned him against rational thought. I talked to his denizens throughout the land, and while some wished for better treatment, none desired the trappings of the crown.

"What proof have you brought me of this great deed?" King Odgeir asked.

I pulled Bjarngimur's head in front of me and held it up for the king to see. "His head, my liege. He will never bother this kingdom again."

"Hrm," the king grunted, leaning in to study the specimen. "Very good. I knew you would not fail me, Akta.

Since you were lain on our doorstep, you have never disappointed our kingdom."

"Thank you, my king," I said, bowing my head.

King Odgeir pushed off his throne and glided to his feet. "Except in one way, of course."

"And what way is that, my king?"

"You still keep the secrets of your pixie magic hidden from me. Dozens of my best men died fighting that horrible Cyclops. Meanwhile, you threw a handful of dust from that magical bag and vanquished him without breaking a sweat."

"I think it was more than that, my grace." I raised an eyebrow. "I have trained for years to develop the skills to fight monsters as I do."

"Yes, yes," the king scoffed. "But imagine what an army could do with that kind of power. Would you let us use it to vanquish our enemies?"

"I can imagine what you would do with it, my liege," I said through a clenched jaw. "Which is why you shall never have it as long as I still draw breath. I'm sorry, but I must once again deny you. It brings me no joy to do so, but it is for the good of the kingdom and all of humanity."

King Odgeir walked down the stairs of his throne and toward me. "Of course. But I had to ask. You can't blame me for that, can you?"

"I suppose not, my king," I said, grumbling under my breath. We had waged this battle since before his coronation, back when he was only a prince and still willing to be seen in public with me.

He claimed that if his soldiers could wield the power of pixie dust, he could expand his kingdom and protect his people from all who would seek to do them harm. I, for my part, did not want to see humanity with that kind of power. I was unsure if they could actually wield it, even if it were given to them. Even then, I knew they would not wield it wisely.

"Will you have a drink with me to celebrate this auspicious occasion?" King Odgeir said, walking through the back chamber of his throne room and into a small room where a plain wooden table was piled high with food and drink.

The king used the room to take breaks during long sessions on the throne. Though it only involved sitting for hours, the amount of intense focus needed to attend to his kingdom was enough to tire him out, as it did my father, which was why the solace room had been my father's favorite in the whole castle.

"I prefer not to drink, as you know."

King Odgeir picked two steins out of a cupboard and placed them on the table next to a keg of mead. "How can you deny your king?"

"Is it my king asking, or my brother?" I asked, frowning.

The king poured the mead into the steins. "They are one and the same. You cannot deny one without denying both."

"If that be the case, then I accept, my king."

"Perfect," my brother said, handing me the mug. "A toast to your good fortune, brave Akta of the Forest."

King Odgeir raised his glass to the air and smiled at me. It was the slightest of smiles, but it was there. It was the first time I'd seen him smile in many moons. I tipped my stein to him and smiled back.

"And to you, good King Odgeir. May you rule another hundred years." I tilted back the stein and took a deep swig.

The cold mead felt good on my parched lips. The honey coated my throat, and for a moment, I was happy, sharing a drink with my brother, as we had so often in our youth.

"May the gods forever smile on you for the rest of your days," my brother said, placing down his drink. His smile turned into a scowl. "Or should I say 'day'. I guess how long you draw breath depends on how much poison you just drank."

"Excuse me?" I asked. "What are you talking about?"

The king lunged at me, grabbing me hard by either cheek and pulling me close to his face. "I am saying I poisoned you! Did you really think you could deny me forever? I am your king, and you are simply a stubborn monster who has outlived her usefulness."

The stein felt heavy in my hand, and my eyes started to blur. My knees wobbled out from under me, and I fell to the ground.

"What did you do to me?" I asked, short of breath. "How could you—"

"I gave you every opportunity to help me, sister. And in every instance, you denied me. You denied your king like I was some common street urchin. Well, the time has come for you to see how powerful I truly am. Today, I am a king." My brother knelt and pulled the pixie dust pouch off my belt. "With this, I will be a god."

I tried to swipe him away, but my eyes wouldn't focus. "I'll kill you!"

"Headstrong as always," King Odgeir said, passing one of his knights on his way back toward his throne. "If she's not dead in two minutes, take pity and slit her throat." King Odgeir turned back to me with a smirk. "Be merciful...for old time's sake."

Four more guards funneled into the small room as King Odgeir, my brother, whom I loved above all others, disappeared from my sight, having poisoned me for the simple act of denying him.

I wished that it was hard to believe he poisoned me, but he hadn't really been the same man I knew since he took the crown. Since then, his only goal had become the accumulation of power.

It always bothered him that I had something he couldn't have; that in some way, I was more powerful than he could ever be because I was a magical being, and he was merely human. He was spoiled and arrogant, egged on by the sycophants that surrounded him. He saw what he wanted and took it, no matter the consequences, no matter who he had to hurt.

"By the gods," I said, wobbling to my feet. "I will have my vengeance."

I lifted my head and connected my eyes with the strongest of my brother's guards, Sir Jay, who stared back at me dead-eyed as if he had never met me before, as if we hadn't fought together on many occasions.

"Let me through, Sir Jay."

"I can't do that," Sir Jay replied. "Orders."

"Do the battles we fought together mean nothing to you?"

"Compared to orders from my king, they mean less than nothing," Sir Jay replied.

I lunged toward him. "Let me through now, and I will spare you! Otherwise, you will meet your end!"

Sir Jay pushed me backward. "Your empty threats no longer scare us, pixie."

My hand instinctively reached into my belt for my pixie dust, but I didn't have it anymore. I would have to beat them the old-fashioned way. It had been a long time since I fought without the aid of my magic, but it was still possible to beat them without it.

Sir Jay lunged, and I flew over him, out of the door and into the throne room. The knights rushed after me, their metal armor clanging together. They were slow. That was why I only wore leather armor for speed and agility.

"Stay back!" I shouted, pulling out my throwing knives and firing them at the knights.

That took all my energy. I landed back on the ground and knelt, catching my breath. I looked up just as a knight swung his sword at me, and I rolled to avoid the blow. Sir Jay was right not to be scared. The poison coursing through my veins had weakened me.

My eyes lost focus again, and I couldn't see. The poison had taken my sight from me. Just then, the light from one of the stained-glass windows fell on my eyes. I could still see light. And it was a way out. All I had to do was follow the light. I unfurled my wings and lifted off the ground.

"Look at the mighty monster slayer run like a scared chicken," Sir Jay said as I rose into the air. "Run, chicken! Run!"

I could barely fly straight, but I let the sun guide me up to the circular stained-glass window. I flew as hard as I could and smashed through the window with all my might. I could no longer see the light, but I could feel it on my face. All I had to do was follow it as far as I could.

"Velaska," I whispered as I rose into the air. "Velaska. Queen of the underworld. Help me. Guide me true. Bring me justice."

My wings flapped one final time and then gave out on me. I fell to the ground and crashed through the forest trees before bouncing on the grassy ground below, skidding to a stop next to the edge of a lake. My breathing was labored. I felt my heart slow. Every move was agony.

"Velaska," I breathed. "Queen of the underworld. Help me."

The last sound I heard was the lapping of the lake next to me. I felt my soul unlatch from my body and drift into nothingness.

# CHAPTER 4

"Help me," I whispered weakly. As my strength came back, my soft voice grew into a yell. "Help me!"

My eyes fluttered open, and I shot up onto my knees. "Oh my god. Where am I?"

All I could see was the flames of damnation. I sat atop a hill, looking out over the fire and brimstone of Hell. In the distance, the great, fiery mouth of a demon skull stood at the front gate to the afterlife. All around me, sharp rocks jutted out of the ground and hung from the top of the cavern.

I had long dreamt of the afterlife and my place in it. There were stories of Heaven, of Valhalla, and Mount Olympus. There were stories of the great warriors finding their rest in the great peace of the eternal beyond. I hoped that my life, my pathetic life, would have been worth enough to avoid the fires of Hell. However, looking out at the scorched pits that surrounded me, I knew that I had not been righteous enough or noble enough to find that end.

"This is not very helpful, Velaska," I grumbled under my breath.

I wanted to be angry about my plight. I wanted to curse the gods, but I knew that my predicament was my own fault. I had no idea what I needed to do to reach a more righteous end, but I had not done it. That was unfortunate, but it was a simple fact of life and death, that not everything was fair. If my brother-murderer had taught me anything, it was that.

I stood on top of the cliff and watched the thousands of damned souls below wandering down a sinewy, rock path toward an unknown fate in the distance. A giant stone wall stretched into the distance and connected to the cliffs on opposite ends of Hell's cavern. In the center of the wall, a barricade of fire shot up from the screaming mouth of that giant, black, metal skull. A great behemoth of a man sat shrouded in shadow at its base. I felt drawn to it. Somehow, I knew that was where my destiny lay.

Behind me was a chasm spewing people out of it; the newly arrived. On either side of the rock path, a river of lava flowed, and sharp spikes stuck up into the sky. There was no way to go except forward, toward the skull and the figure at its base.

Perhaps Velaska heard my call and brought me here. She was the Queen of the Underworld, and if she heard my prayers, so what better place to find her than in the domain where she ruled?

According to legend, Velaska had ruled over Hell for the last three thousand years. She took over after Hades abandoned Hell to seek adventure across the universe. In my travels, I heard story after story of Velaska sending people back from Hell to fix their unfinished business, and I certainly had unfinished business. If that meant traveling through Hell itself to get there, then that was what I was going to do.

I floated down to the path, taking my place among the damned, plodding toward an eternal destination. None of them made eye contact with me as they stumbled forward, barely able to hold together their bruised, cadaverous bodies.

"Excuse me?" I asked a tall man with half his face missing. "Do you know where we're going?"

The faceless man didn't answer. Instead, he just turned from me and continued up the path. A group of soldiers pushed past me and walked up the path in a single file line.

"Men! Don't deviate! We have work to do, and we must not be late."

An old man carried a basket down the path, and I fluttered my wings forward to catch up with him.

"Excuse me," I asked the old man. When he turned to me, I saw that he had no eyes. "Do you know where we're going?"

"Where we're going?" the old man asked. His eyes were completely white. "I can't see where we're going."

"Never mind," I replied.

"To be judged by Petrus," I heard from behind me. I turned to see a brown-skinned woman with olive eyes and matted, black hair scowling at me. Her teeth poked through a large hole in her jaw. "Don't you know anything?"

"I know some things," I replied. "But I do not know what's going on here or who Petrus is, either. Can you tell me more?"

"He judges all the souls in Hell, determines their worth, and the extent of their crimes. Then, we are punished for as long as he deems fit."

"What if we didn't commit any crimes?"

"Everybody has committed crimes." She gave me a hard look. "That's how they get you."

I spent my life stopping crimes, so I truly did not think that I would be judged harshly by Petrus, no matter what the woman said to me. But I couldn't tell her that and retain any purity in my soul.

I saw the fear she had of her pending judgment and didn't want her to feel like I was bragging about my life. It's just that I literally devoted myself to foiling crimes and stopping monsters from hurting people. What could be more virtuous than that?

I floated back into the air and toward the front of the line, now confident that Velaska had, in fact, called me to her. Otherwise, I would be in Valhalla, where I belonged, and if I completed my mission, I would finally find peace there.

*

"Next!" Petrus shouted out from the front of the line. After a few moments, he bellowed again. "Next!"

I was sick of waiting my turn, so I flew in the direction of his voice. When I reached the front, I saw not a vicious, evil-looking man, as you might expect from Hell. He was twenty feet tall if he was an inch and sat cross-legged in front of the black skull which breathed fire.

However, this giant man was not ominous like others of his ilk, with his soft face, balding scalp, and bushy beard. He ran his blue eyes down a parchment scroll that extended a thousand feet behind him into the mouth of the fiery demon.

"Next!" Petrus shouted. "I don't have all day, people. This is how the line gets backed up."

At the front of the line was a short, squat soldier dressed in armor and holding his own bearded head.

"Hey!" I yelled. "He's talking to you."

"I know," he said. "But if I don't move forward, I can't be judged."

"Quit being such a baby," I said, shoving him with all my might. "You're holding up the line. Some of us have places to go."

Petrus looked down from his paper and saw the soldier in front of him. "Ah, there you are. What is your name?"

"Norius," he replied. "Norius the second."

"Just so you know," an old woman said to me. There were deep wrinkles on her face. "You aren't going to be cutting in line. Not today. Not with me."

"Easy, lady," I said. "It's not like we're going to get good news."

"Norius." Petrus's deep, grumbling voice carried across the line. "Yes, here we are. Norius the second. Oh, this is good. Died in battle. High points for valor. Oh. Oh no. Many innocents killed. Not good."

"They were the enemy!" Norius shouted in his defense.

"Yes, yes, well that doesn't matter, now does it? Women raped. Villages pillaged. No, no, no. This is not good." Petrus beckoned forward two red-skinned imps with thick horns and black, leathery wings. "Level five. Eligible for re-examination in 250,000 years!"

The two imps whisked Norius away despite his crying and whimpering. He really didn't believe he was the bad guy. What a sucker. You can't kill a bunch of humans and not expect to get what you deserve. Luckily, I've never killed one.

"Next!" Petrus shouted.

The old woman saw me step forward and pointed, shrieking, "No cutsies!"

I nudged the old woman back. "Come on, lady. It's just a couple more seconds."

The woman elbowed me in the rib. "Then you won't mind waiting."

"Next!" Petrus shouted.

I pushed the woman back into the line of souls. "I'll only be a minute."

"I've been waiting three hundred years to ascend to Valhalla!" the woman screamed.

"And it won't kill you to wait a little longer." I floated up into the air above her. "Yes! I am here!"

"Very good," Petrus said. "Quick. I like that. Name?"

I stuck out my chest proudly. "Akta of the Forest."

"Last name?"

"I don't know. Forest, I guess? Of the Forest? I'm not really sure, to be honest. My father died a long time ago. My mother when I was only a few days old, and I have never met any members of my family."

"Very well," Petrus said, looking through his parchment. "Pixie, yes?"

"That's right."

"We don't get many of those." Petrus scanned through his list for a moment before stopping. "Ah, yes, here we go. Died this morning, yes?"

"That's right," I replied with a nod. "So, if you could just point me to Velaska. I'll be on my way."

Petrus either didn't hear what I said or ignored it outright. "We must be getting more efficient."

"No!" the old woman said. "She cut."

"Come on, lady!" I rolled my eyes. "Why are you so excited to be judged?"

"Why are you?" the old woman shot back.

"I have business with Velaska," I replied.

"Pfft," the woman sneered. "Like Velaska would deal with the likes of you, pixie."

"What's that supposed to mean?" I growled, taking a step toward the old woman. "Do you wish to be gutted from neck to navel?"

"Bring it on, pixie!"

"Enough!" Petrus pounded his fists. "There will be no fighting today! We will deal with you both, in turn. Since Akta is here, and I found her file, she will go first, yes?"

"Whatever," the old woman said. "This better count against her. That's all I'm saying."

"I see some nice things here," Petrus said, looking through the parchment. "Fought valiantly for king and country. Saved several towns from slaughter. Oh. Oh, dear. Did you disembowel an orc child?"

"There was a good reason for that!" I shouted. "I mean, I don't remember it, but there was at the time."

"And you brutally murdered a goblin family two months ago?"

"But they were evil," I replied. "Wait, what does that matter? Monsters aren't human."

"They are living things," Petrus said. "And all living things count in the grand equation."

"That's stupid!" I started to say something else, but Petrus wasn't even listening. He was too busy examining his notes. I started to realize that maybe I wasn't here to see Velaska. Maybe instead, I would be judged harshly. I wanted to leave, flee, and run, but I couldn't do that. Not now. Not when I was standing before Petrus.

"Your sentence is level six!" Petrus said. "Possibility for re-evaluation in three million years!"

"Justice!" The old woman clapped her hands as two imps flew toward me.

"No!" I shouted. The two leather-winged demons grabbed me by either arm and whisked me away. "I have to see Velaska! Take me to her now!"

But Petrus was already looking past me. He had finished with me, and there was nothing I could do about it. "Next!" he shouted, and the old woman marched forward as I disappeared behind the gates of Hell to carry out my sentence.

# CHAPTER 5

"Let go of me!" I struggled against the two demon imps. They didn't respond at all. "Did you hear me? I said get off!"

Underneath me, a chorus of grunts and moans filled the air. When I looked down, I saw hundreds of bodies, each one suspended on a long, wooden stake stuck through their stomachs. The people oozed down the stakes and into the fiery pits below. I wondered what level of Hell this was and what crimes they committed during their lives, but mostly, I just wanted the demons to let me go.

"Get off!" I flipped my legs up over my head and flung them around the demon's necks, one on either of them and squeezed them tightly until they loosened their grip on my arms.

With my arms free, I kicked my legs away from the demons and flew toward the ground. The demons chased after me as I zigged and zagged through the stakes. I swung at one of them until it snapped in half and fell toward the demons. The woman impaled on it screamed as she disappeared into the fiery lake below.

I slammed into another of the stakes, and when it fell, it connected with one of the demons and sent it crashing into the lake below. The second demon broke off its pursuit and chased after his friend as I disappeared into a thatch of thick brambles below me.

"What is this place?" I said aloud, stepping into a thorny maze. The thorns covered the path above me and on either side, leaving me in near darkness. They seemed to ripple and ooze as I walked forward. The only light came from my wings, which shone a golden glow on the thorns.

At the end of the path came a choice to go left or right. In my brain, I heard a sweet, angelic voice whisper to me, "Go right."

"Who said that?" I asked, spinning around.

"Trust me," the voice replied.

"There is nothing in Hell that I trust." I turned left down the sinewy maze.

"Ha!" The voice gave a chortle. "I like you."

"Who are you? What is this place?"

"The brambles of agony, dear," the voice said. "Made from the unending suffering of my subjects. Every thorn an evil deed tortured away from a soul."

The sweet, melodic sound of the voice in my head was too perfect to be a demon or any creature that worked in the pits of Hell. It could only be that of a goddess.

"Velaska!" I said. "Is that you?"

"Of course, my love. Who else would it be?"

"I have business with you!"

The thorns closed in on me with a throbbing pulse. The low rumble that came from their dark spindles seemed to call out to me.

"Don't anger them, dear," Velaska said. "They feed on the evil in people's souls. Your hatred nourishes them."

"I don't care!" I snapped. "I have slain dragons and fought armies. I can take care of some overgrown brush."

"You think so," Velaska said. "Better than you have tried, and the thorns have dragged them all into the abyss."

"I don't believe you," I said. "There are none better than me."

"I certainly do like you," Velaska said. "A pity my vines will soon devour you."

The thorns tightened on me, and I flew away to avoid them. I made a sharp right turn as they scraped my leg, and then I made another left while the path collapsed upon me.

"Give up, my dear," Velaska's voice said. "You cannot win."

"It's not fair!" I shouted. I flew left and then made another right. "There is so much left to do!"

"Life is not fair," Velaska replied. "Why should death be?"

She made a good point, but I wasn't in Hell for a debate. I was in Hell to find Velaska and get back to Earth. I reached into my belt and grabbed at my dagger. A vine of thorns wrapped around my leg, and I cut it off. Another went for my arm, and I sliced through it, too. The vines snapped at me with precision and force, but I sliced through them as fast as they came upon me. With every swipe of my dagger, a groan escaped from the thorns, and they receded for a moment. Each time they fell away, though, they returned with even more force and vigor.

The vines in front of me weaved together, blocking my way forward. I saw a small opening to my right and stepped into it, cut through the vines, and tumbled into a clearing where the vines did not grow.

All around me, the vines covered the exits, but they did not chase after me anymore. Past the clearing, a rock cliff rose a thousand feet into the air. A ledge jutted out over the clearing where I stood and cast a dark shadow over it. The vines cowered from its looming presence. On the ledge, a dark purple door was carved into the cliff itself. The door's knocker was the same shape as the demon skull which guarded the entrance to Hell, except for a large, metal, bull ring that hung from its nose.

"Isn't this interesting?" Velaska said, giggling to herself inside my head.

"I'm not sure what you're going on about," I replied. "Nothing about this has been interesting."

"Come now. That can't be true. You might not like what is happening to you, but you can't say it isn't interesting. You must give it that."

I threw my head back and shouted. "I don't have to give it anything! Now, show yourself!"

"That's not really my style," Velaska said.

There was a snap, and the ground rumbled underneath me. I rose into the air just as it split open. Lava bubbled up to the surface, filling the clearing with molten, hot magma. As quickly as it came, it receded into the earth, leaving in its wake a glowing lava monster made from the fires below it, covered in flaming scales.

"She is my pet," Velaska said. "If you defeat her, you might have a chance at finding me."

I don't know how I knew, but something in my gut told me that Velaska rested behind the purple door above me.

"You're behind that door, aren't you?" I asked.

"If you defeat my pet, you might just find out."

"I'm not sure you remember," I said. "But I can fly, so no thanks. If you won't come to me, I will come to you."

I took off toward the purple door. The brambles chased after me, and I cut them off as they shot at me. Below, Velaska's pet spat fireballs after me, which I ducked and dodged until I was above the brambles and the fire monster. I landed on the rock platform and nearly fell off again when

I saw the gray lizard. It wore a red robe and sat in a wooden chair, resting its head on a long, silver staff as it slept.

"My, my, my. Don't you have spirit?" Velaska's voice said.

"I'm not interested in being mocked."

"Who's mocking you? I hardly ever see this kind of fire anymore. Most people are resigned to their fate. It's quite droll. I haven't had anything interesting happen in a millennium."

"This is where you are, isn't it?" I pointed to the door. "Behind this door? I can feel you behind there."

"Fine. You're right. That door is one way into my chambers," Velaska said. "It is a back entrance, unknown to most, and used by even fewer. I force concubines to use it if they seek my company…it's my way of testing their virility. If they can make it through all my challenges without being torn to shreds by my pets, they are worthy of a night with me."

"And how many make it?" I asked.

"Less than you think, but more than you imagine. Those that do, though, are scrumptious. My guard is the only one who can let you in, so don't bother trying to open the door without his approval. It simply won't work."

"Excuse me?" I asked the sleeping lizard creature in front of the door. "Excuse me?"

"You can't be so nice," Velaska replied. "It's just not in our nature to care about nice."

"Hey!" I shouted. "Get up!"

The lizard creature popped her eyes open and focused them on me. "Oh my. This was not planned or scheduled. I don't like this. No, the great Devil Velaska is not accepting visitors today."

I growled at the monster. "Do you know what I have done to get here today?"

"I am sure I don't care, but my answer is the same no matter what you have done. The queen of the underworld does not take unsolicited house calls. Please turn away and go back to your punishment."

I stepped closer, gripping my daggers tighter in my hands. "Either you open that door, right now, or I gut you from naval to neck and leave you to rot in the heat of Hell."

The lizard scurried forward, holding her staff tightly in its hand. "No matter what you do, it will be nothing compared to what my punishment is if I let you through, so the answer is no."

I didn't stop walking until the lizard stepped in front of me to guard my path. "HALT!" she screamed.

"I am not stopping until I see Velaska," I said. "You can stop me if you care to try, but I've felled foul, worse beasts than you with my eyes closed."

"Oh," the lizard smiled a malicious smile at me. "You have no idea how foul I can be."

Without another word, the lizard slammed her staff on the ground. A shockwave knocked me backward, and I fell. When I looked up, the lizard's head had grown four sizes, and her rippling muscles tore through her robe. Her legs shot up a dozen feet, and her chest expanded until every inch of the great beast was covered in slime.

"You have really done it now," Velaska said. "Quinn does not like being ignored."

The great lizard, Quinn, screamed. Fire shot out of her nose as her jaw opened and a giant forked tongue flopped out. She slammed one clawed hand down after the other and growled at me.

"I warned you," the lizard monster said. "Now, prepare to meet your end."

"Wait," I said, holding up my hands. "Is Velaska really worth fighting for?"

"Of course she is!" Quinn shouted. "My life is to fight for the honor of my queen."

I was known as a fighter, that was true, but that didn't mean that every battle needed to be a fight. Just as often, I beat my opponents with my words instead of my actions. I was tired of fighting. I had fought for so long. If I could avoid a battle, even this once, it would be a great personal victory for me.

"And isn't that sad?" I asked. "I mean, seriously. Both of us have fought our whole lives in service to our masters. How long have you guarded this door?"

"I have guarded this door since the first Devil, Anubis, was but a mere child in the eyes of the universe."

"That sounds…incredibly boring," I said. "And you just sit here all day…waiting for somebody to come here, and you what, fight them?"

"That's right," Quinn said. "Unless the master tells me to let them in."

"Not a great way to make friends, is it?"

"Friends?" Quinn rolled the word over her forked tongue. "I don't know that word."

"You know, somebody to tell things to, to laugh with, to have a conversation with?"

The monster lowered her head. "This is the longest conversation I've ever had."

"Oh." I offered a faint smile. "So, I guess that means we're friends, then."

"Friends?" Quinn asked. "I've never had a friend before."

"Well," I said, holding out my hand, "now you do…if you'll have me."

"A friend?"

"That's right," I said, inching toward Quinn. "But friends don't fight. Not like this at least, and friends definitely don't kill each other."

"Hmmm…friend."

"What do you say? Would you like a friend?"

Quinn thought for another moment before shrinking back down to her original form. Her robe was tattered now, but she was back to her regular, small shape, holding the same staff she'd used to grow so large in the first place.

"I think so…friend," Quinn said, holding out her hand. "I think I would like to try this."

"Good," I replied, shaking hands with the lizard. "I don't have any friends here, so you are my first."

We shook hands for a moment before Quinn looked down at her robe. "Oh my, what a fright I must be. Please give me a moment."

Quinn waddled back to her chair and pushed open a lever hidden in the rock wall. Inside, there was a closet full of red robes. The lizard took off the old, ripped cloak and put on a new one, then pushed the closet closed again.

"I must look a dreadful mess," Quinn said, hobbling back over to me. "And to greet my first friend, no less."

I smiled. "Friends don't care so much about that kind of thing. Last time I came back from a quest, I was covered in blood, and my friend took me into his open arms nonetheless."

"Yes," Quinn replied. "I think I will like this friend thing."

"Well, you know, friends do favors for each other, too."

"Do they?" Quinn asked. "What's a favor?"

"It's something that can help the other person in the friendship. Like, for instance, I could really use a favor right now."

"Oh, yeah? And friends do these for each other?"

"That's right."

"And what favor would you ask of me, friend?"

"I really need to be allowed through that door to see Velaska. It would mean the world to me if you would open the door for me."

"That is a big favor. She will not like it," Quinn said, biting her fingers. "No, she won't like it at all."

"Well, what if I do something for you then, friend? Maybe I can do you a favor."

"A favor?" Quinn asked. "For me?"

I nodded. "That's right. For instance, when was the last time you went on a vacation?"

"Vacation?"

"Took some time off from guarding this door. Went somewhere nice. You know, treated yourself to something nice."

"I have…never done that. It sounds very nice."

"Well, how about this…if you let me through that door to see Velaska, then I will ask her about sending you on vacation. How does that sound?"

"You would do that for me?"

"Of course, because that's what friends do."

A smile crept across the lizard's face. This was not an onerous or malicious smile like I had seen before, but a contented smile. "Very well, friend, if you do that favor for me, then I will do my favor for you."

"It's a deal," I said with a smile.

"My, my, my," Velaska said in my head. "Aren't you full of surprises? Maybe today won't be so boring after all."

# CHAPTER 6

Quinn placed her scepter on the bull ring hanging from the black demon skull on the door and chanted, "*Ilvasian Neblosa*." The purple door swung open, revealing a passage that led into the darkness beyond.

"Good luck," Quinn said. "For all those that go into the darkness, few come out the other side."

"Thank you," I said, smiling at Quinn. "That's creepy but helpful."

"I can't always help," she replied. "But I can be helpful."

I stepped into the darkness and took a deep breath. I didn't like the dark, but that wasn't an uncommon trait up on Earth. Most people didn't like the darkness because it hid monsters from them. If people knew what was truly out there, I doubt they would ever leave their homes.

I didn't like the darkness because I knew what evil lay in the world, and the darkness only masked it from me, making it harder to defeat. I wanted to see what was waiting for me. In the light, a monster was laid bare.

My eyes were more attuned to the dark than most, but I still couldn't see very far in the dark of the cave. My wings normally gave me more light, but this was the kind of blackness that ate away the light. Since they could not do anything to help, I hid them. They would only be a beacon to whatever lurked in the darkness.

I held out my hand, trying to scrape the wall or find something to steady myself, but I felt nothing but air. There was no protection around me, in any direction. Whatever waited for me in the dark could attack from anywhere.

"Don't be scared, my child," Velaska said.

"Who's scared?" I glared in the dark. "I'm just walking in the eternal darkness. What's not to like about that?"

"Anything you fear will manifest in the dark," she replied. "It is best to keep happy thoughts."

I chuckled to myself. "This is still Hell, right?"

"Of course," she said. "However, I prefer not to deal with mopey, dopey people. They are such bores. I prefer to deal with those who have conquered their fears."

I heard at least a dozen voices, then. First, a snarling wolf echoed in the distance; then, the roar of a tiger. A wasp hummed past my ear. "These parlor tricks will not scare me. I have valiantly fought worse than you could throw at me."

"That I know, Akta of the Forest," Velaska's voice replied. "Legend of your deeds has reached my ears. I thought they were embellishments or outright lies. Now, I take them more seriously."

"Everything you heard of me is the truth, I am sure."

The darkness swirled around me, and it took the form of a giant dragon snarling at me. I recognized the beast as Aziolith, one of my greatest conquests. We fought for days until I weakened him by slicing open his belly, sending him to the great beyond.

I pulled my daggers out of their sheaths and knelt, ready to strike. "Is this what you would have me do? Defeat all my old conquests one by one?"

"It would be exciting," Velaska said. "However, you are a learned fighter. I doubt it would do much good to have you relive your victories."

The dark dragon vanished, and again I was alone. I walked forward more quickly than before, hoping that a light would appear in the shadows.

"That is wise," I said. "I never showed fear in the face of great obstacles."

"No, when you were given a task, you accomplished it, didn't you?"

"That's right," I said, feeling around for traps in the air around me. "I never failed my duties to king and country."

"Then, how did you end up here?" Velaska said. "If you never failed."

"I never failed my country," I replied. "I failed my duty to myself, though, by trusting the wrong person."

"Tsk tsk tsk, a tale as old as time," Velaska said. "I can't tell you how many wind up in my kingdom because they placed their trust in the wrong person. Knights, priests, kings, and paupers alike."

"Then I am in good company," I replied.

"Quite," Velaska said. A tiny light appeared in the distance, growing larger with every step I took. "Very well, Akta of the Forest. I suppose you are worthy of an audience with me, even if you have made a mockery of my kingdom."

I ran toward the light, confident that it would lead me to Velaska and my audience with her. When I broke through into the light, I expected to see a hellish landscape, not unlike the one I'd left before entering the purple door. Instead, I came upon a meadow of bright flowers, replete with a waterfall that emptied into a babbling brook. A pagoda, wrapped in green vines, stood in the middle of the meadow. Inside, a thousand plush pillows cushioned Velaska while she ate grapes.

Depictions of Hades saw him rough, gnarled, and mean. Velaska, on the other hand, was soft. Soft and beautiful. Her long, blond hair fell to her knees. Resting atop her hair was a black crown. The purple jewel at its center matched her violet eyes, which shimmered in the light.

"Your behavior has truly been shameful." She ate another grape. "You know that, right?"

"I meant no disrespect," I replied, walking down the marble steps in front of me.

"Whether you meant it or not," Velaska said, chewing on a grape, "I am still put out by how easily you found me. I will have to review my security measures post-haste once you have been dispatched."

"My apologies, my queen." I knelt on the grass at the bottom of the stairs. "I could not wait three million years to see you. My business is urgent."

"Yes, yes," Velaska said, plucking another grape. "Well, get on with it then."

"I have only one request."

"And what would that be?" Velaska asked.

I bowed my head to her. "Send me back to the surface."

"Oh." Velaska spat out her grape. "Is that all?"

"Yes," I said. "It is but one small favor."

Velaska pushed herself up from her pillows. She wore a two-piece toga which showed off her taut, toned stomach. "Do you know how many people request favors from me daily?"

I shook my head. "No, my queen. I do—"

"So many that I can't sit in my throne room without being bothered. Instead, I must escape here, to this place, with every chance I get, just to get some peace and quiet."

"I didn't know that."

"And do you know what the most requested favor is, by any chance?"

"No—"

Velaska clasped her hands together. "To be sent back to Earth, to complete some stupid unfinished business or another. I mean, these people have all of eternity to suffer, and all think if they can change just one thing on Earth, everything will be okay," Velaska scoffed. "Isn't that silly?"

"No," I replied. "I understand it completely."

"That doesn't make it any less silly. You have three million years of torture, and yet you are consumed with thoughts of your old life. Tell me, what could possibly be worth returning to Earth for?"

"Revenge," I growled.

Velaska yawned. "Oh, sorry. I thought it would be something interesting. Silly me."

I slammed my fist on the ground. "It is the most important thing in my life!"

"No, my dear," Velaska said, sighing. "It is the most important thing in your death."

"I cannot rest until my brother is killed," I said.

"Time will take care of that eventually," Velaska said.

"I cannot wait."

"My dear," Velaska said. "There is so much suffering in Hell. You will soon forget your brother even exists."

"You are wrong," I replied. "Nothing could compare to the suffering I feel knowing my coward brother still draws breath."

Velaska stepped down from her pagoda and walked toward me. "Your brother. Oh my. I have never heard that before. So, who is your brother? A carpenter? A soldier?"

"He is King Odgeir."

The smile wiped from Velaska's face. "Oh, really? Well, that changes things a bit. I do love a king. They are so fun to break." Velaska was in front of me now, close enough that I could touch her. "Tell me, is this king old and feeble?"

I shook my head again. "No, my lady. He is brash, young, and virile."

Velaska bent down and tilted my chin up with her index finger so that I could look upon her brilliant violet eyes. "Even better. The old ones have accepted their fate. Their eyes are hollow. There's no sport in breaking them." Velaska pulled me close to her cheek. "But those young ones! How exquisite it is to watch the last drop of hope vanish from their eyes."

"Can you let go of me, my queen?" I said. "I don't like being touched."

Velaska let go of me. "Very well. I will make you a deal. I'll return you to your body. In exchange, you promise to bring me this king of yours. Do this, and I will let you live out whatever miserable existence you have on Earth and wipe clean your past transgressions."

"And if I fail?" I asked.

"Should you fail, you'll carry out his sentence on top of yours. Deal?"

I took a deep breath. There was no reason to think about whether it was a fair deal or not. It was the only deal I had. I was already on the hook for three million years of torture, and this was the only way to get my revenge.

"Fine," I replied.

"Quick and decisive," Velaska said. "I like that. Well, off you go then!"

"Wait!" I said. "Can you consider giving Quinn a vacation?"

Velaska choked back a laugh. She hadn't expected that. "I'll take it under advisement."

With a snap of her fingers, everything went black, and I collapsed onto the ground. My final thought was a peaceful one, knowing that when I woke, I would set out to get my revenge.

# CHAPTER 7

"Wake up, pretty lady." Someone with a low, growling voice was speaking.

"Uhhhh," I mouthed back. I was groggy. Next to me, I heard the lapping of the lake, and the grass underneath me tickled my arms.

"Come on," the voice said, rocking me gently. "Wake up."

"Uhhhh!" I growled it this time.

"WAKE UP!" Now the gruff voice was shouting.

Two massive hands dug into my side and shoved me hard into the water. I splashed around, trying to gain my bearings. My arms were stiff, and my joints ached, but I managed to find my footing on shaky legs.

"What the hell, man?" My voice sounded different. I never liked it much, but now it crackled in the air, like a cat hissing. "What is wrong with you?"

Across from me, on the bank of the river, sat a blue troll. Ugly, fat, and smiling as wide a grin as he could muster. I had never seen a troll smile before. His fanged teeth rose from the bottom of his mouth as his lip curled up, almost touching his bulbous, protruding nose.

"Hi, pretty lady!" the troll yelled, proud of himself.

"You can't just throw people in the lake!" I waded to the edge of the water. My whole body was sopping wet.

Perhaps I should have gone for my daggers, but I didn't. This troll wasn't aggressive. If anything, it was kind and polite, despite tossing me into a lake. I didn't know why, but I didn't feel threatened by this troll. I had fought dozens of trolls in my day, and they always made my hair stand on end. They were loud, and dumb, and quick. They grew more powerful the angrier they got, so you needed to finish them quickly to prevent them from overpowering you with their rage.

"I like your eyes," the troll said as I crawled onto the shore.

"Shut up," I replied. "I'm going to lop your head off when I get dry."

"Please don't," the troll said. "Pretty-eyed lady."

"What's so special about my eyes, anyway?" I asked.

I had never thought much about them. They were emerald green, which was different from the brown of the other villagers. Nobody ever commented on them, though, and certainly not to call them pretty. Sir Cleybourne, my mentor, called them cold and steely once, but that's not the same thing as pretty.

I turned back to the lake. It was now calmer than it had been when I was thrashing around in it. In the reflection of the lake, my jaw dropped. No longer were my eyes their emerald color. Instead, they were dark black, with tiny white irises. My face was no longer brown but a decrepit blue, as if it had been deprived of oxygen for years. I looked like a hideous monster, like the kind I'd fought for so long.

"Oh my gods, Velaska," I whispered. "What have you done?"

"I like it," the troll said with a goofy smile.

"I don't care," I growled.

The troll shrugged.

"Velaska!" I screamed, beating the water in front of me. "What have you done to me?" I slammed my fists into the lake again and again. "Answer me!"

The current flowed out into the middle of the lake, creating a great wall of water. Velaska's reflection shimmered in the water.

"Velaska!" I shouted.

"Of course, it's me." Even in the water, Velaska's smile looked smarmy. "You've been screaming my name loud enough to wake the dead. No offense." Velaska sighed. "So, what do you want?"

"Look at me, you snake! I'm a monster."

Velaska raised an eyebrow. "That's a harsh word."

"You tricked me!" I screamed.

"I did nothing of the sort. You wanted to be returned to your body, yes?"

"Well, yes, but…"

"And were you?"

I cocked my head to the side, confused. "Yes, but…how could you return me like this?"

"Time flows differently for me than it does on the surface. Even though it seemed like only a few hours passed in my realm, you have been rotting up here for a week."

"A WEEK!" I splashed the water in front of me.

Velaska shrugged. "Give or take."

"How am I supposed to kill a king if I'm a rotting corpse?"

"I'm sure you'll figure it out," Velaska said, smiling as she faded from the water. "Or suffer the consequences. Either way, it's a win for me."

"Bitch!"

"I heard that," Velaska said from the ether.
I stomped away from the water and collapsed in front of the troll, whimpering. "What am I supposed to do now?"

"Are you okay?" the troll said, wrapping his meaty paws around me. I didn't mind his touch. If anything, it was nice.

"No," I replied. "I'm doomed. Nothing is okay. Nothing."

I cried until I couldn't cry anymore. My body ached so much that I could barely breathe, and in my pain, I drifted off into a fitful slumber. I hoped to wake up again but did not know what to do if I did.

*

Usually, I dreamt of great battles and conquests, but there was nothing but blackness in my dreams now. By the time I woke up, it was dark out. My body ached as it had never ached before. It was difficult to bend my legs and arms. Every inch of me throbbed.

However, I was never one to wallow in self-pity, and now wasn't a good time to start. My body was stiffening more with each passing minute. Soon, I would be unable to use it at all, and I had to find the King before then unless I wanted his eternal sentence tacked onto mine.

"Is it night already?" I asked the troll, who lay behind me and whom I had used as a pillow. "I've wasted an entire day."

I heard soldiers in the distance, talking to each other, as a wagon wheel rolled behind them. "I'm tired," one of them said.

"Quit your belly aching!" another replied. "We're almost at the inn, you wimp."

I stood up as quickly as my bones would allow. "That must be Hogarth's caravan, making its way to town. I'm starving. I'll bet they have food."

The troll shook his head nervously as I spoke. "No like Hogarth."

"Come on, you big baby," I said. "Let's rustle up some grub."

"Uh uh. No."

"Don't tell me you are afraid of humans."

"Uh huh. Humans have fire. Fire bad."

"Fine. Wait here while I wow these folks. I'm a bit of a legend around these parts. People love giving me free stuff."

I walked through the brambles and the brush until I stepped foot onto the main road. Hogarth had always been so nice to me, and I knew he would understand my plight now. After all, I saved his caravan countless times, and we'd spoken at length when he gave me rides into town.

"Hi, guys!" I raised my hand in greeting. "It's me, Akta. Remember when you drove me into town a couple of days ago and when I helped you fend off a pack of goblins last month? I'm in a bit of a pickle, and I could use your help."

The guards surrounding Hogarth's caravan didn't look happy to see me. My voice was raspy and low. My body was scabbed and blue, but I was still the same Akta underneath it all. I hoped at least Hogarth would recognize me.

"Monster!" one of the guards shouted.

"Outside the Veil?" another asked.

"Who cares?" a third one said. "Just kill it!"

"Wait!" I looked up at Hogarth, whose dark brown eyes stared at me with horror. "We're friends, you and me. Don't you remember?"

Hogarth once looked at me with such kind eyes. Those days were gone, though. Now he narrowed them in suspicion and anger. "Don't try to trick me, monster! You will not get my caravan. Attack!"

The soldiers gathered around me, unsheathing their weapons, ready for a fight. There was no doubt that I could have killed them once without a second thought, but my body felt different now, stiffer, and besides, I preferred not to fight the soldiers I'd sworn an oath to protect. "Guys. I'm not a monster. This is all just a big misunderstanding. I don't want to hurt you."

The guards weren't receptive to my pleas. They advanced on me. If they attacked first, I had no choice but to defend myself. I reached into my belt and pulled out my daggers. As the soldiers advanced, however, my troll friend leaped out of the forest in a rage, blocking them from me.

"Leave pretty alone!" he screamed.

"Wait!" I called out to him. "Don't hurt them!"

"Troll!" a soldier shouted. "Use the fire to scare it off!"

Two of the guards brought forward their torches, and the troll cowered in fear. "NOOO!"

"That's enough!" I stepped in front of the troll. "Back away from him or suffer my wrath."

"I'll lop your head off!" one of the guards shouted.

"Get back to the Veil where you belong!"

I unfurled my wings behind me and leaped forward, stealing the staff from one of the soldiers and kicking him to the ground. When I stood up, I turned back to them with a sneer. "Last chance."

"Go to Hell!" the guard shouted.

"I was hoping you would say that," I replied.

I had to fight, but that didn't mean I had to kill anyone. If I incapacitated them all, I could escape all the same, without their blood on my hands. I tossed the lance behind me and punched one of the guards in the face. As I did so, I watched my pinky break off from my body and fly across the battlefield.

"AHHH!" I shouted. I tried to run toward it, but my legs stiffened under me. I fell to the ground and crawled to my finger as the guards focused their attack on the troll. When I picked up my finger, I held it in my hand and stared at it. It reeked of rotting death. My body had sat in the sun for a week, and it smelled like it. How was I going to force this body of mine to work to kill a king if I couldn't even punch a guard without pieces of me falling off? "What have I become?" I muttered to myself.

"We'll kill you ugly mugs!" one of the guards shouted to the troll behind me.

"Ugly?" the troll said. "Ugly? NOT UGLY!" He rushed forward, toppling the guards in his path. He ripped one of the wheels off Hogarth's caravan and flung it at the guards. "You ugly!"

Hogarth leaped from the caravan as it toppled over. The troll stomped toward him with fire in its eyes. I fluttered my wings to stand and pulled on the troll's arm.

"ENOUGH!" I shouted.

All around us was nothing but carnage. The wagon was destroyed. The soldiers collapsed on the ground, writhing in pain. There was no way for them to hurt us anymore. We were now the monsters that I once fought. Stories would be told about us, and a bounty would be placed on our heads. My brother's monster hunters would chase us to the ends of the Earth now. What an ironic twist of fate.

"Let's just go," I said.

"You okay, pretty?" the troll said, walking behind me.

"I'm fine. Just remind me never to call you ugly."

"Never call me ugly."

I chuckled. "Thanks."

*

Was that how monsters were always treated when people came upon them? The soldiers didn't give us much choice but to fight, did they? I mean, they just launched into battle, and no matter what I said, I couldn't convince them to stop. If they had just been reasonable, we could have worked it out. Why couldn't they have listened to me?

"What a nightmare," I said to the troll as we walked down a dirt road away from the caravan. "You live with that kind of hatred every day?"

"Uh huh."

"That's sad," I replied.

The troll nodded. "Uh huh."

"Thanks, by the way."

"You welcome."

"You're nowhere near as awful as the other trolls I've met."

The troll smiled. "Thank you."

"Hey," I said, "can I ask you a question?"

"Sure," the troll said.

"Why…did you throw me into that lake? I mean, I was dead."

"Your eyes opened. You wouldn't move. I threw. Seemed right."

"How long were you there?" I asked. "Before I woke up, I mean."

"Two days. Trying to get back to the Veil. Men hunted me. Found a safe space. Then, you there."

"So, you just watched me rot for days?"

"Uh huh," the troll said. "Until you opened eyes. Then, I throw."

"Yes," I said. "That part I remember." My stomach grumbled loudly. I hadn't eaten since I was killed more than seven days ago. "I'm so hungry…I'm ravenous. Are you hungry?"

"Very," the troll replied.

Through the clearing in the road, I made out a tavern in the distance. It was the same place I had saved just a week before, except it wasn't full of holes from Bjarngimur's attack anymore. They must have been able to hire out construction workers quickly because it looked brand new. Even better than brand new, in fact.

"All right," I said, stopping near the front door. "This place has to remember me. I just saved the owner's family last week. They don't like trolls, though. So, wait here for me, okay, and I'll bring back plenty of food."

"Okay."

I opened the front door and walked inside. I knew I looked different than the last time they saw me, but I wasn't a monster. I was a hero. I was the same pixie that saved their tavern. "Hi, everybody!"

The talking stopped, and all eyes turned to me.

"Don't be alarmed. It's just me…Akta. I saved your inn recently. Remember that? Please remember that."

The innkeeper walked out from the back room holding a tray of beers. At the sight of me, his body convulsed, and the tray crashed to the floor. He lifted a trembling finger. "M-m-m-monster!"

"No," I replied. "I'm not. I'm not a—"

The innkeeper's curly-haired son stepped in front of his father, holding a mop handle. He swung it in the air violently. "Get out of here, monster! We're not scared of you!"

"I'm not a monster!" I screamed. "I'm Akta! Remember when I saved your life!"

They didn't hear me. Or maybe they heard me but didn't listen. The little boy swung the mop handle at me and smashed it against my hip.

"Take that!"

"Ow!" I heard a cracking in my hip, but nothing flew off, thank the gods.

"Leave us alone, you big, mean monster," the boy said, shaking his mop handle.

"I'm not a monster," I replied. "I'm your friend."

"You are no friend of ours!" he shouted.

I backed toward the door slowly. "I can see you guys are angry, so I'm just gonna go."

"KILL IT!" the innkeeper shouted, and the dozen drunken people in the bar scrambled to their feet and ran after me.

I hobbled through the door on my gimpy legs and unfurled my wings, flapping them to get more distance between myself and the mop. "Time to run!" I shouted to the troll.

"People chase pretty?" he said. "I smash them!"

I grabbed his arms. "No, no, no! They aren't bad. They're just stupid. You don't have to smash everything, okay?"

"Okay," the troll said, turning to me and running away into the forest.

I pulled down my wings so they wouldn't be a beacon for the mob chasing me and ducked into an overgrown bush, pulling the troll in with me. I breathed hard while I watched the bar patrons scamper down the road.

"This stinks," I said after the innkeeper and his son ran past us.

"I know," said the troll with a soft sigh. "And I still hungry."

"How do you put up with people trying to kill you all the time?"

"I hide," the troll replied. "Just like this."

From above me, I heard a voice in the trees. "Well, well, well, Akta of the Forest. You have finally started to understand the truth."

"Who was that?" I replied, looking up to see who was speaking to me.

"After so many years of betraying your own people, it's nice to see you so humbled." I followed the voice deeper into the woods. It grew louder the further I stumbled. "A pity that it took your master growing sick of you before you learned the error of your ways."

I stepped into a clearing where the voice was the strongest. "Come out and say that to my face!"

"Of course," the voice said, making the bushes rustle and shake. "Where are my manners?"

"I'm gonna stab you in the throat," I growled. "Fair warning."

Three dozen monsters popped out of the woods holding crossbows and swords, all aimed and me and my troll friend.

"I highly doubt that."

A one-eyed pixie emerged into the clearing. His golden wings shimmered behind him, and his one remaining emerald eye glowed brightly in the night.

He was a pixie like me. I had heard tales of him before but never seen him with my own eyes. His skin was dark, like mine, and he wore the same leather armor. One of his eyes was covered in a patch, and a deep scar ran down the right side of his face. Even though we were both pixies, he and I couldn't be more different. I fought for justice and humanity while he led a bunch of cowardly monsters.

"Unless, of course, you *like* being riddled by arrows." He raised his bow toward me.

"Who are you?" I asked.

"My name is Rasmus," the pixie said with a smirk, brushing his brown hair out of his face. "You killed my boss's son. Now, I'm here to take you to him."

# CHAPTER 8

Every step I took through the woods was pure agony. Gas bubbles grew on my arms and legs, slowly. With each step, my body became harder and harder to control and more painful to move.

"Where are you taking us?" I asked Rasmus as he walked us deeper into the woods. Goblins, ogres, and orcs followed behind us, and two trolls guarded me on either side. They were neither nice nor kind like my troll friend, who walked next to me, swinging his arms freely, without a care in the world.

"Do you know where we're going?" I asked him.

"Home," the troll replied. "I haven't been home in a long time."

"Where is home?"

"You'll see," Rasmus said. "It's a surprise we don't often share with outsiders."

"I hate surprises."

"Then you must be miserable right now."

My legs and arms had stiffened on the walk. It was as if I'd slept wrong for a whole week, and I couldn't massage the aching out of my joints. A gas bubble grew large on my left forearm and struggled to break free against my skin.

"You have no idea," I told him.

"Good," Rasmus said, his voice filled with contempt. "You worked with our greatest enemy to kill our people. Those you let live came back maimed and broken. They've never been the same. I hope you suffer greatly."

I looked down at the giant bubble on my left forearm. It was painful to the touch. "Then you are in luck."

"Do you know how I got this scar, Akta of the Forest?" He pointed to the large scar that cut down the right side of his face. "That last name. You don't deserve it. You are not from here."

"Maybe." I tugged at the gas bubble on my arm until it popped like a balloon, leaving no blood behind, just an open wound with a noxious smell seeping out of it. "But it is my name, and you know I have no idea how you got that scar because we only just met."

"I was young, alone, tired, and hungry," Rasmus replied. "One day, I stumbled into a town outside the Veil. I saw a shopkeeper throwing away a loaf of stale bread. So, I took it."

"Was it yummy?" my troll friend asked.

"I wouldn't know," Rasmus sighed, lowering his head. "Odgeir's men found me before I could eat it. They laughed while they poked holes in my wings, and they joked with each other as they dragged a knife down my face. I screamed and begged for death, but they only laughed harder."

"That sad," my troll friend said after a long silence.

A twig snapped in the distance, and Rasmus's ears twitched. "What was that?"

"I'm not sure," a burly orc with a long mallet said. "It's not one of ours."

"Careful, men. Be on the ready. Odgeir's men could be anywhere."

"What are you scared of?" I asked. "Odgeir's men have never breached the Veil."

"That was true once, but not anymore. This week alone, his soldiers have made off with a dozen of my best men. Your friends have decimated our ranks."

"They aren't my friends!" I said, pounding my fist in my hand. "They betrayed me, poisoned me, and turned me into this. I have nothing but hatred for them."

Rasmus chuckled. "Then maybe we won't kill you after all. Now quiet. Be on the ready."

The woods came alive with purple and pink explosions of smoke around us. Rasmus struck one of the guards in the shoulder with his saber. Another soldier grabbed a goblin and vanished with a second puff of smoke.

I recognized the helm of King Odgeir's men, but I had never seen them move like that. They were quicker than I could track, and I was only too glad they didn't attack me before they vanished again as quickly as they had appeared.

"Is it over?" Rasmus asked his orc lieutenant.

"Looks that way," the orc replied.

I looked down at a dead goblin soldier on the ground below me. The scent of blood rippled through my nostrils. I had never favored the stench of blood before, but now it made me lick my lips. My stomach gurgled and ached for something to eat. I wanted raw meat.

"What just happened?" I asked.

Rasmus didn't answer me. Instead, he turned toward his orc lieutenant. "How many did we lose?"

I couldn't give in to my baser instincts. I wasn't a monster, and I didn't eat raw flesh, no matter how tempting it might be to my undead stomach.

"Seven dead. Five missing," the orc replied.

"Seriously," I asked, "what was that?"

Rasmus scowled. "Dammit! Did we at least get a couple of them?"

The orc looked at the ground, shaking his head. "Not enough."

"HEY!" I shouted. "What just happened here?"

Rasmus turned to me. "Can't you recognize your own pixie dust when it's being used on you?"

"Impossible," I said. "That kind of magic can only be harnessed by pixies and fairy folk, and I certainly didn't help him."

"Odgeir found a way," Rasmus said before turning to his troops. "Carry the wounded. Loot the dead. Let's move out quickly before they return."

*

For decades my brother-king's greatest desire was to weaponize my pixie dust, and now he had done it. He had created the elite fighting force of his dreams, and it had become a nightmare to the monsters who called the woods their home.

"I want you to know," Rasmus said, "that they attacked us while we were behind the Veil."

"So?" I replied. "You attack us all the time from beyond the Veil. Half my job is fighting you monsters back to the Veil where you belong."

Rasmus smiled. "It's cute that you still use the word 'us', as if you are one of them, instead of a monster like us."

"I am one of them. I spent my whole life serving and protecting their way of life. They love me."

"And yet they disavowed you the moment it was convenient for them to do so, didn't they, monster?"

"Don't call me that."

"Why not?" Rasmus said. "You are a monster, just like us." The word "monster" dripped off his tongue with such ease and without a single ounce of disgust.

"Now, maybe," I replied. "But that wasn't always the case. Once I hunted monsters like you."

"No," Rasmus said. "You were always one of us, and you know it. They just let you think you were on their side. That is the difference between you and me, Akta of the Forest. I have always embraced my monster lineage."

"I am not a monster!" My hands shook with anger. "I am not like you."

"Yes, you are, but luckily, we accept monsters here. So…welcome home."

We stepped through the thicket and into a great tree city where monsters of every type walked freely amongst each other. On every branch was a sturdy wooden house connected to the tree and other houses with ladders and rope bridges. At the base, doors were carved into the trees.

"Where are we?" I asked, staring up at the canopy filled with homes and bridges.

"Shangri-La. The last free home of monsters. The only place we can exist without being hunted by your friends, for now at least. Before King Odgeir created the Veil, factions of monsters warred with each other constantly. Since he began to hunt us to extinction, we have had no choice but to band together for survival."

Rasmus walked down a hillside toward a mud hut erected in the middle of the treetop town. "Our people have no food, no school, and no money, not even the most basic medical care. Our elders try their best, but they are not healers. So, we suffer, and when we suffer, we attack those who have more than us, those that oppress us."

"You mean humans," I replied.

"They are the ones with the means, and they refuse to share, so we take them for ourselves. Would you do any different, given the circumstances?"

A little orc girl and goblin boy fought over a raw chicken thigh. An old goblin shaman peered into the mouth of a troll boy with chicken pox. A pretty, young ogre with pigtails played soccer with her friends.

"Yes," I replied, but I wasn't sure. All around me, the monsters looked so normal, as if they could live in any human village. What would I have done to protect them if our roles were reversed, Rasmus and mine?

"This is where I leave you for a moment," Rasmus said at the front of the hut. "I will go inside and make sure Ylfingur is ready for you."

Rasmus disappeared inside the hut. I looked around at the monster city. I had seen hundreds of cities in my life, and theirs could have been the rival of any human city. Completely normal.

The pretty ogre child dribbled her ball toward a mesh goal in front of her, just like I've seen human children do a thousand times before. A boy tried to stop her, but she spun around him.

"Gulma dribbles downfield," the girl said, imitating a commentator. "She shoots…" She kicked the ball, and it flew above the goal and bounced on the ground, rolling to a stop at my troll friend's feet. "Little help?" Gulma shouted.

The troll reached down and picked up the ball. "Huh?"

"You kick it," Gulma said. "With your feet."

The troll looked over at me quizzically.

"Go ahead," I said.

The troll dropped the ball and kicked it with his foot. It soared over Gulma's head and into the tree canopy, disappearing into the thatch.

"Too hard!" Gulma shouted. "Oh, man. That was our only ball."

"Sorry," the troll said.

"You trolls are nothing but trouble," Gulma said with a wave of her hand. "Just help me get it back."

The troll looked over at me, and I nodded at him. "Go for it. I'll be right here."

He walked away with Gulma as Rasmus emerged from the hut. "What happened to the troll?"

I pointed toward the thatch. "He's helping a little girl find her ball."

"Whatever. Ylfingur doesn't want to see the troll anyway," Rasmus replied. "He will see you now. If he desires you to live, I'll meet you again. Otherwise, well…it was unpleasant."

"Likewise," I replied.

I disappeared into the tent, hoping that if it were my turn to die again, I would at least have a chance to say a proper goodbye to my troll friend before I went. I had grown quite attached to him. He might have been the best friend I ever had, which says more about me than about him. Still, as I ducked into the hut, I missed him already.

# CHAPTER 9

I have never wavered when confronted with death. I went into every battle expecting to live but resigned to die. There were only ever two options whenever I fought: either I would win, or they would. I never really thought about death until my untimely demise, but now, with every creak of my neck and throb of my knees, I heard it calling for me. Part of me hoped that the monster Ylfingur would kill me and prevent the onerous torture of my slow and agonizing death.

The hut was larger on the inside than I expected. Torches burned around its perimeter, giving it a warm glow. Toward the back, a Cyclops sat cross-legged between two roaring fires with a fur cape draped over his shoulders, fastened with a silver skull pendant. Metal bracers ran down each of his arms, but his chest was bare. Like all Cyclops, his muscles were hard enough to stop a sword, which allowed him to be cavalier with his armaments.

He opened his eye and stroked his thick, grey beard. "I am Ylfingur, father of Bjarngimur. I welcome you, Akta of the Forest."

I was not too big to admit his gruff voice terrified me. I was not frightened easily, but the sight of the massive behemoth sent a shiver down my spine. I could have handled Ylfingur when I was alive, but in death, I had lost many steps, and with each hour that passed, my body stiffened more. Still, I could not show weakness in the eyes of my foe. "I won't go down without a fight, Ylfingur."

"You are in no condition to fight, pixie."

"True." I nodded. "But I have no intention of letting you kill me, either."

Ylfingur laughed. "Kill you? I have no wish to kill you. Do you take me for a savage?"

"Rasmus said you would decide my fate. I just assumed—"

"He is young and brash, not to mention prone to theatrics. I mean you no harm. You are my guest. Please, sit."

I bowed my head. "I'm sorry, but I prefer to stand if you'll allow it. I fear if I sit, I will not be able to get up again."

He nodded. "As you wish. Now, tell me, how did you wind up captured by my men, pixie? You are supposed to be the most fearsome warrior in King Odgeir's army."

"It is a long and complicated story, my liege."

Ylfingur held up his mammoth hands. "There is no need for such formalities."

"I'm sorry. I have been under the watchful eye of the king for so long."

"I am no king," Ylfingur replied. "However, I would like to hear your story."

"Then I shall tell it."

And I did. I told him everything, from the moment I was brought to King Odgeir as a baby, through my training to be a great monster hunter by Sir Cleybourne, and up through my death and resurrection. I told him everything, and he sat patiently and listened.

"A harrowing tale," he said when I was finally finished. "If you wish to kill the king, then I believe our interests are aligned." Ylfingur smiled. "Rasmus! Enter!"

Rasmus walked inside the hut. I didn't know how much he had heard, but he looked at me with a knowing look that said he had been listening to everything. "What can I do for you, boss?"

"Our new fairy friend will be joining us," Ylfingur said. "For a time, at least."

"Now wait," I said, my hands in the air. "Who says I want to join you? I was just telling you a story. I'm not ready to join your ranks."

"You have little choice," Rasmus replied.

"Sure, I do. I could find the king on my own."

"And you will die trying," Ylfingur said.

"I have already died once. It isn't so bad."

Ylfingur stood and leaned forward until I felt his hot breath on my face. "You killed my son, Akta of the Forest. Join me, or I will lose my temper and rip you in half, ending your quest for revenge right here and now."

"Fair enough." I sighed, throwing up my hands again. I didn't have much choice but to join them. "I'm in."

"Good. It is nice to see your stubbornness has a limit…even if it is a high one," Ylfingur said. "Now, let us discuss strategy."

"I have an idea," Rasmus said. "If we bring a small fighting force across the plains in the cover of darkness, we can sneak past the king's defenses, scale the wall, destroy the pixie dust, and get out before anybody knows better."

"After we kill the king, of course," I replied.

"Of course," Rasmus replied. "After we kill the king."

Gulma rushed into the hut, short of breath. She leaned over and placed her hands on her knees. "They're here! They're here!"

"Who's here?" Ylfingur asked.

"The king's soldiers!" Gulma replied, pointing to me. "And they have the troll. The one the dead lady brought."

I gnashed my teeth together. "Show me where."

Gulma ran out of the hut, and I hobbled as closely behind as I could. I unfurled my wings to help with my pace, but even with them, I could hardly get off the ground.

Gulma led us to a cliff overlooking a clearing where twenty guards huddled around a campfire in the valley. Monsters were tied to every tree, and soldiers patrolled the perimeter. Hogtied in the middle of all the soldiers was my troll friend.

I peered down at the guards below us. "How do you want to do this?"

"We should go in hard," Rasmus said. "If we wait much longer, they might jump away, and then we'll never get them back. I think we use the element of surprise to our advantage."

I looked down at my withered hands. "I don't know how effective I will be in a fight."

"Then don't fight. Just kill and disappear back into the woods."

I nodded to him. "I can do that, I think."

"You go down first. Cut our men free one by one. Once they're free, I'll come down and lead the brunt of the attack while you free the troll. Got it?"

I slid down the cliff into the basin below. In front of me, two guards monitored the perimeter, but they weren't doing a very good job. It was easy to sneak past them toward the first tree which held one of Rasmus's men.

"Don't do anything yet," I whispered to him as I cut his rope free. "When Rasmus appears, be ready to attack."

I waited for the orc to nod before I rushed as fast as I could to the next tree, closer to the center of the camp. I cut another soldier free then waited for an opening to move again. It was hard to scuttle across the open space, but I was still able to run for short bursts without my thighs burning or feeling like they were about to fall off.

"Be ready to attack on my signal," I said to the pair of goblins I was cutting free.

I darted to another tree, which stood next to the raging fire at the center of the campsite. I watched a blond-haired soldier kick my troll friend in the stomach.

"One of ye ugly mugs killed me mum!" he shouted. "I'm gonna enjoy watching you get ground up!"

I couldn't let him hurt my friend. I should have stayed in the shadows, but my anger overtook me. I used to be able to control it better when I was alive. Now, white-hot rage controlled every inch of me.

The soldier wound back his leg, but before he kicked, I threw a dagger into his neck. I leaped forward and sliced another soldier across his throat. I stood valiantly in the center of the clearing and watched him fall to my feet.

"Let him go, or I'll rip the rest of you to shreds!" My body was wobbling, and I was starting to feel woozy.

The guards moved to get their weapons, and Rasmus jumped down from the trees and landed in front of me. "Or don't," he said. "I'll shred you to pieces either way."

"Now!" I shouted, and the prisoners dropped their ropes and jumped into battle.

Rasmus swung his sword and chopped the head off one of the soldiers. The other monsters rushed in as well, but I had a different mission. I ran toward my troll friend.

"Akta come for me?" he asked.

"That's right, buddy," I said, cutting through his rope. "You ready to fight for your freedom?"

The troll leaped up as I unbound the last of his rope. "Ready!"

"Then charge!" I shouted, and we both ran into battle. I sliced open a soldier's chest before my bones got the better of me, and I had to lean back against an old oak tree to catch my breath.

Rasmus's soldiers attacked with grace and elegance. I had never seen monsters so coordinated in their attacks. I was used to monsters being slow and oafish, even comical. These soldiers were elegant and smooth. I was lucky I had never run into them beyond the Veil. They would have given me a lot of trouble.

From behind me, I heard a whoosh and ducked to avoid a great hammer aimed for my jaw. I spun around and uppercut the soldier with my dagger, and he fell down dead. I survived. However, my knee locked in place and wouldn't come unstuck. I grabbed the hammer and tried to use it as a crutch to stand up, but I wobbled as I tried to stand. I didn't have much longer in this body, I feared, before I couldn't use it at all. If I wanted victory, it needed to be soon.

"RETREAT!" One of Odgeir's soldiers shouted, and with a purple puff, he vanished along with a half-dozen of his men. The rest of them remained dead on the ground, their blood shimmering pink and purple, infused with the pixie dust.

"Soak it in, men!" Rasmus said. "We won! We finally won."

I wasn't so sure, and as my eyes scanned the horizon, I heard a bugle in the distance. I pulled myself up onto a cliff and peered over it, into the valley below, where thousands of Odgeir's men marched toward us.

"Hrdubally. TIj Apsbent sebven begun."

"Excuse me?" Rasmus said, turning to me. "Oh. Uh, your jaw. It's hanging out."

"Whub do shis dot, dyur," I said, feeling for my jaw. "Oh by dobs! By daw diz hambing out!"

I grabbed onto the sides of my jaw, which dangled from my mouth. It was true. I was falling apart. My whole body was dying slowly, and I was barely any closer to the king than when I woke up.

I snapped my jaw back into place. "OW!" It hurt badly, but at least it locked into place, and I was able to move it again.

"Now, what were you saying?" Rasmus said.

"The King's men are coming. We have to bring Ylfingur here right now. Otherwise, we'll all be killed. Some of us for a second time."

"Go! Bring every man you can find," Rasmus said, and a goblin hobbled up the cliff of the encampment to bring back Ylfingur's men. I hoped they would return before Odgeir's men razed the forest to the ground.

# CHAPTER 10

I killed a lot of monsters during my time on Earth. I would watch the life drain from their eyes, their blood drip on the ground; I was the harbinger of their doom.

Truth be told, however, I never thought about death much during my life. It was simply a necessary part of my job. I always knew it was possible for me to die, but I never let that fact hold me back from any task assigned to me.

I was blessed with a muscular frame that rarely ached or gave me trouble. I could fly. I could fight. I could love. My body was lithe and limber. There was little I couldn't do. There was a time when I could defeat anyone and anything in front of me, from dragons to goblins and everything in between. There might have been a time not long before when I could have taken on an entire army by myself.

But now, as the scouts ran to find Ylfingur and bring him back to us, I realized that I would not live to see the end of this battle. Looking down at my weak hands and frail body, I knew I was looking out at my doom. My body could not hold together long enough or well enough to defeat them. I did not even have the strength to ride to the castle, let alone survive an army's violent attack. If I had my pixie dust, perhaps it would be a different story.

I knew what awaited me on the other side of death, and I did not look forward to it—my eternal damnation. Worse yet, I had agreed to suffer King Odgeir's sentence on top of mine if I failed.

"And you couldn't find any of the pixie dust?" Ylfingur asked. He had wandered around the battlefield for the past hour, trying to devise a plan.

"We searched everywhere," I said. "If we had any, I could jump some of your men to the castle and end this."

"That is very troubling," Ylfingur said. "You have no idea how they vanished, then?"

"Rasmus has an idea," I said, pointing back to him as he leaned against a tree. "But I think it's crazy."

"And what idea is that, my son?" Ylfingur said.

Rasmus put his hands on his hips. "It's because the dust is in their blood."

"It's impossible," I said. "I have never heard such a story in all my travels."

"Maybe you haven't heard tales where you come from, but I have, as one who grew up in the trees," Rasmus said. "There have always been whispers in the forest of pixies who could vanish at will. That has been true since before my time."

"And how did they get it into their blood?" Ylfingur asked.

I rolled my eyes. "Don't encourage him."

"They snorted the dust, injected it, spread it on their food. Anything to get it into their bloodstreams. The dust slowly drove them mad, but for a time, they were the most powerful fairies in the world, able to vanish without a trace at a moment's notice."

I looked down at the ground. There were pools of blood all around me, and I had to admit the blood was like none I had ever seen before. It sparkled and shone when it came in contact with the light from the sun. Pink crystals twinkled inside the blood. I fought my stiff knees and bent down to the ground to look a soldier in his dead eyes. His pupils glistened with the same pink flakes.

I placed my finger on the ground and dipped it into the blood. When I pulled it up to the light, it sparkled, just like my pixie dust did when it met the sunlight. The smell of the blood was intoxicating.

"Orcs, goblins, zombies, pixies, and monsters of all types!" a voice blared from the front of the army underneath our position. "We have allowed your kind to exist and to hoard our most precious resource for far too long. Your power! Now, we come to claim what is rightly ours as your betters!"

I sighed. "I can't believe I used to work for them."

"Yes," Rasmus said. "You died working for them."

"Don't remind me," I said, staring at the shimmering blood on my fingers.

"Surrender now," the voice continued, "and you will be spared the humiliation of torture and given a quick death. For those that resist, may the gods have mercy on your immortal souls!"

"They intend to slaughter us like sheep," Rasmus said to Ylfingur.

Ylfingur shook his head solemnly. "Then we will fight 'til the last man. We have no other option!"

"Maybe we do," I said, still staring at the blood. "This is going to be disgusting, but if Rasmus is right, then…"

"So, now you think I'm right?" Rasmus scoffed.

"I said if," I replied. Every word scratched against my throat. Everything hurt.

"And what happens if I'm right?"

"We can enact your plan," I said. "The one you talked about in the hut. We take a small group of men behind enemy lines, destroy the pixie dust, and kill the king."

"That was just my first plan," Rasmus said, looking worried. "I was spitballing. I figured we would think on it."

"There is no time for that now," I replied. "It's as good as we're going to get."

"And how do you think we'll get behind enemy lines? It's not like we can snap our fingers."

"No, you're right." I looked down at the rotting bodies below me. I had never thought dead bodies looked appetizing when I was alive, but now, in my undead state, I couldn't take my eyes off them. They would make a delicious dinner. "But maybe we can have the next best thing…"

The soldier's flesh looked delicious. I had been trying to reject my animal instincts since the first moment the sweet smell of blood reached my nostrils, but my body longed for the taste of man-flesh. All that held me back were my principles. Ripping through the skin of a human would truly make me a monster. Could I live with myself if I turned into everything I hated? On the other hand, could I live with myself if I let King Odgeir get away with his betrayal?

"Just do whatever you have to do already!" Ylfingur said. "We don't have much time."

I couldn't hold back my desire for one more second. I ripped the throat off one of the dead soldiers with my teeth and gnawed on his flesh. I sunk my teeth into the soldier again and again until his blood ran down my face and covered my clothes.

"My god!" Ylfingur said. "What are you doing?"

For the first time since I came back from the dead, I felt good. Really good. Better than I had since…maybe ever. I felt the flexibility come back to my joints and my shoulders loosen. I stood without needing help to do so. Wiping the blood from my mouth, I heaved and felt raw power coursing through my veins.

"Stand back."

I closed my eyes tightly and tried to vanish. My body shook, and my mind vibrated, and then, in a puff of purple smoke, I was gone, only to appear again a few moments later.

"It worked," Rasmus said.

"Yes," I replied. "It worked. Now, I can use the pixie dust flowing through my veins to bring a small group of your men past King Odgeir's army and right up to the gates of the castle. While your men fight here, we can make it to the throne room, kill the king, and end this. Then, I will have my revenge!"

"That's incredibly risky," Rasmus said. "We barely have enough men to fight one battle, let alone two."

"You don't have enough to fight even one," I replied. "You will be wiped out by that army in hours. You cannot win."

"Then why try?" Rasmus said.

"Because it's the best plan we have."

"It's a suicide mission!"

Ylfingur held up a hand. "We'll all die if we do nothing. We'll likely die if we do something, too, but at least we have the choice. We won't live through this day, but we can live while we are here."

Rasmus paused for a moment, absorbing all of this. "I suppose given the options, it is better to take this risk and at least take our fate into our own hands."

"My sentiments, exactly," Ylfingur said.

"Okay," Rasmus said. "So, if we take a small squad of men to the town, we can cause a distraction, maybe get the guards to call some soldiers back, and buy you time to evacuate Shangri-La."

"It could work, but it would be incredibly risky. Who knows if there are even enough soldiers left in the city to call for help. It looks like every soldier in the king's army is out there."

"I know it's risky, but so is this whole plan. If we can draw away some of the king's soldiers, it will leave more of our men to help evacuate Shangri-La, and if that's all we get out of it, then it will be worth it. Then Akta and I can infiltrate the castle and destroy the pixie dust by ourselves."

"Won't you need more men?" Ylfingur asked.

Rasmus looked over at me. "No. I think Akta and I can handle it, don't you?"

I nodded. "Even at my worst, I can kill the king with my bare hands."

"Then pick your squad," Ylfingur said. "You have my support."

"Me coming!" my troll friend shouted, running up to me. "Me coming!"

"It's very dangerous," I replied. "We're all gonna die."

The troll grabbed me around the shoulders. "Me coming, too!"

"All right, buddy. You're coming too. Help Rasmus round everybody up while I prepare."

"Prepare?"

I didn't reply to him. I dropped to my knees and started to eat all the flesh I could find. The pixie dust had soaked into every inch of the men's flesh, and I needed as much as

I could get if I was going to jump people to the castle over twenty miles away.

There was a rule about pixie dust. You had to know where you were going so perfectly that you could envision it in your mind's eye. If you could do that, you could move thousands of miles in an instant, but if even one detail was wrong, you could be lost in the vacuum of nothingness forever.

Luckily, I remembered every inch of the castle walls. I could never forget even one centimeter of my home, no matter how long I lived in Hell.

"Will none of you surrender?" a voice screamed from the head of the army. "Do you truly wish all of your bodies to be broken before you die? Well, we can arrange that!"

The sky turned black as the army let loose a thousand arrows, blotting out the sun. They landed all around us, but I was too consumed with the flesh of the soldiers to care. I knew I had enough pixie dust to survive the jump, but I wanted more. I wanted to feel human again. I wanted to feel alive, and every ounce of flesh I ate brought me closer to feeling like I was normal, even though the feeling could never last.

"Akta!" Rasmus shouted from under a tree, hiding from the volley of arrows. "We have to go now."

I didn't answer. I clung more tightly to my meal. As Rasmus grew closer, I growled at him like a wild dog.

"Akta, let's GO!"

"GRAWWWW!" I snarled and turned to him with blood around my mouth and fire in my eyes. I had never felt so much power coursing through me before. The strength of a god was in my veins.

Without a word, Rasmus smacked me across the face, hard enough that I winced in pain. However, the slap also brought me back to reality and the mission at hand.

"Better?" Rasmus asked.

"Better," I replied.

"Then let's go." Rasmus dragged me up to standing. "Will you be okay, Ylfingur? You will be here alone, with few troops."

"Don't worry about me," Ylfingur said. "I have fought many battles."

"Very well," Rasmus replied. "Then off we go."

I looked back at Ylfingur as Rasmus's troops gathered around. "Good luck."

"You as well," Ylfingur said, nodding to me. "Godspeed."

I focused my mind, closing my eyes and imagining every inch of the castle I had called my home for so long. It would all be over soon, and I would find peace. The king would be dead, and with that thought, I smiled, vanishing, taking the rest of Rasmus's troops with me.

# CHAPTER 11

This was it. The culmination of my entire life, or at least my second life, led to this moment. Every day of my training, every ounce of my skill, every cold night in the wilderness alone. It all came to this. It was a sobering fact that all I had gained from my years on Earth, and two lifetimes, was the ability to kill a king. A sobering truth, but a truth nonetheless, and since my eternal soul depended on the successful completion of my mission, I was ready to oblige.

Our troop of monster soldiers reappeared in front of the castle in a puff of purple and pink smoke. Usually, troops guarded the doors to the castle, but now they were bare.

"King Odgeir must have sent all his troops to the front lines," I said as Rasmus's men huddled around me.

Pixie dust travel wasn't easy for many people, and half of Rasmus's men fell over vomiting when we rematerialized. Rasmus wasn't affected by the travel, nor was my troll friend.

"Get up, men!" Rasmus shouted. "This is no time to get sick."

Rasmus's men rose shakily to their feet and gripped their weapons. Even though they were sick to their stomachs, they were ready to fight for their home.

"What now?" the troll said to Rasmus.

"Now, we split up," he replied. "We need some of King Odgeir's troops to come back here to split them up. Ylfingur won't last long against a barrage of their entire army. It's up to you all to cause a distraction and make whatever guards are left call for help. Meanwhile, Akta and

I will climb the tower, destroy the pixie dust, and kill the king."

"Me go with pretty?" the troll asked.

"No," I said. "I need you to stay out here. Cause a distraction. As big a distraction as you can manage. Can you do that?"

"That will help?" he asked.

I nodded. "More than you know."

"Then me do it!"

I smiled at him. "If we don't see each other again, know that I will miss you and cherish your friendship."

"Same," the troll said with a grin before bounding off toward the town.

"And try not to hurt the innocents!" I shouted after him.

"Sure," Rasmus said behind me. "If you can find any innocents, try not to hurt them."

"Good luck!" The troll barreled into the side of a building as the townsfolk shrieked at him.

"All right," Rasmus said. "The rest of you, follow the troll. You must buy Ylfingur as much time as possible to evacuate the monster town. The more troops we draw to us, the more time he has. That's up to you, so go, and the gods' speed to you."

The rest of the troops ran forward toward the town, brandishing their weapons in the air, leaving only Rasmus behind with me.

"This is a dumb plan," I said.

"I'm not disagreeing with you," Rasmus replied. "But as we've already pointed out, it's the only one we have."

I looked up to the castle. All the archers that usually guarded its walls were gone. The king must have wanted to cleanse the monsters from the world in one battle, using every soldier he had at his disposal. I just hoped there were enough left to call for reinforcements.

I pointed to a window at the top of a tower above us. "That window is our best shot. It's close to the king's bedchamber."

"Can you climb?" Rasmus asked.

My arms were stiff again, and I could barely move my legs. All the energy I'd gained from the pixie dust blood had run its course and left me with nothing but tired, old, undead bones. "No, but what choice do I have?"

"Fair enough," Rasmus said, nodding. "Let me at least give you a boost."

He bent down and placed his hands together. I stepped onto them, and he flung me into the air. I unfurled my wings and tried to rise as high into the air as possible, but I couldn't get further than halfway before I latched onto the tower.

It was torture to place one hand over the other and pull myself up. I felt my tendons loosen in my arms with every pull. Rasmus climbed above me, quickly and easily, as quickly as I used to move when I was alive, and soon he was through the window above me.

"Come on," he said to me. "You've been stuck down there forever. We don't have much time."

I willed my arms to move, but when they did, I felt a snap in my shoulder. I could barely keep my other hand on the wall as my left arm dangled at my side.

Rasmus reached down for me. "Grab onto my hand! I'll pull you up!"

I swung my throbbing arm up to him, but I was just out of reach. I summoned all my strength and heaved my arm in one last show of strength. Rasmus grabbed it and started to pull. That's when I felt the arm detach from my body. It didn't hurt. It was like watching a piece of paper rip down the middle, except that piece of paper was my body.

"Stop!" I shouted, but it was too late. My left arm dislocated from my shoulder, and the force pushed me from the wall. Rasmus didn't know what to do. He used all his energy to fling me toward an open ledge below me just as my body tore from my arm. I sailed down the tower and crashed into the ground, rolling into a dark room at the bottom of the castle. I had never seen this place before.

Tears streamed down my face. "Velaska," I whispered. "Why have you forsaken me?"

"Hello," a raspy, female voice said from the darkness in the room. "Is somebody there?"

I pushed myself to my knees with my one arm and looked at the figure sitting next to a roaring fire at the far side of the room. "Who are you?"

"Please," the voice said. "Please, I can't make it any faster."

"Stay there," I said, rising to my feet. I pulled out my knife and hobbled through the room. "Don't move."

"Please don't hurt me."

"I make no promises," I replied. "Tell me who you are!"

I stepped into the light of the room and was able to make out a plump, old woman with dark skin and green eyes. She wore a head scarf and a long apron covered in dark stains. Her eyes might have been kind if they weren't so scared at the sight of me.

Admittedly, I was hideous, ambling along on my knobby knees. My jaw hung on by a thread. One of my arms was missing, and my eyes were shrouded in blackness. Had I looked upon myself for the first time, I would have been scared as well.

"Please," the old woman said. "I have done everything you asked."

"Who are you, old crone?" I hissed, moving further into the room until I was bathed in the light of the fire.

The old woman squinted at me for a long moment. She cocked her head to one side, then the other. "My gods. Is it really you?" She rushed toward me. "Akta? My dear, sweet Akta? What have they done to you?"

"Don't change the subject," I said, batting her arms away from me. "Who are you?"

"My child," she said, her hand on my rotting shoulder. "I know it's been a long time, but don't you recognize your own mother?"

I grabbed her by the fingers with my one remaining hand and squeezed until she dropped to her knees. "Do not lie to me, old crone. My mother is dead."

"No! That's not true. I swear to the gods that's not true."

"You lie!"

The old woman stood and removed her head scarf. Underneath her ears were long and pointy, like mine. Then, she removed the cape from her back and two, beautiful, golden wings unfurled behind her.

"No, Akta," she said. "It is King Odgeir who has lied to you your whole life. I tried to protect you. I tried to save you. I watched you grow. I am your kin, child. Of that, I am positive."

My mind raced back to my childhood. I seemed to remember an old, black woman nursing me when I was a child and taking care of me, but then she vanished, and I never saw her again. I assumed she had died, but could it have been my mother all along?

"That…was you?" I asked. "You took care of me all those years?"

"Yes, my child. None of the other nursemaids would touch you, so the king let me care for you in your youth until you could care for yourself." She wrapped me in a hug. "Do you feel it, child? Only a mother's embrace can be so powerful."

When she wrapped me in her arms, it was as if all the evils of the world vanished. I was transported back to being a baby, before I ever held a knife or killed a monster, and well before I died. For decades, I had believed my mother was dead, and it took until my untimely demise to realize that wasn't true.

"Mom," I said. Tears streamed down my face. "It really is you, isn't it?"

"Yes, child."

I pushed back from her. "But…what are you doing here?"

"I have been the King's prisoner since the last great war. I fear that he is planning to march on our kind again. King Odgeir has been forcing me to make pixie dust for him. I had long told him that I forgot the recipe, but finally, he told me to either make more, or he would kill you."

"And then he killed me anyway, didn't he?" I said, snarling.

"It would seem that way," she said, stroking my cheek. "I'm so sorry, my love. I only thought I was protecting you."

"Well, King Odgeir is using the pixie dust to hunt monsters. His men are fighting them now, near the Veil."

"That's horrible. He told me that it was to expand our kingdom and protect the monsters inside of it. I never thought—"

"You never thought he was a liar," I replied. "It's okay, Mom. Even kings lie. I understand that now."

"I would have still made him the dust, even if I knew," my mother said, looking up at me. "I would have traded all the monsters in the forest for you to be safe."

A loud horn rang outside. It was the call of the guard tower, demanding reinforcements. The monsters outside had done their job. The soldiers would be back soon, and now it was time to do my job. Kill the king.

"Akta," Rasmus shouted. "Are you in here? It took a while, but I found your—" Rasmus and my mother's eyes connected. "Mom? What are you doing here?"

"Mom?" I said. "That's impossible. If that's your mom, it would mean you're my—"

"He is your brother," my mother said.

My brother. I had a mother and a brother. I had a family. My whole life, I thought I was alone, the only pixie in the world. I had never met another like me. Now, I had a family.

I thought I was alone, that my parents had died. That turned out to be a lie. Both King Odgeirs, my brother-king and father-king, let me believe that. They were no longer my family. They had taken my family from me. They had taken my life from me. And they had to pay; one with their life, the other with the end of his lineage.

"Where is King Odgeir hiding?" I asked.

"He does not hide. He comes every day," my mother said, "to check on my progress. He will be here any minute." A long shadow fell over the room as the door swung open. "That's him now. Please, hide."

"I will not hide," I replied. "I will end him quickly."

"You're in no condition," my mother said. "Please hide…for me. I can't lose you again."

"Fine," I grumbled. "But only for a moment." I stepped back into the shadows with Rasmus and listened as King Odgeir's boots stomped through the room.

"Dear, sweet, Zabina," the king said. "Good day to you. What ho?"

"What ho, my king," my mother replied with a smile, trying to hide her anger at him.

The king leaned in and kissed my mother on the forehead. "Just another day."

My mother didn't shudder or flinch. She would have made a good king, as comfortable with lying as she was. "It is loud out there. I heard the horn of war blow. Is something the matter?"

"Nothing for you to concern yourself with," the king replied.

I leaned out from the darkness. "I can kill him while he's distracted."

Rasmus held me back. "It's too dangerous. Mom said—"

"Don't try to be my brother now," I said, shaking him free. "This is all too dangerous. That's why I'm dead. I'm going."

"Fine, but be careful."

"No."

I inched out of the darkness toward the king, careful not to make any sudden moves. It wasn't hard since I could barely move my legs. I pulled the dagger out of my belt.

"How is production on the pixie dust coming?" the king asked.

"Slow, my king, but I am making progress. I hope to have more for you to use soon. I am very close to unlocking the original recipe used by the ancient pixies."

"So, you have no new dust for me to use?"

My mother shook her head. "No, my king. Nothing more than what you gave me, of which only a small fraction remains unused."

The smile drained from the king's face. "That is disappointing. You told me if I found you a sample of pixie dust, you could create an unlimited quantity for me. I scoured the world to bring you not only a small sample but an entire bag to study, and now you claim to need more time." The king stepped forward toward my mother menacingly. "I get the sneaking suspicion that you are lying to me."

"I'm not, my king. I have always been loyal to you and your family."

"Then what is taking so long? You gave me the first batch mere days after I brought you the dust to study."

My mother gulped loudly. "I used the powder you gave me to create a potion for your soldiers, as you asked.

However, there is a difference between stretching the uses of existing pixie dust and making more from scratch."

"Then stretch it some more!" The king growled.

"I can't. The existing supply is finite and nearly exhausted. I cannot rush production of more."

"Why not?"

"If I get the recipe wrong by even a drop, I risk killing all your troops in an instant or transporting them across the world with no way for them to get back. We wouldn't want that, king, would we?"

The king shook his head. "No, we wouldn't want that."

"Then, I'm afraid you'll just have to trust me. I can only go as fast as I can go."

A sinister smile grew across his face. "You have my trust for now, but my patience wears thin. It would be a shame if your daughter should suffer because of this delay."

My mother swallowed loudly. "So, my daughter, she's okay?"

"Of course," the king replied. "I am a man of my word, am I not?"

This was my chance. I raised the dagger over my head. "No! You are a liar!"

I swung the dagger down as hard as I could, but my decaying body had lost so much speed. I was just slow enough that the king dodged my attack. I tried to stop my hand when I knew the dagger wouldn't connect with its target, but I could not, and the dagger plunged deep into my mother's chest. Her blood oozed onto my hands, and her wounded eyes looked at me for a moment before she fell to the floor.

# CHAPTER 12

"Mom," I whimpered, collapsing next to her. "Mom, mom, mom. Please, no. No. I just found you. Please don't go."

I had never known sadness, true sadness, until that moment. Really, I'd never had anything to lose. When my father-king died, he was old, and he went peacefully. When my mentor died, it was valiant in battle with an ice giant. I had mourned them in my way, but I knew it was their time to go. This death was completely preventable. I wept bitter tears.

"It's okay, Akta," she whispered back, her blood pooling on the floor under her.

"I'm so sorry, Mom," I said through my tears.

"It's okay. I'm just glad I got to see you one last time."

The last of the air went out of her lungs, and she collapsed next to me. Her eyes lost the sparkle of life, and I knew she was dead. She was now doomed to wander the same rock bridge I did, meet with Petrus, and be damned for eternity. It was all my fault. No, not my fault. It was King Odgeir's fault.

"What have you done!?" the king shouted.

I spun back to him with anger in my veins, rage overflowing until I lost all feelings of pain in my body. I had only one mission left, to kill King Odgeir.

"What have I done?" I choked the words. "I killed my mother! And now I'm going to kill you!"

The king looked at me for a moment, wondering if I was capable of killing him in my current degraded condition, but it didn't matter. He was a coward, and cowards ran away. That was exactly what he did. He burst through the door of the room and out into the hallway.

"I'm going after him," I said to Rasmus, who looked down at my mother, our mother. "I know this is hard, brother, but we have a mission to take care of now."

"She told you to hide," Rasmus said, dropping to his knees. "She said to hide. That's all you had to do, and she would be alive right now."

"Hey!" I shouted. "We can mourn later. Right now, we have a mission. Destroy the pixie dust. I will find the king and end him. Can you do that?"

Rasmus nodded through his tears. "I can, but how can you be so matter-of-fact about it?"

The only solace was that my life would soon be over, and I could find my mother again in the great beyond. The corners of my lips turned up. "Because I know I will see her again soon enough. And so will you."

I hobbled out of the room and headed toward the throne room. I knew that was where I would find King Odgeir. He was weak-willed and cowardly, so he would escape to the only place that made him feel safe. It was where he felt the most powerful.

It was inevitable that I would die soon. It was agony to walk, and when I did, I could hear my skin crack and break under me. I could barely lift my single remaining arm over my head, and my hand was stuck holding the dagger inside of it.

In truth, I wanted to die. I was sick of this world and its endless pain. Even if I had to suffer for ten million years, it would not have been as horrible as walking around in a useless body. It wasn't long ago that I flew like a bird out the window of the throne room, and now, I could barely hobble into it. The only thing keeping me alive was the thought of killing the man—my own brother—and sending him to Velaska.

I stepped down the stairs into the throne room. Sure enough, King Odgeir stood there hunched over, trying to catch his breath, next to a sheathed sword he kept for ceremonies.

"What will you do now?" I said. "Your men have been driven from the castle to fight your battles."

The king spun around with a smug look of superiority on his face. He drew his ornate sword, decorated down the blade with ancient runes, and pointed it at me. "They may be gone, dear sister, but I do not need them. I can take care of you myself. I have done it before."

"By poison, the coward's weapon."

King Odgeir gripped his sword tightly. "It worked, though. I tried for years to kill you, by all manners. I sent you on ridiculous missions and suicidal plots, and yet you always returned."

"You could have just sliced my neck open with your bare hands, like a man of honor."

King Odgeir chuckled. "And now I will."

"You are foolish to try," I replied. "It is my destiny to kill you."

"And it is my destiny to destroy every one of your accursed kind!" The king raised his sword. "One of our destinies will go unfulfilled today!"

He swung the sword. I tried to parry it with my dagger, but I was too slow. I dove out of the way, but the sword sliced through my right leg. Now, I was legless and armless. I could not stand. I could barely crawl. I felt my tendons twist and tear each time I moved to pull my body away from the king. There was a time when I could have killed King Odgeir easily, but now I was painfully close to losing everything.

"You have failed, sister," the king said, smirking. "What a story it would have been if you triumphed. A pity, that. I suppose my destiny was greater than yours on this day!"

King Odgeir raised his sword again to strike me down. He lowered it toward my head, but the blow never came. Instead, a puff of purple smoke plumed from around me, and I heard the loud clang of a sword as it met Odgeir's. I looked up to see Rasmus's saber blocking the king's steel from my neck. My brother.

"How did you get here?" I asked.

"I might not have ever been to this castle before," he said. "But you are my sister, and I will never forget you. I just remembered everything about you until I could picture you in my mind's eye, and then I vanished. I ended up here."

"You could have died or been lost in the void forever."

"I could have, but, thankfully, I didn't," Rasmus said, still blocking the king's weapon. "Now, end this."

I pushed myself up to sit and pulled on Rasmus's back, so I could stand by leaning on him. With a heave, I unleashed my trusty, ivory dagger, which cut through the air and caught the king right in his neck, sending blood flying everywhere.

The king fell to the ground, gurgling on his blood as he convulsed, dead.

*

The king's body hit the ground outside the palace with a thud. Rasmus had carried it to the ledge outside the castle that overlooked the town square and tossed it over. Across the town square, monsters fought with soldiers, but when the king's body landed amongst them, the fighting stopped.

"Your king is dead!" I shouted. "The fighting will cease now."

Rasmus stood next to me, hanging onto my body. It was the only way I could stand, and it was hard, even with his help.

"Give me the pixie dust you used to help me," I said.

Rasmus handed me a blue bag with stars on it. I recognized it as my own. I never thought I would see it again. "Here you go."

"Is this all of it?" I asked.

Rasmus nodded. "I destroyed everything else."

"Good," I said, turning to the ledge. I turned over the pouch, and the pixie dust poured out. "This is the last of the pixie dust." I coughed. It was hard to talk. Every word was agony. "Very soon, whatever is left in your veins will run its course, and you will be mortal once more."

I leaned over the balcony. No matter how hard I tried to push myself back up, my arm would not move to my command. "I have slain the king. By the law of our land, I may now appoint his successor."

All the townspeople, monsters, and soldiers gasped at the thought of it. It had been generations since the old laws were put into effect, but they were iron clad. Whoever I chose would be respected and given their place as the rightful heir to the kingdom and the throne.

"I name my brother, Rasmus of the Forest, as your new lord. Kneel before your king!"

"What are you doing?" Rasmus said. "I don't know how to lead a nation."

I smiled. "You'll figure it out. I have faith. You will be a great king. Kind, noble, and patient." I turned back toward the crowd. All of them—even my troll friend, who somehow made it through the battle—rested on bended knee in honor of their new king.

"This is a great day for our kingdom!" I shouted. "From this moment hence, all species and races will be looked upon as equals!" I pointed to a soldier, strong-jawed and baby-faced. "Soldier, go tell the generals they are to stop fighting at once."

"Yes, ma'am," he said, disappearing into a purple cloud of smoke.

With that, I was spent. I had no more energy left to give. My jaw clenched shut, and I slid down the wall. I could not move my arm, my leg, or my head. My jaw and tongue barely moved when I talked. "It is your turn now, brother. I have no more words to say. My time is over."

My eyes closed, and my breathing labored. I felt Rasmus kneel next to me. "No. Please don't go!" His voice broke into sobs. "I have no idea what I'm doing. I don't know how to lead. Stay and help me. I order you to stay and help me."

I let out my final breath. "I. No longer. Take orders. From kings."

*

I expected to wake up in the pits of hell, but instead of darkness, I was surrounded by shimmering white light. All around me, the light pulsed, and I felt overwhelming happiness. I no longer hurt. I looked down and saw not my disgusting blue body but my original one. Behind me, my two beautiful, golden wings flapped flawlessly and beautifully.

"You did better than I could have imagined, my child," Velaska's voice whispered. "I will enjoy my pet for the rest of eternity."

In front of me, two golden wings flapped in time with mine. From the light, my mother emerged, holding out her arms for me. I flew into them, and she wrapped me in her warmth.

"Now is the time to rest, my child," my mother said, and I couldn't agree more. For the first time in as long as I could remember, there were no more battles to fight. I was at peace.

# BOOK 2

*"Fallen"*

# CHAPTER 1

"More mead!" I shouted. My voice rang through the great halls of Valhalla. "More mead for my friends and me!"

I sat in the castle that the greatest warriors of all time called their eternal home. Upon my death, my true death, I had been awarded the greatest honor in the universe, the ability to live out my eternity in the hall of Valhalla, telling stories of my conquests and battles for all time, as was befitting a warrior of my stead.

"Another story!" I shouted. "Who will regale us with a tale of bravery?"

The great Danish warrior, Bjorn, a fat, jolly man with a bearskin coat, stood up. "I will! This be the tale of how I slaughtered the Centaur of the Green Isle."

For the last five hundred years, I had been gleefully, exuberantly happy. All I had to do was wait until I died for it to happen. In my twenty-six years of life on Earth, I had experienced many emotions, including what I thought was happiness, but nothing compared to what I felt in Valhalla. No, I didn't know true happiness until I was killed.

Well, not the first time I died, of course. The first time I died was at the hands of my adopted brother, King Odgeir. He poisoned me so that he could weaponize the magical pixie dust which I had refused to give him. He murdered me for it. And I returned from the grave to enact my revenge, with the help of the devil Velaska. Revenge—a tale as old as time.

A statuesque, blond Valkyrie, tall as she was fair, ran over with a new stein of ale and slammed it down in front of me. I picked it up and held it up to the Viking warriors sitting with me.

"A toast!" I yelled. "To the hunt!"

The Viking warriors smashed their glasses against mine. None of us had a care in the world anymore, nor any obligations, except to drink, eat, and be merry.

"And to you, Akta!" A blond Viking with braided hair held up her beer. "The noblest pixie I ever had the pleasure of knowing."

I appreciated their acceptance of me because I was not, by any account, a person they would usually have shared an ale with. I wasn't a person at all, even though I looked human. Fairy folk are all humanoids, but I could not say that a pixie was a person, at least not without confusion, derision, and possibly execution.

In fact, in most cultures of the world, including the Vikings with whom I drank, it was legal and even encouraged to hunt pixies. Many of the men in Valhalla, and a few of the women even, gained acceptance into the great hall by killing hundreds of my kind for sport. Though Petrus, the gatekeeper of the Underworld, frowned upon such practices now, there was a time when hunting monsters like me was a noble venture worthy of veneration, which was why fairy folk had been hunted almost to extinction.

"Mother," I said. My mom sat across from me with crossed arms. Aside from me, she was the only dark-skinned woman in the whole hall. Our pointed ears and bright-green eyes set us apart among the blue eyes and rounded ears of the other warriors. "Isn't this the grandest day you have ever had?"

"No. It's not." Mom stood up. "In fact, I'm going to bed." She sighed and pushed away from the table, then squeezed her way through the tables full of fat, jolly men.

"Mom!" I pushed through the crowd after her. "Wait!"

I felt bad for my mother. She wasn't supposed to be in Valhalla. She wasn't a warrior, noble or otherwise. However, after I completed my mission to kill my murderer and was successful, Velaska rewarded me with a life of ease and comfort and allowed my mother to join me. But Velaska had not considered my mother's needs when she rewarded me. My mother was not one for talk of battle or conquests, and that was all the other warriors cared to discuss.

"Mom!" I shouted as I ran up the stairs after her. I was exceedingly drunk, to the point of falling over, but I managed to squeeze through the bulbous men filling the hall and up to the stone stairs which led up to our chambers.

"I said I'm going to bed," my mother said, her tone impatient.

"You don't have to do that!" I climbed the stairs after her, swaying to either side as I tried to steady myself on the banister.

"I know I don't," my mother said. "But I want to. I can't hear another story about hunting today, sweet child."

"We can…stop—I think," I said, not confident that was true. "It's possible to talk…about other things. I guess."

"You haven't stopped talking about murdering monsters in five hundred years," she replied. "Why would you stop now?"

"How about a walk?" I asked. "Let's take a walk to the gardens. You always liked that, yeah?"

She sighed. "It's the only thing about this place that I like."

"It's a might bit better than Hell," I said. "You can trust me on that."

My mother hadn't gone to Hell after her death, so she didn't know its horrors, but I did. I had seen the lakes of fire and heard the ungodly screams of the tortured as they writhed in agony. There was no end to their suffering or their torment, and it was a great blessing that Velaska kept my mother from that fate.

Mother shook her head. "I don't think you can understand how I feel about this place." She looked out over the Vikings toasting their mead. "These men, many of them, hunted our kin, and they were rewarded for it. Just look at them, laughing and drinking. If anybody deserves to be tortured for all eternity, it's these murderers."

I looked out at the horde of men and women singing songs and laughing. Their fur capes covered their broad shoulders, and their thick beards hung down to their waists. The bar stretched along the far wall for the entire length of the castle. Ten Valkyries manned the tavern, gathering drinks, working tirelessly to quench the unquenchable thirst of the Vikings.

On the wall above the bar hung a hollowed-out skull suspended on a wooden plaque—a troll skull, mouth open, forever screaming in pain. It looked just like a friend of mine who had protected me on my second journey to Earth. Around the hall, red-headed men with bad teeth wore necklaces of tiny scalps, no doubt gathered from the fairies of the Northern Isles before they'd been massacred to extinction. A few of the women wore earrings made from the bones of a gnome, and I saw a brooch made from fairy's wings.

Trophies of hunted monsters decorated the hall. They had surrounded me for eons, but I had never truly seen them until that moment. As I stared into the eye sockets of the troll skull, screaming silently at me, a soft hand pressed against my shoulder. I understood then how such a sight could be horrifying to my mother. For the first time since I had entered the great hall, it turned my stomach.

"You know," my mother said, touching my shoulder, "I think I feel like a walk after all if the offer still stands."

I smiled at her. "That sounds nice."

# CHAPTER 2

"I'm not sure how I never saw it before," I said, walking with my mother through the tulip fields outside of Valhalla.

When you were inside the castle, you couldn't get a sense of its scale against the surrounding mountains. From the gardens, though, the behemoth size of Valhalla was impressive. You could not see the top of the highest tower, not even if you craned your neck up to the sky.

"You didn't see it because you didn't look, my love," my mother said, smiling. She always enjoyed the field of multi-colored tulips that stretched out from the castle's base into the horizon.

"But it was staring me right in the face," I said. "I feel so foolish."

She shook her head. "We are all fools for that which we allow to blind us."

"But how can I make you go back in there?" I asked, bending over to catch the soft smell of the tulips. "How can we sit among them, and eat among them, and laugh with them?"

My mother held up her hand. "You were once a monster hunter as well, my love. Do not forget that. And yet, still, I sit with you."

"I am ashamed of it. I fought monsters because I thought it was in service to a greater purpose, one higher than myself."

My mother picked a glittering purple tulip flower off its stem. Within seconds another had rematerialized in its place. "And I am sure those warriors in there will tell you the same sort of story."

"Then how can you condemn them?" I asked.

Mother placed the purple tulip in the lapel of my green tunic. "I am not condemning them. I don't want to sit among them, though, while they tell tales of slaughtering my people."

I dropped my head. "No, you should not have to do that."

It was only after I came to Valhalla that my mother told me about the great extinction of monster kind throughout the world. It was not only King Odgeir who hated monsters. Men all over the world vehemently despised monsters just as much as he, from the great orcs and trolls of the world to the fairy folk who were my kin. Over the centuries, ninety percent of my brethren were hunted to death, leaving my kind nearly extinct in the world of men. It was hard to believe there were any monster species left. No warrior had come through the doors in Valhalla since I arrived, though, so it was impossible to know for sure.

"Had you known," my mother said, "you wouldn't have done any different. That King Odgeir, both father and son, they turned you into a weapon, and you can't blame a weapon for being used like it was designed."

"That's true," I replied. "I have to admit, a big part of me enjoys the talk of conquests. I understand you do not, and I understand why I should not, but that does not make the tales any less glorious in my eyes."

"This is paradise to you," my mother said. "And I respect that. But to me, it is a personal hell."

"If you hate it so much here," I said, "maybe there is somewhere else we can go, just the two of us."

My mother shook her head. "There is no 'we.' You like it here, so there's no reason for you to leave. Besides, you don't want to hang around an old, broken woman for the rest of eternity, not when you could be among people who understand you."

I gave her a smile and was about to respond when the sky crackled. Lightning struck the rainbow bridge, which led away from the castle and into a great fog. I had been on that bridge just three times before, and each time filled me with a foreboding sense of panic. Whenever I planted my foot on the bridge, the echoes of a thousand haunting voices whipped upon me like the wind, and the air grew colder. I had never gotten more than a few steps before turning back to the sanctity of the castle, but I knew it extended out into the distance of the great beyond, somewhere past the horizon. We all knew in Valhalla. The bridge was legend and truth wrapped into one. One day, we told each other we would find where the bridge led.

"What was that?" my mother said, startled. Her head snapped around as she watched the ground sizzle where the lightning had crashed upon the bridge.

"I don't know," I replied. "But I'm going to find out."

I started walking in that direction, but my mother latched onto my arm with a death grip, her fingernails digging deep into my skin. "Don't you dare."

She was scared, as was to be expected, but my instincts overpowered her trepidations. I was trained to take action, and no matter how many centuries had passed since I first came to Valhalla, I was still ready to charge into any new challenge headfirst.

"It will be fine, Mother," I said. "There's nothing here that can hurt me."

"Whatever just happened didn't come from here, child," my mother said.

I grabbed her hand and peeled her fingers off my arm. Her grip would have left welts on my arm if I could have been injured anymore. "I'll be back. Wait for me here."

"You better be."

She worried for me, but she didn't need to. If anything, my skills as a warrior were sharper now than they were when I arrived. While there were no monsters to slay in Valhalla, there were plenty of warriors who wanted to get out their aggression, and I was happy to oblige with a tussle now and then.

I unfurled my golden wings and floated into the air, flying toward the entrance to the castle at great speed.

*

I landed at the end of the bridge where it met with the grassy field of Valhalla. A tall, broad angel with a long beard and angry eyes pushed open the tall doors of the castle and stomped down the steps to meet me.

"Janus," I said as he stalked toward me. "What is happening?"

"Nothing to concern yourself with," the Valkyrie growled back. "Get inside the castle."

I looked back to the castle doors, a hundred feet tall and intricately carved with flowers and dragons. Only the strongest men and women in the universe, those worthy of a warrior's reward, were able to push them open, and yet Janus had flung them open like they were made of feathers.

"I'm not going anywhere," I replied.

Two Valkyries guarded the door to Valhalla, and two more stood just inside to keep the warriors in the hall from escaping to join us. The warriors milled about, trying desperately to get out, but even with their strength, they were no match for their Valkyrie guardians.

"I said turn back, pixie," Janus growled, but he didn't slow his gait. "I can handle this."

"No way," I said. "I am not leaving."

"I need none of your help."

"I'm not coming to help you. I'm coming because it's the first interesting thing that's happened around here in five hundred years."

"Suit yourself," Janus said. "It's your funeral."

"I've already had two of them," I said. "I don't fear a third."

Janus couldn't help but give me a small smile. "I did not particularly care for letting you into the halls of Valhalla at first, especially given your monster blood, but you have a warrior's spirit. I will give you that."

That was the most Janus had spoken to me since I had come to Valhalla.

"What's that supposed to mean?" I asked.

"Let us focus on the problem at hand," Janus said. "If we survive, there will be time for tales later."

We neared the edge of the rainbow bridge. The sky over the bridge was black and foreboding, with dark, swirling clouds. Crystals of every color comprised the intricate design of the bridge. On the best days, when the clouds receded a bit and the sun could reach the gems, they sparkled in a myriad of colors and danced upon the light. Now, though, the bridge was dark, and no light touched it.

"Be on your guard," Janus said, pulling a broadsword out of a sheath he kept hidden under his blue cape.

I pulled my ivory daggers out of their scabbards and gripped them tightly. They still fit perfectly in my hands even after five hundred years. "I am ready."

Out of the darkness, a figure emerged. His long, white wings extended across the entirety of the bridge's expanse and shimmered. Unlike the fur and leather bracers of the Valkyrie of Valhalla, he wore a loose-fitting, white toga, and instead of a bushy beard, his face was clean-shaven. His hair wafted in the breeze as if it were taking a stroll through a pleasant meadow.

"Speak your piece!" Janus shouted, raising his sword. "And step no further."

The intruder held up his arms. His aura glowed like a star. With every small step he took, the darkness receded from him before collapsing again when he walked past. Wherever his feet touched the bridge, the gems shimmered under him, lighting him with a brilliant rainbow everywhere he stepped.

"I'm sorry, brother," he said. "I mean you no harm. I am sorry for the intrusion, but we have been looking for you for many moons."

"And who is we?" Janus growled.

"We of Mount Olympus, your kin."

"We recognize no kin from Mount Olympus."

"Of course," the intruder said. "But there was a time when you did. I have business with you and those you protect."

"Speak your name so that I might know whom I will slay."

He held his arms higher. "I am the angel Gabriel. I come with a message from our God."

"And what message is that?" I asked.

Gabriel looked down at me as if he hadn't seen me before, which was likely true. Up until that moment, his eyes had been locked with Janus's.

"You must be her," he said with a smile. He wasn't afraid or angry, unlike Janus. He seemed at peace, in a way I hadn't ever seen, not in all my time on Valhalla. "You are the pixie, yes?"

I nodded. "Possibly, friend. Why?"

"I have a great mission for you, Akta of the Forest. We have scoured the world for another who could complete this dangerous mission for us, but we now believe you are the only one who can. No matter how many others we send, they all meet their doom. We believe you will succeed where they failed."

I frowned. "And what mission is that?"

"We need you to go back to Hell."

# CHAPTER 3

I laughed a lot after my death, a lot more than during my life, but I doubt I ever laughed as hard in my five hundred years than I did when Gabriel asked me to go back to Hell. I didn't even know people could laugh so hard that it was painful. I hadn't felt pain in decades, and yet, my side literally hurt as if it were split in two.

"I'm sorry," I said, wiping the tears from my eyes. "I thought you asked me to go to Hell again."

"That is what I said, Akta of the Forest," Gabriel said to me. "Your God needs you to enter Hell and retrieve something precious to him."

"All right," I said. "First of all, no. Second of all, what are you talking about, *God*, as in singular? There are at least a hundred gods!"

"That was true, once," Gabriel replied. "However, in the many years since you have been away, the gods have mostly abandoned Earth, and now all that remains is a small cadre, who have ceded power to the one God who will oversee the development of Earth from here on out."

I looked at Janus. "Is he…all right in the head?"

Janus shook his head. "No, he's not. But he's not telling a lie, either. There was a time when my people, the Odinson line, resided on Earth as well. However, thousands of years ago, a cleft emerged, and they abandoned your planet, along with the Old Gods, to make their way across the universe. They left me and my kin here to look after the last warriors in their hall for the rest of eternity."

I looked back at the palace. The Valkyrie did their best to contain the hundreds of warriors who pushed and prodded to get a glimpse of what was happening beyond the walls. I hadn't seen a new person in over five hundred years, which meant they hadn't either.

"How long ago did they abandon you?" I asked.

"Long enough," Janus replied. "Before you, we had not seen a new warrior in a long while. Since my kin vanished from here, all warriors have been dealt with by the devil instead of our illustrious Hell." A tear rose in his eye. "Did you know she was the reason it was named such? Anubis had such kind things to say about his paramour."

"They have been gone for many eons," Gabriel added. "All that are left are Velaska in Hell, Bacchus, and the last remnants of Mount Olympus."

"Of course, she would be the one that remained," I grumbled.

"And that drunk!" Janus said with a laugh. "They are leaving Bacchus in control of the planet? Wow, it won't last the millennium."

Gabriel smiled. "We have all taken bets on that. My money is on two thousand years before the Hellmouth opens and consumes the world for good. Good riddance. It is not one of the gods' better attempts at life."

"Agreed," Janus replied. "I will be happy to be rid of it."

"Hey!" I shouted. "That's my planet you're talking about."

"Yes," Janus said, lowering his head. "It is a pity it was so poorly conceived. My apologies."

"Sorry," Gabriel said, dropping his eyes to the ground.

"If you're so sure it's going to end," I said. "Why do you want my help at all?"

"It is not my call to make," Gabriel replied. "I am merely the voice of God."

"Feckless totem is more like it," Janus said, growling.

"Whatever you call it," Gabriel said with a glare, "I only go where I am told and do as I'm told. My current mission is to come here and deliver you to God himself. It is a great honor. Most mortals never set foot on Mount Olympus."

"Yeah," I replied. "Well, if it involves going to Hell, you can count me out."

"Please," Gabriel said. "I have been instructed to offer you anything you desire."

"I've got everything—" I caught my mother flying toward the castle with the corner of my eyes. Maybe I didn't want for anything, but she, on the other hand…I did have a wish for her. "Very well. I think we might be able to work something out."

*

"I don't want you doing this," my mother said. "There is no reason. There's nothing to gain from helping them."

I was sitting on my bed, sharpening my blades. I stopped to look at her. There was something to gain, her freedom from this place. Her happiness mattered more than mine, and I was willing to endure the flames of Hell to make sure she didn't have to live in Valhalla anymore.

"There is always something to gain," I said, careful not to tell her why I was going, lest she feel guilty about my decision. It wasn't her fault, of course, but mothers always bore the guilt for their children's decisions. They wore it like a boulder on their backs.

"You have everything you want right here," my mother said, placing a hand on my shoulder.

I brushed her off and stood. "That is not true. I have not had the thrill of a hunt, or the allure of danger, in five hundred years."

"That's what this is about? Danger! Adventure! You have all you could ever want right here, and you would give it up to satisfy your bloodlust?"

"Yes!" I shouted. "I would. What is the point of having everything if you can never feel alive?"

I was surprised at the veracity of my words. I told myself that I would go on Gabriel's mission to save my mother, but perhaps a part of it was to satiate something inside myself as well. After all, I enjoyed drinking and cavorting in the great halls of Valhalla, but there was never any risk.

Perhaps that was why the liquor flowed so easily here, to numb the gnawing voice in the back of each warrior's mind, one that longed for adventure. Craved it, even.

"I will be back soon," I said, placing my daggers in their scabbards.

"You could be back now if you didn't leave," she replied.

I wrapped her in a hug. "When I come back, it will all be different, you'll see. No more drunken nights filled with people you hate, hearing stories about your people being massacred. I swear it."

My mother pulled away from me. She cocked her head to one side and squinted suspiciously. "Is that what this is about? Are you doing this for me?"

I stepped away with a shrug. "No, of course not. I'm doing it because I have been summoned."

"You do not have to answer every person that summons you."

I sighed. "Old habits are hard to break, even after five hundred years."

She smiled a pained smile. "Be careful, okay?"

I shook my head. "I'm not sure that's possible in the bowels of Hell, but to the degree that I am able, I swear I will."

"Please don't go," she said, tears in her eyes.

I bit my lower lip so hard I thought it would puncture the skin. She was in such pain, and it was because of me. I wanted so desperately to stay with her, to tell her it would be okay, and to deny the will of the gods…but it was not in my nature to do so. Even if it were, some things were more important, like the eternal happiness of the mother I loved, the only thing, maybe, that I ever truly loved.

"Goodbye, Mother," I said, opening our bedroom door. "I will be back before you know it."

I didn't wait for her to answer before closing the door behind me. I didn't bother looking back, either, because the tears welling in her eyes, streaming down her face, would have broken my heart and shattered my will.

*

I stomped down the stairs of the tower and into the hall of heroes. Usually, the warriors in the hall were drunk, laughing, and cavorting, but when I entered the great hall, they were silent. All their eyes followed me as I walked down the middle of the room toward Janus, who stood at the front door.

"What is happening?" I asked Janus as I neared him.

Janus chuckled to himself. "They are all jealous. Very jealous."

"Of me?" I said. "They know I'm going to Hell, right?"

He nodded. "That makes them even more jealous. Each of these warriors has been without a battle for eons, and it kills them inside."

I laughed. "Perhaps I can convince Gabriel to trade my place for one of them."

Janus turned and pushed open the door. "Don't say that too loud, or they will take you up on your offer."

We walked outside, where the crisp night air brought the sweet scent of tulips wafting across my nose. I felt my lapel for the flower my mother had placed there earlier.

"The last time I was on Mount Olympus," Janus said, "there were thousands of angels milling about and gods working together. I miss it. I must say that I, too, envy you."

"The last time I was in Hell, I nearly fought a giant lizard and a flame-spitting fire monster. It was horrible."

"Sounds grand," Janus said. "Oh, the stories you will tell after this adventure. I long to hear them."

"Yeah," I said, tipping my head. "I long to tell them, my friend."

Gabriel was waiting for us on the rainbow bridge. His tunic blew in the wind. The darkness of the night engulfed everything, but his aura emitted a white light that shone down a beacon upon him.

"Champion of the gods, I bring you Akta of the Forest," Janus said.

"Is that my new title?" I said with a smile. "I rather like that."

"Akta," Gabriel said, walking forward. "Do you willingly accept the burden being placed upon you and agree to follow me to Mount Olympus and speak with God?"

I looked him in the eyes. "Do you agree that my mother and I will find a new place to rest for eternity in exchange for my help?"

"I do," Gabriel said.

"Then so do I," I replied.

"I will miss you," Janus said, clearing his throat. "I haven't heard a new story in over five hundred years, and I was quite looking forward to this one."

I placed my hand on Janus's shoulder. "And you will hear it, somehow, of that, I am sure."

"It's time to go." Gabriel beckoned. "Please, Akta of the Forest, there is little time to waste."

I nodded. "Then let's go."

I followed Gabriel onto the bridge. As it always had when I set foot on the bridge, my breath grew shallow, and my will abandoned me. It was the only time in my existence I felt powerless and weak.

"Don't be nervous," Gabriel replied. "Mount Olympus is a grand place."

"I'm not nervous about that," I said, stepping onto the bridge next to him. "This bridge is the only place where I've ever been nervous in my entire life."

Gabriel smiled. "As it is intended. It is a safety precaution built into the bridge to prevent warriors like you from walking upon it. Otherwise, anybody could cross the bridge into Mount Olympus. We couldn't have that, now could we?"

"Wait," I replied. "This bridge will take us to Mount Olympus?"

Gabriel smiled. "Yes. However, it is quite a long walk. Would you mind if we flew? It will cut our time drastically."

"Can't we just go by lightning bolt?" I asked.

Gabriel laughed. "I'm afraid that was more for theatrics than anything else."

"Then I suppose flying will do, then."

Gabriel unfurled his wings, and I followed suit. Together, we rose from the ground and flew across the bridge, toward Mount Olympus and my destiny.

# CHAPTER 4

We flew for what felt like endless miles, the wind whipping at our faces as the bridge led us further and further into the darkness of the clouds. I hadn't felt cold, true cold, since I was on Earth, but the way the wind thrashed across my body on the rainbow bridge, I lost feeling in my face immediately, and the frost worked its way through my body until I was numb from head to toe. Had I blood in my veins, it would have surely solidified, and had I flesh, it would have been rock hard. Only my lack of a corporeal body kept me from dropping out of the sky like a ball of ice, but if we had to contend with the wind much longer, I feared even that would not prevent me from becoming a popsicle.

"This path was lost to us for eons," Gabriel said as we fluttered against the headwinds. "We thought that Valhalla was gone, along with their Odinson line."

"How did you find it again?" I shouted across the howling wind. The creases of my mouth cracked with every word.

"Our informant in Hell. He told us of your ascension to Valhalla some years ago, and it sent us on a quest to find the bridge."

We smashed through the cloud cover and popped out the other side. As we did, the wind died down, and the beams of sunshine warmed my frozen body. It was as if we had broken through the ceiling of the storm and left behind all the forces that had conspired against us.

In front of us, beautifully painted columns lined the clouds. I had traveled to Greece twice during my life, and the architecture reminded me of the great city of Athens.

Two colorfully decorated statues stood at either end of the rainbow bridge, and hundreds of angels in togas wandered across the clouded plains, carrying baskets and tools.

"You have an informant in Hell?" I asked.

We landed on the rainbow bridge. It sparkled with translucent jewels of every color that glittered in the sunlight. Beneath us, I could just barely make out the curvature of the Earth, peeking through the clouds.

"I suppose 'informant' isn't the right word. It makes him seem like he's sinister in some way. A better word would be envoy. Just like I am an envoy to you, so he is an envoy to the Devil in Hell."

"And he's the one that told you I'd been sent to Valhalla?"

"Correct. The envoy cannot come to Mount Olympus himself for fear that he will taint our perfection with the essence of Hell, but he does communicate through me, the messenger of the gods. I can withstand the fire of damnation for short bursts, so I travel there periodically for his updates."

"I thought Hermes was the messenger of the gods?" I asked. "With the fast shoes and such."

"Ugh, what a dreadful god he is, and no. He was given his own planet to govern several million years ago. Since then, the charge of messenger on Earth has fallen to me."

"I see."

We reached the end of the rainbow bridge, and Gabriel looked back at it, shaking his head. "To think, it was here the whole time, if only we had looked for it."

"Why didn't you?"

"Well, our alliance with the Odinson line was broken, and when they left Earth, the bridge vanished with them. So, we assumed Valhalla was gone. It was only after thousands of years that we found the spell to reveal it again."

"And what was the spell?"

Gabriel chuckled to himself. "It's quite funny, actually. It was *Sesam öppna dig.*"

"Why is that funny?"

"It means 'open sesame' in Swedish."

"I don't get it."

Gabriel sighed. "It's just an old, stupid, godly tradition to make things both easier and harder than they have to be at the same time. Now, let us on. We don't want to keep our God waiting."

"No," I replied. "We wouldn't want that."

*

I expected Mount Olympus to be some sort of ethereal haven for the gods, filled with parties and booze, but it was much like any other city I had ever been to. The only difference was that instead of humans and monsters doing the hard work, it was the angels.

A blacksmith's forge, for instance, was tended to by a sweaty angel whose assistant stoked the fires by puffing air into them. Across from their shop, a group of angels worked to erect a column high into the air to stand with the six others they had already raised next to it.

"You don't look impressed," Gabriel said as we walked through the cloud across the plains of Mount Olympus.

"Should I be?"

"Many would kill their firstborn son to see the plains of Mount Olympus with their own eyes. Hercules completed twelve labors to win his way into Mount Olympus, and when he was granted entrance, he fell on his knees and wept with joy for three days."

"Hmm," I replied. "It doesn't look that much different than Earth, honestly. Just with a lot more clouds."

"Well, that may be because humanity, and pixies to some extent, were fashioned after the gods themselves, so what they do, you also do."

"I thought that saying we were made in the image of god was utter nonsense. The kind of nonsense religious people told their congregations just so they could steal money from them."

Gabriel laughed. "They do stretch the truth quite a bit, I must admit. Still, the essence of their teaching is accurate, even to this day."

A mammoth, bearded man lumbered toward us. He was covered in soot. Compared to the effortless beauty of the angels, the lumbering beast walking toward us was gnarled and deformed.

"Hephaestus!" Gabriel smiled. "What ho, good sir?"

"What ho," Hephaestus grumbled back.

"Something wrong, my friend?" Gabriel said.

"We're two centuries behind schedule," Hephaestus said with a sigh. "And Zeus is insistent we leave this planet within the decade. There is so much left to do."

Gabriel threw up his hands. "There is only so much you can do, though, my friend. At some point, it is out of your hands."

"Ain't that the truth," Hephaestus replied. "I just wish Bacchus would quit sashaying around like he owns the place, you know? Barking orders like he wasn't Zeus's thirtieth choice for God of Earth."

"Well, can you blame him? This is the most power he's ever held. For the first time ever, we are forced to take him seriously."

"He is an impetuous snot, and I can't wait to be rid of him. The only positive thing about him taking over this backwater planet is that I never have to see him again, ya know what I'm saying?"

"Unfortunately not, my friend." Gabriel sighed. "My orders are to stay here for the duration."

"Oh," Hephaestus said. "Tough break."

Gabriel shrugged. "Well, maybe it will all go to pot soon, and then we can be reunited again."

Hephaestus smiled. "I will have the mead ready when we do." He lumbered off down the lane before disappearing down a column and out of sight.

"Who was that?" I asked.

"He is the blacksmith god," Gabriel said, continuing to walk. "Every time the gods create a planet, he is there to make sure they have everything they need. Then, when the build is done, he goes off to the next planet."

"Wait," I replied. "What do you mean, the next planet?"

"This is what the gods do," Gabriel replied, continuing to walk through the cloud streets. "They create planets. Or, should I say, Zeus creates planets, and then the other gods help make sure the planet is sustainable for human life. It takes an incredible amount of energy to create life, and Zeus does not use that power lightly."

"I just figured life sprung from nothingness," I said.

"Nothing springs from nothingness, my friend," Gabriel replied. "It is a carefully orchestrated process to create something, and the gods are there to make sure it goes the way Zeus intended."

"So, the gods are really just highly regarded contractors?" I asked.

Gabriel chuckled. "Something like that."

"This is blowing my mind," I replied. "So, does that mean there is life on other planets?"

"Yes," Gabriel said.

"What's it like?"

"Surprisingly, it's a lot like Earth. The gods are not incredibly imaginative in their creations, so their planets always end up…just like this. Each planet is at different stages of development, but in the end, they all wind up the same."

"And this God, Bacchus, he is the one who will—"

"Make sure this planet keeps evolving and progressing in the way the gods intended. You are familiar with kings, I assume."

My lip curled. "I have known them."

"Well, think of Zeus as the king of the galaxy, and Bacchus, and the other gods who rule the planets around him, his dukes, earls, and lords. They make sure that his will is carried out across the galaxy."

"That is the first thing you said that makes any sense," I replied. "This Zeus, is he terrible, like most kings?"

Gabriel shrugged. "He carries great burdens—the galaxy, the universe…the fate of these things rests on his head. That would be enough to cause even the greatest being insurmountable stress."

"I'll take that as a yes," I said. "And this Bacchus, he's not very good then?"

"He is the god of wine and drink, and he lives his life as if those were his patronages. I would not trust him with the simplest of tasks, and here he has acquired an entire planet to rule."

"That doesn't sound good. I can see why you bet on the planet facing destruction in two thousand years."

"I hope I am wrong," he said.

"Me too," I replied.

# CHAPTER 5

Gabriel led me across the plains of Mount Olympus and toward a huge circular structure, surrounded by pillowy clouds, standing apart from the rest of Heaven.

"These are called the Elysian Fields," Gabriel said as we flew over the vast, empty space between the town and the structure.

"They look like clouds to me," I replied.

"It's important that the god of each world have a place to conduct and meet with emissaries in private, away from the angels and other prying ears."

"Why not just build them a place with walls, then?" I asked. "Where nobody can hear them."

Gabriel smiled. "Because that is not how it is done."

The giant, white cylinder in the center was encircled with columns, and the whole thing was raised thirty feet into the air by a large marble slab foundation. A stone staircase floated in midair around the structure.

Gabriel landed at the base of the cylinder, and I followed him up the steps. I expected the stairs to wobble, but they never wavered when I placed my weight down upon them. I looked out into the distance as I climbed. The Elysian fields spanned in each direction, and I barely made out the skyline of the angelic city we had walked through earlier.

"This is very important," Gabriel said as we climbed. "Do not meet Bacchus's gaze. He is very insecure about his new position as God, and great insecurity matched with great power is a dangerous combination. He believes that direct eye contact is a challenge to his power and will act accordingly to protect himself. More than one angel met their end that way."

"I have dealt with enough kings to know the type," I said. "If he meets my demands, then we will have no problems."

"Quite," Gabriel said. "And make sure to kneel at his feet before he speaks to you. Otherwise, he will take it as a sign of disrespect."

"Like I said, I've met kings before. They are rarely ever different than your Bacchus. Infinite power, but full of bluster and insecurity."

The platform at the top of the stairs was intricately tiled, a mosaic of the Heavens depicting men and women, smiling and laughing, reaching out their hands. In the center of the platform, a rock rested, with a flaming sword embedded deep inside it.

On the far side of the platform, a man with dark brown hair and a tight beard, dressed in a gleaming, ivory toga, hovering cross-legged in the air, was drinking wine straight from the bottle.

"Keep your eyes low," Gabriel said. As he stepped, the tiles lit up underneath his feet the same way the gems had on the rainbow bridge.

I watched the different colored tiles as they danced under my feet as well. "Yes, sir."

"Gabriel! My old friend. What ho? What ho?" When the man shouted, his words slurred together.

"Bacchus," Gabriel replied with a bow. "Or should I say, my God?"

"Please," Bacchus said, swatting his hand toward Gabriel. "No need for such formalities. Would you like a drink?"

Bacchus held out his wine bottle toward Gabriel, but the angel refused it, saying, "I'm sorry, Bacchus. I am here on official business."

"Of course," Bacchus replied, taking a swig of the wine. "Everybody is here on official business. Do you remember when we stayed for a century drinking wine and playing cards? How wonderful that was! I miss those days. Don't you miss those days?"

"Quite, your grace," Gabriel said.

"Now, visitors only come when they want something from me or need me for an official matter. How droll!"

"Certainly," Gabriel replied. "As you know, now that you are the God of this world, that is the expectation. If you do not like it, you didn't have to accept the post."

"Sure, I did!" Bacchus said, taking another deep swig. "Zeus told me I had to accept it. You think I want to be God? No, but I wasn't pulling my weight, he said. You think I don't know they're just trying to stash me somewhere out of the way? I know their games, but I'm gonna show them. I'm gonna be the BEST god. You wait. I have a lot of ideas. Did you know that?"

"I am sure you do."

"For one thing, I never liked the name Mount Olympus. After all, we're not even on a mountain. I'm thinking of renaming it. What do you think of Heaven?"

"It sounds…fine, my lord."

"Yes, Heaven. Has a nice ring to it, don't you think?"

"Quite."

"I have a lot of other ideas too, Gabriel. There are gonna be big changes. Big, big changes. I am going to fix the problems of the past, that's for sure."

"I'm sure you will, sir," Gabriel said, gesturing toward me. "To that end, I would like you to meet Akta of the Forest. She is here per your request."

Bacchus was a drunk, a lush, who had come into his power without truly earning it. I had dealt with many kings like him in my life, and the secret to winning their affections was in acting as if you were powerful yourself. Despite what Gabriel told me, I could not cower from him. I needed to be respectful but also forceful. If you cowed down to them, they would never respect you; if you showed you weren't afraid of them, you could earn their begrudging admiration.

Then again, they were just as likely to kill you. That was the chance you took with unstable leaders. They might kill their own mothers, given the inclination. That was the thing with power, it corrupted, but it also brought out the childish tendencies of cowards who wielded it…and the only thing cowards respected was power.

I stepped forward and knelt before Bacchus. "An honor to meet you, sir."

"Akta?" Bacchus said, mumbling to himself. "Akta? I don't know an Akta. You sure I called on her? Sounds like something I would remember."

"Yes, sir," Gabriel replied. "To find the angel Zharaqiel, if you remember, sir."

"Ah yes," Bacchus said, slapping his forehead. "This is the one who has been through Hell and lived to tell about it."

"I'm not sure I lived, sir," Akta said. "That is why I'm here."

There was silence on the platform for a moment, and my gut tightened. Bacchus leaned forward and squinted at me. Then, after a long pause, he slapped his knee with his free hand and laughed.

"I like her!" Bacchus said. "She's funny. You didn't say she was funny."

"I didn't know she was funny, sir," Gabriel said as he bent down. "Please stop being funny," he whispered.

"So, you think you can find my missing angel?" Bacchus said.

"I'm not sure, my lord," I replied. "I don't know much about the details of what happened, but if I can help you, I will."

"Good, good," Bacchus said, taking a long swig of wine. "I can't have my angels getting lost in Hell, you see. That would be a bad look for my reign, you know?"

"Of course," I replied. "Could you tell me…what happened?"

"Oh no, I simply couldn't," Bacchus said. "I'm not good at that kind of thing. Have Gabriel fill you in. I'm just here to snap my fingers and send you on your way."

"Yes," Gabriel said. "Well, it seems that one of our angels, Zharaqiel, found a portal to Hell and has gotten quite a bit lost. We've been trying to find her for the last three hundred years, to no avail."

"How hard did you look?"

"Not very. Honestly, angels do not like Hell one bit. The intense heat does dreadful things to our complexion, you see, and no hero we recruit can make it past Petrus without being burned alive in the pits of damnation."

"You're sacrificing mortals because Hell makes your skin dry?"

"There are…other reasons…"

"Name one?"

Gabriel shook his head. "No."

"Whatever. So, you need me to go to Hell and find this angel for you?"

"Would you?" Bacchus replied. "That would just be…so great if you could do that."

This was the moment of truth. I had made him feel comfortable. I had treated him with respect, now was the time to show my power and hope that he didn't kill me on the spot.

"Of course, my liege," I said. "I am at your command, granted, of course, that you can meet my price."

"Price!" Bacchus shouted. "I pay no price, except the reward of my countenance."

"Actually," Gabriel said. "I may have offered her something else."

"Oh?" Bacchus said. "And what would that be?"

"My mother will leave Valhalla and enter Mount Olympus to live out the rest of eternity."

"What!" Bacchus said, spitting out his wine. "Mortals can't live on Mount Olympus! That's against, like, fifty rules or something."

"Sixty-four actually, sir," Gabriel replied.

"Then why would you make this deal, Gabriel?" Bacchus said. "Are you trying to make me look like a fool?"

"No," Gabriel said. "But I made a calculated decision that if I could bring her here, you might be able to persuade her to abandon her foolish request. I, of course, am only a humble servant, bound to follow your orders, which were to find Akta and bring her to you."

"You demon!" I said, standing to face Gabriel. "You lied to me."

"I delivered a message and fulfilled my charter to bring you here. My methods are not in question, only my results, and by that metric, I was successful in my mission."

"This is crazy," I said, turning to Bacchus. "Listen, I'm willing to go to Hell and find an angel for you. I already have eternal bliss. I don't have to help you, but I'm willing to if you meet my demands. Otherwise, I'll just go home and drink more."

"Nobody ever speaks to me that way anymore," Bacchus said with a dark look. "I love it! Ugh, I'm surrounded by sycophants."

I gave a slight bow with my head. "I am sorry for being so curt, but the truth is I hold the power here in this negotiation. I'm willing to walk away at any time and return to Valhalla."

"You do know I could blink you out of existence now, right?" Bacchus said, turning his smile into a scowl. "You only hold the power which I allow."

I had overplayed my hand, but I couldn't turn back, not if I wanted his respect. "Then, I think we are done here. I will be going."

I spun to leave and walked toward the end of the platform. There was a snap, and my body refused to move any further. I fought to stretch out my leg, but it would not budge. Instead, I found myself being dragged back across the platform through the air. My body turned around against my will, and I was again face to face with Bacchus.

"Gabriel," Bacchus growled. "Is she really our best option?"

"I believe she is our only option, my lord. No other hero we employed has been able to make it past Petrus, but she has not only entered the Gates of Abnegation once, but she also met with Velaska and lived to tell about it."

"What are the Gates of Abnegation?" I asked.

"You remember the gigantic, black, fire-breathing skull sitting behind Petrus, the giant, while he sentenced people for their crimes?"

"The one demons flew out of to carry me off to the pits of Hell?" I said. "Yeah, I remember."

"Those are the Gates of Abnegation."

"Ah," I replied. "Well, if I'm the only hero who's passed through them, then I'm afraid you are at a bit of an impasse."

Bacchus scoffed. "I have all the power of a god, and yet I must bargain with a mortal."

"It is not a bargain, sir," I said. "You can meet my demands or ask me to leave. Those are your options."

"Or I can snap my fingers and vaporize you into oblivion."

I smiled. "I fail to see that as a threat."

The pressure on my arms and legs increased until I could barely feel my fingers. My eyes rolled back in my head as the air choked out of my lungs. And then, just as suddenly as it began, I was dropped to the ground, and the tension in my body fell away.

"Fine," Bacchus said. "If you help me, I will allow your mother to reside on Mount Olympus with the angels. Should you succeed, of course."

I kept my eyes on the ground. "Then I will help you, my lord."

"Yippee," Bacchus said, taking another chug of wine. "Gabriel, do the thing! Prepare her so I may send her on her way and out of my sight!"

Gabriel pulled me to my feet and brought me to the opposite edge of the platform from Bacchus. Sweat glistened on his brow.

"Very good," Gabriel said. "My, that was very exciting, wasn't it?"

"Was it?" I replied with a smirk.

"Frankly, I thought you were going to be vaporized for sure. Why were you so curt to him? I thought you had said you dealt with a lot of kings before?"

"I have," I replied.

"And were you always so…insolent?"

"Only when I had something they wanted, and I knew they weren't going to pay me fairly. At that point, I was very stern because I knew they had no other choice."

"And if he had another choice?"

I shrugged. "Then, I suppose, he would have vaporized me on the spot."

"You were willing to take that risk?"

I nodded. "Without the risk, there can be no reward."

"Very well, then. I suppose it worked out for you, so I can't fault your logic. Now, your mission. We cannot send you to meet your contact in the walled city of Dis. He is behind the Gates of Abnegation, which Petrus guards. However, we can send you into Hell, before the Gates. You will have to make your way through Petrus to the city of Dis, where you'll meet up with your contact. He will tell you what he knows and be your guide through Hell until you find the angel."

"And who is this contact? An orc, an ogre, another pixie?"

"No," Gabriel said. "He is an angel, like me."

"An angel? I thought they didn't like Hell."

"Generally, we don't," Gabriel replied. "Lucifer is…different than the rest of us, but I will let him tell you that story. There is no time to weigh you down with details."

I nodded. "So, go into Hell, make it through the Gates of Abnegation, find Lucifer, and go from there. That it?"

"Correct."

"One last question. How am I going to find him?"

"He spends most of his time in Dis," Gabriel said. "It shouldn't be hard to find him if you just ask around. He's the only angel who's been in Hell for almost two hundred millennia." Gabriel took me by the elbow and headed back toward Bacchus. "But do not tell anyone why you are in Hell, lest you alert the demon spawn that you do not belong."

"Right," I replied. "I wouldn't want that."

"No, you wouldn't," Gabriel replied. "Lucifer is an envoy to Mount Olympus, so he is off-limits to the monsters of Hell, but you are not. The demons of Hell hate goodness and light. They will rip you apart for pleasure if they discover you are working for us."

"All right," I said. "I get it. Don't reveal my secret identity to anyone."

"Good," Gabriel said, turning back to Bacchus. "My lord, she is ready now."

"You've told her everything?" Bacchus replied.

I nod. "I got it."

"Oh good," Bacchus said. "Then off you go."

Bacchus snapped his fingers, and before I could say another word, everything went black. My stomach dropped like I was falling through a great abyss. When the world came into focus again, I would be in Hell, and I hoped to the gods I would make it back to Valhalla before it was all over.

# CHAPTER 6

My eyes fluttered open, and I felt the heat of Hell all around me. The moans and screams of eternal damnation filled my ears, and my body recoiled from them. I had spent the last five hundred years in the pleasantness of Valhalla and was ill-prepared for the insufferable pain of Hell. The heat.

I pushed myself to my knees and looked out over Hell's fires. A great stone wall blocked the entrance of this damned place. The only way through the barrier was guarded by Petrus, the behemoth who determined the fate of all who entered. Behind him, a fiery, black skull marked the Gates of Abnegation. Hundreds of demons with black, leathery wings waited there for Petrus's final judgment before leading the condemned to their tortured ends.

A long, black path led the condemned across a cavern of Hellfire from the black void that spat them into Hell to the Gates of Abnegation. On either side of the path, twisted stalagmites rose from the fiery lava like jagged teeth waiting to swallow the condemned.

The last time I came to Hell, I hadn't known where to go or what to do, but this time I had no doubt. I fluttered into the air.

My first death came at the hand of my adopted brother King Odgeir. I wondered what fate awaited him in the pits of Hell. After I sent a dagger through his throat, Velaska promised to torture him for eternity. In Valhalla, I never thought of his suffering, but now, I wanted to know what wicked pleasure the queen of the underworld had found for my evil, adopted brother.

I was not a torturer by nature. I preferred my victims killed quickly and painlessly, even if they were miserable jerks. None deserved a slow, painful death, but I made an exception for my brother-king.

As I landed on the black rock of the path leading toward Petrus and the Gates of Abnegation, my mind turned from my adopted brother to my true brother, Rasmus of the Forest. I had only known him for a few days after I was resurrected but before I met my final end, and yet, when I finally killed King Odgeir and sent him to Velaska, I appointed Rasmus, my brother, my true brother, as the new king of the land, and bade its citizens follow him.

I hadn't thought of that moment in five hundred years. In Valhalla, I told stories of my conquests, but I avoided the one about my revenge against King Odgeir. I did not like to remember my body so frail and so weak, as it was after Velaska reanimated me into my decaying body. I preferred to tell tales of my endurance and strength, like when I singlehandedly fought and killed ten mountain trolls without taking a hit. Nearly being beaten by a human, especially one so cowardly as my adopted brother, was nothing to be proud of, nor was being tricked by Velaska into accepting a hopeless situation. Even if I wound up winning in the end, I avoided the subject at all costs.

*

Thousands of souls packed the path leading toward Petrus, waiting for their final judgment. In my last trip to Hell, the line was backed up for over three hundred years, but it was longer now.

People shuffled forward as slowly as possible, hoping to stall their final judgment. The moment Petrus's demons brought them behind the flaming gate, their fate was sealed. While standing in line, there was hope. Hope that you were a good, kind person. Hope that you would be spared. Hope that your fate wasn't sealed. Once you stepped up to be judged by the giant Petrus, all that hope vanished.

Of course, I could not wait three hundred years to get through the Gates of Abnegation. One thing I forgot about Hell was the overwhelming hopelessness that seeped into your pores with every passing second. More than the heat, it was the hopelessness in the air that weighed on my soul. I wanted to get out of there as quickly as possible. Just like I'd done during my first trip to Hell, I lifted off the ground and flew toward the front of the line. While those who stood in line clung to their hope, the pits of Hell worked to rip it away from them, leaving nothing but a hollow shell in return.

I finally planted my feet back down on the ground at the front of the line. Ahead of me, a weary, old man with a cane hobbled forward toward the giant Petrus. I'd forgotten how large the giant was up close, upward of thirty feet tall. He stroked his long, bushy, brown beard. His face was kind, which I didn't expect when I first met him, and smooth like a child's, but even his boyish looks were terrifying on a body so massive.

"Name!" Petrus said in a booming voice that echoed across the path.

"Olfrick of Padua," the man replied.

Petrus picked up a scroll which stretched thousands of feet behind him, piling up nearly as high as the wall itself. The frayed parchment flecked off in Petrus's hands as he searched for the name of Olfrick of Padua.

"Ah yes, here we go. Been waiting long?"

"I'm not sure," Olfrick replied. "What is long?"

"Well, it says here you died…oh my. Five hundred years ago. That is not good. I thought we had improved…well, I'm sorry for the wait."

Five hundred years ago. The man in front of Petrus died the same time I did, yet he was only just getting his judgment now. If I had not completed my mission for Velaska, or if I stood in line instead of cutting to the front of it on my last trip to Hell, I could have been that man. We may have reached the front of the line together.

"It's okay," Olfrick said. "I mean…I know what's waiting for me."

"Nonsense," Petrus replied. "There is every chance that you will be spared. Not a good chance, mind you, but there is a chance. It has happened before. Not for some time, though." Petrus took a deep sigh. "Now, let us see here. Oh, yes. Yes. I see that you were a cobbler. People seemed to like you quite a bit. High marks for customer service, and you did plenty of pro bono work, it looks like. Well, that is nice. See, this is going so well."

The man started to smile. "Really?"

"Yes, yes. Oh, oh my. Did you cheat on your wife…with the blacksmith's daughter? And…then accuse her of being a witch when you confessed?"

"I—"

"Oh my. That is not good at all."

"But—" the old man said.

"I'll commute five hundred years off your sentence for the wait, and you'll be sentenced to LEVEL TWO, for seventy-thousand years." The man looked on in horror. "Oh, my apologies. 69,500 years! See isn't that better?"

The fiery gate fell. Two demons with dark, black, leathery wings flapped forward and grabbed Olfrick by the arms. He cried for justice as he disappeared behind the black gate, but his cries fell on deaf ears.

"Next!" Petrus shouted. "And be quick about it!"

I looked over at a scared little girl whose hair was matted to her head. Dirt smudged her face and her tunic, and she shivered as she willed her quivering body to take a step forward. I bent down to her.

"Do you mind if I go first?" I asked with a smile.

"Whoa," the girl said, looking up at me. "You don't got no dirt on you or nothing."

"That's right, I don't."

"And you wanna go ahead of me?" she said.

I nodded. "That's right. Is that okay?"

"I guess," she said. "You sure are brave."

"Well," I said, standing back up. "I have an advantage. This isn't my first time."

I stepped forward and presented myself to Petrus. "I'm back again, Petrus."

Petrus looked down at me. "That isn't really a name, is it? I'm afraid I haven't seen that one before."

"No," I said. "It is I, Akta of the Forest."

"Ah," he said. "And what is your last name?"

"We have already done this," I said. "I came here five hundred years ago. You sentenced me to three million years on level six. And now I am back, so you might have a hard time finding me."

"Hrm," Petrus said. "I don't remember that. You must have been pardoned at some point or something, though. I don't follow the comings and goings of Velaska's—Ah, here is it. Akta, you say, of the Forest. Pixie, is it? We don't get many of those here."

"No, I don't imagine you would. Now, I know this is a little weird, but I'm hoping we can come to some sort of understanding. If you'd—"

"In fact, monsters aren't even supposed to come in this way anymore. You have an entrance over at the mouth of the river Styx. Oh, why can't they figure out this damned bureaucracy?"

"Sorry, what's happening now?"

"You have to go," Petrus replied.

"Where?"

"To processing…you know, I'm just not in the mood to deal with this today. Look at all this work I must get done. Just go in already. Go in. Let the damned demons deal with you."

"So, I can just…go?" I said.

Petrus nodded. "Yes, yes. And please, don't come through this way anymore. I won't be responsible for sending the next monster I see to the bloody pits for the rest of eternity, damn Velaska's orders."

"Okay," I replied, stepping toward the Gates of Abnegation. The flames stood in front of me like a wall. I dared not walk through unless I wanted to get burned for my troubles.

"Excuse me?" I said. "A little help."

Petrus turned around and eyed the flames. "Ah, yes. FRANK! Would you be a dear and help our monster friend out. She doesn't want to walk to the right entrance."

"I didn't say that!" I replied.

"Sure, sure, but you thought it loudly, and that's all that matters to me. Now, unless you want me to revisit your original sentence, I suggest you leave. NEXT!"

The wall of flames licked the air, and a dark-skinned demon with thin glasses walked out to greet me. His face was sullen but not snarling, and he held a clipboard which he looked down at with great interest.

"Are you Akta?" the demon said.

"Yes," I replied. "Are you Frank?"

"Follow me," the demon said, turning on his heels. "I swear, you monsters cause more paperwork than you are worth. Better to just burn the lot of you, but can't do that, can we?"

"I...guess not."

Frank stepped back through the flames, and I followed. Once I walked through the gate, the wall of flames rose to cover the entirety of the skull entrance. Behind the gate, dozens of demons sat in small circles with each other. Some played cards or dice. Others read thick, leather-bound books. Still others slept against the stone walls of the gate.

"Three hundred years!" Petrus's voice boomed.

"Johnson. Edwards. You're up!"

Two demons, who had been busy playing Go Fish, pushed themselves up from the ground. They slapped each other across the face as they jumped up and down in a frenzy.

"You ready for this?" one of them screamed in a shrill voice.

"Ready!" the other replied.

"Let's do it!"

The demons snarled and snapped at each other, then rose into the air. The fire from the gates fell for them, and I listened to the little girl shriek as the demons picked her up into the air and flew her toward her eternal demise.

"What the hell is going on here?" I asked, scratching my head.

"Theatrics, my dear," Frank replied. "You'll get used to it. Don't worry. The first century is always the hardest."

A horse-drawn caravan sat before us, one of several. Their carriages were made of wrought-iron cages, and moaning souls screamed out from inside them. Two demons flew over the wall and deposited the little girl—the one who'd let me cut in front of her—into one of the cages.

"Level one. Three hundred years," one of the monsters said, as they threw her into a cage with a bunch of burly men.

"Come on," the other said, slapping his partner on the back. "Let's get a beer."

I wanted to ask questions. I had so many, but my eyes focused on the driver of the carriage where the two demons had deposited the little girl moments before. He had dark-skin and pointy ears, just like me. He wore a patch on his left eye, and a deep scar fell down the other. I recognized him instantly, even though time ravaged his once youthful appearance.

"Rasmus?" I said, inching toward him.

"Oh my gods," he said, catching my eye. "Akta!"

My brother. My only blood brother. Fate had brought us back together for the first time in over five hundred years.

"Oh good," Frank said. "You know each other. Driver! Bring this woman to central processing in Dis. Do not let her out of your sight until then or suffer the consequences. As you know, we demons are very good at suffering. Understood?"

Rasmus nodded, beaming wider than his mouth would allow. "Understood."

"And wipe that smile off your face," Frank added. "This is hell for the Devil's sake. Show some pride in your work!"

# CHAPTER 7

"What is going on here, Rasmus?" I asked once the unicorn pulling the cart had trotted away. "I'm not saying I'm an expert in Hell, but this is a lot different than I remember."

The last time I'd been in Hell, the demons were not sitting around playing cards. They were responsible for bringing you all the way to your final torture. They didn't throw you in cages and have pixies drive you to your final destination by unicorn-driven cart.

It wasn't just pixies, either, who were driving the carts. We passed orcs, ogres, gnomes, dwarves, gorgons, and trolls all waiting for damned souls, although unicorns didn't pull all of those carts. Some of them were too heavy, it seemed, even for a magical creature to pull. The trolls and orcs were responsible for pulling their own carts.

"A lot changed since you came here the last time, Akta," Rasmus replied. I couldn't get over how white the whiskers on his face were or how wrinkles covered every inch of his cheeks. "Velaska has implemented a lot in the last five hundred years to revolutionize the place."

The carriage popped onto a cobblestone street which led straight down into the fiery plains. A walled town dominated the horizon.

"I'll say it's changed. I remember all the monsters being…well, quite a bit scarier."

Rasmus laughed. "Yes, that was just an act, of course, going all the way back to Anubis. The truth is we all just work here. It's not much different than any other kingdom if you really think about it."

"Except it revolves around torturing people."

Rasmus chuckled. "You have not been part of many kingdoms, sister. Most of them revolve around torturing people. Hell is just more blatant about it. In that respect, I almost prefer it. No subterfuge."

"And how did you get out of torture, good brother?" I asked. "If so many kingdoms are built around torturing their people?"

"Good fortune, I must say," he replied. "I wasn't a great king, Akta, but you weren't wrong about picking me. I was fair, or at least I tried to be, and kind when I could be. I built a thriving kingdom where monsters and humans alike could live freely. Other kingdoms feared our ogre armies, so they let us be, and in return, we lived in peace, as best we could, with humanity."

"I am glad to hear that, brother."

"It was not all good. I still had to dole out justice and order the deaths of my people when they broke the law. Those sentences weighed on my soul. They never left me. When I died, I was sure that I would be judged for my crimes, and I was willing to accept the blame."

"But you escaped that somehow."

"I'm sorry to say it was by luck. As Petrus no doubt told you, monsters are no longer condemned in Hell, good sister. Instead, we work the land for the Devil, and in exchange, we are not condemned like humanity."

"Why would such a thing happen?"

"Humanity, sister, has blossomed and grown since even during our time. Demons cannot breed, so there are only so many of them. Out of fear, the gods prevented the Devil from making more soldiers for their army. There were simply not enough hands to go around, so Velaska pardoned us monsters, all of us."

"It seemed like there were plenty of demons milling around by the gate."

"Unions," Rasmus said. "They sprung up after we were pardoned. Monsters are non-union labor, so we can be worked until our backs break, but demons…well, they claim they've earned a little comfort in their job."

"I hear the bitterness in your voice, brother. You do not agree?"

"I have no say, my sister," Rasmus said. "I lived a good life on Earth, and if this is my row to hoe, I shall do so to the best of my ability. It is a far cry better than the fate of those who ride with us."

I looked back into the cage Rasmus, and his unicorn pulled behind them. I made eye contact with the little girl who had let me cut in front of her.  She was crushed between a dozen other sweaty men and women, crying to herself. I pitied her, but at the same time, I praised the gods I wasn't in her shoes.

*

Rasmus's job was simple and banal. He took souls from the gate and brought them to their destination for torture. During our journey, we spoke of many things, but he never asked about why I came to Hell. I appreciated his discretion since Gabriel told me I should not reveal my reasons.

"There are thousands of different tortures in Hell, and they are divided into ten levels," Rasmus told me as the unicorn steered his cart down the cobblestone streets. "The level pertains to the severity of your crime, but the specific torture itself is determined by what atrocities you committed during your life. For instance, an adulterer might have their penis ripped off for all eternity in level three, but in level seven, he could be required to have sex with a cheese grater in perpetuity."

"Oh god," I replied. "Are those really…things that happen?"

"I mean, yeah, just two of them, out of thousands, but a lot of it is customized for each individual soul."

"And you're okay with them just being tortured?" I asked. "It doesn't bother you?"

"Not anymore," Rasmus replied. "It used to a little bit, but this is Hell. There must be a good reason for them to be here, right? I mean, it's not like Velaska is torturing people for the thrill of it, you know?"

"Don't count on that," I said. "I've met her before. That sounds like the exact kind of thing she would do."

"Maybe, but it is not my problem. You can't shoot the messenger."

"I have watched messengers get shot multiple times in my life. Often out of a cannon."

"What I mean is that I'm just delivering these souls to their final destination. I am not doling out their punishment. Besides, it's better than being one of them, right?"

"Are those the only two options?"

"It seems like it."

"Well, then I agree with you. I fought for my life to avoid being tortured. I cannot say I wouldn't make the same choice again."

*

Rasmus turned his cart onto a dirt road and headed toward a dark pit at the end. "Level six!" he shouted. "The goblins will come and count you out. Don't try to hide. This is Hell. We know everything."

A shiver went down my spine. We pulled to a stop and three goblins hobbled up to the cart. A mournful dirge escaped the black pit as wind and bile flew out of it. Level six. If I didn't fight to find Velaska, this was where I would have ended up.

"These the Hopkins lot?" one of the goblins asked in a deep voice.

"That's right," Rasmus said, hopping off the cart and handing the goblin a clipboard. "There are seven who get off here." The goblin muttered something back to him. "No, I don't know where they are. You have to take it up with Frank up at the Gate. Or maybe they are on a later transport."

I looked back at the cage. Even the bravest and toughest men cried out for mercy. They begged and pleaded for a second chance, but there was none to be had. The back of the cart opened, and the goblins filed out the people onto the dirt path. The little girl ran forward and grabbed the bars next to me.

"I don't want to go," she said.

"You don't have to go, little one," I replied. "I don't think this is your stop. It's for very bad men."

"I am bad."

"No, you're not."

"Then, how did I end up here?" the girl asked.

"What's your name, little one?"

"Agathe." She was crying.

"That's pretty. Is it Greek?" The young girl nodded her head. "I have been to Greece before, beautiful country. Do you have a patron god, Agathe?"

"Hera," the girl said. "She was my favorite."

"She is very strong and powerful, isn't she?"

"Yes!" Agathe said.

"But bad things happened to her, too, didn't they? Even though she was big and strong. Even though she was a god?"

"I guess so," the little girl said.

"But just because bad things happened to her, did that make her a bad god?"

Agathe shook her head. "No. She was great."

"Of course she was. I'm sure she blessed your family with many great harvests, didn't she?"

"Many great ones," Agathe said. "But not all of them were good. Some were bad."

"And during those bad times, your mother suffered, didn't she?"

"Yes," she replied.

"But does that mean your mother was a bad person?"

"No!" the girl said. "My mother was the best!"

"Mine, too," I replied. "So, if neither Hera nor your mother was bad, just because bad things happened to them, do you think you are bad just because bad things happened to you?"

"No," Agathe replied. "I guess not. But the big man said that I was bad. He said I had to suffer for three hundred years!"

"Do you know how long I've been dead, little one?"

"Five days?" the girl said, guessing.

I laughed. "Over five hundred years. And let me tell you, it goes by like the snap of a finger. Before you know it, your suffering is going to be over. Some of these people, the real bad ones, they are going away for millions of years!"

"Wow," Agathe said. "That's so long."

"I know," I replied with a sigh.

"How do you know that?" she asked.

"Can you keep a secret?"

She nodded. "Uh huh."

"Because the first time I was here, I was sentenced to this very pit."

"You?" she said. "But you're not bad."

I smiled again. "Thank you, Agathe. That means a lot to me."

*

My brother made stops at each level of Hell, and at each stop, fewer and fewer people remained in the cage. Rasmus said it didn't bother him, but I saw his eyes droop with the weight of their suffering. By the time he got to level one, only Agathe was left in the back of the cart.

"All right!" Rasmus said. "Level one. Last stop. Everybody off."

A floppy-eared goblin with a gnarled nose and a wart on its forehead ambled up to the cart. Agathe reached out through the bars and grabbed at my shirt.

"He's a bad man!" Agathe said.

"He's not bad," Rasmus said. "He's just doing his job."

"She doesn't know that," I said to him before turning back to her. "Would it help if I walked you over?"

"Yes!" Agathe said. "Please."

I hopped out of the cart and opened the cage in the back. Agathe ran over to me and leaped into my arms. She was heavy, and I let out a deep but contented sigh before I dropped her to the ground.

"Hold my hand," I said. She latched on tightly. So tightly that I would have feared the blood flow would be cut off to my hand if I had any blood flow at all. "Now, we have to be brave, okay?"

"Okay!" Agathe said with a smile. It broke my heart. She was being so courageous, and I feared that I had led her astray, but her attitude wouldn't stop the horrible things that would happen to her in the pits.

The goblin ambled toward the pits, and when we reached the edge, I knelt next to Agathe. "Now, this goblin is going to take you the rest of the way. I need you to be brave, okay?"

"Brave like you?"

I smiled. "No, brave like you. You're braver than me. I couldn't have done what you're going to do, but it will be over before you know it, okay?"

She nodded. "I'll be brave."

"Come, child," the goblin said, holding out its hand. "It's time."

Agathe wrapped me in a hug and squeezed tight. Then, she let go and took the goblin's hand, and it led her toward the mud stairs, which would lead her down to the pit.

"What's going to happen to her?" I asked as they descended.

"You don't want to know," the goblin replied. "It would only break whatever heart you have left."

"Come on, sis," Rasmus said, walking up to me. "Let's go. There's still a ways to go before we reach Dis."

# CHAPTER 8

The road to Dis was mostly silent, save for my brother occasionally yelling at his unicorn to move faster. I wanted to speak to him, but there was nothing to say. I had so many questions, but none that he could answer. I wanted to know how the world could be so cruel, and then Hell could somehow be even crueler, but I was afraid of the answer. There was so little hope left in me. I couldn't watch it diminish even further.

"When we get to Dis," Rasmus said as we neared the walled black gates of the city. "Do as I tell you. It will save your life."

"Sure. I'll do whatever you say," I replied.

The walled city of Dis looked like any other metropolis I had been to in my years on Earth. Outside, a small river led water out of the grates under the city and into the surrounding lava. The walls stretched high into the sky and wrapped around it, funneling all visitors to a large gate.

I hadn't seen water since I arrived in Hell, and a small part of me wondered how it could even exist in such oppressive heat. Then again, I figured, with all the other magic I'd seen in my life, this was just another thing that I didn't need to question.

A glowing, blue wraith floated above the bridge in front of the city and checked each traveler in as they passed. Behind it, a dozen fat orc guards held spears at attention, ready to pounce on any that didn't meet with the wraith's approval.

"Hello, Gil," Rasmus said, pulling on the reins to his unicorn. "How's the family?"

"Very funny, Rasmus. As if I would ever have a family," Gil replied. "Who is the girl?"

"I am Akta of the Forest," I replied.

Rasmus chucked a casual thumb over his shoulder at me. "Frank said she needs to get checked into central processing and fitted to work."

I wanted to tell him that I wasn't here to work, but I knew this wasn't the time. I was here to find the fallen angel and return to Mount Olympus as quickly as possible. There would be time for protest later. I promised Rasmus I would follow his lead.

"You know where to go, right?" Gil asked.

Rasmus nodded. "Of course. This isn't my first new recruit, you know."

"I have to ask."

"I'm going to board my unicorn in the stables, then I'll walk her over."

"Don't take too long. You know how Velaska gets about monsters working."

Rasmus nodded. "Oh, yes. I know."

Gil waved us forward. "Move along, then."

Rasmus snapped the reins on his unicorn, and it started to trot forward. "Not too fast, Snowflake."

"What was that about?" I said under my breath.

"This is not the time or place to discuss it. Wait until we are inside the walls, away from prying eyes, and then I will explain."

"I trust you, brother, but barely," I said as we disappeared through the city gates and passed the orc guards, who eyed me with contempt.

*

"Thank you, Gregor," my brother said, shaking the hands of an elf who tended the stables. "You will take good care of her, won't you?"

The tall, thin elf nodded. "As if she were one of my own children."

"Thank you, my friend." Rasmus pulled me out of the stable and into an empty alley. "And thank you for not causing a scene."

I folded my arms across my chest. "I appreciate your help, brother, but I will not be given a job today, not by demons or by anyone."

"All monsters must be assigned a job. Otherwise, they are tortured and left to rot with the rest of the condemned. If you refuse work, then you choose damnation. Please, think about the consequences of your actions."

"I do not choose death, brother. I have another task assigned me."

Rasmus looked exasperated. "And what task is that, dear sister? Tell me!"

"I should not say," I replied. "I am bound to secrecy."

"If you want my help, I need to know the truth. The full truth."

I looked around me to make sure the coast was clear. When I didn't see anybody coming, I turned back to Rasmus. "Fine. I am here to meet an angel named Lucifer. I was told to meet him here, in Dis."

"By whom?" Rasmus asked.

"By—" I replied. "By the gods."

Rasmus snorted. "Please don't insult me."

"You are correct. I misspoke. It was not by the gods. It was by THE God. Singular."

"Oh really?"

I nodded. "Yes, my mission is to find a displaced angel who fell from Mount Olympus into Hell three hundred years ago. Now please, I need your help. You must know of a way for me to stay in Hell without being caught or assigned a job."

"Perhaps," Rasmus said. "Come with me. And let us hope we don't get spotted along the way."

*

The thatched homes and mud huts of Dis reminded me a lot of the kingdoms I had visited on Earth during my twenty-six years of life. Rasmus weaved me through the dirt streets of the city, passing ogres, orcs, demons, imps, wraiths, ghosts, elves, satyrs, sprites, zombies, gnomes, and all manner of monsters from Earth and Hell. They walked with each other as if it were the most normal thing in the world. Some even seemed…downright happy with their lot in life.

"Why are so many of them smiling?" I asked Rasmus as he led me through the crowded streets. Merchants peddled their wares in poorly-constructed, wooden boxes lining either side of the street.

"Because down here, we are normal. On the surface, humans treated us like second-class citizens, but down here, we can be free."

"I guess that makes sense. After all, they do get to torture humanity now, after they hunted our people across the world."

"They didn't just hunt us, Akta," Rasmus said with a sigh. "They hunted us to extinction."

"Did they? I had wondered if that were the case, but I have not heard from Earth in five centuries."

"There are no more monsters on Earth. Some humans carry on the bloodline of a monster in their ancestry, but there are no pure-bred monsters on Earth anymore."

"Carry on the bloodline?" I asked. "How is that even possible?"

"Easily," Rasmus said, stopping by a stand to sniff a bushel of flaming flowers. "My wife was a human, and our children are half pixie, half human."

"You married a human?"

"I did," he said. "To consolidate power between my kingdom and a neighboring one, I took a wife and loved her for all my days."

"And she gave you children?" I asked.

"Four." He turned to the florist. "I'm sorry, but how much are these?"

"Ten Quan," a fat, gray troglodyte grunted.

Rasmus reached into his pocket and tossed a small gold coin to the merchant. Then, he picked up the bushel of flaming red flowers and turned to me. "Nice, aren't they?"

"They're fine," I replied.

"Fire daisies," Rasmus said. "The flame carries the fragrance all over the street. They are the only thing that can puncture the stale fire of Hell. When they bloom, it makes me remember home. My wife. My children. My old life."

"Your kids," I asked. "Have you ever seen them…down here?"

"No," Rasmus replied. "That's why driving the chariot weighs so much on my soul. Each time I carry someone to their final torture, I think to myself—that could be my wife or one of the kids."

"Well," I said. "They are five hundred years backlogged at the Gate. Maybe they'll have a different job for you by the time they come through."

"They might," Rasmus said, starting to walk down the street again. Nobody gave a second thought to the flaming flowers in his hand. "But I hope I never see them. I don't know what I would do if I saw my sweet wife at the gates of Hell, and I had to deliver her to her final damnation."

"I pray you never find out."

"Me either, but in some ways, I am blessed. My job is easy by comparison to many monsters. Most of us never get the chance even to see a human," Rasmus said as he continued his leisurely stroll. "Most monsters work keeping the bowels of Hell functioning. They are construction workers, alchemists, janitors, plumbers, blacksmiths, stable boys, and the like. Many haven't left Dis in hundreds of years."

"I never thought I would hear somebody say they were blessed while walking through Hell, my brother. This day continues to surprise me."

"Then, let us keep the surprises going."

*

We walked down the streets of Dis until I heard a little girl's voice blaring from the end of a dirt-filled street. She stood atop a wooden stand, holding shoes in each hand.

"My daddy's the best cobbler in Dis!" she shouted. "Get your shoes here! Don't wanna go walking on the rocky terrain of Hell without nice shoes, do ya?"

Her ears were pointy, and two of her teeth were gone from the front of her mouth, but that didn't stop her from screaming loud enough to reach over the din of the street. Behind her, a kindly, old elf with even longer, pointier ears slaved over the stitching in a pair of loafers.

"Where are you going?" the girl hollered to an ogre who passed by her booth. "I see those old, dirty shoes. They're gross!".

"Beatrice!" the old man hissed. "Don't insult people."

"I'm not insulting!" Beatrice said. "I'm just stating a fact. His shoes are uuuuuuugly."

The old elf shook his head. "True or not, that isn't polite."

"Who cares about being polite, Dad?" Beatrice said. "I'm trying to sell shoes."

"You catch more flies with honey, Bee."

"Not in Hell, Dad!"

"Beatrice!" Rasmus shouted across the crowded street. "Are you harassing customers again?"

"You say harassing," Beatrice folded her arms across her chest. "I say selling. Whatever it is, it's why I sell more shoes than anybody on this street."

Rasmus cocked his head. "You are also the only cobbler on this street."

"That's because nobody else sells shoes like me, and nobody makes them like my dad. Everybody buzzed off when they realized they didn't stand a chance."

"I suppose I can't argue with that," Rasmus said, walking me up to her booth. "After all, I have been wearing your shoes for hundreds of years."

"Yeah," Beatrice said, looking down at the worn, frayed leather shoes on my brother's feet. "You could use a new pair. We'll give you a good deal. We'll call it a friend discount."

"Maybe later," Rasmus said, holding out the fire daisies. "Here, I got these for you. They're your favorite."

Beatrice hopped down from her booth. "Thanks, buddy. That's nice of you. I'll make sure I put them in some magma when I get home." Beatrice smacked her dad lightly on the arm. "Dad, Rasmus is here, and he's bribing me. It must mean he needs something big."

"It's good to see you, Clovis," Rasmus said.

Clovis looked up from his spectacles and sighed. "It would be nice to see you if you weren't always bringing me strays. Who is this?"

"This is Akta," Rasmus said. "She's my sister, and she needs your help."

Clovis stood and wiped his glasses. "Of course she does. Well, any friend of Rasmus's, as they say, is a client of mine."

"Can we talk somewhere more private?" Rasmus asked.

"Not now, you mook!" Beatrice said. "We have shoes to sell."

"We'll close up early. Meet me at my house in an hour. Try not to get in too much trouble until then."

"We'll try," Rasmus said. "Thank you. I can't stress this enough. You are a lifesaver."

"Technically, he's a death saver," Beatrice said. "But that's picking nits. Just make sure you bring money this time. We're not a charity."

Rasmus tapped a pouch on his belt. "I have plenty."

"Let's hope so," Beatrice said. "For your sake."

# CHAPTER 9

Clovis and Beatrice's house rested in the middle of a long alleyway lined with row houses. It took barely five minutes to walk there from the street where we'd met them, but it felt like a whole different world. Their street was lined with cobblestones instead of dirt, and all the houses were built with brick and stone instead of mud and sticks. Even the stench of Hell didn't hit my nose as hard as it had on the main street.

"I don't understand," I said. "How would Frank—or Velaska, or anybody—even know that I wasn't supposed to be in Hell anyway?"

"I'll show you." Rasmus pulled down the collar of his cloak. On his chest was a brand of a code of arms, with a horse and carriage in the middle of it. "Every monster in Hell is branded with one of these badges. They are attached directly to our soul, with dark magic. Any demon can request to look at it at any moment. They glow blue with the utterance of a spell. The badges cannot be forged or duplicated, except by very skilled hands. It is dangerous work, and the slightest mistake could alert every demon in Hell that you are a spy. You don't want to know what happens then."

"Yes, I do," I replied.

"Then we will all face the pits of Hell, if we are lucky. If we are not lucky, then we will face the wrath of Velaska herself."

My heart beat fast in my ear. It was a reflex I knew and a trick of the mind, but that did not make the sound any less irritating. I no longer had a heart, after all. But just like an amputee could feel their phantom limb, so too could the dead feel their hearts and their breath, even though they no longer had either.

I turned my attention from the brand on Rasmus's chest to a long, ornate, golden pendant hanging from his neck. It was inlaid with emeralds and rubies, and a silver rose grew from the middle of it.

"That's beautiful," I said.

"Thank you," Rasmus replied, stroking it. "It is the last memento of my wife, Rosemary. I feel close to her every time I touch it."

Behind us, four footsteps clopped on the cobblestone street. I turned around quickly, ready to draw my daggers, but relaxed when I saw Beatrice and Clovis walking toward us. Clovis held a briefcase while Beatrice waved the fire daisies happily.

"Sorry we're late," Clovis said. "Beatrice was busy accosting people again."

"Making sales," Beatrice corrected him. "I was busy making sales, and I don't like to leave while I'm on a hot streak. I even got a wraith to buy a pair, and they don't got any feet. I mean, I am that good."

"Quite," Clovis said. "Shall we go inside?"

Clovis walked to his front door and clicked the lock with his key. Inside, a long staircase led to the kitchen above.

"Your house is very nice," I said. "Nicer than any I have seen in Hell yet."

"Thank you," Clovis replied, pushing open the door. "Just because we live in Hell doesn't mean we can't be civilized about it."

"I bust my butt all day so we can live here," Beatrice said, walking up the stairs. There was a kitchen at the top of the landing.

"They also make money…other ways," Rasmus said. "Which is why we're here."

*

Beatrice, Clovis, Rasmus, and I sat around a wooden dining room table in the kitchen of his house. The fire daisies flamed in a vase of magma between us. The room was bigger than most of the huts we had passed on our travels through Hell, and yet, Clovis and Beatrice still resorted to selling their wares on the streets with the other monsters, as if they lived among them in the same squalid conditions.

"Now," Clovis said. "What can I help you with?"

"I need a brand," Rasmus said. "For my sister."

"Magical brands do not come cheap," Clovis said. "But if you have the money, then I have the expertise."

Rasmus reached into his belt and pulled out a pouch. The gold coins rattled together when he laid them on the table.

"One thousand Noo," he replied.

"So, she already has a brand, then, and she just needs it changed?" Beatrice said. "Let's see it."

"I have nothing of the sort," I replied. "I just arrived here and would rather avoid anybody knowing I exist if you know what I mean."

"Of course we do," Beatrice said. "We're shady people, in case you didn't notice."

"I had, actually," I replied. "They are often the best kind of people, I have found."

Beatrice smiled. "Me too. But if we are making a new brand from scratch, it's double. Two thousand Quan."

Rasmus sneered. "You know I don't have that kind of money."

"Then it appears we're at an impasse," Beatrice replied. Clovis fell silent, letting his daughter negotiate for him.

Rasmus placed his hands on the table in front of him. "There must be something I can offer you as payment for your time."

"Her daggers are pretty nice. I'll take those."

"Never," I replied, growling at them. "I would rather die."

"You already have," Beatrice said. "But if you don't want a brand, that's your choice. Of course, you're almost guaranteed to be caught and tortured, but it's your afterlife."

"Wait," Rasmus said, standing up. "Make the brand. I will be back. You have my word that I will return with the money."

*

"Where do you think he's going?" Beatrice asked me as she walked me through the kitchen and into a study. It was filled with curio cabinets displaying statues and relics—from hand-carved reliefs of beautiful women to fat buddhas and even daggers so old I couldn't place their origin.

"I'm not sure. I am not my brother's keeper."

"If you ask me, I say he just disappeared and left you here," Beatrice replied. "That's what I would do."

"Really?" I said. "You would leave your own sister without help?"

"I don't know," Beatrice shrugged. "I guess. I mean, I don't have a sister, so I couldn't tell you."

"What about your father? Would you leave him?"

Beatrice stomped her feet. "Well, no, of course not. But that's different."

I bent down to look at a statue of a jade dragon breathing fire. "Why?"

"Because my dad's awesome, and the jury's still out on you."

I had to laugh. "Fair enough. Where did you get all this stuff?"

"People traded it to us over the years," Beatrice said. "Or we found it. Dad's always had a thing for old junk, like your daggers."

"My daggers are not junk. They have helped me slay many things, even dragons."

Beatrice's eyes went wide. "You fought dragons?"

I nodded. "Not only fought but killed them as well. The dragon Aziolith was my greatest conquest."

Beatrice laughed until she had to hold her side. "Aziolith? Really? That's your greatest win as a monster hunter?"

I stood up. "That's right. Why do you mock me?"

"Nothing," Beatrice said with a snicker. "It's just...well, he's kind of a softie, at least these days."

"A...softie?"

"Yeah, like, he lives up in the hills. Keeps to himself. Doesn't bother anyone. He's not really all that scary."

"Aziolith...is here. In Hell?"

"That's what I'm saying," Beatrice replied. "And he's not that scary, to be honest. I mean, lots of other people are scared of him because he's a dragon, but I'm pretty sure I could take him."

"What are you two doing in here?" Clovis asked, walking in from the kitchen. "Gossiping?"

"Just talking about Akta's…conquests," Beatrice said with another snicker.

"Well, come along," Clovis gestured. "Your brother's just come back."

I walked back into the kitchen just as Rasmus came up the stairs to meet us. He placed a leather coin pouch on the table.

"Twenty Loo, as promised," Rasmus said. "That's equivalent of 2,000 Quan. So, get moving on that brand." I'd noticed a heaviness about him when I arrived in Hell, but now there was something more. A deep sadness in his eyes.

"What did you do?" I asked.

"Don't worry about it," Rasmus grumbled. "Just make it happen, Clovis."

"As you wish," he replied with a slight nod.

*

It took twelve hours for Clovis to cast the mold for the brand. He asked me all sorts of questions about my strengths and weaknesses, and he finally decided that I should be branded as a scout. Scouts traveled the fields of Hell, looking for those who had escaped the pits.

"Do people escape the pits often?" I asked.

"Not often," Clovis told me as he carved into the plaster mold that would be used to create my brand. "But with trillions of souls in Hell, there are always bound to be a few who escape. It's not a perfect system."

"And it's the scout's job to track them down?"

Clovis nodded. "There is a whole department of monsters and demons whose sole job is to catch escaped souls."

"So, this will prevent that department from finding me."

"If I do it right," Clovis said.

"You don't sound too confident," I replied.

"Well, I haven't been caught yet, so that means I haven't screwed it up yet, so let's just say I'm cautiously optimistic."

After the plaster was cast, Clovis melted a glowing metal rod in the magma that flowed under the stove in their kitchen. The room looked innocent enough, but what I found was that every piece of it had a purpose used for Clovis's forgery. Once the metal was melted, Clovis poured it into the cast and covered it, then placed it in the bath of cold water Beatrice had prepared in the sink. Watching them work was like watching a beautifully choreographed ballet.

"Do you want to know something funny?" Rasmus asked me as we waited for the metal to cool.

"Always," I replied.

"I would bet if we went to the ministry and got you an assignment, a right proper assignment, you would have been made a scout anyway."

"I was thinking the same thing," I said with a smile. "It sounds like the perfect job. But now I don't have to tell anybody I'm here, which has its own benefits."

"Assuming he made it correctly, of course," Rasmus said. "If not, everybody will know."

"Hey!" Beatrice said from across the kitchen. "How about a little faith? There's all sorts of magic going on here, and the last thing we need is for your bad mojo to seep into the brand and give it bad juju."

"Sorry," Rasmus said. "I won't say another word."

"Now, now," Clovis said. "Let's not make promises we can't keep."

*

When Clovis finally finished his brand, he placed it at the tip of a metal poker and held it over the magma until it was red hot.

"You have a choice of where to place it. On your chest, on your arm, or on your wrist."

I unbuttoned my coat and pulled my shirt, revealing my collarbone. "I choose my chest, like my brother."

"Are you sure?" Clovis said. "If you should ever need to show it again, you will have to bare your breast for all to see."

"I'm not concerned about who sees my breast," I replied. "Just do it."

Clovis nodded. "Open your mouth."

I obliged, and Beatrice placed a towel in my mouth. "This will imprint on your soul, so it's going to sting. Bite down as hard as you can. You might pass out."

I would not pass out. I was strong-willed, as was my soul. I narrowed my eyes as they met Clovis's gaze. He took a deep breath and pressed the brand into my chest. The scalding fire from the poker gushed across my entire body and consumed my soul with flame.

My body jerked and convulsed on its own as the heat from the brand grew and grew until finally…it stopped, and Clovis pulled the brand back from my chest and tossed it into the cool water of the sink.

Beatrice pulled the towel from my mouth and replaced it with a cool, damp rag on my head. "It's over now."

"Did it work?" I replied.

"Seems like it." Clovis walked up to me. "*Inacta Zambri.*"

He waved his hand over my chest, and my brand glowed blue. At its center, a blue eye shone out for all to see.

"The mark of the scout." Rasmus was giddy. "It worked."

"*Renacta Zambri,*" Clovis said, and the glowing stopped. "Success. None but the greatest wizards in Hell would be able to tell it was a forgery. I dare say it is a masterpiece."

"Thank you," I said, standing up with wobbly knees. "I am forever in your debt."

"Nah," Beatrice said, pointing to the coin purse. "Your debt is clear."

"If you will excuse us," Rasmus said, standing up. "We must adjourn as we have business to attend at the Old Hat."

"That's a dangerous place, old friend. Only the worst of the worst in Dis hang out there."

Rasmus smiled. "I'm counting on it."

# CHAPTER 10

Rasmus walked with me back to the main road of Dis, where we originally met Beatrice and Clovis. We zigged and zagged through alleyways and passed vendors packing up their wares while others were just setting theirs up. Rasmus was silent except for a few "turn left" and "right here."

Finally, I stopped in my tracks. "What is going on with you?"

"Nothing," he said. "We just have somewhere to be, and I want to make sure we get there."

"I don't have anywhere to be with you. My only mission is to find Lucifer, track down the fallen angel, and get back to Mount Olymp—"

Rasmus stopped and covered my mouth. "Don't say that here. Don't ever say that here. You have no idea who is listening."

"Pus," I spat out when he moved his hand. "Why are you so pissy? Is this about the money?"

"No," Rasmus said. He wasn't very convincing.

"I don't believe you. Tell me the truth."

"Fine!" Rasmus replied. "I sold it, all right? Is that what you want me to say? We needed money, and so I sold it."

"Sold what?" I asked, but then my eyes tracked down to his neck, and I realized the gold pendant which once rested there was gone, the last memento of his dear Rosemary.

"Oh, Rasmus," I breathed. "Why would you do that?"

"We needed the money more than I needed a silly pendant."

I shook my head. "No, we could have found another way."

"There was no other way. You're my blood, and I needed to know you were safe. We do for family, sister."

I placed my hand on his shoulder. "Thank you, brother. Your kindness will be rewarded."

"We do for our own, and that is its own reward," he replied, avoiding my eyes. "Now, come, we have somewhere to be."

*

Finally, we reached the Old Hat. Above the building, there was an old, wooden crest with a beat-up top hat carved into it. Next to it, an old clock tower told me that it was almost eight PM. Clocks were the only way to tell the time in Hell. There was fire but no sun. The flames licked the top of the cavern, where twisted stalactites dripped down toward us. Their sharp points looked like the claws of a deranged monsters, reaching to rip us apart.

"Now, this is the toughest bar in Hell," Rasmus said, holding the metal latch of the wooden door. "It's no place for the faint of heart."

I chuckled. "I think I'll be fine."

"You say that, but you've been in…well, up there for five hundred years. Things work a little differently down here."

"Just open the door," I replied. "I'll take my chances."

Rasmus smiled at me. "You asked for it."

He pushed open the door and held it for me to walk inside. The minute I did, I was met with the laughter and excitement of about two dozen voices.

"Oh yeah," I said, rolling my eyes. "Looks really treacherous."

Monsters hollered and cavorted with each other like old friends. A ragtime piano sat in the corner, played by a long-fingered goblin, as orcs and ogres sang all around him.

"Over here," Rasmus said, walking toward the dimly lit back of the bar, where booths lined the wall. As I sidestepped the raucous patrons of the bar, I heard a familiar voice.

"The problem with Hell isn't the monsters," it grumbled. "It's the management."

It wasn't long before I recognized the long beard and single eye of my cyclops friend Ylfingur, the cyclops warlord who helped me kill King Odgeir so many centuries ago.

"Ylfingur," Rasmus said. "I have somebody here I think you'll remember."

"Well, well, well," he said, standing. "If it isn't Akta of the Forest. I haven't seen you in nigh on five hundred years. Where have you been?"

A quick shake of Rasmus's head told me it wasn't safe to tell him the truth. "There was a mix-up, and I was sent into the line with the humans. Took five hundred years, but I finally made it here."

"Fascinating," Ylfingur said. "It's good to see you, old friend. Please, come, toast us with a drink."

Ylfingur sat back down in the booth. Next to him, another cyclops glared at me with venom in his eyes.

"Bjarngimur," I said. It was Ylfingur's son and the last monster I had killed before King Odgeir betrayed me.

"I heard you dragged my head through the woods and up to the king's throne room," Bjarngimur growled.

"I did."

"Did it scare the little human children? Did they run and flee at my awesome might?"

"No," I replied. "A couple of them thought you were squishy though when they touched your eye, and I did drag your head over a courtesan's dress, which certainly destroyed it."

"Hrm," Bjarngimur said with a huff. "The only joy I have is that you learned the error of your ways, even if it was after my death."

"Akta!" I heard behind me. "Akta! Akta! Akta!"

I turned to see a big, blue troll lumbering toward me. I recognized his crook-nosed face anywhere. It was the troll who found me in the woods when I returned after my first death and the last, and possibly only, true friend I ever had on Earth.

"Akta!" he said, wrapping me in a big hug. "Akta!"

"Hi, buddy," I replied. "Good to see you, too."

He dropped me to the ground and studied me. "Like your eyes better the other way."

"Yeah," I said. When I was resurrected after my first death, my eyes had turned from emerald green to black with little white dots in them. "I…don't."

"Smell better now, though," the troll added.

I laughed. "That I will agree with, and I can move much better, too."

"This color better. I like," he said with a nod.

When I was undead, my body was not its normal dark, rich mocha. Instead, it was a disgusting blue, as if all the life had drained out of it…which was exactly what happened.

"Thank you," I replied. "So, how have you been?"

"Good," he said, sliding into the booth with Bjarngimur and Ylfingur. "Dig ditch. Make hole. Drink beer. Good life."

I smiled. "Sounds like a good life."

"No hunt," he replied. "No humans hunt."

"But there is fire," I said. "I know you don't like fire."

"I get used to it," the troll replied, sipping his ale. "No human hunt me. So, fire okay."

I nodded. "That makes sense." I turned from him to Ylfingur. "And what about you, Ylfingur? Are you digging ditches as well?"

"Lord, no!" Ylfingur said. "I work as a constable."

"Head constable," Bjarngimur added.

"Yes. Well, I don't like to brag, but I bring law to this lawless town."

"I disagree. You're a stooge to the bureaucracy. The monsters of Hell can police themselves," Bjarngimur said. "It sullies everything we did on Earth to turn around and police your own people."

"That is neither here nor there," Ylfingur replied. "If I were to deny my job, I would be burned alongside the humans."

"And therein lies the rub," Bjarngimur said with a scoff. "They hold eternal damnation over our heads to make sure we do our jobs. Gods forbid we think for ourselves."

"But that is not the problem of the everyday demon!" Ylfingur said. "It is a systemic problem with the gods themselves. They designed a system in which they win, and we are treated like garbage."

"Guys!" Rasmus shouted. "This is getting a little intense. How about I buy you all another round, and we settle down, okay?" Rasmus pulled me away from the group and toward the bar. "I love them, but they will never stop talking about their problems with the gods as if we had any way to change it."

"This has been fun and all, Rasmus, but please tell me there's another reason you brought me here other than to have a drink with friends."

"Oh, I did. This is the bar Lucifer visits every evening. Drinking with friends is just a bonus."

I smiled. "Then, bottoms up."

*

When I was alive, I wasn't much of a drinker. The first drink I'd had in three years was also the one that killed me. However, spend five hundred years in the bars on Valhalla, and you learn a thing or two about booze. The piss swill they drank in Hell was much weaker than the mead on Valhalla, but it did the job all the same.

"And, so you arrest people in Hell?" I asked Ylfingur. "For what?"

"All the same things they would have gotten arrested for on Earth," Ylfingur replied. "Just because we're in Hell doesn't mean we can't be civilized about it. Dis needs order, just like anywhere else."

"Order," Bjarngimur sneered. "That's what they used to call it on Earth, too. Humans enslaved our people everywhere we roamed in the name of order."

"True," Ylfingur said. "For years, we had monsters from Africa and India, and all over the world, really, who didn't understand what it meant to be civilized."

Bjarngimur slammed his stein down on the table after he'd emptied it. "That is a Eurocentric definition of what civilization means. Plenty of perfectly functioning civilizations would be barbaric by your definition. I swear, you're no better than the kings back on Earth."

"I take offense to that!" Ylfingur shouted. He slammed his hands on the table and nearly woke up my troll friend, who had fallen into a drunken stupor.

As they argued, the door swung open, and a tall, statuesque man with a clean-shaven face sauntered into the bar. His immaculate white suit shimmered like sunlight as he walked. All its patrons stopped what they were doing and stared at him, except for Bjarngimur and Ylfingur, who were engrossed in their own conversation.

"That's him," Rasmus said. "That's Lucifer. Let's go."

"What about them?" I asked, pointing back to Ylfingur and Bjarngimur.

"They can go on like that for hours," he replied. "Do you want to wait for them?"

I jumped up. "Hell no."

I walked around the slobbering drunks and up to the bar, where Lucifer's light shone bright enough that nobody dared come within two feet of him. In fact, the other monsters at the bar looked downright frightened of him.

"Why are they all so scared?" I asked.

"If a demon encounters God's light, they will be evaporated in an instant. There's nothing that says monsters will be disintegrated, too, but no monster has ever tested it."

"Well, I will."

I sidled up to the bar and leaned against the open spot next to Lucifer. My skin basked in his glow, but it did not burn. It actually felt quite pleasant. I missed the glow of Heaven, and I suddenly felt at peace in a way I hadn't since I left Mount Olympus.

"You are Lucifer?" I asked.

"What gave me away?" he replied.

"I've been looking for you."

"You must be the one Bacchus sent," he said, looking me over. "Ashley, is it?"

"Akta," I replied curtly.

He threw out a dismissive wave. "Whatever. It doesn't matter. You're wasting your time."

"Why do you say that?"

"Because I know exactly where the angel is."

"Great," I replied with a smile. "Then this should be easy."

"On the contrary, there is no more heavily guarded place in Hell than where she is being held."

"And where is that?"

Lucifer smiled. "Velaska's personal prison, of course."

The smile disappeared from my face.

"Exactly," Lucifer replied. "Come, let us talk somewhere a little more private."

# CHAPTER 11

"So," I started, sitting down with a piss-warm beer across from Lucifer. "How are we going to have a private conversation in this place? I'm not really supposed to be here in Hell, you know."

"Don't worry about that." Lucifer gestured to the ray of light that fell on everything around us for two feet in any direction. "This orb of light is completely soundproof. One of the advantages Heaven afforded me."

"That's nice, I guess," I said. "All right then, so what you're saying is that you know exactly where Zharaqiel is, but you didn't tell Bacchus or Gabriel?"

"No," Lucifer replied. "What I'm saying is that no matter how often I try to communicate what I know, Gabriel doesn't believe me. He thinks I'm incompetent, but I'm very competent at my job. I've been here almost two hundred millennia at this point. I know this place like the back of my hand."

"Then what am I doing here?" I said, trying to take a sip of the disgusting beer in front of me.

"Here," Lucifer said, grabbing the glass and holding it until ice crystals formed on the sides. "It's the only way I can drink it."

"Thanks." I took a swig. It was cold, which made it slightly better, but there was still a distinct aftertaste of urine. "That doesn't answer my question, though."

"I don't know what you're doing here," Lucifer said after taking a sip of his beer with a pained expression. He didn't seem to like it any more than I did. "I don't know why they sent down any heroes. The others couldn't even make it past the front gate without being thrown into eternal damnation. It's simple. Unless somebody can reason with Velaska, then there's nothing to be done, and if that person isn't me, it's definitely not any of them."

I sighed. "That must be why I'm here. Once, I convinced her to send me back to Earth after I died so I could get revenge on the king that killed me."

"Ah," Lucifer said, nodding his head. "Yes, that is the kind of simplistic thinking that Gabriel and Bacchus would use to find me a hero who wouldn't be burned alive."

"Whoa. I'm no kind of hero."

"Well, sure you are," Lucifer said. "You left Mount Olympus, or, I'm guessing, Valhalla, since humanity can't live on Mount Olympus."

"That's right."

"I knew it. You smell like mead and Viking sweat," Lucifer said. "But you came from Valhalla down to Hell on a rescue mission of your own free will. If that's not a hero, then I don't know what is."

"I don't know if I would take my definition of a hero from somebody who has been in Hell for so long." I took a sip of beer. It had already returned to room temperature and was again undrinkable, so I pushed it away. "Or somebody who can drink this swill."

"Your taste buds have softened in Valhalla, my friend."

There was a bitterness in Lucifer's tone as he spoke. With every sip he took of the beer, his eyes narrowed, and he bit his lip harder.

"You don't sound happy about being here," I said.

"Would you be?" Lucifer replied. "Look around you. There are demons and imps everywhere. It smells foul, and the heat, my gods, the heat. Curse Zeus for making me with the ability to withstand such infernal temperatures."

"Why don't you just tell Bacchus you don't want to be here anymore?"

Lucifer sighed. "I tried. I even begged Gabriel to let me out of here. They have been less than receptive. Apparently, none of their other angels is willing to volunteer."

"Did you volunteer?"

"Of course not, which is what makes my internment here wholly unfair."

"Why don't you just say screw it and leave, back to the surface. Just abandon it all and walk away if you hate it so much."

"That is not an option for me. Angels are sworn to obedience to the gods for all time. I could not break my vow if I tried. Please, do not pity me for it, though."

"I don't."

"You do a little. I watched your eyes soften as I spoke." He sniffed and gestured at the room around us. "I have become very accustomed to my lot in life. Though I am in Hell, I am afforded luxuries that other beings do not have. I am not subject to torture or manual labor. I am simply an envoy. Some would consider it a great honor to be given such an important task, to be plucked from the ranks for this mission."

"Then they should do it," I replied. "If they are so honored."

He smiled. "This thing you are doing, trying to bond with me. I like it. This is the most interaction I have had in quite some time. There are not many who understand my plight, but you—you have seen the majesty of the heavens and the horrors of Hell. You are unique among the monsters with whom I normally interact."

"Does that mean you'll take me to Velaska?"

Lucifer laughed. "And you are singularly focused. Is that what got you killed?"

"Yes. Both times, in fact."

"It is a blessing and a curse. Very well. Find a way to abandon your post and meet me at the North gate in two hours. I will bring you across the molten river to see Velaska. Perhaps you will have more success with her than I, though I doubt it."

"I doubt it as well, but I have a lot riding on my success, so I must at least try."

Lucifer gave me a doubtful look. "Trying has sent better men than you to eternal damnation."

"There are none better than me," I said with a smile. "Of that, I am sure."

Lucifer scoffed. "We'll see about that. Two hours. The North gate. Do not be late."

*

"Stop dragging behind me," I shouted to my brother as I pulled him across the dirt street, away from the Old Hat. "You're way too heavy for me to carry you."

"Don't tell me what to do," Rasmus said. His voice slurred, and he was barely able to place one leg in front of the other.

I understood why he drank. It was blatantly obvious that Hell was still the worst. Even if nobody hunted monsters in Hell, they were still little more than slave labor to Velaska. They could not say no to her any more than Lucifer could say no to the gods on Mount Olympus.

"I have to throw up," Rasmus said, falling to the ground.

"Do you even do that here in Hell?" I asked. "I didn't know souls could vomit."

"We throw up. We don't do anything fun, but we can throw up since that is onerous."

"I don't envy the hangover you will have in the morning, my brother."

"At least it will be something to distract me from the smell of burning flesh."

I knelt next to him as he wretched with his whole body. "I'm sorry this fate has come to you. If there is anything I can do—"

"You are going to Velaska, right?" he asked between convulsions. "You will see her?"

"I don't know if I will see her, brother, but I will do my best to get an audience with her, yes."

"My wife," he said. "My wife and my children. Please don't let them suffer. Please, do something to help them."

I looked down on him, and my eyes softened. "I don't know if I can do anything to help them."

"They are everything I have. I can't bear the thought of their damnation."

I reached down to help him to his feet. "I am sorry. Please, don't torture yourself—"

"Don't tell me what to do!" Rasmus curled his lip and slapped my hand off him. "And don't look at me like that. I don't need your pity."

I pushed myself to my feet. "I'm sorry, brother, but you are lying in your own sick in the dirt streets of Hell. You are piteous. Now come, let me take you home."

"No!" Rasmus shouted as I stepped toward him. "I do not need your help. I have accepted my fate. My family. Do not forsake them, Akta. Do not forsake them!"

I sighed. "Very well, Rasmus. I cannot promise to help them, but I can promise to do my best. Now, please, let me help you to your feet."

I held out my hand toward him. He stared at me for an unusually long time. His eye color had dulled since I saw him last, but I still recognized the green hue of my family in them.

After a long moment, he locked his hand with mine, and I yanked him to his feet. I was sad this would likely be the last memory of my brother. Still, I would have a story to tell my mother. It would make her smile.

Of course, I would leave out the part about him lying in his own vomit.

*

After dropping off my drunken brother at his mud hovel on the outskirts of the walled city, I made my way toward the North gate. I wasn't sure where north was at first, but the nice thing about being around monsters was that I didn't have to hide my fairy wings. I released them so that they fluttered on either side of me and lifted me high into the air.

Far in the distance, the outline of a sinewy black castle sat on an island in the center of a molten lake of fire. A river of lava ran from the lake out across Hell, and two sheer rock faces barricaded either side of it. A dark, black gate rested at the top of the cliff.

Behind me rose the Gates of Abnegation, with Petrus sitting at the base, guarding the entrance to Hell. To my left rose a sheer rock wall that extended to the top of Hell itself, and to my right, ceaseless darkness which I couldn't see beyond.

Speckling the rocky countryside, pits of Hellfire, and bogs of darkness created an ominous glow. My stomach sunk into my knees when I imagined the horror that those who suffered inside them must face.

"Are you going to stay up there all day?" a voice boomed below me. "We have places to be, you know."

I looked down to see Lucifer flying toward me, his beautiful, white wings a stark contrast to the dirty grime of Hell. Light escaped him so brightly it was hard to look at him directly.

"I forgot you could fly, too," I said.

"Yes," Lucifer replied. "But the locals don't like it. It makes them uneasy. It's bad enough I am an angel without having to rub it in their face by literally flying above them."

"And your glow," I replied, "can't help either."

"Ah yes," Lucifer said. "Well, that is on purpose. I don't particularly like demons, and they don't particularly like light, especially light from Mount Olympus. I tend to keep myself bright, lest some demon or another tries to pick a fight with an angel to make a name for himself."

"So, it doesn't have to be that bright?" I asked.

"Of course not." Lucifer took a deep breath, and the light from his body faded. He was a beautiful specimen of a man, truly flawless in his effortless good looks, but he no longer glowed like a firefly.

"Better?" he asked.

"Thank you," I said. "Much better."

"Shall we away?" he asked. "I chartered a carriage for us."

"Can't we just fly?" I asked.

"Better not to risk it. I am an angel and all, so I can take care of myself, but you don't want to draw too much attention."

"I can handle myself," I said.

"I'm sure you could," Lucifer replied. "However, it is best to keep a low profile."

# CHAPTER 12

Lucifer spared no expense when it came to our carriage. It had gilded accents affixed all around and intricately carved oak doors. I had never ridden in a carriage with doors before, let alone silk curtains which prevented us from being seen by prying eyes. The driver, a regally dressed imp, sat atop the carriage, and four black unicorns with glowing, yellow eyes were latched to the front, their red leather reins sparkling with golden runes and jewels.

"I hope you don't think it's too garish," Lucifer said.

"This is nicer than any I have ever seen before," I replied. "I'm used to riding in the back of rickety, old, wooden carts full of hay and livestock."

"Well, there will be none of that today. It's half a day's trip to the lake of fire, and I won't be riding like a common swine."

"You're kind of pretentious, aren't you?"

"Only in some things, my dear. In others, I'm downright common."

I chuckled a bit as the ostentatious carriage, and its driver idled patiently behind Lucifer. "Whatever you say."

A flaming, blue wraith floated up to us as we continued toward the carriage. "Name?"

"Lucifer," he said. "Morningstar."

"Destination," the wraith said.

"The castle of Velaska, by means of the lake of fire. Charon shall meet us there in four hours hence."

The wraith sighed. "Passengers?"

"Myself," Lucifer said. "And this woman. I'm sorry, I don't recall her name."

"Akta of the Forest," I grumbled.

"She's not on the manifest," the wraith said.

"Last minute changes were made," Lucifer said. "However, she will be my guest."

"Hrm," the wraith said, looking me up and down. "I recognize you. Didn't you come in through the south entrance yesterday?"

I gulped. "I did."

"And did you get your assignment yet?" the wraith said.

"What does that have to do with anything?" Lucifer said, indignant.

"It's just a little weird, is all. A pixie comes to Dis yesterday, brand new, and today she's leaving with the Morningstar?"

"And yet, that is what happened. Is there a problem?" Lucifer said.

"No problem," the wraith said. "I just need to see her brand and make sure she's not trying to shirk her duties to Velaska."

"Even if she weren't branded, it is my decision who I ride with—"

"Enough," I said, unbuttoning my shirt and pulling it down to reveal the scout brand on my chest. "There you go."

"*Inacta Zambri*," the wraith said, waving his hand over my chest.

I closed my eyes and prayed to whatever god was listening for it to work. It worked when Clovis spoke the incantation, but what if it didn't work this time? Luckily, the brand glowed blue, and the wraith noted it in its notes.

"Ah, there we go," the wraith said. "You're a scout. Good, good. Not enough of them. It's so hard to find good ones, I'm afraid. Very well, be on your way."

"Can you…make it stop?" I asked, looking down at the glowing brand.

"Oh, of course," the wraith said, turning back to me. "*Renacta Zambri.*"

The wraith floated away, and we continued to the carriage. "A scout, huh?"

I nodded. "That's right."

"It's very good work," he said. "Who forged it for you?"

"None of your business," I replied.

"Still, the choice of location is stellar," Lucifer said with a smile, his eyes glancing down the opening of my shirt. "You are full of surprises."

I pressed my shirt closed and rebuttoned the clasps. Still, I couldn't help but smile. I hadn't been flirted with in many years, and Lucifer's subtle charm was a nice change of pace from the brutish warriors and their oafish attempts to flirt with me.

*

"Can I ask you a question?" Lucifer said. We had been riding toward the lava lake for over an hour in near silence.

"As long as you don't expect an answer," I replied, watching the sterile wasteland of Hell pass by.

"That flower, on your lapel," he said. "Is it from Valhalla?"

I looked down at the purple tulip. It hadn't moved an inch since my mother placed it there, nor had it wilted in the heat of Hell.

"It is from my mother. She gave it to me right before Gabriel came and summoned me. Why do you ask?"

"No reason," he said. "I was just homesick and recognized the smell."

"Well, I'm glad I could remind you of home, then, I guess," I replied with a slight smile. "Although, I fear you are looking at more than my broach."

"My dear, I was just admiring the flower."

"Whatever you say," I smirked.

"I know what you're thinking," Lucifer said as the carriage jolted over a bump in the road. "But it's not true."

"And what am I thinking?"

"You think I only complimented you because you're new to Hell, and you have the stench of Mount Olympus all over you."

"Oh, do I now?" I said. "Is that what I am thinking? Should I be worried that somebody else will catch a whiff, too?"

"Don't be absurd," Lucifer scoffed. "Demons don't know the smell of Mount Olympus, but I remember it all too well. No matter how long I am in this infernal place, I will never forget the sweet smell of home."

"And is it an aphrodisiac as well?"

Lucifer laughed. "No, it is not. At least, not that I know of. You'll have to forgive me. I know I was being forward earlier, but I haven't seen one so lovely as you in a long time."

"All right," I said. "Keep it in your pants."

"As you wish," Lucifer said.

"Can I ask you a question?" I said. "Since we're being open and honest."

"Now would seem like the perfect time."

"Why are you down here? I mean, why are you really down here? I don't buy the fact that you were just made unlike every other angel."

"Well, you should because it is true. However, they did not know that when they assigned me here. They just didn't like…my power or the way I wielded it. Let's leave it at that."

"No, we can't just leave it at that. You can't just say something like that and then close up. What do you mean?"

"I was the most powerful angel on Mount Olympus in my day. I was the one they would call to defeat any unbeatable foe. Over time, they grew wary of my power, so they sent me here. They told me it would be temporary, but then ideas grew in my head, which my higher-ups didn't appreciate, so they never relieved me. Thus, I have remained in Hell for all this time."

"Like what kind of ideas?"

Lucifer took a deep breath and gestured out the window toward the plains of Hell. "Like this, okay? Like this whole thing. Like how angels get cushy lives in Mount Olympus, and demons have to spend eternity in Hell. Or how we're all just servants to the gods. I mean, weren't we made for more than this? Seriously, does any of this seem fair to you?"

"No," I said. "It doesn't. It didn't seem fair when I was condemned here, and it sure doesn't seem fair now that I've been saved. Being back here, I can't believe it, honestly."

A geyser of black smoke shot from a pit on the right of me. Behind it, a demon, three-hundred-feet-high, worked diligently, pulling people apart by their stomachs and gluing them back together.

"I have always honored my vow to the gods," Lucifer said with a sigh. "I never wavered in my devotion to them, but over the years, I became more and more disillusioned with how they deal with mortals, especially when they shuffle off their mortal coil."

"I understand," I said, watching two demons impale damned souls with their tridents. "Those people will have to suffer forever, won't they?"

"Yes," Lucifer said, pulling down the blinds on his side of the carriage. "It's best not to think about it, honestly. That's what I have found in the last two hundred millennia. The only way to survive is to put it out of your head."

"How can you not think about it when you're surrounded by torture every day?"

"I drink, and I pray. I pray for the salvation of the gods so that they see the error of their ways."

"How is that working out for you?" I asked.

"Poorly," Lucifer admitted.

"In my experience, prayer does very little."

"You said that Velaska granted your prayers to return to your body, so it must work sometimes, right?"

"No," I replied. "Velaska didn't hear my prayers. It was only by traveling through Hell and demanding she act that she heeded my request. Without action, prayer is meaningless."

"Perhaps," Lucifer said. "But it was the first step to your salvation."

"I'm sick of talking about prayers. Can we talk about something else?"

"Fine with me," Lucifer replied. "But you do realize you're talking to an angel, right? Prayer is kind of my thing."

"Yeah, but one that's bound to Hell, so even his prayers have fallen on deaf ears."

"Touché," Lucifer said, turning his head and staring absently out the window.

*

The carriage lurched to a stop in the middle of a large field. Unlike the other fields we passed, this one had grass in it and flowers blooming all throughout. I placed my feet on the ground and brushed my hand on the grass, feeling its gentle sway in my hand.

"How is this possible?" I asked Lucifer. "All I have seen of Hell has been a barren wasteland."

"This is the Field of Yilir, a great sorceress who once worked for the gods. She offended Zeus by falling in love with Charon, the ferryman. He was promised to the siren Thelxiepeia for her great service to the gods. However, Charon refused to marry his betrothed and instead ran off with Yilir."

"What happened to them?" I asked.

"Nobody knows. When the demon scouts finally found Charon, he was clutching Yilir's prized silver mirror next to his bosom, sobbing in these very flowers. This field has bloomed since that day, and since that day, Charon has been bound to the Devil to ferry those who seek an audience to their chamber."

"So, she just vanished? Like that?"

"It seems that way."

"But why?"

"Perhaps she thought that with her gone, Charon would marry Thelxiepeia and avoid a curse. If so, she did not understand the depth of Charon's devotion to her. He would rather live a cursed life than take another into his bed-chamber." Lucifer shrugged. "Of course, it might be another reason altogether. If you ever find her, you can ask her yourself. However, if a thousand demon scouts cannot track her down, I doubt you stand a chance of doing so."

"You would be surprised what I can accomplish."

The imp snapped the reins of his unicorn, and the carriage took off. As it crested a footbridge over the river of magma, a gondola appeared and floated toward us. The ferryman wore a black cloak, and nothing but glowing yellow eyes escaped his ragged dress.

"Charon!" Lucifer said. "What ho?"

The boat came to a stop at the dock, and the ferryman ambled out onto the shore. His voice was gruff and raspy, and he spoke with long, drawn-out words. "My old friend. What can I do for you today?"

"I need passage for myself and my friend to Velaska's castle."

"Is she expecting you?" the voice growled slow enough to catch every syllable. "I hope she is expecting you."

"If she were expecting us, we would have used the Gate," Lucifer replied.

"I am duty-bound only to carry those who have business with the Dark Mistress and with whom she requests to do business."

"Forget this, Lucifer," I replied. "Let's just fly over."

"That is quite impossible, impetuous one," Charon replied.

"He's right," Lucifer added. "The lake surrounding Velaska's castle is protected by magic. If we tried to fly over the great cliffs that guard the lake, we would sink into the lava and burn."

"Better than you have tried," Charon said. "And failed."

"Why do people keep saying that?" I replied angrily. "How do you know I'm not as good as somebody else? Better, even?"

"Two hundred millennia of experience," Charon replied. "Of course, you are welcome to try and die, just like the others, if you wish."

"We do not wish to try," Lucifer said. "I apologize for my friend here. What will it take to secure our passage?"

Charon's hand lifted, and his bony fingers pointed to my lapel at the purple tulip which rested there. "My Yilir…she so loved flowers, and that is like none I have ever seen."

I pressed my hand down upon it. "It is from my mother. The last thing I have to remember her in this place."

"Then, I suppose you can take the Gate of Ulthar and risk your luck with the great eye. Of course, it's a three-day hike through mountainous terrain, as opposed to an hour-long boat ride—quite a pleasant one too, if I do say so myself. It's your choice."

"Just give it to him," Lucifer said. "It's the only way."

"You knew this was going to happen, didn't you?" I sneered. "That's why you asked the question about the flower earlier. You knew he would ask for it."

"I know many things," Lucifer said. "But that does not change our current dilemma. If you want to complete your mission and return to your mother, you must give up the flower. What will it be?"

I pulled my hand off my lapel and grabbed the flower which resided inside of it. I handed it to Charon, who took it in his bony hands and brought it to his face. "Fine."

"It smells…heavenly," Charon said.

"You have no idea," I said as Lucifer elbowed me in the ribs.

"Yilir would have appreciated this. Thank you. Please, step inside."

Lucifer nodded slightly to Charon as he boarded the gondola. "Thank you, old friend."

Charon held up his bony hand when I tried to step on the boat. "I'm afraid you will have to leave your daggers and other weapons here. Nothing that might damage the Devil may find its way to her castle."

I pulled my daggers out of my belt and stuck them into the ground, along with the throwing daggers I kept in my leather breastplate. "These better be here when I get back."

"They will be," Charon said. "My Yilir will see to it."

# CHAPTER 13

Charon pushed the gondola slowly down the lava river. I sat at the front of the boat, Lucifer in the middle. The lava bubbled and brewed underneath us as Charon's oar cut through it. Along the shores, demons and imps tortured damned souls, whipping them against the rocks as they screamed in bloody agony.

"You've been here for a long time, right, Charon?" I asked.

"Longer than most, save for Lucifer and his ilk."

"Yeah, but I mostly confine myself to Dis these days," Lucifer said, pointing to the demons on the shore. "This torture, it really doesn't sit well with me anymore. I don't like to see it."

I spun around to face them. "Did it sit well with you before?"

Lucifer dropped his eyes. "There was a time, before Velaska, and even Hades, when I thought what we were doing was necessary. Human souls were tainted and needed to be purified."

"That's the dumbest thing I've ever heard."

"It's really not," Charon replied. "All energy in the galaxy comes from the Source, which sits in the middle of the universe, or so they say."

"So idiots say," Lucifer grumbled.

"That is what the gods have said since I have known them," Charon said. "And the source is full of incorruptible energy. When we die, that energy becomes reabsorbed into the Source. However, it must be pure. If that energy is corrupted, then it corrupts the whole system and can destroy the universe."

"Or so the story goes," Lucifer said. "Of course, with every successive Devil, they talk about it less and less. Velaska doesn't talk about it at all. Hell, she offers pardons for good behavior."

"That is a fallacy," Charon grumbled. "She will dangle the carrot, but she has rarely offered a pardon to any mortal, even if they carried out her wishes to the letter."

I frowned in disbelief. "That sounds even worse than not offering a pardon at all."

"It is not as much worse as it is evil," Charon replied. "The goal of the previous devils was to purify the dead so that they could return to the Source. It was a dirty but necessary business. However, Velaska gets pleasure from the torture. She feeds on it, and there is nothing more torturous than giving hope of salvation."

"But isn't that what the other devils were doing, too?" I asked. "I mean, if everything returns to the source, then everyone will eventually have salvation."

"Sure," Lucifer said. "But you don't have to offer it to them like a carrot. That's just cruel. It is better not to offer any hope, in my opinion. If I ran Hell, I would have a big sign out front of the gates that said, 'Abandon hope, all ye who enter here.'"

"What if hope's the only thing you have left?" I asked.

"Then it should be the first thing to die," Lucifer replied.

I turned away from Lucifer and Charon and watched the lava. It circled and swirled under me. It did not make anyone suffer. It did not care about hope. It just flowed past, and for a moment, that thought brought me comfort.

Charon made another push with his oar, and we sped into a chasm with rock walls on either side of us. I looked up and saw the black gate looming over us. Lucifer had told me about it earlier.

"Be still now," Charon said. "The Gate of Ulthar is ever watchful of the river."

"I thought that it wouldn't attack us on the lake," Lucifer said.

"I never said that," Charon replied. "It will not attack if you are invited, as you have always been in the past, but I do not know what will happen with an uninvited visitor."

"And what if it kills us?" Lucifer said.

"Then I will meet my Yilir again."

We eyeballed the cliffs above us. The black gate extended across them and shot down a thousand feet, splashing into the lava ahead of us and causing waves that rocked the boat to either side.

"Make no sudden movements," Charon said. "The eye sees all."

A giant, red crystal shone at the center of the gate at the top of the cliff. From it, a beam of red light emerged. The light washed over us for a long moment, flashed quickly, and then disappeared again. With the light gone, the gate rose and receded into the top of the cliff.

"That was interesting, wasn't it?" Charon said.

"If I knew we would have to deal with the Gate of Ulthar even if we rode with you, I would not have bothered."

"You can get off any time. It's a one-thousand-foot climb up sheer rock. Even your wings would tire before you reached the top. Not to mention that once you get there, you would have to deal with Cerberus, too. Or, you can have a pleasant ride into the lake. It's your choice."

"I choose the lake," I said. "I do not need a fight nor a long climb. I just want to get this done as quickly as possible, so I can go home."

"That is a good choice," Charon assured us.

*

The river of lava bent, ebbed, and flowed until it emptied into a molten lake swirling with eddies; Velaska's castle stood on an island in the center. The onyx and obsidian façade weaved up every turret and across every parapet. The black drawbridge was designed in the shape of a mouth, and two windows carved on either side created the look of a skull. Nothing lay beyond the castle except a rock wall.

"That is the furthest corner of Hell," Lucifer said. "Making this castle the perfect defensible position. None can attack it and live. Between the Gate of Ulthar above and the fact that only this gondola may ride on this river, combined with the dozens of guards that fortify the position, a hundred legions of angels could not attack the castle and hope to live."

When I had seen the castle from the sky above Dis, I did not give credit for its enormous size, but from the dock where Charon parked his gondola, the castle's size screamed at us from hundreds of feet above.

"I wish you good fortune," Charon said. "And a pleasant journey."

"This is Hell, buddy," I replied. "There is nothing pleasant about it."

"I very much enjoyed our time together," Charon replied. "So, it was pleasant to me."

"That's because this is the only conversation you ever get, buddy," Lucifer said, stepping out onto the dock. "But, for what it's worth, I had a pleasant time as well."

"You see," Charon said, turning to me. "It is possible to have a pleasant time in Hell after all."

*

Fourteen burly demons wearing black chain mail armor stood on the stairwell leading up to the black front door of Velaska's castle. They didn't speak or look anywhere but straight ahead, and their beady, yellow eyes glowed as they fixated on a point in the distance.

"Do not be deceived," Lucifer said. "If you make a false move, they will strike, no matter how stoic they appear right now."

The stairs were steep, and I had to use my arms to pull myself up to the next ledge. "Can we fly?" I asked.

"No," Lucifer replied. "If we do, the guards will strike. The way up to Velaska's castle is meant to tire us out so that we have no energy by the time we reach the top."

"I have not been tired in five hundred years," I said.

"The boiling heat from the lava combined with the strain of the stairs will change that before we reach the top. I have never felt exhaustion so deep as when climbing these stairs."

Lucifer was right. Each step was more agonizing than the one before. My arms burned, and my legs throbbed as I pulled myself up the unending staircase. I lost count after six hundred stairs. My energy was completely depleted, but I had made it. I turned and looked down at how far I had come and could barely make out Charon's boat at the dock.

"Is he waiting for us?" I asked.

"Unless someone calls for him. However, few have the gumption to ask for an audience with Velaska these days, and even fewer are granted one."

If I thought the demons guarding the stairs were big, they were nothing compared to the behemoth guarding the door to Velaska's castle. The beast stood nearly half the size of the gate itself. A bull ring dropped from its nose, and its arms dragged on the floor. Sinewy horns rose from the sides of its oblong head, where sharp fangs protruded down from its lip.

"State your purpose," the monster grunted.

"Ardwina," Lucifer replied. "Good to see you as always. I'm here to see the queen, of course. If you could just let me in."

I looked past Ardwina and toward the black door behind her, which was decorated with the bones of hundreds of skeletons, their skulls screaming out as they looked out from the castle for eternity.

"Do you have an appointment?" Ardwina asked.

"No, my dear. I don't. But if you could just—"

"If you don't have an appointment, angel, be gone with you."

Lucifer smiled and raised a finger to contradict her. "Now, you know that's not true. As envoy to Mount Olympus, I am to be granted an audience with the Queen whenever I deem it necessary, and I deem it necessary right now."

"She doesn't want to see you," Ardwina replied.

"Now listen here. I have allowed this impetuousness to stand for far too long. Velaska has denied my requests to meet for years, and I simply won't have it anymore. I demand to have an audience with her this instant."

"You can demand all you want, but it ain't never gonna happen."

The snap of fingers boomed through the castle and echoed out onto the lake. A voice spoke from inside the castle as the doors swung open. "Just let them in. It's so much easier to tell him to piss off to his face. Come in, you spineless coward, and let's be done with it."

"Velaska!" I said, smiling. "It's good to see you."

"Ah yes," Velaska's voice replied. "The pixie. Well, maybe today won't be so boring after all."

# CHAPTER 14

Five hundred years ago, I found myself in Velaska's palace, begging her for a chance to return to my body and vanquish the king who had killed me. But that part of the palace was nothing like this one. Then, I had used a back entrance, one which only her concubines used. It hadn't looked much like a castle, either. It was just a garden, tucked away from the world, nestled in a perfect, little corner of the universe.

The front entrance of Velaska's castle was much different. The black bones continued from the door and lined every wall of the grand foyer, up into the ceilings high overhead. Paintings of demons, skeletons, and nude reliefs hung on the walls, below stained-glass windows much like the ones I remembered from King Odgeir's kingdom. These ones, though, depicted monsters, gods, and demons instead of kings. Black carpeting extended into a dark hallway. Empty suits of armor guarded the entranceway, lining either side.

"Come," Lucifer said. "Velaska awaits us."

"I wouldn't say I am waiting for you." Velaska's voice echoed off the walls. "I am consigned to your appearance, however. It has been so boring these last years without either of you. Perhaps you can cut through the doldrums."

We stepped through the foyer and into a long hallway. Yellow, beady eyes glowered at us from the dark, and even though I couldn't see them, I knew there were demons lurking around, watching our every move. We emerged from the hallway into a throne room, where Velaska sat on a throne of bones, strumming her fingers.

She was just as beautiful as the last time I saw her. Tall, statuesque, with blond hair flowing down to her knees and piercing, violet eyes that matched the jewel in her obsidian crown.

"Come closer," Velaska said. "Let me have a look at you."

I followed the black carpet to where it dead-ended at the throne, and then I knelt in front of her. "It's nice to see you again, your majesty."

"Oh, please," Velaska said. "Don't try to butter me up just because it worked the last time. I'm a lot older than I was last time I saw you."

"You don't look a day older."

Velaska smirked. "All right, that one I liked. I suppose a little kindness really does go a long way. Of course, it's nothing compared to the kindness I bestowed during your last visit to my castle."

"I am forever appreciative for what you did for me, ma'am," I replied.

"You should be. Do you know what it's like to spend three million years trapped in the pits of hell?"

"No, I don't," I said. "And that's because of you."

"That's right," Velaska replied, smiling. "Because of me. And also because of me, you ended up in Valhalla. Do you think that was easy to swing? No. It was not. They don't just let anybody in there. In fact, you were the last person I pardoned because of the hassle."

"And thank you for that as well, and for reuniting me with my mother. How is my king?"

"Odgeir?" Velaska said. "Piffle. He was fun for a hundred years or so, but just like all the others, once they succumb to my will, they are…not funny anymore. Still, I enjoy hearing his screams of agony in my dungeon whenever I visit my sanctuary.”

“You built your garden sanctuary near your personal dungeon?” I asked.

“Well, it wasn’t built for me, per se, I’m just its latest occupant, but yes, my sanctuary resides right next to my dungeon,” Velaska said. “How else would you design your castle?”

“Well, for one, I wouldn’t have to pass the screams of my prisoners to reach peace,” I replied.

“To each their own,” Velaska said. “The screams from my dungeon soothe me.”

“Your dungeon is exactly why we are here, Velaska,” Lucifer said, stepping forward. “If you forgive my intrusion.”

“You know, it is courtesy to kneel before your queen.” She was right. He had not bowed or genuflected.

“Beg your pardon, ma’am, but you are not my queen. I work for the gods, not for you.”

“Yes,” Velaska replied. “You have made that very clear, and yet, here you are, with this pixie, clearly to ask a favor of me, and you don’t show me any common courtesy. Well, go ahead, tell me I’m wrong.”

“I will not, Velaska,” Lucifer said. “For that would be a lie.”

“And you, Morningstar, are afraid of lying, still? I see you are still little more than a puppet. I would have thought the horrors of Hell were enough to break you of such blind devotion.”

"I lie only when it is critically important," Lucifer replied. "It is not so in this instance. Whenever I am able, I try to be forthright and honest."

"You are no fun," Velaska said. "I thought you might entertain me at least for a little while, and yet here I am, bored as ever. Go ahead and ask your favor already so that I may deny you like all the others."

"The fallen angel, Zharaqiel. She is locked in your dungeon, is she not?"

"She is. She was brought to me, a truly wretched dear, and I have been nursing her back to health."

"We would like her released," Lucifer said, "and sent back to Mount Olympus."

"Oh, this old chestnut again? I thought you would bring me something more interesting this time. Request denied."

"Please," I said. "Your majesty, the gods would see it as a personal favor if you would release this angel back to them."

Velaska smiled. "Now, this is an interesting development. You've never brought a pixie here with you to aid in your groveling." Velaska cocked her head toward me. "And what have the gods offered you for your service?"

"They called on me, my Devil, and I answered them."

"Yes," Velaska said, leaning forward. "For what price?"

"I prefer not to say, Devil."

"Then I say again that your request is denied," Velaska said with a smirk.

I sighed. "My mother, she does not like Valhalla. Bacchus agreed to let my mother live on Mount Olympus if I was successful."

"Blasphemy!" Lucifer shouted. "No mortal may live on Mount Olympus. It's bad enough Bacchus let you walk on its hallowed ground. This is heresy, and I won't allow it."

Velaska opened her eyes wide with delight at the angel's outburst.

"You can leave then," I said. "Once I recover the angel and bring it back to Heaven, Bacchus owes my mother and me eternity on Mount Olympus. That's the deal we struck. I can do this with or without you."

"You make a mockery of the gods' laws!" Lucifer said.

"Those laws are stupid!" I replied. "Are you really defending the gods after everything they've done to you? After everything you told me?"

"Exactly!" Velaska said, clapping her hands together. "That's what I've been telling him for centuries. His blind devotion to the gods is ridiculous, especially since he seems to disagree with everything they say. Isn't that right, Lou?"

"Don't call me that!" Lucifer said. "I know well your mind games, witch, and I will not succumb to them."

"You'll help her, then?" Velaska said. "Since it is the will of the gods?"

Lucifer gnashed his teeth. "The gods' will be done."

"Is that a yes?" I asked.

"If it is the will of the gods, then it is my sworn duty to make sure it is done."

"And it is the will of the gods, yes?" Velaska asked me.

"Of Bacchus," I replied. "Sworn ruler of Earth, it is."

"Hmm, I wonder what the other gods would say to such a plan. I doubt they would like it. No, I know they wouldn't. Of course, I am a god, and I like it quite a lot, actually. I hope they let all sorts of people up into Mount Olympus, really open the place up. Make it livelier and more fun."

"Heresy!" Lucifer said. "The gods and mortals must remain separate for all time. It is law!"

"Even if it is Bacchus's will?" Velaska asked.

"He is but one god. He does not speak for the entire pantheon."

"He does, though," I replied.

"The pixie is right," Velaska said. "Soon, he will be the only god left on Olympus, and his will shall be absolute. He will rule in Zeus's stead, and his will shall be the law of this planet."

"NO!" Lucifer said. "I will not stand for it. Bacchus is wrong. He is wrong, and I will not be part of this heresy against the gods."

"So," Velaska said, "you will go against the sworn ruler of this planet?"

"It is against the wishes of the gods to allow mortals into Mount Olympus," he said. "It has always been and always will be. So yes, I denounce him. He is no king of mine."

Velaska leaned forward. "Well, this has been interesting, but if you have no business to discuss, then I suppose you should leave, so I can speak with Akta alone."

"Do not do this," Lucifer said, grabbing my arm.

"Don't tell me what to do." I pulled away from him. "You do not own me. I have a mission, and I will see it completed."

"Fine!" Lucifer said, storming off through the black tunnel and out of my sight.

"Good riddance," Velaska said. "He was always a wet blanket. You, on the other hand, are a lot of fun. You like to make deals."

I shook my head. "Not this time, Velaska. I remember what your deal did to me last time I made one with you."

"What! You said you appreciated everything I have done for you," Velaska said.

"I, unlike Lucifer, have no problem with lying to further my ends."

"How could you not appreciate our bargain? You were successful, were you not?"

"I was."

"And you got more than you could ever want in return. I don't see how you could complain, honestly."

"I was successful despite you, not because of you."

Velaska scoffed. "Excuse me, but without my help, you wouldn't have even gotten back to Earth. And I promise you have enjoyed the last five hundred years in Valhalla more than I enjoyed the king you bartered for me. If anything, I got the worse end of this deal."

"Worse end of the deal!" I shouted. "You sent me back to Earth in a decrepit body! It literally fell apart on me while I was using it."

"Well, that wasn't my fault. It's not my fault that bodies just fall apart like that. It's really a flaw in Hera's design if you ask me. They should be heartier."

I shook my head. "I will not make a deal with you."

Velaska shrugged. "Then you will not get your angel."

My voice deepened. "I will find another way."

Velaska gripped the skulls embedded in the hand rests on her throne, and her eyes narrowed. "Do so at your own peril."

"You don't scare me."

"Oh, but I will," Velaska said, her voice a low whisper. "I promise you that. Do not cross me."

"Don't make me," I replied. "Give me back the angel, and let me be on my way."

"That angel will never leave Hell. Not ever. Do you hear me?"

"We'll see about that."

"Guards!" Velaska shouted. "Throw this filth outside. If she tries anything, toss her into the lava."

Four massive demons, their skin burning like coal, stomped forward out of the darkness and grabbed me by the arms and legs. They squeezed me so tightly I couldn't move an inch and marched me out of the throne room.

"Ta ta, darling!" Velaska said, waving to me as I left. "Maybe this will teach you." Her voice became gravelly, and the smile left her face. "Never mess with the Devil."

# CHAPTER 15

The demons tossed me out the front door of Velaska's castle, and I slammed down on the hot stone outside. All around me, demons sneered at me as if I was the worst piece of garbage in the universe. I could tell they wanted to rip me apart. Their teeth gnashed together, and their eyes burned into me.

"Come, now!" I heard from the bottom of the stairs.

I squinted to see Charon in the distance, standing on his gondola, waiting for me, and I couldn't help but smile. I knew Lucifer told me not to use my wings on the stairs, but I didn't care anymore. I expanded them and floated down. As I did, the demons guarding the landings locked onto me and started to howl. They chased me down the stairs, so I moved faster. With one final burst of energy, I landed in Charon's gondola, just as an army of demons arrived on the dock.

"Now, now," Charon chided at them. "You know the rules. None are allowed on my gondola unless I should invite them." He paused. "And none of you are invited."

The demons chomped and howled, but there was nothing they could do. I stuck my tongue out at them as Charon pushed off from the docks.

"That's not very polite," Charon said. "Do not make me regret coming back for you after dropping off Lucifer."

I sat down in the middle of the gondola. "Sorry."

"I suppose it didn't go well," Charon said.

"You could say that," I replied. "It couldn't have gone much worse."

"A pity," Charon replied. "You know my Yilir designed that castle for Anubis so many centuries ago. She made every nook, cranny, and crevice. It's a pity it is now inhabited by a queen who is so stubborn and hard-willed. Yilir would turn over in her grave if she knew."

"And Lucifer? What happened to him?"

"He was furious when I delivered him across the river. He said many nasty things about Velaska and you as well."

I shrugged. "I suppose that is the price of following the will of the gods."

"Yes, my Yilir knew that all too well."

"How long…" I asked, "since she left you?"

"She has never left me," Charon replied. "She is always in my soul. And one day, we will be united again, in the great beyond."

"How did she…die?"

"I prefer not to talk about it. I will talk about her pleasant memories for the rest of her days, but there is no reason to recount the bad ones and allow them to linger."

"I respect that," I said. "Tell me a good memory, then."

"Whenever she created something, she always tried to plant a garden inside of it. Even if it didn't fit aesthetically inside the building, she jammed it in there anyway. She always wanted to be surrounded by plants." He touched the purple tulip I had given him, which was pinned like a broach to his cloak. "I have never known anyone who loved plants as much as she did or were more attuned to giving life and beauty, even in a place like this. But she thought that even in the worst of places, there could be beauty. That castle is a perfect example."

"How?" I asked.

"Even though it was the home of the devil, she thought there should be light and life, so she designed a garden sanctuary under the castle which could serve as a respite from the burdens of Hell for all time. Devils still use it to this day."

A lightbulb went off in my brain. I had been to the sanctuary before, through a back entrance to the castle. If Velaska wouldn't let me in the front door to retrieve Zharaqiel, I would have to enter through the purple door in the back of it.

"Charon, do you know the Brambles of Agony?" I asked.

He nodded. "Of course."

"Take me there."

*

The first time I came to Hell, demons had chased me, and I hid from them in the Brambles of Agony. When I found my way to the center of their circuitous maze, a monster of fire tried to burn me alive. I escaped to a ledge above the brambles, where there was a purple door. This was the door to a back entrance into Velaska's castle and to the garden sanctuary which Yilir had built before she was killed.

After taking me to retrieve my daggers, Charon parked the boat at the edge of the lake of fire nearest the brambles.

"I do not like long goodbyes," Charon said.

I nodded. "Me either."

Without another word, I stepped out of the gondola, and he drifted off. We didn't need to say more. Still, I watched him until his gondola drifted out of sight. I hoped I would never see him again, which filled me with sadness because Charon was filled with goodness like few others I've met in my travels. He deserved better than an eternity in Hell. Perhaps one day his service to the gods would end, and I could meet him again on Mount Olympus. When he was out of sight, I spread my wings again and flew toward the great ledge that held the purple door. It extended from the sheer cliff above the Brambles of Agony.

As I flew, the thorns twisted and curled underneath me. They were alive and ever-growing. Every evil deed tortured away from one of Hell's damned souls became a new thorn on its branches. The brambles stretched beyond the horizon, but I didn't care much about them. I only cared about the ledge. I breathed a sigh of relief when I landed on it. The sheer cliff behind it rose for hundreds of feet into the air. On the other side of the cliff, hidden from my sight, the lake of fire bubbled and brewed. I didn't care much about that, either. I was looking at the purple door with its black demon knocker. It would lead me into Velaska's castle.

In front of the purple door was a small, wooden chair, and on top of that chair sat a lizard creature shaped like a large salamander. She was dressed in a red robe and resting on her staff, asleep. Her name was Quinn. She had become my friend the last time I visited Hell when she let me through the purple door into Velaska's chamber.

"Quinn," I said as I inched up toward her. I didn't want to startle or anger her. Even though she looked cute and sweet while she was asleep, she had the ability to turn into a massive lizard creature with giant, sharp teeth, which I wanted to avoid at all costs. "Quinn."

The last time we met, I had promised her I would ask Velaska to give her a vacation. While I fulfilled my promise to ask, I had no idea if Velaska approved her leave request or if she had instead poisoned Quinn against me.

I pressed my hand against her shoulder and shook her. "Quinn."

Quinn's eyes popped open. "Huh?"

Her lizard eyes blinked, first horizontally, then vertically. As I came into focus, her hands waved wildly in the air, and she fell backward, rolling off the chair and smashing against the cliff wall behind her.

"Ah!" she shouted, scrambling to her feet. "Who are you?"

I stepped back. "Easy, Quinn. It's me. Akta. Do you remember when we met five hundred years ago?"

"Akta?" Quinn said, stroking her bearded chin. "I don't remember."

"We were friends, you and I. Remember friends?"

"Friends?" Quinn replied, squinting at me. "Friends."

"You let me through the door you guard, and I asked Velaska to give you a vacation. Do you remember that?"

"Vacation?" Quinn said excitedly. "Oh yes. I do remember. Vacations are so lovely."

"Yeah?" I replied. "So, she gave one to you?"

"Oh yes, yes," Quinn replied. "I spend two weeks in Dis. It was lovely. I petted a fire turtle and drank beer at a tavern. I've never had so much fun. Of course…"

"Of course what?"

Quinn sighed. "It made it even more torturous when I came back here and still lived alone. I haven't been back to visit since."

"You haven't had a vacation in five hundred years?"

Quinn shook her head. "Sadly, no. And nobody comes to visit me anymore, either."

"Well, I'm here," I replied. "And that's pretty good."

"Pretty good," Quinn said. "Yes, I would say that is pretty good."

"And maybe, if you can help me, I can grant you another favor, maybe a vacation for you to somewhere nicer than Dis."

"Another vacation!" Quinn said. "Oh, I would like that very much. What do you need, my friend?"

"Have you ever been to Velaska's dungeon before?"

"Oh yes, yes. I used to be personal maid to Hades before I was posted here, so I know the whole castle like the back of my hand."

"Can you lead me there?" I asked. "There is something there I very much need to retrieve from the castle."

Quinn's eyes narrowed. "And my queen did not give it to you herself?"

I shook my head. "No, my friend. I'm afraid the queen refused my request that she return it, even though it is rightfully mine to take."

"Then, how will you help me if the queen does not want you to enter?"

"Because the favor will not come from her, it will come from another god, one who sits on the throne of Mount Olympus right now. Velaska is wrong to deny my request. The gods of Mount Olympus want a fallen angel returned to them, and Velaska has refused."

"She refused the will of the gods? Never! We are in service to them for all time."

"I know we are. All of us. Even you. And the gods want me to retrieve this angel and return her to Mount Olympus. If you help me, the gods will owe you a favor."

"The gods, like the real gods? Up in Mount Olympus?"

I nodded. "That's right. The real gods. All of them, but I can't get you a favor with them unless you help me. Will you help me?"

"If it is the gods' will, I will surely help you. And you will get a favor for me, yes?"

I nodded. "I will."

"I would like to no longer guard this door. I want to live in Dis forever."

"An odd request," I said. "Given that you could have anything, but I will do my best to make that happen for you if you help me."

Quinn walked toward the purple door. "Then let us away."

She tapped her staff on the door, and it creaked open. She walked into the darkness, and I followed close behind. As the door closed behind me, I heard the echoes of the nightmares that haunted the darkness. They were getting louder.

# CHAPTER 16

"Stay close," Quinn said, hobbling through the dark. "And think pleasant thoughts. The Nothings draw strength from bad thoughts."

"What is this place?" I asked.

"Have you ever had a feeling of emptiness or loneliness that cannot be explained? It just comes on you seemingly from nowhere?"

"Yes," I said.

"This is where it comes from, the Nothing, and where it returns once the Nothings have finished feeding off your bad thoughts."

"So, they can pass the veil between Hell and Earth?"

Quinn slammed her staff on the ground. The quake shook the air around us. Her staff now glowed enough to create a barrier around us, like the one Lucifer had around him when we met at The Old Hat.

"The veil between our worlds is semi-permeable, like a membrane. That is how ghosts can escape to Earth and how the Nothings do so as well. Too many have made their way back to Earth, and when they do, they cause all sorts of trouble."

"*Gitvaru Manstrasa.* Light the path. Light the way. *Gitvaru Manstrasa. Gitvaru Manstrasa.*"

A bolt of lightning struck out from the staff and exploded in front of us. A bright light shone down, and I recognized where we were from my last trip through Hell. It was Velaska's grotto. I hoped she wasn't there when we came calling.

"Hurry. The door will not be open long."

*

We pushed through the nothingness until the light enveloped us and spat us out in a beautiful meadow. It was unlike anything else in Hell, except perhaps the fields of Yilir.

Thousands of flowers bloomed in the garden and gave a pleasant, fresh smell. A waterfall led water down a cliff and trickled into the stream below. A white gazebo with thousands of pillows rested in the center of the meadow, where birds chirped, giving a peaceful sound…almost heavenly. It was the closest I'd felt to Valhalla since I left the Great Hall.

"Don't dawdle," Quinn said, pressing down the stairs in front of us. "The queen is not here now, but she is never far."

I followed Quinn through the field toward a wooden door which I had not seen on my last visit to the grotto. She pushed it open, and we were once again in the castle, the dewy, stone walls bare and dark. Horrible sounds came from the stairs below us: screaming and suffering.

"The dungeon is down the stairs this way," Quinn said. She lit her staff again, and the light bounced off the walls of the hallway. At the end of the staircase, we ended up in a cell block, complete with dozens of wooden doors. The moans of the prisoners were loud and continuous. Small cutouts were made in the doors and covered with bars, so the prisoners could see out but never get out.

"This is Velaska's personal dungeon. It is only for people who have personally wronged the queen, and she delights in their torture—at her convenience."

"We're looking for an angel," I said. "Zharaqiel. You should be able to recognize her easily. She'll likely be the only angel in this place. Look for a shimmering glow emanating from her body. Call out to me if you find anything. You take that way, and I'll take this way."

"Right," Quinn said. "The god's speed."

*

My feet echoed on the cobblestones as I checked each cell for a glowing angel.

"Akta?" I heard a rasping whisper. "Akta? Is that really you?"

The voice was weak. I opened my wings so they could light the path. "Who are you?"

"Akta? It truly is you," the voice replied. "Thank the gods you have come for me."

The glow from my wings lit the face of the man who called to me. He was dirty, his beard covered in mud and sweat, but I recognized my brother-king's face behind the bars of the cell.

"Odgeir," I said. "It's nice to see you living in such filth, brother."

Odgeir gripped the bars of his cage and pushed his face against them. "My gods, Akta. How long it has been?"

"Five hundred years."

"Five hundred?" he replied. "It feels like a million. Look at you. You have not aged a day."

"I hope your time in Hell has treated you poorly, brother." I spat.

"Why do you spew venom on me?" Odgeir asked. His voice was a pitiful whine.

I scoffed. "You murdered me."

"You did the same to me and sent me here on top of it. Yet, I do not spew venom on you."

"Then, perhaps, in that one way, you are better than I."

"It has been horrible, Akta. They have done unspeakable things to me. Unspeakable. I would have never done what they have done to me, not even to my worst enemy. And yet, they did it with such glee—" His voice caught in his throat. "But now, that does not matter. You are here, and I am rescued."

I chuckled. "I am not here for you, dear brother, and if I were, it would only be to take you to the worst ring of Hell and watch you suffer ever greater for the next million years."

"Akta!" Quinn shouted from the other side of the hall. "I found her!"

"Goodbye, brother."

"No! No! No!" Odgeir shouted as I walked away. "Please! Don't do this to me! Akta! I am your brother!"

I spun around, satisfied at the utter disgrace righteous King Odgeir made of himself. "No. You are just a king I killed once."

*

"Here she is," Quinn said, holding up her staff so I could see inside Zharaqiel's cell. "This is her, yes?"

I could tell from her glow that she was an angel, but Zharaqiel looked nothing like her brethren. She was small, dirty, and shaking uncontrollably. Her hair was matted and black. Dark marks dabbled her skin and blackened her face. When she looked at me, her eyes were dark, nearly black, and the glow around her was a faint blue.

"Zharaqiel," I said, looking inside the dingy cell.

"That name," the angel said. "I answered to it once. Long ago."

"Stay there," I replied. "We'll get you out." I turned to Quinn. "You can get her out, yes?"

Quinn nodded. "Of course. This staff can open any door in Hell." She placed the staff on the doorknob, and the door clicked open. I ran inside and knelt next to Zharaqiel. She was cold to the touch and trembling. Her arms were thin and weak, and I could see her bones under her loosely hanging skin.

"Zharaqiel, can you walk?" I said. "We have to get you out of here."

"Walk?" Zharaqiel said. "I think so. It has been so long since I have been asked, though."

I reached under her arm and lifted her to her feet. She took a shaky step forward, and then another. Soon, we were at the staircase, where she pressed her hand against the wet wall to steady herself as she climbed.

"Do you know why Velaska held you captive for so long?" I asked.

"No," she replied. "I don't even remember how I got to Hell. It has been so long. So very long. I begged her to let me go, to return to Mount Olympus, but Velaska always said no. She screamed at me that I would never leave Hell again. I don't remember why."

"Evil," I said, shaking my head. "Well, don't worry, we will get you home soon."

We reached the meadow after ascending the stairs from the prison and walked toward the door that would lead us back to the Nothing. The cries from the prisoners lessened as we made our way through the grass and then were silenced completely.

"You must be strong now," I said. "I know that you are tired and scared, but we have to make it out of the castle, and you cannot think bad thoughts. If you do, the Nothings will attack us, okay?"

"Bad thoughts?" Zharaqiel said, her blue light flickering as she walked. "I will try not to think bad thoughts."

With each step she took, the grass beneath her feet turned black, dying. I didn't know what Velaska had done to torture her so, but I hoped the gods of Olympus would make her pay.

I tried to be encouraging. "I know it's hard, after all you've been through, but soon we will be back on Mount Olympus."

"That will be nice." Her voice was so weak I could hardly hear her.

"Hurry up!" Quinn said. "The queen won't be far behind."

Zharaqiel and I hobbled up the stairs, arm in arm, and made our way to the door. Quinn disappeared into the darkness first, and we followed close behind.

"Are you ready?" I asked.

"Yes," Zharaqiel replied. "I am getting stronger by the moment. My mind is growing less foggy, too."

"Good," I replied. "Remember to think good thoughts."

We disappeared into the darkness, and the door slammed behind us. I saw nothing except the faint glow of Quinn's staff for guidance and the glow of Zharaqiel's blue body to put a target on our backs for the Nothings to find us.

"Are you okay?" Quinn asked.

"Yes," Zharaqiel said. "I am starting to remember now. I didn't fall here by accident. I came by choice."

"Excuse me?" I replied, but Zharaqiel was lost in thought.

"I was looking for something…answers. I wanted to know why we follow the gods. And then…and then I learned…I learned…I learned of the past…I learned of the light… that we didn't…"

The echoes from the Nothing grew louder with every word Zharaqiel spoke. Her blue aura glowed brighter.

"We didn't have to follow. We could be…be free. Then, I tried to return to Olympus and tell the others…but Velaska. She trapped me. She said I could never leave."

Wind swirled all around us. Thunder echoed in our ears. A crack of lightning filled the sky for a moment, and it illuminated the dark, twisted shadows of the Nothings. Horror filled me.

"Get us out of here!" I shouted to Quinn.

"*Gitvaru Manstrasa.* Light the path. Light the way. *Gitvaru Manstrasa. Gitvaru Manstrara.*"

The light crackled from her staff and shot forward. In front of us, the purple door creaked as it opened for us, and we ran for it. Zharaqiel struggled with her gait, so I unfurled my wings and rose into the air, carrying her by her armpits. Behind us, the shadows snapped and shouted.

Finally, I reached the light, and it enveloped me. Quinn closed the door, and the howling stopped. I looked down at Zharaqiel, who had a tranquil smile on her face.

"We made it," I said, smiling with her.

"Not quite," a booming voice replied.

I looked up and saw Lucifer. He stood at the end of the ledge, snarling at me. His beautiful wings extended fully, and he held a flaming sword in his tightly clenched hands. "This ends now," he said. "The fallen angel shall not leave this place."

# CHAPTER 17

I stepped in front of Zharaqiel. I wasn't about to let Lucifer hurt the angel I worked so hard to save, not when I was so close to completing my mission.

"Back away," I growled.

Lucifer grinned slowly. "Do you not see the enormous sword in my hands and the lack of one in yours? It will be you who backs away."

I pulled the ivory daggers out of their scabbards and gripped them tightly in my hands. "Do not make me do this."

"I'm not making you do anything," Lucifer replied. "You can move out of my way peacefully at any time."

"What about your oath to the Gods?" I asked. "If you kill her, you will break it."

"No," Lucifer said. "I will break the command of a fat, drunken slob. The pantheon is more than any one god, and it must be protected. You will not enter Mount Olympus again, and neither will your mother. That is holy ground."

"Then, it seems we are at an impasse," I replied, opening my wings.

"It seems so," Lucifer said.

I shot forward as fast as I could. Lucifer swung his sword, and I ducked to avoid it. I rose into the air and slashed at him, but he blocked me with his flaming sword. He flapped his wings and rose higher into the air before coming down on me with the entirety of his force. I rolled toward Zharaqiel to avoid him.

"I was the greatest warrior in the heavens," Lucifer said. "They were so frightened of my power they sent me here, and you dare challenge me."

I flung two of my throwing daggers at him. He caught them in his hand and crushed them like they were nothing.

He looked at me and laughed. "Pathetic!"

"I'll help you!" Quinn said. She slammed her staff on the ground, and it quaked. Her arms grew to ten times their normal size. She rose into the air as her body expanded with rippling muscles. When she finished, she threw her head back and screamed into the bowels of Hell.

A behemoth Quinn charged toward Lucifer, kicking up dirt as she lumbered across the ledge. Her tongue sprung out and caught him by the arm. He swung his sword and cut off Quinn's tongue before spinning away and slicing off her head with one motion. Quinn's head fell into the Brambles of Agony, and her blood seeped out of her headless neck and oozed across the ledge.

"Quinn!" I shouted, tears welling in my eyes. "No!"

"She can't hear you," Lucifer said. "Quinn is dead! And soon you will be, too!"

Lucifer flew into the air, and I rose to meet him. He cocked back his arm and smashed his fist against my face. I flew backward and crashed into the cliff wall, sending rock and debris crashing down on me as I fell to the ground. I was pinned there and could only watch when Lucifer landed gently on the ground and confronted Zharaqiel.

"Sister."

"Brother," she said. "You don't have to do this. We can be free. We can all be free."

"No," Lucifer said, pulling back his sword. "We cannot. Service is our lot in life, for better or worse. I'm sorry, sister, but this is the gods' will. I kill you to protect all we hold dear."

"I hold nothing dear, brother," Zharaqiel replied, stoic.

With a great swing of his sword, Lucifer sliced Zharaqiel in half. The halves of her fell away onto the ground and evaporated into dust.

"What have you done?" I shouted.

"I killed my sister," Lucifer replied. "I defied the will of God, and I am still here. I half expected to be struck down, but I was not. In fact, I feel amazing, like I can do anything."

"At what cost?" Velaska's voice floated through the air. "You have killed your kin."

"I have protected my kin!" Lucifer shouted.

"Velaska?" I looked around me, confused.

"Yes, my dear. It is me. You have made quite the mockery of my kingdom, haven't you?"

"It was not my intention," I replied.

"Intentions matter not," she replied. "Now, what to do with you?"

The mountains quaked, and the ledge shook under our feet, and then there was blackness. Velaska called me to her, and I would have to answer for my betrayal.

*

"Do you know how angry I am with you?" Velaska said as I reappeared inside her throne room. She paced furiously in front of a wall covered with paintings of the Devils who came before her.

"I'm sorry," I said.

"No, you're not," Velaska replied. "You're sorry you got caught."

"That's true," I replied. "I never meant to deny you. I only wanted to carry out my mission."

"And you almost destroyed Mount Olympus in the process. I kept Zharaqiel from my kin for a reason. Because I knew she would infect the other angels and destroy them."

"Why didn't you tell me that?"

"Because you didn't need to know!" Velaska shouted. "You are a mortal, a nothing in the eyes of the universe. Your five hundred years in existence is but a day in my eyes. You are a child, and I do not concern myself with the needs of children."

"Why didn't you tell the other gods?"

"Because they would have ordered her killed, and I did not wish to see Zharaqiel killed. I had grown quite fond of her before she turned. I was still fond of her, even at the end."

"So, you were protecting her?" I asked.

"That's correct, and now she is dead, along with my darling Quinn. Lucifer has taken the life of his kin, and all because you couldn't leave well enough alone."

"I'm…sorry." I really was. I lowered my face, and my head drooped.

"Now that sounds like you are sorry," she said, walking toward me. "My ways are my own, but I do always want the best for humanity, and even for you."

"I have ruined everything," I said, hanging my head in shame.

"Well, not everything," Velaska replied. "But you certainly haven't made things any better while you were here, have you? Now, the question is, what to do with you?"

I looked up. "What do you mean?"

"Well, you know what happened here, which means I just can't have you going back to Mount Olympus or Valhalla and telling people what transpired in my domain. There would be too many questions."

"Sure you can!" I said, standing up. "What about Lucifer? What will happen to him?"

"He took the life of an angel. He disobeyed the will of a god. He will never say a word, lest they kill him."

"And you think I will say something?" I replied.

"Yes, because that is the way of the warrior," Velaska said. "Your type cannot help themselves but boast and brag about every battle. If I let you go back to Mount Olympus, you're sure to let it slip. I can't have that. I must protect Lucifer and my kingdom."

"Even now, you protect him?"

"I do," Velaska said. "It is the burden of the throne. If the gods were ever to find out about the murder of his kin, they would destroy him."

"Then what will you do with me?"

"I'm not sure. It's probably easiest just to evaporate you."

"You wouldn't do that."

"Sure I would. You think you matter to me, you insignificant whelp? I should kill you now for all you've done."

"What if," I said with a sigh. "What if I stay here, in Hell, of my own will, and agree to never consort with Mount Olympus again." I couldn't believe the words were coming out of my mouth, but it was the only way to avoid being killed or captured for all time…and then it would be my choice to stay in Hell, not Velaska's.

"Hmm," Velaska said. "Well, that is interesting. You would give up a chance to return to Mount Olympus, to remain here."

My mind raced back to all I had done since I came here. It raced back to Lucifer, to Ylfingur, to Bjarngimur, and to Rasmus.

"Yes," I said. "If it will make things right. On one condition."

"Pfft," Velaska said. "You and your conditions. Well, out with it then."

"I will give up my claim to Valhalla, and work for you, here, as penance, for as long as you shall ask it of me. However, in return, you must commute the sentence of my brother's wife and her children."

"Are you kidding?" Velaska said. "Just like that, you want me to go against the rules of Hell and let your brother's family roam free."

"Not just like that," I replied. "His children are half monster."

"And his wife is not!" Velaska said. "You are setting a dangerous precedent here."

"No," I replied. "Petrus offered me parole when I came the first time. He said I was eligible in three million years. He told the little girl I met she would be eligible in three hundred."

"That is just a thing we say," Velaska said. "We don't mean it."

"It does not have to be," I replied. "Perhaps, my brother's wife could be a beacon of hope, proof that redemption is possible. Except—"

"Except they can never receive the redemption they seek," Velaska said with a smile.

"Decades, centuries, eons would pass, and still none would receive their pardon. They would keep the hope of reprieve as long as they could muster the strength until it finally drained from their eyes. I know you love to watch the hope fade."

"It is," Velaska said, nodding, "my favorite thing."

"And you can give them hope and then whisk it away again," I said, taking a step toward her. "Forever."

Velaska smiled. "And what is to prevent you from welshing on your promise and returning to Valhalla?"

I pulled a dagger from its scabbard and cut into my palm. "My blood oath that I will not."

"You know," Velaska said, "that is legally binding here."

My blood dripped on the ground in front of Velaska's feet. "I swear that I will work in Hell until you release me."

"Very well," Velaska said. "I accept."

"Then I am yours," I said, pressing my hand against my chest.

"Good," Velaska smiled. Then her face changed, and she was laughing. "My, my, my, you are very easy to manipulate, aren't you?"

"Excuse me?" I said.

"All I had to do was plant a seed in your little head, and just like that, you gave yourself to me. I thought you would be more of a challenge than that."

"Wait," I said. "This was your plan all along?"

Velaska walked up the stairs to her throne and took a seat. "Not all along, but once you disobeyed me, this seemed like an apt punishment. Every day, for the rest of eternity, you will linger and long for Valhalla, but you will remain stuck here, surrounded by withering agony. It is a delicious punishment, and one day, the hope will dwindle from your eyes as well."

"You bitch!" I screamed, rushing toward her.

"Guards!" Velaska yawned. "Get her out of here." Two demon guards flew forward and grabbed me before I could reach Velaska.

"I hate you!" I shouted, kicking and screaming against the demon's thick bodies. It was futile. "I hate you!"

"I'm okay with that," she said. "And make sure that brand on her chest is put to good use. We can always use a good scout."

Velaska laughed to herself as I was carried brutishly out of the room. Her shrill pitch echoed through the chambers as she vanished from view. I had given myself over to her service for as long as she deemed worthwhile. I had sold my soul to the devil.

*

I hopped slowly down the mammoth stairs in front of Velaska's castle. The monsters of Hell were ready to pounce on me if I made a sudden or wrong move. They wanted so badly to rip me to shreds, and I wished they would. At least then, maybe I would cease to exist. Maybe I would return to the Source, or maybe I would go somewhere else, but I would not be stuck in Hell due to my own idiocy.

Finally, I arrived at the docks and looked down into the magma. I could just jump into the lake, I thought. What was the worst that would happen if I did? I would burn for eternity, maybe. It wasn't any worse than living in Hell until Velaska released me, which would likely be never.

"Please don't," I heard through the fog that had fallen over the magma lake. A moment later, Charon's gondola cut through it. "I promise you that it's worse than you think."

"I think it's pretty bad right now," I replied.

"The lava will make it worse," Charon said, docking his boat next to me. "You will descend into the Nothing, and that is the worst torture imaginable."

"I'm stuck here," I said to him. "I'm stuck here forever. How could any torture be worse than that?"

"In so many ways. I told you already—Hell, well, it's not so bad," Charon replied. "You can have a rather pleasant time here if you let it."

I chuckled. "I still don't believe you."

"Then hop on board," Charon replied. "I have a lot to show you."

I sighed and stepped into the boat, sitting down in the middle seat as Charon pushed away from the dock. As he rowed, I looked up at the cavern of Hell, my new home, for as long as the Queen of Hell wanted me here. Until she released me, I would never see my mother again. I hoped she would forgive me for my foolhardiness. At least, I thought, I would be able to take care of her son for her and make sure no harm came to him. That was a little comfort. And perhaps I could at least visit my niece and nephew, and we could create a sort of family here, in the horribleness of Hell, together.

That did sound nice, I thought. Perhaps Hell wouldn't be so bad after all. That was a stupid thought, of course, but I hoped it was true, and hope was the one thing Velaska could never take away from me.

# BOOK 3

*"Hellfire"*

# CHAPTER 1

The barren wasteland of Hell crunched under my feet as I sprinted across the cracked desert. Every time my feet slammed against the ground, flecks of the warped terrain exploded and rose into the air.

"Slow down!" I shouted. I was chasing after a tall, lithe goblin. "I'm not going to tell you again!"

The goblin had escaped the tenth and most horrible pit of Hell, where he had worked for the past four hundred years. He was faster than most, but he wasn't any more intelligent. Intelligence, however, wasn't required to work the pits of Hell. There really wasn't any requirement to work the pits of Hell, except being either a monster or a demon.

"Just let me go already!" the goblin shouted back. "I ain't doing nothing to nobody!"

He wasn't wrong, but that wasn't the point. Abandoning his post didn't hurt anybody directly, and yet, it hurt the entire structure of Hell. Nobody could abandon their post in Hell. He couldn't, and neither could I. We were all assigned a job, and it was up to us to carry it out for as long as the Devil favored that we do so.

Favor was a funny word. Favor. As if it were a benevolent gift that the Devil forced us to work his infernal torture pits or chase after deserters. Then again, when the other option was burning alongside the humans, it really was a magnanimous gesture.

"You will go back!" I shouted at him.

I didn't view being used as a slave like it was some gracious gesture, but it was a job, and I was good at my job. I had been a scout in the Devil's army for three hundred years, ever since I was tricked into abandoning Mount Olympus to remain in Hell forever at the behest of Velaska and then retained by her successor, Lucifer.

Working for the Devil was tiring and trying, but it was never boring. For the last three hundred years, it was my job to find those who had escaped the pits of Hell and bring them back to face their punishment. It was a lot of long, lonely journeys into the wasteland, but having spent my life on Earth as a ranger, I was perfectly suited for it.

"You can't escape!" I called after him. "I haven't lost a target in three hundred years, and I don't plan on starting now!"

I unfurled my wings and rose into the air. One of the advantages of being a pixie in Hell was the ability to fly, though I tried not to use it. Flying gave me an unfair advantage over my prey, but I was tired of this chase, and it was time to end it.

"Yeah, well, those dummies were different," the goblin shouted. "They weren't me!"

They always said they were different or at least thought it loudly, but they were all the same: nothing but dumb, ugly cowards.

I pulled a bow from around my shoulder and grabbed an arrow from my quiver. "Don't make me hurt you!"

"You couldn't do any worse than they'll do to me back in the pits!" the goblin shrieked.

He was right. The moment I returned him to the pits, the demons he served would rip him apart and reassemble him in the most painful ways possible, again and again, for the next several decades, until he learned his lesson. It was cruel, but it also wasn't my problem. I was simply a blunt instrument, a cog in a machine. A horrible machine, for sure, but a cog nonetheless.

I pulled back my bow until the string rested next to my pointed ear. I closed my right eye and focused on my target. The trick with hitting a moving target was to aim for where they were going, not where they were at the moment.

I let go of the arrow, and it flew through the air, whooshing past my ear as it traveled toward the goblin. The bow had never been my weapon of choice while I was alive, but during my time in Hell, I had found it to be an elegant weapon and a fine complement to my daggers.

The arrow met its target, flying straight into the goblin's leg. "Ahhh!" he shouted. He immediately fell to the hot, dirt ground, where he writhed in pain. I no longer needed to fly. A brisk walk and I had caught up with him, even as he struggled to pull himself along the ground.

"Do you yield?" I asked the sniveling goblin.

"Yes, I yield! Are you proud of yourself, pixie?" the goblin asked. "Are you proud that you have caught a worthless servant trying to make a better life for himself?"

"Pride is not an emotion I have felt since I returned to Hell," I replied. "I felt it in Valhalla, though, and because of that faint memory, I can tell you I take no pride in taking you down. However, there is a certain satisfaction in a job well done."

Before I was tricked into the Devil's service, I lived in Valhalla, along with the greatest Viking warriors of all time. We drank, cavorted, and laughed together, but we never hunted, which was the one thing that Hell had over my previous home. In every other way, it was worse.

"You cannot believe the horror of the pits," the goblin said, trembling. "I did terrible things in my life, and it chills even me to the bone. Do you know what we do to them?"

I cocked my head, considering this. "I have a vague sense, but I try to keep myself out of the affairs of demons."

"You are lucky that you can be so willfully blind, having been the pet of two Devils in your time here," the goblin spat. "Most of us are not so lucky."

"I am no pet," I spat.

"Believe whatever you want," the goblin said. "I know what I have heard."

I knelt next to the goblin and pulled my arrow out of his leg with a single yank. "Do you know how I came to Hell?"

"Everyone knows the story of the fallen pixie." The goblin rolled his eyes. "The one who chose Hell over eternal paradise."

I chuckled. "That is not quite how it went."

"I don't care, pet," the goblin said, his voice a growl. "There is a reckoning coming, and you will be consumed."

"I've heard that one before," I said, pulling the goblin up to his feet. "And yet, Hell still stands."

"For now," he said. "For now."

*

Hell was mostly a barren wasteland, speckled with pits of suffering for damned souls, worked by the demons and monsters in the Devil's service. There were ten levels of Hell, based on the severity of crimes committed. The goblin I had bound on the back of my unicorn was from the tenth pit, where the evilest of the evil dwelled for all eternity: Kings who slaughtered whole civilizations, pirates who raped and pillaged with glee, conquerors and mongrels who decimated continents in the name of their own vanity.

"Please don't make me go back." The goblin was still pleading from the back of the unicorn. "I can't work in that pit for another moment longer."

During my time in Hell, I had ridden many steeds, but unicorns were by far my favorite. It took me a while to get used to riding them, but once you overcame the stubbornness of the wild beasts, they ended up being excellent companions. Perhaps even better than my beloved horses on Earth. Their gait was milder, and their ride was smoother, which made for far less cramping after a long ride.

As a pixie, I could fly across the wastelands of Hell if I wanted. I preferred to ride, though, just as I had in my time on Earth. It yoked me to the ground and made me one with the soil. It also meant I didn't have to hold criminals in my arms for hundreds of miles.

"I don't have any say in the matter," I replied. "I have my orders to return you to the pits. We all have to do what we all have to do. That's the rule."

I almost felt bad for him. He drew the short straw when it came to assignments. Most goblins didn't work in the pits. If they did, it was simply to process new souls at their entrance. Goblins, with their fastidious nature, were well suited for bureaucracy.

For the most part, monsters worked to make sure Hell functioned properly without too many hiccups. People told stories about the demons of Hell and the cruelty of the pits, but they didn't think about the industrial complex behind the scene required to make the whole place function.

"Come on," the goblin said. "Like you've never broken the rules before."

"There are no exceptions, goblin," I replied.

"Yancy."

"Excuse me?"

"My name is Yancy," the goblin said. "I'm not just some goblin. I have a name."

"Sorry," I said. "I try not to remember that you have names."

Yancy studied me for a moment. "I understand that in a weird way. I have to forget that those people we torture had names and lives on Earth before they died. Otherwise, the guilt eats away at me. Truthfully, it eats away at me no matter what I do. This place has a way of doing that to you, stripping everything good about you and leaving you just...just empty."

He was right. The longer I did the job, the less I saw the individuality of anyone I chased. They were simply deserters, and it was my job to bring them back. Any more thought than that might make me hesitate. Hesitation led to errors, and I couldn't afford any of those.

"I'm not a pet, either," I replied. "My name is Akta, and I am trapped here, just like you. Three hundred years ago, I was asked to do a favor for Bacchus, God of Earth."

"What kind of favor?" Yancy asked.

"He asked me to come to Hell and find an angel. In doing so, I ran afoul of Velaska and was cursed to remain here in her service."

"Then why do you remain loyal to the Morningstar?"

Lucifer. The Morningstar. The only angel stupid enough to attack a god. Two hundred years ago, he marched against Heaven. His army fell in a single battle, and Bacchus, God of Earth, cast him back to Hell to face eternal punishment.

"I was never loyal to him or his stupid crusade. I am loyal to the Devil."

"Velaska?" the goblin replied. "The deserter? You pledged fealty to her?"

Velaska continued the line of Devils that started with Anubis, led to Hades, and finally to her. She abandoned Earth soon after Lucifer's failure to conquer Heaven, and in her last act, named him to become the Devil after her. It was her last screw you to Bacchus, the drunken buffoon ruler of Earth.

"That's the one," I replied. "And yes, I did."

"If you hate her so much, then why did you stay with Lucifer when she named him the Devil?"

"No more questions," I said, hanging my head low. "We have a long way to go, yet."

The truth was that I didn't know how to break the spell Velaska had cast on me all those years ago. She bound me to her and disappeared across the galaxy. The angels tried to break the curse countless times, but their attempts proved useless. Unless Velaska came back and set me free, I had no idea how I would ever stop my service to the lord of Hell.

*

"I know you're tired, Winter," I said as the light from her horn blinked wildly. The one thing I never got over with riding unicorns was the multi-colored lights their horns gave off when they were trying to tell you something. "We're almost there, okay? It's just one more hill, I promise."

The unicorn whinnied.

"I know I said that three hills ago, but just trust me this time."

She was named Winter ironically, as she was black as night and born from Hellfire. She was ornery, but we got along just fine. Nobody else could tame her wild ways, but that's because they didn't understand her. Winter couldn't be tamed. She had to join you willingly.

It wasn't easy to build trust in Hell, but Winter and I had been together for the past hundred years, and over that time, we'd developed a bit of a shorthand. She always had my back, and I had hers.

"Here we are," I said, cresting over the hill. "See? I told you, buddy."

Below us, the pit to the tenth level of Hell coughed noxious fumes into the air. They bubbled up into the sky hundreds of feet into the air. Dark black clouds plumed out like geysers and mixed with the orange hue of Hell, creating a terrifying haze that spread across the valley.

And the stench. Dear gods, the stench. Like a million rotten corpses festering in the hot sun. I felt the need to vomit up everything I'd ever eaten in the last hundred years.

"Please," Yancy said, clutching at me. "Don't make me go back."

I looked down at the bog fuming out of the pit and then back to the goblin, and I couldn't help but sympathize with him. I had never seen the tenth level of Hell before, and looking down upon it was enough to break my will. I could not imagine living in it for hundreds of years.

"I can't," I replied. "I have orders."

"What if I helped you?"

I scoffed. "How could you possibly do that? You're bound like a prize pig."

"I have information," Yancy said. "If you let me go, I will give it to you. All of it."

I turned to him. "What information could you possibly have that would make me shirk my duties to the dark lord?"

"It's specifically because of your duties that you need to let me go," he hissed. "A plot arises to take down the Morningstar."

"Lucifer?" I frowned. "There is a plot to murder him?"

"That's right, pixie," the goblin nodded, his eyes gleaming. "And I will tell you everything if you bring me to Dis and away from this place."

"Many others have tried and failed to kill the Devil," I said. "Why should this plot be taken any more seriously than the others?"

"Those who plot against him seek the weapon that can destroy the Devil."

"No such weapon exists," I said. "The Devil is both immortal and invulnerable."

"Says you," Yancy replied. "But they claim the weapon they seek can kill the Devil so that they can rule Hell themselves."

"What's to stop me from beating the information out of you and bringing you back to the pits anyway?"

"There is no punishment you could give me that is worse than returning to the pits."

He was right about that. It was my responsibility to protect Hell and thus the Devil. If there was a plot afoot, I needed to hear it.

"Name your terms."

Yancy didn't skip a beat. "Safe passage to Dis, and never having to return to the pits again for the rest of my days."

"If I bring you to Dis and find you other work, you will tell me everything?" I said. "Those are your terms?"

"Bring me to Dis, and everything I know will be yours," Yancy replied.

"Very well. But turn on me, and I will not hesitate to send you back to the pit myself."

# CHAPTER 2

The great city of Dis was erected in the dead center of Hell—and that's not even a play on words. It was the only city of its kind across the barren wastelands surrounding it. Small shacks and towns speckled the horizon, but no more than a dozen monsters inhabited any of them. If they ever got too large, enforcers from Dis forced the town to disband and its inhabitants to relocate back to the city.

With all the monsters confined to the walled city of Dis, Satan could monitor them all and move against any who became too powerful. He wanted all his workers in one place, lest they rose up and attacked him.

Dis was home to 95 percent of all the monsters and demons in Hell, including me. After long shifts in the pits of Hell, or riding across the barren wastelands delivering souls for torture, or cleaning out toilets, the inhabitants of Dis went to their homes and lived normal lives full of families, fun, and frivolity…at least as much as we could have in the bowels of unending suffering.

It surprised me how quickly my life normalized after I was stranded in Hell. I thought my days would be filled with torture and death, watching mutilated souls filleted in front of me. It wasn't like that at all, though. It was much like my life on Earth. My job was that of a scout, which meant I monitored the plains of Hell and made sure nobody escaped the pits.

However, there was always work for me. You would think the security would be better, but my services were constantly enlisted to track somebody down. Either souls or monsters would escape the pits or run away from their post, and it was my job to find them and return them for punishment. Usually, that meant bringing them back to the pit they escaped from. Sometimes, I brought them straight to Dis and the constables who engaged my unique talents.

"Papers!" A fire-blue wraith shouted as I inched Winter across the wooden drawbridge over the moat surrounding the city.

The great wall of Dis stretched hundreds of feet into the air, its obsidian facade looming over us. I remembered the first time I saw the great gates, and they were just as impressive and hostile, even hundreds of years later.

"I don't have papers," I said. "I left them back at the tenth pit. Please don't make me go back there and retrieve them. The tenth is a horrible, dreadful, no good, very bad place."

The wraith shook his head. "You can't enter without papers, Akta, you know that."

"I live here, Gil. Cut me some slack." I threw my hands in the air. "I need to get this guy to the Central Precinct for processing, and I need to do it without a lot of questions, okay?"

Gil looked up at me and sighed, his hollow eyes filled with fire. "Rules are rules for everybody who leaves Dis, even inhabitants. If I let you pass without papers, I have to let everybody else pass, too. It would be bedlam. Hell runs on order. Don't you know that?"

I shook my head. "Not true. You could just let me pass and tell everybody else to shove it up their ass."

It took me a long time to realize the shrill shriek which pierced the air was a laugh escaping the wraith's lips. It sent chills down my spine.

"You're a pain in the ass," Gil said. "But you are funny."

"Please," I replied. "Pain in the ass? I've caught more escapees than any other scout, which makes your job easier, not harder."

Gil sighed and waved me forward. "Just go. I tire of looking at you."

I snapped the reins on Winter's bridle, and the unicorn trotted forward. "You're the best!"

"Remember that when I burn you to the spot next time you come through without papers."

"You won't do that, Gil," I replied. "You like me too much."

*

I hated to admit it, but I was kind of happy in Hell. At least I wasn't miserable. It's not that I didn't love Valhalla, but there was very little to do in the way of mental stimulation. You could eat, drink, or have sex, which was all fine and well, but it didn't have the thrill of the hunt, and I missed that. Hell certainly wasn't all that pleasant. Charon once told me that it could be if you let it, and after three hundred years, I kind of knew what he meant. Hell was what you made it, and I was determined to make the best of my horrible situation.

"Come on!" I shouted, pulling the goblin down from Winter's back. "I don't have all day."

Yancy slammed onto the ground, and I picked him up by the scruff of his neck. "That's not very nice, you know."

"I didn't bring you to the pits, goblin," I replied. "I have run out of nice with you. Now shut up before I change my mind."

"I'm still Yancy, you know."

"And I still don't care."

The Central Precinct was the largest and busiest in all of Hell. While my job was catching escaped souls, the constables kept the peace in Dis. It was a thankless job, as neither monsters nor demons had any interest in playing nice.

The constable's office buzzed with life when we walked through the door of the precinct. Convicts sat in thick shackles on the wooden benches in the front of the room, waiting solemnly for their time of reckoning.

Behind them, dozens of desks lined the floor. Constables sat behind them, filing paperwork and interrogating potential witnesses. Trolls, orcs, and ogres made the best constables because they were the strongest in Hell, aside from the demons, and the only monsters who stood a chance against them. Still, their methods were cruel and vicious at their very best. That was what was needed to keep order in Hell. For all its flaws, Dis was nearly crime-free, despite being filled with demons and all manner of villainous creatures.

I pulled Yancy toward the front desk. A bearded dwarf sat behind the counter, dressed in a flowing, pink dress covered in lace. It was impossible to tell whether a dwarf was a man or a woman since they were all built the same— thick and boxy, with long, bushy beards to boot.

"Patty," I said, walking up to her. "I need to see Ylfingur. Is he in?"

"Is he expecting you?" Her voice was nasal.

"Is he ever?"

Patty shook her head. "He told me next time you showed up unannounced to tell you to pound sand."

I smiled at her. "That's not very nice, Patty. I thought you were supposed to be nice."

"Who ever said that?" Patty waved a hand dismissively. "My job is to treat people with the respect they deserve, and I've done that. Unfortunately, you don't deserve that much respect, and that's a you problem."

"That's definitely not very nice," I muttered. "Now come on, is he here or not? I don't have all day to stand around and hold this asshole."

"I assume this…thing is for him?" Patty asked, pointing at the goblin.

"Yancy," the goblin said.

"He is," I said. "And his name is Yancy, not asshole. He's very adamant that you know that about him. Though asshole would be more appropriate."

"You think we have room to hold another monster in here? We're all full up. Just bring him back to the pits and be done with it."

"Luckily, you are no constable," I said. "Which means I don't have to take it up with you. I'll take it up with Ylfingur. Is he here or not?"

Patty sighed. "He's here. He's here. If he asks, though, I'm going to tell him you knocked me out and had your way with me before you ran back to him."

"You're not my type, Patty," I replied.

"I'm bored now," Patty said, picking up the knitting needles she kept on her desk. "You are boring."

I grabbed the goblin by the scruff and pulled him forward.

"Does anybody like you?" he asked. "It doesn't seem like it."

"I don't need to be liked." I shrugged. "And I only need to be respected enough to get my work done. To that end, I have been very successful."

Ylfingur was a Cyclops and once the leader of a band of monsters that lived in the forest outside of King Odgeir's kingdom. That was how we met. He was one of the few monsters in Hell that I first encountered during my short life on Earth.

When I was alive, I killed his son Bjarngimur, but we quickly made peace with that, and he helped me exact my revenge on the king who murdered me. When I returned to Hell the second time, Ylfingur had been made the head constable at a small police precinct on the outskirts of Dis. In the ensuing three hundred years, he moved from that outpost to head constable of the biggest precinct in the city. Ylfingur didn't like his job, but he did respect his position and worked to make Dis as safe as possible.

His office was in the back of the precinct so he could look out on all the monsters that worked for him, which he did with little joy. A waist-high partition separated him from the rest of the precinct, which allowed him to survey his wards while remaining separated from them. His face dropped as he watched me cross the precinct toward him.

"Go away," Ylfingur said when I walked into his office. "I have no favors left for today. At least not for you."

I shook my head. "I'm afraid I can't leave. This goblin—"

"Yancy," the goblin added.

"This…Yancy here says he has information about a plot to assassinate Lucifer."

"Hmm." Ylfingur's single eye narrowed to focus on the goblin. "That is more interesting than most of the wayward monsters you bring in here."

"It's true, sir," Yancy replied. "There's a big plot coming down the way, and if you don't stop it, the Devil's gonna be killed. Half the monsters in Hell are ready to move against Lucifer for what he did, and the other half ain't in the mood to protect him if you catch my drift."

"I suppose I should look into something like that," Ylfingur nodded. "What do you want for this information?"

"I want not to go back to the pits. I hate it there."

"Well, that is outside of my control. We have all been given our orders."

"Easy for you to say," Yancy said. "You got a nice desk in the middle of Dis. Try singing that tune when you're pulling mutilated souls outta the Bogs of Bile or listening to the sound of eternal agony in level ten for a couple hundred years. We aren't all built to do what we're supposed to do. I thought Lucifer knew that. I thought he was on our side. I thought things were gonna change after he took over, but nothing's changed, sir, and we're fed up with it."

Ylfingur pushed back from his desk. He was massive. His broad shoulders were as long across as I was tall and barely fit the confines of his chair and desk. They put a visible strain on the tight, blue shirt he was forced to wear as head constable. That type of hulking frame would have made a wonderful construction worker, like his son, but the Devil had assigned him to a different purpose, and just like the rest of us, he dutifully accepted.

"Very well," Ylfingur said with an impatient sigh. "If your information checks out, then we will find another use for you. Dis can always use more janitors, after all. I hope you don't mind cleaning shit."

Yancy shook his head. "No, sir. After where I been for the past millennia, that will be a welcome sight, I'll tell you that."

Ylfingur reached out his massive hand. "Then we have an accord."

# CHAPTER 3

The city of Dis had improved drastically during the three hundred years that I lived inside its walls. When I first came, the streets were mostly mud and dirt, with cobblestone streets reserved only for the wealthiest areas. Since those days, the whole city had been paved with stones, and in the poorest areas, ramshackle huts were replaced with stone and brick, insulating us from the heat of Dis and giving us a respite from the merciless fire that burned ceaselessly.

Rasmus and his family lived in the stone tenements that lined the walls of Dis, and so did I. My house didn't have more than a cot made of hay and a small fireplace. It was a single room, but it was mine, and I didn't owe anything to anyone for it.

The commission I earned from catching escaped souls afforded me more than my humble tenement, but I didn't need much, so I didn't get much. Besides, I was rarely at home, and when I was, I was usually holed up at the Old Hat or with Rasmus and his family. They fed me and mended my clothes. They made sure I was as healthy as possible, and it was because of them that Dis was bearable. I would have loved to have my mother with me as well, but that would have meant pulling her from Heaven. I couldn't be that selfish.

My mother. I often wondered how she was doing in Heaven. Gabriel, God's messenger, sometimes came with news of her, but it was rarely more than a couple of words. I wished desperately to see her once more, but my oath to Velaska bound me to Hell.

"Akta!" Rasmus said as I walked toward the home he shared with his wife, Rosemary. He wrapped his arms around me and hugged me close. "When did you get back?"

Rasmus drove the carts from the Gates of Abnegation, where tortured souls first came into Hell and were sentenced by the giant Petrus to their final torture in one of the ten pits of Hell. It was long, boring, lonely work, but at least it allowed him to be home every night with his family.

"I just now finished with Ylfingur," I said. "I brought a goblin to him for protection."

"Ylfingur?" Rasmus drew back with a quizzical look on his face. "I didn't think he muddied himself with scout affairs."

"He doesn't, usually," I replied. "This was a special case. There is a plot afoot to kill the Devil, and a plot like that affects us all."

"Good riddance," Rasmus said, scoffing. "Lucifer has done nothing of value since he took over. I would welcome a change."

My brother did not like Lucifer any more than the other denizens of Dis, but he did not usually mock him openly, either. It was not wise to do so. Many monsters had been taken from their home and thrown in the pits for talking out against the Devil.

"Don't say that too loudly, brother," I said quietly. "The Morningstar has ears everywhere."

"I do not scare easily, sister."

"I know," I said. "Neither do I, but I would like you around for a long time. The thought of you in the pits due to a slip of the tongue does nothing but fill me with dread."

"Then I will keep my opinions to myself."

"For the best," I said.

Rasmus smiled. "Come on in. Rosemary is just finishing making supper."

"You know we don't have to eat, right?" I replied.

Monsters did not have to eat in Hell, but we often chose to indulge anyway. It brought us back to our roots and grounded us to Earth. It reminded us that at one time, we did not do the Devil's bidding and that for a brief moment, we were free. Besides, it was a good excuse to be with family.

"We don't have to eat," Rasmus replied, "but we get to. That is the joy of family and food. It brings us together."

"Very well," I said. "I haven't had any food since the last time you invited me over. Let's eat."

*

Rasmus, Rosemary, and I sat on the ground around a small wooden table. His house was no fancier than mine. A stew boiled in a metal cauldron on the hearth, and a small hay bed lay in the corner. Otherwise, the house was sparsely decorated.

"This is wonderful," I said to Rosemary. I knew she'd spent all day slaving over the stove to make it.

"Thank you," Rosemary replied. "It took many hours to gather the ingredients. It's not easy to find a shop in Hell that sells fresh herbs, especially to somebody like me."

Rosemary was one of the only humans allowed to live in Dis. As a condition of my deal with Velaska, I asked that Rosemary be spared the horrors of Hell. Though Velaska agreed to my request, none of the monsters liked it, or her, very much.

One of the reasons they enjoyed Dis was because it didn't have any humans, and Rosemary reminded them of the discrimination and death they faced at the hands of people for thousands of years. That did not make her well-liked or well treated.

"Well, you did a fine job," I replied.

"Thank you," Rosemary said. "It's the only thing that keeps me sane here."

Because she was a human, the Devil had no need for her in his army, which meant that she didn't have a job, or a brand, like all the monsters of Hell. However, even if she wanted to work, nobody would hire her or even associate with her. It made her life lonely, save for the occasional family visits.

"Anything to keep you sane, right?" I asked.

"That is a good way to put it," she said with a sigh.

"What about the children?"

It was hardly fair to call any of Rasmus's four children such, as they had died in their old age after having children of their own. In fact, seven generations of Rasmus's lineage roamed through the pits of Hell, working odd jobs.

Rasmus slid his hand over to hers and squeezed it softly. "It's not been easy, as you know, being here. We have often thought about leaving Dis and forming another city that would be free of the prejudice that Rosemary faces. But it's virtually impossible, even if we took the entire family with us."

"Couldn't you leave, just the two of you?" I asked. "I'm sure you could drive your wagon from anywhere in Hell, and there must be a little town that's welcome for you."

"No," Rosemary said. "I would not want to leave my children. Who knows when I would see them again once I stepped out onto the wasteland, or if I could ever step foot into Dis again."

"I wish I had better words for you," I told her. "I don't know if I could have dealt with what you have faced. I admire you for it."

She smiled sweetly. "It's better than the pits, right?"

I nodded. "Anything is better than the pits."

*

After leaving Rasmus, I had more pressing business with old friends who I hoped could fill me in about the plot on Lucifer's life. They were more tied into the Dis underground than anybody else I had met since coming here. They were also excellent cobblers.

I stopped by my house to sharpen my daggers and refill my quiver, then walked to the main street of Dis, where artisans and merchants sold their wares from stands on either side, hollering to potential customers as they passed.

Even from the bottom of the main street, Beatrice's voice echoed above the din of the other merchants. The young elf had died young and maintained her youthful visage when she came to Hell. Even though her brain aged, her body stayed the same. Luckily, no one in Hell cared what you looked like. It was the years you spent in Hell that mattered.

She screamed at the top of her lungs, standing atop the wooden stand which displayed their shoes. "BEST SHOES IN ALL OF DIS!" Beatrice never lost her enthusiasm to sell her father's shoes, which made them one of the richest families in Dis. Their house was on a nicer street and had a full kitchen. They could afford the niceties of modern living.

"Beatrice!" I waved, walking up to her stand. Beatrice's smile never faded from her face, which brought a smile to mine.

"Akta!" she shouted. "What do you want?"

"Do I always have to want something?"

She shrugged. "No, but you always do."

"I do not."

"And you don't bring any bribes when you come, either," Beatrice added. "Your brother always used to bring us bribes, but not you. You just expect something for nothin'."

"I pay you, don't I?"

"That you do," Clovis replied from behind his daughter, where he worked on sewing a heel onto the leather hide of a brown shoe. The older elf didn't speak much. He let his daughter do that, but when he spoke, I listened. "What can we help you with today, Akta?"

"What do you know about a plot to assassinate Lucifer?" I asked.

Clovis looked up from the shoe he was cobbling and smiled. "Which one? There's always talk, but nothing serious. Not since Velaska made him the Devil, at least."

When Lucifer was just an angel, hundreds of attempts were made against his life. However, once he became the Devil, those plots stopped. It wasn't because the monsters of Hell hated him any less, but because the Devil was an immortal being that couldn't be killed by any method known to Hell. Part of me believed Velaska did a kindness for Lucifer by making him an immortal Devil so that he couldn't be harmed by normal means. Of course, that was crazy because Velaska doesn't have a kind bone in her body.

"There is one that has come anew," I replied. "One that would have made it to the pits at level ten no less."

"*Pfft*," Beatrice said. "That's a new one. Nobody talks to those jokers. They're messed up in the head, you know?"

"And yet, somebody did this time," I replied. "I picked up a goblin that deserted his post, and word of it had reached even him."

"Well," Clovis said, "that does make it a little different from the drunken idiocy spewed by most of these demons. Nobody likes being ruled by an angel, especially one as cowardly as Lucifer."

"A fallen angel," I corrected him. "His former brethren in Heaven no longer consider him an angel. They cursed him to look like a demon and threw him down here."

"I doubt the demons believe they were cursed with their appearance," Clovis replied. "Which I think is one of the problems right there. Lucifer thinks he is better than the rest of them. After they served his use for his plot against Bacchus, he discarded them like trash."

"And you?" I asked. "How do you feel about Lucifer? Are you among the many who aim to bring him down?"

"We don't care about the stupid Morningstar," Beatrice said. "Velaska. Lucifer. Some dumb, old rock. Whatever it is, our lives ain't gonna change. No matter who's in charge, monsters and demons will need shoes, and we'll get by."

"She's right, you know," Clovis said. "One of the great truths about the world is that everybody needs shoes."

"So, you have no information for me?" I asked.

"I have lots of information," Clovis replied. "But you don't have much to go on, and I am not a psychic. Come back knowing more about what you need, and I'll gladly part with some of my knowledge."

"For a price," Beatrice added. "Now get out of here. You're scaring away business."

# CHAPTER 4

I don't know why I had such an affinity for Lucifer. I hadn't even seen him for two hundred years, not since the Fall. However, I'd seen him plenty in the lead up to his war against Mount Olympus. He made hundreds of speeches around Dis, building an army of monsters and demons right under Velaska's nose. An army he used to march on Mount Olympus.

I rarely talked to him in those days, but I saw him around. I always felt guilty for sparking his disillusionment with the gods. After all, I was the one who planted the first seed of revolution inside of him.

When Bacchus recruited me for his mission to find the fallen angel Zharaqiel, my help came with a price. As a condition of my help, I forced Bacchus to allow my mother to live on Mount Olympus. She never liked Valhalla or the warriors that lived within its walls who were constantly boasting about killing her people. I thought that living on Mount Olympus would offer a natural solution to her problem.

I didn't know it was a huge slight against the gods to suggest a pixie live on Mount Olympus. Apparently, that right was only granted to gods or angels, and when Lucifer found out, he went apoplectic.

Not only was it a slap in the face to the rule of the gods, but Lucifer as well. He had been denied entrance to Heaven for nearly two hundred millennia. He argued that if Bacchus allowed pixies to live in Heaven, then he should be able to live in Heaven as well. More so, he believed that every monster in Hell had the right to live in Heaven if they chose to do so.

Because of the spark I lit in his belly, Lucifer took his grievance all the way up to Heaven itself. Bacchus didn't agree with him, of course, and so the Morningstar raised an army and marched on Heaven in one of the most ill-fated moves in all of eternity.

Still, that wasn't why monsters of all types wanted him dead. For a long while, actually, monsters loved him. They felt he was their champion, one that listened to their needs and fought for them. He was their hero, their rallying cry. He was the only one who heard their plight and took arms to help them.

No, losing the war was not why they hated him. They hated him because once he lost the war, in a damning act of cowardice, Lucifer dropped down on his knees and begged God to let him come home. He abandoned all his monster kin and the demons who fought with him for a chance to return to Heaven. For those that followed him, that act was unforgivable. His army fought for him, they bled with him, and they died for him, only to be betrayed by his cowardice. When he returned to Hell with his minions, he had lost their respect.

Many monsters tried to take Lucifer's life in the years after he returned to Hell, but then Velaska offered him a way out. She gave him the chance to take over her throne, and he accepted. He became the Devil, and Velaska abandoned Hell, and Earth, the moment she could coronate him. Since then, Lucifer was holed up in his castle, refusing to see visitors and avoiding the outside world.

As a Devil, Lucifer was immortal. He could not be killed by any being in Hell, not even those who hated him, but their hate kept him from the world outside his fortress. It was the hate that caused him to isolate himself.

*

I returned to the police station to see how successful Ylfingur's interrogation of Yancy had been. I found Ylfingur at the precinct's reception desk, going over the interrogation with Patty. When he saw me, he turned back toward his office.

"How did it go with the goblin?" I asked.

"We haven't gotten a lot out of him, unfortunately," Ylfingur said when we reached his office. "He doesn't know much about anything. I'm afraid he played you to get out of his duties in Hell."

"And nothing he told you lines up with any other open investigations?"

"What investigations?" Ylfingur said. "There are no other open investigations like it. There hasn't been an attempt on Lucifer's life in a long time. Even when there were, it's not like they were well planned out. Usually, it was some drunken imp with a beer bottle. Maybe if they planned better, one of the attempts would have worked, and we wouldn't have Lucifer as the Devil."

"He's not so bad," I said.

"Yes, he is," Ylfingur replied. "He betrayed us after leading our kind into a slaughter. What he did was unforgivable."

"Eternity is a long time to hold a grudge."

"I was there, Akta. My sword dripped red with angel's blood for him. His betrayal will live with me for the rest of my days."

"As is your right, but you still have a job to do."

"And I will do it to the best of my ability," Ylfingur replied. "But your suspect is useless. The guy seems like he's just trying to get out of going back to the pits."

"They will say anything to avoid going back, won't they?" I was starting to doubt my judgment. "He seemed so genuine, though."

Ylfingur nodded. "I've heard every single excuse imaginable for shirking the duty to the Devil, and his just sounds like any other."

"Can I speak to him?" I asked.

"Be my guest. He's sitting in the cell at the end of the hallway, on the right. Do you want to see his statement?" Ylfingur handed me several pieces of parchment. "I don't think it's going to do any good, though."

"No," I said, turning toward the door. "I would rather hear it directly from him."

"Suit yourself." Ylfingur's eye rolled up to the ceiling.

*

I was hit by a cold burst of wind when I stepped foot in the damp and cramped corridor behind the reception area. It felt nice against my skin. It reminded me of Valhalla and the cold days of drinking mead with my warrior brethren. I wondered, absently, if they pitied me or envied me for being back on the hunt while they drank away their eternity.

Most of Hell was hot and muggy, but the jail cells running down either side of this hallway were unnaturally cold. The monsters of Hell didn't like the cold. It dampened their powers and forced them to cooperate. The moans of prisoners echoed louder the further I walked down the long, dirty hallway.

Yancy, the goblin, sat on the floor. His cell was empty, without so much as a pile of hay for comfort. He shivered, staring blankly into the darkness of the hallway.

"Is this better than level ten?" I asked.

Yancy nodded, his teeth chattering. "Anything is better than level ten."

"Is that why you are lying to Ylfingur and his men about a plot on Lucifer's life?"

Yancy crawled toward the front of the cell. "Of course not! I've been telling the truth. It's just that…well, I don't really know much. I just overheard a conversation or two between demons while I was working. I ain't no criminal mastermind. I just know what I know."

"So, you did lie," I said.

"Only about how much I knew," Yancy said. "In Hell, that's like telling the whole truth, ya know?"

"It's not going to be good enough to save you from the pits. I'm getting shackles and taking you back there." I turned to leave.

"Wait!" he shouted, scrambling to his knees. "Okay, I got one more thing I've been holding back. I was saving it for a final bargaining chip, but if you promise not to bring me back to the pits, I'll tell you."

"Let me see if your information pays off. If it does, Ylfingur will grant you safe passage here in Dis. I will make sure of it."

"That's what he said, too," Yancy scoffed. "But I don't trust no cop."

"Then trust me," I replied. "I swear to you that if your information checks out, you will never see the pits again."

There was a long pause, longer than I would have liked, before Yancy swallowed hard and spoke again. "At the front gates, there's a demon named Tygil. The demons I was telling you about, the ones from the tenth pit, they mentioned her by name."

I nodded. "I will go to the Gates of Abnegation and verify your story.'

"What am I supposed to do until then?"

"Try not to freeze," I said with a shrug and started back down the hallway.

"Be careful," he called after me. "Tygil is nobody to be trifled with."

I stopped for a moment and smirked. "I didn't know you cared about me so deeply."

"I don't, but you're the only one who can get me out of here, so I'm rooting for you."

"I will return when I know more."

*

The Gates of Abnegation sat at the front entrance of Hell. It was the only way in and out of Hell for human souls and was guarded by the giant Petrus, who read the history of their time on Earth and assigned them a punishment to fit their crimes.

The gate itself was designed to look like a black skull breathing fire, with long, impenetrable walls on either side which stretched to the edges of Hell's cavern. There was no way to scale the wall without wings, as immediately in front of the wall was a chasm that led to Hellfire.

There was no way around the wall, the only way into Hell was through Petrus, and the wait along the narrow, rock path could stretch for five hundred years or more. Luckily for me, at least, monsters could leave through the Gates of Abnegation at will. Most monsters did not use this power, and few even knew about it. I learned of it from Lucifer, who often met with Gabriel on the rocky cliffs outside the Gates during his tenure as envoy to Hell, a position he held for almost two hundred millennia before his war against Mount Olympus.

After Lucifer lost his war, however, all his communication with Gabriel ceased. Since then, I was the only monster in Hell that God—Bacchus—trusted. After all, I wasn't even supposed to be there. I was supposed to be in the halls of Valhalla, with the greatest warriors of all time. Gabriel knew that too, and it was the reason he trusted me. He was the one who'd found me in Valhalla and brought me to Bacchus. It was he who sent me on the mission, which ended with being bound to Hell, but I tried hard not to hold it against him.

"Frank!" I called out, walking toward a thin, lithe demon. Frank was Rasmus's boss. He ran the Gates of Abnegation and managed the other demons who brought the damned souls through the gates and the monsters who carted them from the gates to their final punishments. He was surly and no-nonsense, qualities I appreciated in just about anybody.

"I don't have time for you today," Frank said in a huff. "If you're after a runner, they didn't end up here."

Runners liked to leave through the Gates and try for the black void at the entrance to Hell, where all human souls entered into oblivion. Unfortunately for them, however, it was a one-way void with no exit back to Earth.

"I know that, Frank. I'm looking for one of your demons. Name's Tygil. Have you seen her?"

Being a demon at the gates had once been a hard job. They were expected to lead the condemned all the way through Hell to their final punishments. However, with the addition of monsters as a labor force, the demons only had to fly out of the gates and drag people to the waiting cages. Not all demons could fly. The ones who could were afforded the most prestigious jobs in Hell, like bringing the condemned through the Gates of Abnegation.

Monsters dealt with the rest of the trip to the pits because it was slow, banal, unglamorous, and thankless work. It's what my brother Rasmus did.

Carts, dragging cages behind them, lined the road on the other side of the gates. Damned souls moaned and screamed for mercy inside the cages, but there would be none. Even if there was mercy to be had, the only one who could grant it was Lucifer, and he hadn't been in the mood for visitors for a few centuries now.

"I run a tight ship, Akta," Frank snarled. "I haven't had a demon not show up for a shift in seventeen thousand years, did you know that?"

"I did not," I said. "Could you just check anyway? Please?"

"Very well." Frank flipped through his clipboard. "Tygil, Tygil, Tygil…now, this is weird. She's not had a shift in three weeks. Odd. I'd never approve that kind of leave."

"Who would?" I asked.

"Nobody, except for…No, he would never…it's impossible."

"Who wouldn't what?" I asked.

"My lieutenant, Uglath. He's been with me for millennia. Leave it to me. I'll get to the bottom of this."

"If you don't mind," I replied. "I'd like to question Uglath myself."

Petrus's voice boomed from beyond the other side of the gate, announcing the final judgment for some poor soul. "Two million years!"

"Fine," Frank shrugged. "I have work to do, anyway." The great fire dropped from the black skull's mouth, and Frank looked down at his clipboard. "Anter. Glor. You're up!"

Two demons flew through the Gates, pulling an old woman behind them. She was kicking and screaming. I watched as they tossed her into one of the gates along with a half-dozen grimy souls and slammed the door shut.

"What did she do?"

"Who cares?" Frank didn't glance up again from his clipboard.

"Fair enough," I said. "Where's Uglath?"

Frank pointed behind him. "Barracks. You can't miss him. He'll be the ugly one with buck teeth and gnarled horns."

# CHAPTER 5

Frank wasn't wrong. Uglath was the first thing I saw when I entered the barracks. He was nearly as tall as the building itself, and I wondered how he entered and exited through the normal-sized door at its entrance. Usually, only imps handled bureaucracy, so I was surprised to see a hulking demon, with long, twisted, black horns, working in the office. Being fastidious wasn't generally in their nature.

"Uglath?" I said as I walked inside the barracks. Inside was sparse and clean. Cots filled with hay lined the floor, and a small desk, covered with pieces of parchment, sat at the front.

Uglath busied himself cleaning the floors of the barracks between the perfectly made cots. "How can you be so dirty?" he muttered to himself under his breath.

"Uglath?" I said again. "I'm sorry, but are you Uglath?"

"Yes!" he hissed. "I thought if I just ignored you, then you would go away, but clearly, that is not the case."

"I'm sorry," I replied. "But I need your help."

Uglath turned to look at me, and for the first time, I saw his sharp, buck teeth. The skin on his face dragged lower than the bones on it, and his jowls shook as he swayed back and forth with the mop. "I'm very busy."

"Yes," I said, nodding. "Aren't we all?"

"I don't know about anybody else, but I am terribly busy." Uglath sighed deeply. "Well, ask your questions, then. Let's be done with it."

"You made the schedules for Frank, right?" I asked.

"I do everything for Frank except yell at his troops. Yeah, I make the schedules."

"Is there a reason you gave Tygil three weeks off in a row?"

His jowls made an audible slap against his neck when he shook his head. "Not that I can recall."

"Frank said it was very strange. He said he would never approve something like that."

"Frank doesn't have the first idea what goes on around here," Uglath said. "I mean, technically, he is the boss, but all decisions run through me first."

"And there's no reason Tygil got three weeks off in a row. None at all? It's just coincidence?"

"I'm afraid I just don't know," he said. "If I knew, I would help you, but sometimes…things just slip through my fingers. Maybe this was one of those flukes. It happens every now and then, especially when you've been here for so many thousands of years."

"I can imagine," I said. "How long have you worked here?"

"Since before there was a Hell," Uglath replied. "I helped build these gates, and it is my duty to maintain it for eternity."

"Can I ask you one last question?" I asked.

"If you insist," Uglath growled.

He was lying. I couldn't prove it, but I knew in my bones that he had a hand in whatever attack was being planned. It was in the way he didn't look at me when I spoke and how his hands wrung the mop so tightly that sawdust plumed out from under his fingers. He was lying.

"How do you feel about Lucifer being the Devil?" I asked. "After all, he is not a god, and he betrayed you all for a chance to return to Mount Olympus. He lost his battle with Heaven, and yet he still rules over you."

Uglath's response was mechanical. "I feel fine about it. Better him than me."

"Were you one of his soldiers during the great battle?"

"I fought with Lucifer once, yes," Uglath said. "I fought many battles, though. So many battles I cannot pull out any one as significant above the others."

"So, you don't hate him, then?"

"I don't think about him," Uglath replied. "My stead has never changed. It is to protect this place and the Devil. It was the same under Anubis, and it will be with whoever is the Devil in the future."

Another lie. Uglath dug his buck teeth into his lip as he spoke. His words came out the side of his mouth as he tried to hide his anger at the mere mention of Lucifer.

"Understandable." I watched him carefully as I spoke. "Do you know where I can find Tygil?"

Uglath sighed. "I thought you only had one more question."

"I lied," I replied. "There seems to be a lot of that going on today."

Uglath growled at me. Demons had short tempers, and I knew I was angering him. I had never beaten a demon before, and I had no desire to try my luck now. Luckily, after a moment, he calmed himself. "She doesn't live in the barracks. A few of the soldiers live in a little town near here called Voxel."

"Thank you," I said. "You have been a big help."

"Hopefully not too big, monster," Uglath replied, turning back to his mopping.

*

The town of Voxel had a grand total of five thatch-roofed homes in it, arranged in a circle and facing each other, with a pentagram drawn in the center. As I flew closer to the city, I noticed that it glowed a dim blue.

The town was a twenty-mile flight from the Gates of Abnegation, and there was nothing between there and here. I had decided to leave Winter at the Gates of Abnegation stables. If I was chasing after demons, I didn't want to risk her being hurt or worse. Besides, I needed to remain agile, and flying afforded me that luxury.

A deep, gurgling hum filled the air as I landed on the ground outside the town. I tiptoed to the nearest house to hide myself. Inching along, I made my way to the side of the house and peered toward the center of town, where the pentagram was drawn into the ground. In its center, an ugly, fat demon hummed loudly.

One point of the pentagram touched the entrance to each house. A different demon sat at the tip of each one, cross-legged, eyes glowing the same pale blue as the pentagram itself. They all hummed loudly, like the demon in the center.

I snuck around the corner of the house and peered into the window. On each wall of the house, someone had drawn a crude plateau with a temple on the top of it. The symbol throbbed blue in time with the chanting of the demon townsfolk. I crept across the perimeter to the next home.

This one was set up the same as the first, except for a giant, wooden table in the center of it. On the table sat a huge, leather-bound book. I couldn't read the text from where I stood, but I wanted to get a better look. I crept through the window silently and placed my feet on the floor.

The walls of the small shack pulsed and glowed, and the symbol drawn on them seemed to pulsate faster when I walked to the table and studied the book. On the open parchment page, I saw the outline of a curved dagger. The caption read, "The Dagger of Obsolescence." I looked closer. In smaller text and in a different hand, somebody had added, "can kill the Devil."

"What are you doing here?" a low voice growled.

I hadn't noticed the humming had stopped. I looked up to see a muscular demon with snarling teeth and a thick jaw staring at me from the entrance to the shack. The symbols drawn into the walls no longer glowed, and the demonic faces of those who had been seated and chanting now peeked in from the windows.

"Nothing," I said, tearing the page out of the book quickly. "I just wanted some reading material."

"You dare steal from the Necronomicon!" the demon screamed, its tongue lashing out in every direction. I turned toward the window, but it was blocked by another demon and the front door by two more.

"Is one of you Tygil?" I asked.

"I am!" One of the other demons at the front door crawled ominously toward me on her hands and knees. "You dare to disturb us?"

"What is this?" I asked, pointing to the page. "What is the Dagger of Obsolescence?"

"Nothing you need to concern yourself with," Tygil said. Her neck was contorted horribly, and her eyes rolled. "You'll be dead before I could finish telling you anyway."

"I'm already dead," I replied. "We all are."

"We're not!" the demon guarding the window shouted so loudly it shook the walls of the shack. As the house quaked, a small ray of light peeked through from the thatched roof.  It was my best chance of escape.

"This is our home, monster, and you invaded it, just like the usurper Lucifer!" Tygil shouted, stomping toward me. "Now, give back the page to me, and we shall eviscerate you quickly! Deny us, and we will torture you for as long as we are able."

"Come get it," I replied, unfurling my wings and leaping upward just as she grabbed for me.

I broke through the thatched roof and into the air. Tygil threw two fireballs after me, setting the house on fire before following me into the air. Before long, all six of them were flying after me, their leathery wings flapping in the wind.

My wings were short, which made me quick and nimble. I could turn on a dime, but I wasn't fast, at least not by a demon's standards. The demons' long wings allowed them to cover huge distances quickly, and soon one of them was on top of me, clawing at my leg.

I grabbed a dagger out of my scabbard and dug it into the demon's eye. It fell away, but not before the rest of the demons surrounded me. Luckily, I was nimbler than they were, so I spun around and dove down toward the ground before they had a chance to grab onto me.

I was trying not to panic. I was an able fighter, but I had never beaten a demon before, let alone six at once. Demons weren't like anything else in Hell. While everything else came to Hell after their death, demons were born there; they grew up in the flames. I was an outsider, but they fed off the horror and the heat. It gave them life.

"You're going to burn!" one of the demons shouted, heaving a battery of fireballs after me.

There was nothing to hide me from them until I got to Dis unless… an idea occurred to me. The Brambles of Agony began across a river of lava that passed nearby. I squinted into the distance, and there they were, every thorn another sin tortured from the living. When I first came to Hell, the Brambles were a thousandth of their current size. Their massive length spanned vast ranges of the barren wasteland.

Often in my days as a scout, I found escapees camped out inside the Brambles, using the thick vines to hide themselves. With any luck, I could lose the demons there with more effectiveness than my targets hid from me. It was a long shot, but I had done it once before, and I had no other option. The demons on my heels would soon overtake me. I turned hard right and disappeared into the thick, thorny brush.

The Brambles weren't a place you wanted to stay for any length of time, not if you had any other choice. They were alive, and they were not happy. They were never happy. They existed as the physical manifestation of pain and suffering. They were as much the embodiment of evil as anything else in Hell.

"You won't lose us that quickly, pixie!" Tygil shouted from above me. "Perhaps lighting these Brambles on fire will draw you out."

"If not," another demon cackled, "At least it will light you on fire, and we will laugh as you burn!"

The demons sent fireball after fireball into the Brambles, but I only disappeared deeper inside the web of vines.

The laughter of demons filled my ears. I had no lungs, and yet I choked as the fire invaded me, penetrating my very soul. I fell to my knees as the Brambles writhed in agony, squeezing tightly around me. My hands fell to the dirt floor, and my head spun wildly. I had no strength. I couldn't move. My eyes closed as the Brambles closed around me.

"Oh, for Heaven's sake," a loud voice boomed.

And then a snap filled the air, and everything turned black.

# CHAPTER 6

"Can't you go a couple of centuries without needing my help?" It was the gravelly voice of Lucifer. I regained my vision, and color came back to the world.

I was no longer in the Brambles of Agony. Instead, I was in the throne room of Lucifer's castle. I had not been there since Lucifer was coronated, but not much had changed. Artwork of the previous Devils adorned the dark stone walls, and bright torches lit the room and gave it a warm glow. Beneath my feet, a black carpet separated me from the cold, stone floor around the rest of the room.

Lucifer sat on a throne made of skulls that rose ten feet into the air so he could look down at all who came before him. Of course, none ever came before him.

"It's good to see you again, your majesty," I said, bowing my head to him.

"Please, no need for pleasantries, my dear. We go back a long way."

"I went a long way back with my brother, too, my Devil," I said, avoiding his gaze. "And the moment he was coronated, everything changed."

"Why won't you look at me?" he asked.

"No reason," I said. That was a lie. I had heard of the horrible disfigurement that Bacchus placed on Lucifer.

"Look me in the eyes," Lucifer said. "Your Devil demands it."

I knew that Bacchus cursed Lucifer after the Fall, but I didn't know to what extent. The last time I saw him, Lucifer was a brilliant, beautiful angel, replete with long, white wings and a bright glow that emanated out from him in every direction.

"I'm sorry, my lord," I replied.

I peered upward, and what I saw chilled me to my bone. Gone was the beautiful angel that once stood before me. In its place, a horrible demon. Lucifer's legs were now the color of blood, and his feet were hooved like goat's. His once lithe body was now bulky and muscled like the demons he governed, and glowing, yellow eyes replaced the soft, kind ones I remembered. Long, black horns protruded from his skull as thick, jagged teeth smiled at me.

"How bad is it?" Lucifer asked. "Be honest with me."

"Has nobody told you yet?"

"None had the guts," he replied. "And I had all mirrors banished from the castle so I might not look upon myself."

I shook my head. "I prefer not to say."

"Please." His voice cracked as he spoke. "I have not heard an honest word in two hundred years."

"You look horrible," I said with a long sigh. "You look like a demon."

"I feel like one. So, I suppose my feelings are accurate, unfortunate as they are."

"It's not so bad, though." I turned away from him. "I mean, it could be worse."

"If it is as bad as you say, so bad you cannot even look at me without recoiling in terror, then I am glad I cannot see myself."

"You should have called me sooner, my friend."

"I have avoided seeing you, all these long years, as you might imagine. I did not want to admit that you were right to doubt me."

"I did not doubt you. I questioned your judgment."

"With good reason," he replied. "I also did not want to see you because of…my own vanity."

"That's stupid," I said. "I don't care about what you look like."

"It's not only because of that," Lucifer said. "The last time we spoke…when we fought."

Our last encounter wasn't a pleasant one. He demanded I join him, or he would destroy me. He screamed at me across the vast wasteland of Hell, pleading with me to see the light, but I would not.

"You were not wrong, my lord," I said. "I should have joined you, but I could not."

"Yes," he said. "I understand that now. Funny that you now serve me, though, isn't it?"

"Not so much," I said. "It was I who started you down this path toward your current state. It is only right that I serve you now."

Bacchus had agreed to grant me and my mother a home on Mount Olympus if I retrieved the angel Zharaqiel for him. A mortal living on Mount Olympus was forbidden by the gods, and yet Bacchus still agreed. Lucifer went ballistic when he found out. He sabotaged my mission and abandoned his post. A deep sense of the gods' betrayal grew in Lucifer over the next two hundred years until he finally unleashed it, unsuccessfully, on Bacchus.

"It was not fair to you," Lucifer said. "Anyway, my anger was with Bacchus, and I paid for it with my eternal life."

"That makes it a little better, truth be told," I said to him with a smirk. "You got yours, in the end."

"Was I so bad to want freedom?" he asked.

"That is what Zharaqiel wanted, too," I replied.

"She wanted information," Lucifer said.

"And she found it," I said. "That information drove her to seek freedom, just like you, and Velaska imprisoned her for it. Then, you killed her for daring to be more than a servant. Was that fair to her?"

Lucifer stood up and walked down the pile of skulls toward me. They cracked and popped with every step he took. He seemed to relish in their destruction, taking each step slowly and deliberately.

"Often, I ask myself if I should just succumb to the Hellfire, but then I remember that Hellfire cannot kill a Devil." Lucifer walked toward the paintings along the wall and stared at one of the yellow-haired Devil Velaska for a long moment. "Do you think she planned this?"

"Who? Velaska?"

"Yes," Lucifer said with a sigh. "She was a cunning one, perhaps too cunning for her own good."

"And you think she did what?" I asked. "Orchestrated your attack on Mount Olympus?"

"I'm not sure what she did. We grew very close in those last years before the attack. We talked for hours about the weaknesses of Mount Olympus. Did you know that?"

"No," I replied, shaking my head. "I thought you plotted alone."

"I doubt I ever could have planned such a thing on my own. She was so angry at the gods for abandoning her on Earth while they galivanted around the universe creating new worlds, and I was angry for being abandoned by Bacchus in Hell. We made a perfect pair. It's all fuzzy, but she filled my head with so much…anger. She could have stopped me at any moment, and yet, she did not. She let me amass an army. She let me march against Mount Olympus. She watched me fail. And when all of that was over, she trapped me in this post forever."

I pushed myself to my feet. "That sounds exactly like her. However, you have only yourself to blame for your actions, just as I only have myself to blame for mine."

Lucifer smiled slightly. "You are not very good at pep talks. Did you know that?"

"I leave the words for your silver tongue."

Lucifer turned to me. "I know there is a legitimate plot to kill me. My enemies have come for me often in the past. However, this new attack feels different. There is a haze that covers it. I could see the others so clearly, but this new one…it is foggy to me. I cannot see who pulls the strings. I hope you can do better than me to find this threat and stop it."

"Can I ask you a question?" I said.

"Of course," Lucifer said. "You may ask me anything."

"Do you want me to stop it?" I asked. "If they are successful, and they can truly assassinate you, do you truly want me to prevent them from ending your suffering?"

Lucifer sighed. "I am miserable here, my friend. However, I still value my life and would like to keep it."

I nodded. "Then I will do everything in my power to keep you safe."

"And I will do all in my power to help you. However, know that I cannot see across the plains as I once could. I only saw you at the Brambles because the intense pain of the thorns pierced through the fog. I do not know how much help I can provide for you."

"I do not know if I can save you, my Devil, but we will both do our best."

"That is all we can do." Lucifer nodded, then exhaled loudly and changed the conversation. "Charon is waiting for you outside. He is eager to see you again."

"Can't you just snap me back to Dis?" I asked.

"I could," Lucifer smirked. "But I don't want to. Besides, if I did not connect you with Charon, I would never hear the end of it."

*

I walked down the corridor between Lucifer's throne room and the entranceway. When I had come to the palace during Velaska's reign, dozens of yellow, demonic eyes would peer out at me from the darkness, but now there were none.

That didn't make the foyer any less creepy. Thousands of black bones lined the walls, and the stained-glass windows shone down horrific images of old gods and monsters. The main entrance room was nearly dark save for the windows, and the black carpet led me past the black knights in their empty armor toward the front door, which was adorned with horrifying skeletons.

With all my might, I pulled open the heavy, bone door and walked out into the fires of Hell. No demonic soldiers guarded the hundreds of steps down to Charon's gondola. The ferryman waited for me there at the bottom of the stairwell.

It was unsettlingly quiet as I flew down the stairs toward the dock. Flight was banned on the castle's steps during Velaska's reign, on punishment of being ripped apart by the demons that guarded the castle, but since there were no guards on the steps, I floated with no fear of reprisal.

"Good to see you again," Charon said, moaning through his black cloak. On his chest, he still had pinned the purple tulip I had given him so many years ago, the one my mother gave me in Valhalla. I caught a whiff of the flower, and it immediately brought tears to my eyes, remembering her and all I had left behind when I came to Hell.

"And you, my friend," I said.

"Lucifer told me that you would need assistance."

I stepped off the wooden dock and into the boat. When I first met Charon, it bothered me that all I could see of his face were two glowing, yellow eyes, but after three hundred years, I had grown accustomed to the oddities of Hell.

"Thank you, my friend," I replied.

"I have missed bending your ear." Charon pushed off from the dock with his enchanted oar. "Tell me, have you had a pleasant stay in Hell since we last spoke?"

"I've had my moments of joy, even in this joyless place."

Charon was always going on about how Hell could be pleasant if you just gave it a chance. For decades I did not believe him, but eventually, well, I found out he was right. Hell was no longer the unpleasant place it once was so many generations ago. You can adapt to anything, I suppose.

"That is good," Charon said. The gondola cut through the fog of the lake.

"And you?" I asked. "Have you had a pleasant time in Hell since I saw you last?"

Charon smiled. "I am close to my Yilir on this lake. So, I am content, and the pleasant flower you once gave me lifts my spirits when my mind wanders to darker thoughts."

"Well, it comes from Valhalla," I said. "So, I'm not surprised."

Charon seemed to muse over this for several moments. "I did not know that. That must be why it hasn't wilted in the heat of Hell."

"Possible," I replied, thinking back to Lucifer. "Though it seems to be the only thing from Heaven that has not wilted."

"Not true," Charon replied. "You seem strong as ever."

I chuckled. "Flattery will get you everywhere, friend."

"That was a favorite expression of my beloved. I never cared for it much, flattery. I simply say the truth, and if it happens to be pleasant, then so be it."

"You and Yilir, you both worked for the first Devil, right?"

"Yes," he replied. "We worked for Anubis when Hell was young. The castle was not even built yet, in fact."

I pulled a piece of paper out of my cloak and unfolded it to show Charon the picture of the Dagger of Obsolescence. "Have you ever seen this dagger before?"

"My word." The oar froze for a moment. "Where did you find this?"

"Do you recognize it?"

"Of course I do. This page is written in the hand of my dear, sweet Yilir. I remember exactly where we were when she wrote it." He brushed the page with a skeletal finger.

"She wrote this page?" I said excitedly.

Charon nodded. "Well, of course. She wrote much of the Necronomicon and designed much of the weapons found in Hell. We made the Dagger of Obsolescence ourselves."

My jaw dropped. "You and Yilir made this dagger?"

"It was mostly my love. I only helped a bit here and there."

"Is it true, then?" I asked. "Can this truly kill the Devil?"

He nodded again. "More than a Devil. They can kill even a god, as before Lucifer, every Devil was a god, by design, of course."

"Why by design?"

"That goes back further than I would care to discuss."

"Please," I said. "For old time's sake."

Charon smiled. "Very well. The Devil's Castle sits upon an ancient evil. A demon so powerful that it rivaled even Cronus's power. The gods bound it to Hell, here, in the outer most habitable planet."

"Wow," I said.

"That is why there is greater magic here than in any other planet in the known universe because the titan slumbers deep in the bowels of this Earth's core. That is why we made the weapons of Hell; to defeat a god, yes, but even more."

"Do you know where this dagger is now? Or any of the weapons?"

"No," Charon replied. "The weapons were forgotten eons ago. They could literally be anywhere—Heaven, Earth, Hell, but they are not mere myths. I have held that dagger in my hand. Why do you ask?"

"There is a plot on Lucifer's life. I found this in the home of one of the possible conspirators." I held out the torn sheet from the Necronomicon.

"That is alarming, my friend. If they are searching for the Dagger, you must find it first, or the Morningstar's life will be in grave danger."

"I plan on it, Charon. I plan on it."

# CHAPTER 7

If the dagger was as old as Charon said, there weren't many in Hell who would know about its existence, aside from hearing about it in legends. Really, I wasn't sure if the dagger was still in Hell in the first place, but I knew who could tell me for sure, and I wasn't looking forward to dealing with the smug angel who sent me back to Hell. Gabriel liked to gloat about information and made it like pulling teeth.

If I were going to talk with him, I'd have to pass through the Gates of Abnegation. That wasn't too difficult since I wasn't one of the damned. Frank and his minions weren't scared of monsters abandoning Hell, after all. Even if we returned to Earth, we would be treated with nothing but hostility and vitriol.

Petrus sat in front of the gate, like he always did, since the days before I knew him. He was twenty feet high, even seated, with a childish-looking face, save for the thick, bushy beard that hadn't grown since my first appearance in Hell almost a millennium ago. Generally, I had very little reason to interact with Petrus, save for waving at him as he went about his work. Today, though, I needed to engage with him. It was possible he had information I could use.

"Petrus!" I shouted as I rose into the air. "Can I talk to you for a moment?"

The giant gave a weary sigh. "Can you wait? I'm already seven hundred years behind today."

"I don't mind!" a young man with one leg hollered at us from his place at the front of the line. "Take as much time as you would like."

"Yes," Petrus said with a groan. "You would say that. Soon I will simply have to arbitrarily assign you punishments. Is that what you want?"

"Maybe you can use a giant wheel," I said. "Make them spin it."

"Hmm," Petrus said. "That's an idea. Now, how can I help you?"

I pulled the illustration of the Dagger of Obsolescence out of my pocket and showed it to Petrus. "Have you ever seen this before?"

Petrus squinted at it. "I can't say that I have, no. Why? Is it important?"

"Yeah," I replied, flying away. "Watch your back until I find it."

*

I soared away from the Gates of Abnegation and over the sinewy rock bridge where tortured souls stood waiting for their day of judgment. The line twisted further and further each time I exited the Gates. The world was becoming more populated, which meant more souls to judge every day. I wondered how Hell would fit them all.

Waiting in line was torturous, for sure, but it was nothing compared to the horrors that awaited the damned once they were judged. The infernal line below me was the best it would ever get for those waiting in it. I wondered if they knew what was about to happen or if they were hoping for some sort of miracle. Hell wasn't the place for miracles.

When I got to the hilltop on the other side of the rock path, Gabriel stood atop it, waiting for me. I could tell by the tapping of his foot that he had been there for a while and wasn't happy about it.

"I don't have all day," Gabriel said. "I've been waiting for hours."

"I don't believe you," I replied, landing on the hillside. "I don't think you're busy. You only have something important to do once every thousand years or so."

"I hope this isn't about your mother again," Gabriel huffed. "I've told you she is fine. She took up playing cards. She has a group of friends, and they play every day. She's getting really good, too. One day soon, she might be able to take on Bacchus himself. Now, if that's all, I'll be leaving. I am very busy these days."

I gave him an even stare. "It's not that I don't believe you. It's just that I…kind of don't believe you."

"I don't care what you believe. I have no reason to lie."

As much as I wanted to smack the smug look right off his face, I couldn't. Gabriel wasn't actually in Hell. No. That would be too gauche for him. He was just projecting himself from his cushy post on Mount Olympus. The mountaintop in Hell where his projection stood was the only place Heaven could break through the crust of Earth into the valley of the damned, which meant whenever we needed to communicate, it had to be on this hillside.

"This isn't about my mother," I said.

"Good," Gabriel replied. "Because I'm only supposed to come for emergencies."

My eyes widened. "And me being stuck here isn't an emergency?"

"It was for the first hundred years or so, but after that, well, is anything really an emergency after a century?"

"Whatever," I grumbled. "This isn't about my interment here, either."

"Then to what do I owe the displeasure of your company?"

I pulled the paper out of my cloak and held it up for Gabriel to see. "This dagger. What do you know about it?"

"Ah, yes." Gabriel squinted at the page. "That dagger is one of five items which could kill a God or Devil, should the need arise."

"Do you know where I can find it?" I asked.

"Well, it's not up here. I can assure you of that."

"Is it on Earth?"

"No. It's not there, either. We would have known if it was. Hell is the only place we don't have eyes, so if it's anywhere, it's there."

"Okay," I replied, putting the paper away. "At least that narrows it down. It's somewhere down here, then."

"Anubis wouldn't have made it easy to find, nor would Hades or Velaska. To protect themselves, they would have hidden it somewhere no sane person would venture."

I looked out at the vast, barren, horrific expanse of Hell. In the distance, a fire raged across the Brambles of Agony. The black smoke plumed up to the top of Hell's cavern and cascaded downward. Aside from the fire, Dis, and Lucifer's castle, the only things that dotted the landscape were the pits of Hell themselves.

"That doesn't narrow it down much further, I'm afraid," I said.

"That's the best I can do for now," Gabriel said. "If I find anything else, I will let you know."

He started to fade out, but I reached for him. Unfortunately, all I swiped was air as I grabbed at him. "Wait!"

He rematerialized. "What is it? I'm very busy."

"I have something else to ask of you," I replied. "Have you ever seen a symbol that looks like a little plateau with a temple on top of it?"

"Hmm," Gabriel said. "Not very descriptive. It could literally mean anything."

"Any idea why it would be on the walls of the demon hut I stole this page from?"

Gabriel shook his head. "I'm sorry, but it's not ringing any bells."

"So, it could mean anything." I was feeling discouraged. I wasn't getting answers to anything.

"As far as I know, but I will look into that as well," Gabriel said.

"One more thing."

"What is it?" Gabriel snapped, impatient.

"Tell my mother I love her," I said with a small smile.

Gabriel's face softened. "I will deliver the message post haste."

*

I made my way back through the Gates of Abnegation and returned to Dis, heading straight for the Central Precinct to tell Ylfingur what I had learned. When I entered, he was deep in conversation with his son, Bjarngimur.

"Three of the men you have locked up back there haven't been processed for four years," Bjarngimur shouted. "How is that fair to them?"

"It's not fair, my son," Ylfingur shouted back. "I never said it was fair. I just said that was the way the system worked."

"Screw the system," Bjarngimur yelled, turning on his heel and stomping past me, slamming my shoulder hard enough to knock me over.

"What was that about?" I asked Ylfingur when I caught up to him. He was rubbing his temples.

"What is it always about?" Ylfingur spat. "He doesn't like how the system is run, and so he blusters, screams, and nothing changes."

"He's not wrong, though," I said. "I mean, is he wrong?"

"Of course, he's not wrong!" Ylfingur flailed his arms. "That's not the point."

"What is the point?"

"We don't have any power to change the system," Ylfingur said. "That's the point. Even I am powerless to do anything except what I'm told to do, just like him, and just like you."

"Depressing," I replied. "True, but depressing."

He closed his eye and let out a deep sigh. "I never expected Velaska to change a thing, but I had hope for Lucifer…I thought the Morningstar might change things when he took power. I knew he was a coward, but at least he was a coward who knew our suffering. I held out hope for so long, you know? He lived among us, so I thought he might change things." Ylfingur looked at me. "For a moment, at least."

"His reign is still young. Things might change yet."

Ylfingur shook his head. "I never figured you for an optimist. I assume you have more information since you're back. Or are you just here to bug me?"

"No, I have something for you," I said, pulling out the parchment. "What do you know about the Dagger of Obsolescence?"

"Never heard of it," Ylfingur said, deadpan, as he examined the paper.

"I'm not surprised," I said. "Only the most ancient demons were around during its construction, no monsters. But it's rumored to be able to kill the Devil himself. I believe it revolves around the center of the plot to kill Lucifer."

"Well, if that's true, then we need to find it."

"I agree," I said. "And what about this?" I drew the plateau with its temple on a scrap sheet of papyrus from a nearby desk and showed it to him. "Have you ever seen this symbol before?"

Again, Ylfingur shook his head. "I'm sorry, my friend, but for all my time in Hell, I never wrapped my brain around any of the mythology of this place. Perhaps you should see our occult expert."

"You think he would know more about this?"

Ylfingur nodded. "If anybody would know that symbol, it's Charlie."

# CHAPTER 8

Charlie's office was in the basement of the central precinct, under the frigid stones that held up the jail cells. The steps were uneven, and the walls damp. I wasn't tall, but even for me, the space was cramped.

At the end of the hallway, the warm light from a candle flickered behind an open door. Books were stacked haphazardly to the ceiling, and papers were strewn about the ground. Ylfingur kept a tidy precinct, so I only assumed he never ventured down to the basement. I was pretty sure he wouldn't fit. If he could see Charlie's office, he would have a heart attack and die for a second time.

"Hello?" I called out quietly as I neared the door.

I heard heavy breathing and a feather scribbling on parchment. The heavy breaths grew louder and faster, along with the scribbling of the paper.

"Hello?" I said again, this time louder and more forceful than before.

"Yeah! I heard ya!" a nasal voice shouted back. "Give me a minute."

I poked my head into the room. A writing desk rested against the wall in the corner. It was covered in even more papers. Seated in the wooden chair in front of the desk was a short imp writing frantically on a piece of parchment. While demons did most of the heavy lifting in Hell, imps were often behind the scenes, doing the work that bored demons to tears. They were much smaller than demons but shared much of the same features, shrunken into a pint-sized frame.

"I'm sorry for interrupting," I said. "Ylfingur told me you could help me. Charlie?"

"Yeah, yeah," Charlie replied. "Ol' One-Eye doesn't know nothing about Hell, and so he sends all his hard cases to me." He finished writing and spun in his chair. "Do you think it's a little insulting that we got a head constable that doesn't even know the first thing about the place he's supposed to be protecting?"

"I hadn't ever thought about it, actually," I said. "But no."

"Back in my day, we didn't even have constables, or precincts, or even jails, and we certainly didn't need protecting," Charlie grumbled. "Demons did their jobs and went home. It wasn't until you monsters came along that things started going sideways."

"I'm sure you'd like to eat away the rest of the day telling me how horrible I am and all, but I really just need help with a case."

"Lay it out for me. Obviously don't have anything else to do."

I pulled out the piece of parchment and handed it to him. "It's from—"

"I know what it's from, lady," Charlie said, snatching the paper from me. "It's from the Necronomicon."

"Akta," I replied, gritting my teeth.

"Excuse me?"

"My name is Akta," I growled at him.

"Does it look like I care?" Charlie gave me a blank stare. "Did you know it's illegal to rip pages from the Necronomicon?"

"I did not."

"It's also insulting. That's my people's most precious book, and you just destroyed it like it was toilet paper. Do you have any idea how hard it is to bind a book in human skin?"

"I do not," I answered. "Should I?"

"It's real hard," he said. "There are only six, maybe seven copies of this book in the whole of Hell, but this one is special," Charlie said, holding it up to the candle flame. "This is the original. Wow. The very first one ever made, written by Yilir and the first Devils themselves, and you destroyed it. Way to go."

"I'm sorry," I said.

"No, you're not," Charlie replied. "And don't insult me by telling me you are."

"Fine, you're right. I'm not sorry."

"Typical," Charlie said with a sigh. "Where did you find this page?"

"I stole it from a group of demons," I said. "They were sitting around a glowing pentagram, and this was in a room with a glowing symbol behind them."

"Were they chanting?"

"Oh yeah. And they did not like being disturbed."

"I wouldn't either," Charlie said. "What color was the pentagram glowing?"

"Blue, a dull blue."

Charlie held up the page. "And this was the page they had opened while they were chanting?"

"That's right," I replied. "But it was in another room in one of their houses."

"It's a locator spell, then."

"A locator spell?"

"Listen, sister. I know some of these occult concepts are hard to understand. I'll grant you that, but this one's right in the name. Locator spell. A spell. To locate. Those guys were trying to find this dagger, and if the legends are true, that means bad news for our fancy pants ruler."

"So you hate Lucifer as well?"

"Sure, I do, but I've hated them all," Charlie shrugged. "Anubis. Hades. Velaska. Lucifer's just the last in a long line of horrible rulers."

"Will you have trouble helping me protect him, then?"

Charlie shook his head. "I never had problems protecting the other fancy pants rulers, so why should this guy be any different?"

I grabbed a piece of loose parchment and drew the plateau and temple on it. "This symbol. Do you know it? It was drawn inside the hut of the demons where I stole the page. It was glowing blue as well, just like the pentagram."

Charlie raised an eyebrow. "You sure it was this symbol?" he said, pointing to it.

"Positive," I replied. "Why? Do you know it?"

Charlie nodded. "I do. It's the symbol of a new terrorist cell called the Godless. Can you guess what their mission is? I'll give you a hint. God less. Less gods."

"To kill the gods?" I answered, but not confidently.

"Bingo, and any sycophants that associate themselves with the gods, too."

"And that means Lucifer."

"And that means Lucifer. The kind of sycophants that goes crying to the gods when things don't go their way."

Charlie hopped down from his chair and waddled toward the door. "Come on. If what you say is correct, then finding the Godless means finding the dagger."

I didn't follow him. "I work alone, generally. I don't like, want, or need, a partner."

"Then you don't solve this case, sweetheart." Charlie stopped at the door and glared at me over his shoulder. "Your choice. The only way you solve this case is with me. As you've already seen, the other monsters around here…well, they don't know much about the occult."

"Will you stop insulting me?"

"No," Charlie said. "I don't like monsters, and I definitely don't like you. I've got all the cards here, darling. If you want my help to solve this thing, I come with you. Take it or leave it but make it snappy. I got plenty of other cases to work."

I took a deep breath. "Fine."

"That's a wise decision," he said.

"We'll see about that."

*

I didn't trust Charlie, not even a little bit. On top of the fact that he was a demon imp, he was also a fast talker who didn't like to explain himself. I never liked those types, even when I was alive. They tried to build your dependence on them and horde all the information so that they could use it to their advantage.

I tried to ask him all sorts of questions as we walked through the streets of Hell, but he just answered, "trust me." Whenever somebody begged me to trust them, it was a pretty good indication that I shouldn't. That kind of person was a natural liar. They kept you in the dark and spun the truth to fit their narrative. I didn't like relying on those kinds of people, but when I had to, I was sure to keep them at an arm's distance.

"Do you know how great this place was before you monsters came along?" Charlie asked. We were walking through the middle of a crowded street. "Dis was only filled with demons and imps, and we didn't care about nobody or nothing. Now, all these 'sters around—"

"Hey!" I shouted. "I don't like that word."

"Sorry, sweetheart. It's just slang."

'Ster was slang for monster, but it meant something worse than that. Demons used it to put down monsters as if we were beneath them. The politics of Hell already made our place in the natural order more than evident. I didn't need a weasely imp rubbing it in that he thought I wasn't good enough to share his air.

"Not to me, it's not," I hissed. "It's not our fault Velaska made us servants down here."

"You're right about that," Charlie said. "You got the better end of the deal, though, at least compared to humans. I mean those humans, man, they have it tough."

"You pity them?" I asked, surprised that an imp would care one way or another about the plight of humanity.

"Not pity, but they got a raw deal. You all got a raw deal. Monsters and humans alike, if you ask me."

"That is the first thing you have said I agree with, Charlie," I replied.

"Then you are gonna fit right in with B'rahg. He doesn't like anything the gods do." Charlie stopped talking for a moment, lost in thought before he continued. "On second thought…don't say anything to him. Let me do the talking, okay? Just because he doesn't like the gods, it doesn't mean he likes monsters either, you savvy?"

"I understand, if that's what you mean."

Charlie turned up a skinny alley that narrowed slightly the further along we went. He turned left, then right, and two more lefts until we ended up in a small square surrounded by tall buildings. In the center of the square, a fat orc, dressed in nothing but a loin cloth, sat on a rug. His green fat rolls hung out everywhere. Jars and vials filled with bubbling and glowing liquids of every color were scattered around him on the exquisitely stitched rug.

"Charlie," B'rahg said. His tone was smug. "I thought I told you never to come here again."

"B'rahg!" Charlie said, his voice a little too loud. "My favorite alchemist. How are you doing today?"

"Worse now," B'rahg said. "What do you want?"

"What I always want," Charlie replied. "Information."

"Always information with you," B'rahg said. "Ten Quan."

Charlie looked back at me. "Pay the man."

I sighed and reached into the pouch on my belt. It was better just to do what Charlie said and see how it played out. There was always time to make more money. I pulled out ten Quan and handed it to the alchemist. "Here."

The folds of his fat barely registered the smile on the orc's face as he took my money. "What can I do for you, pretty one?"

"We're here about the Godless," Charlie said. "What do you know about them?"

"No," B'rahg said. "No, no, no. Sorry, but I don't discuss the Godless. At least not out in the open, and definitely not at my place of business. They've got eyes everywhere. They're crazy, Charlie. You shouldn't even be saying that word out here. Who knows what's listening?"

"We need to know," I replied. "Please."

"That kind of cutesy stuff don't work on orcs, sweetie. You can't just bat your eyes and make them swoon," Charlie said. "All right, B'rahg. How much is it going to take?"

"Twenty Loo."

My eyebrows shot up. "That's highway robbery! I have my own sources, which are way cheaper than your prices."

"Not like this, you don't," Charlie said. "Show her."

The orc lifted the fat fold on his chest to reveal a tattoo of a red plateau with a temple atop it, the same one that I saw at the demon's house.

"You are one of the Godless," I said.

"No, I am a seeker of wisdom, as they are. Just because we share the same symbol does not make us the same. However, in my travels, I have come across their kind, and it has been rather unpleasant for me."

"Fine," I replied, reaching into the coin purse on my belt. I pulled out a stack of twenty Loo coins and handed them to B'rahg. "Here you go. This better be good."

"Oh, it will be," Charlie said, rubbing his hands together. "I know it will be good. This is going to be good, right, B'rahg?"

"It depends on your definition of good," B'rahg said. "It will be information, I promise you that, and the truth, which you can use for whatever ends you see fit. Good or bad, it doesn't matter to me."

I was tired of this whole thing being dragged out. "Just get on with it, okay?"

"The Godless arose shortly after Lucifer's failed attempt to take Bacchus's throne. For eons, the demons of Hell believed they were fated to serve, but Lucifer showed them there was another way. He made them believe they could have free will, and after the Fall, there were many demons who still believed they could take their freedom by force. Those demons became the Godless organization."

"These were types of monsters and demons that tried to kill Lucifer all those eons ago?"

"Yes, but the Morningstar was able to resist their assassination attempts long enough to become the Devil, which rendered all their attacks useless."

"Because nothing can kill the Devil," I replied.

"Not even Hellfire. It wasn't until the Godless found the Necronomicon, a treasure stolen right out from under me might I add, that they found a new way to kill the Devil."

"The Dagger—"

"Of Obsolescence. Yes. Since they learned of its existence, their sole mission has been to track it down and kill the Devil so that they could live free without the gods' interference."

"The other angels though…and God. Aren't they scared of retaliation?"

"The angels will never come to Hell, and the Godless know it. Once Lucifer is dead, the line will end with him, and the Godless will be free."

"Where can I find the Godless?"

B'rahg didn't respond. A sound from the alleyway startled him. I turned around to see a shadow at the end of the alley. I spun back to Charlie and saw another figure on the other side of us, holding out its arms toward me.

"What have you done?" B'rahg said breathlessly.

"Nothin'! I haven't done nothin'!" Charlie shouted frantically.

"You brought the Godless right to me!"

There was no way out. Godless demons blocked the alleyway exits with their enormous bodies. Their chanting vibrated through the air as blue fire grew in their hands. Every alley I looked down, the Godless charged fireballs in their hands, ready to blast them at us.

There was only one way out, and it was up. There was nothing blocking us from escaping into the sky. I spread my wings just as the shadows released fire from their hands that burned down the alley.

I grabbed Charlie in one hand and B'rahg in the other. I tried to lift them off the ground, but B'rahg was too heavy for me to carry.

"Leave me!" he shouted.

"Never!"

"Just leave him!" Charlie shouted. "Or you'll both die!"

"No!" I cried as the fire bore down on us.

"Son of a…" Charlie muttered under his breath. He snapped his fingers, and suddenly everything was black, just like it had been when Lucifer summoned me.

# CHAPTER 9

Charlie, B'rahg, and I reappeared upon a street corner not far from the square where we left. I didn't recognize it, but from the building markers, I knew we were still in the bowels of Dis.

"What was that?" I asked Charlie.

"It's a little thing I can do," he replied.

"I thought only gods and Devils could transport like that."

"When you've been alive as long as I have, sweetheart, you learn a thing or two about Hell and how to manipulate it to your advantage at every opportunity." Charlie brushed himself off. "Now, can we please get the information you need so we can get out of here, and I can get back to work?"

I turned to B'rahg. "Where can I find the Godless?"

"I can't tell you now." B'rahg shook his head furiously. "They'll kill me for sure."

"No, we will protect you," I said. "Go to the Central precinct. Talk to Constable Ylfingur. Tell him I sent you, and he will protect you."

"What if that doesn't work?" B'rahg said. "What if the officers are members of the Godless as well?"

"Find Ylfingur. He will make sure you are safe."

"I don't like constables," B'rahg said, still shaking his head. "They aren't…appreciative of my line of work, if you know what I mean."

"That is all I can offer you," I replied. "It is also the best chance you have of survival. Whether you help us or not, the Godless are after you."

B'rahg's eyes ping-ponged from my eyes to Charlie's and back again. "Fine. I don't know where they are, but I know a name. Aziolith. It is a name that flows from their tongues like the wind flows through the streets of Dis during a sandstorm."

That caught my attention. "Aziolith? The Dragon? Are you sure they said that name?"

B'rahg nodded. "I will never forget it for all my days."

"Crap."

"What is it?" Charlie said.

"I killed him…and I'll bet he's still raw about it."

"Well, I hope he's forgiving, cuz if not, he'll swallow you whole without a second thought."

*

We left B'rahg and set off across the streets of Dis. I wasn't about to take the advice of one of Charlie's informants without verifying it with Beatrice and Clovis.

"I still don't see why we need to get advice from a little twerp," Charlie said as we walked down the main street of Dis.

"You have your sources, and I have mine."

"Your source is a baby," Charlie said.

"She's not a baby. She's a child that's hundreds of years old."

"Whatever. Child. Baby. It's the same thing."

"It's not—look, just let me do the talking, okay?" I replied. "We did things your way and almost got killed. Now, we'll do things my way."

I heard Beatrice before I saw her, but that wasn't unusual. She was bigger than life, laughing on the top of the wooden stand which acted as her storefront and heckling everyone that passed her.

"I know you need new shoes," she shouted. "You're are P-U-uuugly!"

The ogre she insulted passed with a grumpy *harrumph*.

"You aren't going to catch many customers by insulting them," I said.

"You don't have to catch many," she replied. "Just enough."

"And you'll turn off the rest," I said.

"You know anything about sales, kid?" Beatrice asked, cocking her head to one side.

"Kid!" Charlie gruntled. "She looks older than you."

"No, she ain't," Beatrice screamed into Charlie's face. "I've been here longer than that pixie, and that makes her a kid. Who are you anyway? Another stray she's bringing me who needs help?"

"I ain't no stray, kid!" Charlie snapped.

"All right, sorry, sorry," Beatrice said, throwing up her hands in apology. "Don't get your knickers in a twist. It's just you look a little homeless." She held out a pair of her father's loafers. "Maybe a new pair of shoes will help."

Charlie pushed the shoes away. "I ain't buyin' no shoes from a flippin' kid."

"Hey!" I shouted to Charlie. "What did I tell you?"

"I ain't, though," Charlie grumbled as his eyes fell to the ground. "But whatever. I'll shut up, I guess."

"See that you do," I replied.

Beatrice hopped down from her stand. "So, what? Did you find more info out about that thing you were searching for?"

I nodded. "I did. Have you ever heard of the Godless?"

"Who hasn't?" Clovis said from behind the booth. Like always, he was deep in concentration, mending a pair of shoes. "I wouldn't be much of an informant if we hadn't heard of the Godless."

"And yet, they didn't come up last time we talked," I replied.

"They didn't not come up either, if I recall," Clovis said, looking up from his shoes. "I just said I needed more information. What are they after?"

I leaned in toward them and spoke with a whisper. "The Dagger of Obsolescence."

"Whoa," Beatrice said. "They really are going after the big man, huh?"

"Yes, it seems like they do plan to assassinate the Morningstar, and I believe they have found the means to do so," I nodded. "But they don't seem to know where it is, not yet at least."

"So, what? You need a clue to where it might be?" Beatrice said. "Twenty Loo."

"I'll make it fifty," I replied. "If you can give me the location of Aziolith's lair."

"That washed up, has been dragon?" Beatrice scoffed. "Why do you want to go all the way there?"

"Don't you worry about that, kid!" Charlie shouted. "That's need-to-know only."

"And I need to know…cuz I wanna." Beatrice turned to me. "He's sensitive, huh?"

I nodded. "You don't know the half of it. Our last informant nearly got us killed, and he's a little raw about me not trusting a word that fat, little orc said."

"Almost got you killed?" Clovis said with a snarky smile. "Then, thank you for stopping by."

"Do you know where the cave is, or don't you?" I asked, rummaging through the money bag on my belt.

Beatrice held out her hand. "Do you have fifty Loo, or don't you?"

I reached into my coin purse and pulled out fifty Loo. The laughing face of Velaska on the back of the coin mocked me derisively. "There."

"Then we can do business," Beatrice said, pushing the coins into her hand. "You ever been to the caverns on the edges of Hell?"

"No."

"Well, that's where you're going today. Watch yourself. Dragons live all over that place. If you piss off one of them, you'll be digesting in their stomach for the next century."

"Then make sure you give me proper directions," I replied.

"Let me draw you a map."

*

After getting directions from Beatrice, Charlie transported us to the caverns on the edge of Hell itself. From the cliffs beyond the caverns, I could see across all of Hell. The

Brambles of Agony still burned as brightly as they had when the Godless demons set fire to them. If I strained my ears enough, I could make out the sound of their shrieks as they shriveled up.

Few ever ventured to the edges of Hell, and far fewer climbed the cliffs lining the caverns. Dragons enjoyed the solitude and comfort which came with living away from the drudgery of Hell. It made sense why Aziolith would pick such a remote place for his home. Though he made his name attacking villages for their treasures, most of his time was spent in the peace of solitude.

That's why it was so hard to track him back on Earth. He would attack quickly and violently and then retreat to the mountains where he kept his lair. Nobody knew exactly where it was located.  We only knew it was high in the mountain peaks where none dared travel. Even if we could have found it, we would have been so tired from the climb that the great dragon would have slaughtered us easily.

I stalked him for many moons, following his trail of carnage, before I finally came across a town he was in the middle of attacking. The battle was fierce and brutal. It lasted days without rest. Finally, we wore each other down enough for me to land the fatal blow on Aziolith's stomach that sent him down to the pits of Hell.

"There's something I never understood about dragons," I said, pulling myself up the rock cliff. "Why do they get a pass from working a job in Hell?" I asked as Charlie and I climbed up the cliff toward the cave entrance above us. "Why can Aziolith lie around all day without lifting a finger while we're down here slaving away?"

"I don't think he gets a pass," Charlie said, grunting as he hiked himself up above a rock. "Demons tried to put dragons to work for a long time, and most of the time, they were eaten, in one gulp, just as easy as I can snap my fingers. After a while, we just left them alone. They aren't hurting nobody, and it's not like we need a dragon roaming around eating demons."

I laughed. "I have never heard of a demon who feared anything before."

"We ain't scared of him or nothin'," Charlie replied. "We just don't need the headache, all right? I mean, dragons are a pain. They're big, strong, and stubborn. Some of 'em can't wait to torture humans, but others want to keep to themselves, and it's more trouble than they're worth to fight with a dragon."

"I thought demons were the biggest, baddest beings in Hell."

"We are," Charlie replied. "But dragons aren't far behind. Us demons can take the heat, but the dragons, they love it. They make it. They were born in fire and lived in volcanos. This is like paradise to them."

"What about ice dragons?" I replied with a smirk.

"All right," Charlie replied snidely. "I'm not a teacher, and this ain't a lesson. School is over."

"Fine with me," I said. "We're here anyway."

I pulled myself up on the ledge of the cliff. I could have flown us to the top of the cliff, but frankly, I wasn't too excited to see the dragon, not even after eight hundred years. I barely came away with my life the last time we'd met, and I had no interest in being digested in Aziolith's belly for the next hundred years.

"You sure this is the place?" Charlie asked as he peered into the cave.

I looked down at my map. There was a big red "X" right at the cave entrance where I stood. "If Beatrice says this is the place, this is the place."

"Go away," a deep, growling voice echoed out of the cave. "I have no interest in visitors today."

"Aziolith?" I asked hesitantly.

There was a groan. "Go away."

The sound of his voice sent shivers down my spine. I was rarely scared, but Aziolith terrified me to my core. My battle with him was the closest I ever came to death, at least until my dear brother-king Odgeir poisoned me. Still, I could not show him weakness under any circumstances. He would sense it. I was a proud warrior, and if my fate be another death, then so be it.

"I have questions for you, dragon," I said, puffing out my chest. "And you will answer them."

A long streak of fire blew out of the cave, and I dodged to avoid it. "I recognize your voice, pixie, even after nearly a millennium."

I gulped. "And I yours."

"I knew the day would come when we met again. Frankly, I thought it would be sooner."

"I have not needed to call on you until today," I replied. "And thus, I have kept my distance. I do not hunt for sport, only for duty."

The ground quaked under me as the great dragon Aziolith rose to his feet. Fire blew out of his nose, and I caught a glimpse of the beast through the flickering shadow. His neck stretched long in the cramped confines of the cave, and when he snarled with his pointed mouth, a row of razor-sharp teeth showed. Thick, red scales covered him from his head all the way down to the talons on his feet.

A barbed tail swung toward us as I rose into the air, and Charlie disappeared himself to avoid it. "If you want a fight, pixie, I can accommodate. I have been in hibernation for the past hundred years, but I have dreamed of our rematch since I first came here."

Aziolith's only weakness was his soft underbelly. When he rose onto his back legs, I saw an opening to slice him open but did not take it. I was not there to fight. I was there for information, and I would not take his bait to appease his bloodlust.

"I do not come for a fight," I said, refusing to touch my daggers.

Aziolith slammed his front claws onto the ground. For a moment, I thought he would strike, but his head only cocked to one side.

"No," he replied. "You are not here to fight, are you?"

"Are you kidding?" Charlie said, throwing punches into the air. "Take him down!"

"No!" I shook my head. "I vanquished him for his crimes once already. If the need to fight should arise, then I will do so again. Count on it. But all I've heard about Aziolith so far has been rumors and conjecture."

"And what have you heard about me?" The dragon took a step into the light, curious.

"The Godless, and your place among them."

"Oh gods, that group infuriates me," Aziolith growled. "Come inside."

"Are you crazy?" Charlie said. "We're not going inside with him. Please, tell me we are not going inside with him."

I took a few steps after Aziolith, then turned to Charlie. "You do not have to come with me, but I am going inside."

"This is a bad idea."

"I'm already in Hell, imp. What is the worst that can happen now?"

"Digesting in the stomach of a dragon isn't enough for you?"

I shook my head. "Quit being a baby and come inside. We are being very rude."

"Oh yeah, wouldn't want to be rude to a dragon, would we?"

"No, we would not," I replied. "They take offense to that kind of thing."

# CHAPTER 10

Aziolith's cavern was filled to the brim with treasure. Towers of gold balanced haphazardly all around, with beautiful, silver armor strewn about like it was garbage. Bronze swords and axes tossed carelessly around shimmered like gems in the dim light. The dragon seemed to have half the valuables in Hell in his cavern.

"Where did you get all this stuff?" I asked.

Aziolith chuckled as he lit the torches on the wall with his nose. "This is a bit embarrassing to admit, but a fair number of monsters consider me a deity."

I raised my eyebrows, surprised. Then I laughed. "That is funny."

Aziolith's eyes narrowed. "It's not that funny." His nose lit a pile of wood in the middle of the cave, and the whole cavern lit up. "I was seen as a deity by many on Earth as well. You think that I stole my wealth, but much of it was freely given."

"Sure," I said. "But it was given mostly because they feared you."

"Are gods not worthy of fear?" This time, Aziolith laughed. "Besides, monsters did not fear me, they adored me. I did what they could not, single-handedly attacked humans and made them pay for what they did to us."

"And what did they do?" I asked.

"Hunted us, degraded us, forced us to live in squalor. No, not I. I lived like a king. That's a very appealing proposition to a certain class of monster, and why they still worship me here, along with my kin."

"That's crazy," Charlie said, walking cautiously behind us. "They know the gods are real. Why would they worship you?"

"Most have never seen a god before, little imp." Aziolith stretched out behind the fire. "They have seen me, and I have been able to avoid working in hell for the last millennium. If that doesn't make me a bit of a god, then what does?"

"The blood of the gods," Charlie muttered.

"That is simply a matter of opinion." Aziolith gave a sly smile, then turned to me. "Now, what is it you wish to know about the Godless?"

I didn't hold back. "Are you their leader?"

"Wow," Aziolith said. "You always were blunt, I will give you that. Let me ask you, if I were the head of the Godless, do you think I would tell you?"

"Yes, I do," I said. "We have battled in combat, and there is a bond there which requires truth and honor."

"Maybe for you," Aziolith shrugged. "Not for me. Still, I will tell you honestly that I have no connection to the Godless."

"But you know who they are?" Charlie asked.

"Of course, imp," Aziolith replied. "Many see me as a god, as I have said. Still, others see me as the only one who could defeat a god. In that way, many have come to me for help and offered gifts in exchange for my assistance."

"Sounds like they're just replacing one god for another," I muttered under my breath.

"Yes, but the gods demand obedience. I do not."

"No, only shiny things."

"I have a weakness for that which shimmers." Aziolith chuckled. "There is nothing wrong with having particular proclivities, pixie. It certainly does not mean I work with the Godless."

"You're saying you have no affiliation with the Godless?" I asked.

"I have told you no. Asking more forcefully will not change my answer."

"It's impossible you're not one of 'em!" Charlie shouted. "My buddy says you are part of it, and I'm saying he's right. Akta, beat it out of him!"

Aziolith let out a deep sigh. "I tire of this game. I suppose I could just eat you both and be done with it, or you could leave of your own free will. I don't know many gods who would offer a choice like that."

I pulled the page of the Necronomicon out of my cloak. "I believe you."

"Either way is fine by me," Aziolith replied. "It doesn't matter to me whether you trust me or not."

"May I ask you one final question?" I asked, unfolding the parchment.

"If you must, but hurry, the fire in my belly grows for pixie flesh."

I held up the image of the dagger for Aziolith to see in the fire light. "Do you recognize this dagger?"

Aziolith dragged his head forward for a closer look. His eyes lit up. "The Dagger of Obsolescence! It is a fine prize. I would be lying if I said I didn't ache for it. I have many treasures here, but I have longed for that one since I first arrived in Hell."

I folded the picture and placed it back in my cloak. "So do the Godless. Maybe that is why people think you are connected."

"Perhaps. I have desired it for a long time, but I am not willing to pay the price to win it for myself."

"Win it?" Charlie exclaimed. "Does that mean you know where it is?"

"I do, imp," Aziolith growled. "But I will not share it with the likes of you."

I stepped forward. "Then share it with me."

"You killed me, pixie!" Aziolith said. "Why should I help you?"

"If you do me this favor, I will bring you the Dagger once I have no need for it anymore."

Aziolith looked me up and down before letting out a puff of fire at my feet. "Why should I believe the pixie who killed me?"

"I have earned passage to Valhalla and walked upon the plains of Mount Olympus. I would not have done so if I was not bound by duty and honor. Of all the monsters in Hell, you can trust me most of all."

"Why do you seek it?" the dragon asked.

"There is a plot against the Morningstar, and I have sworn to protect the Devil at all costs."

"And you will bring it to me when you find it?"

"By my honor."

"Very well," he said. "It is in the tenth level of Hell, through the Bog of Bile, and through the unspeakable evil which curdles the will of all who pass through it."

The tenth level of Hell. The worst place in all of Hell. A place that would drive mad even the best warrior in the universe in a matter of days. Few could withstand its punishing torment, and yet, luckily, I knew one who could.

"How do I find the dagger?"

"Follow the path to the bottom of the pit, cross the bogs, and you will find the dagger buried in the ground below the far wall of the pit."

"Very well," I said. "I will return when I have it in my possession."

"You had better."

"You have my word." I turned to Charlie. "Take us back to the central precinct. I need to have words with a goblin held there."

And with that, Charlie took my hand, and we vanished into the ether. If we were going to get into the tenth level of Hell, I would need to get back to the Central Precinct for Yancy's help. I only hoped nothing horrible had happened to him yet.

*

Charlie and I reappeared inside the lobby of the Central Precinct, scaring a couple of gnomes shackled to the bench next to reception.

"Thank you for the help," I said to Charlie as I walked away from him. "I will see you around."

"Whoa!" Charlie said, scurrying after me. "If you think I'm just gonna let you get all the credit for this, you're crazy. You're about to track down the greatest treasure in Hell, and I'm gonna be there when you do."

"This isn't about credit. This is about saving the Devil's life."

"And finding one of the greatest treasures in Hell in the process. Do you know how famous I'm gonna be when I find it?" He rubbed his hands together. "So, so famous."

I shook my head. "No, you cannot say anything to anyone about our quest."

"Watch me!" Charlie turned to the crowd of constables. "Excuse me! Can I have your attention? I have some big ne—"

I clapped my hand over Charlie's mouth. "Fine. You can come along on the condition that you say nothing to nobody. Got it?"

Charlie smiled at me as I removed my hand from his mouth. "Who am I gonna tell?"

"Say it," I replied.

"I promise not to tell anybody about anything related to the dagger, all right?"

I stormed toward the back of the precinct. "That almost sounded believable. Fine, you can come, but no dawdling. Time is of the essence."

Charlie followed closely behind me, pounding his stubby legs as fast as he could. "I don't know how good a promise is with you, though, after you just lied to that nice dragon."

"I didn't lie," I said quickly. "How dare you accuse me of such a thing!"

"Please," Charlie replied. "You think Lucifer is going to let that thing out of his sight after you bring it to him?"

"No, I don't," I said. "But I didn't lie either. I promised I would bring it to him. I didn't say I would leave it with him."

Charlie cackled. "That's rich. A lie of omission is still a lie, sister."

"Says you."

"Says everybody!" Charlie sighed a contented sigh. "You know, I like you. You come across as a wet blanket, but you have the cunning of an imp buried deep in your cold, dark soul."

"That is not a compliment."

"Says you."

"Says everybody."

Ylfingur sat at his desk and was filling out paperwork with his quill when we arrived in his office. "I'm very busy, Akta. What do you want?"

"I need to use your goblin, the one I brought in here before."

"I'm afraid I can't help you there," Ylfingur said. "He's gone."

"Gone!" I shouted. "How could you lose him?"

"I didn't lose him." His voice was terse. "A couple of demons from the tenth pit came by earlier today and took him for processing back to the pits. He wasn't very helpful, and I wasn't very patient."

"Oh no," I said. "You have no idea what you've done."

Ylfingur gave me a quizzical look. "No, I don't." He focused on his work again. "Luckily, I don't care either."

I turned to Charlie. We didn't have to speak. He knew what we had to do. I latched onto his arm, and he disappeared us from the police station. If I had stayed another second, I might have ripped Ylfingur in half, but now I had bigger problems. The Godless were going after the Dagger, and I couldn't let that happen. I had to get there first.

We reappeared at the entrance to the tenth level of Hell. The stench was unbearable, even from a hundred yards away. Black bile and green fumes oozed from the pit like a geyser. In front of us were Tygil and her demon lackeys, who nearly engulfed me in flame at the Brambles of Agony, leading Yancy past the security goblins and orcs directly into the pit. There was no choice in the matter. We had to go into the pit after them.

# CHAPTER 11

There were no unauthorized entries into the pits of Hell. Every soul needed to be accounted for in the great ledgers at the entrance to each pit, which were written by the goblins, and transcribed by the imps at the Ministry of Records. They oversaw every soul in Hell. If there was a problem with any of the accounting, the imps sent out one of their own to deal with it, and that's what gave me an idea of how to sneak into the tenth pit and catch up with the Godless.

"I don't want to go in there," Charlie whined as we looked over the cliff above the pit. "The pits are the pits. Besides, do I look like I'm from the Ministry of Records?"

"Kind of," I said. "All you imps look the same, though."

"Oh, look who's being racist now, Akta. We don't all look the same! Imps from the ministry have longer noses and fatter stomachs. Nobody's gonna believe that I'm one of them. Look at how skinny I am."

I poked him in the stomach. "Are you saying you're not a good enough liar to get us into the pits?"

Charlie's eyes flashed. "Well, no. I'm a great liar. Maybe the best there's ever been."

"Now that I believe," I said. "And even if you don't believe it, I need you to lie to yourself, okay? Because you are our only chance. You have to go, and you take me with you."

"How would this work?" Charlie was starting to do the math. "You're not in the ledger. In order to get into the pits, you need to be on the goblin's ledger."

"Figure it out. Say you audited the books and your higher-ups found out I was supposed to be here. I don't really care. Just be convincing."

"You realize if we get trapped down there, you'll be stuck forever, right?" Charlie asked. "Cuz from where I'm sitting, you're really good at getting yourself into trouble and kind of a mess at getting yourself out of it."

"I understand," I told him. "But that doesn't change the fact that we're Lucifer's only hope, so you have to make this work."

Charlie sighed. "If you insist on going into the pits, then I have a plan. You gotta act like my prisoner, though. I'll figure the rest out as we go."

I pulled a length of rope out of my belt and handed it to Charlie. "Tie me up, then."

Charlie grabbed the rope and pulled it taut around my hands. "My pleasure."

"Not too tightly," I warned him. "I don't quite trust you yet."

"That's a good instinct." Charlie finished the knot. "Never trust anybody in Hell."

He pulled the rope, yanking me forward. We walked down the hill and onto the dirt path which led up to the tenth pit's entrance. Its putrid smell made me wretch.

"I despise the stench of the pits," I said as we neared the goblin guarding the gates. "And this one is the worst. I have never smelt a bog so foul."

"That's hope, sweetheart. The smell of hope washing away from every terrible soul in the bowels of the tenth pit."

"It reeks of sulfuric acid and burned man-flesh." I could barely talk through my dry heaves.

"That's what hope smells like…plus they do burn people with acid down there, so it might be a bit of that as well."

I buried my nose in my shoulder. "It smells worse than anywhere else in Hell."

"Well, it should. It's got the worst people in history down there. Think about your Alexander the Great's, your Genghis Khan's, your Socrates, worst of the worst. And the worst punishments are reserved for the worst people, which makes it smell the worst. Now, shut up."

Charlie pushed me to the ground and spoke to the goblin on duty. "I got a live one for you."

The pudgy goblin looked up from her ledger. "I'm afraid you are mistaken. I don't have any new souls expected today."

"This one isn't new," Charlie said. "She was misplaced."

"Hmm," the goblin said, eyeballing her paperwork. "Pixie, is it? We aren't missing one of those. Your records must be faulty."

"I don't think so," Charlie said. "Your records are faulty. We just audited our books, and this one slipped through a thousand years ago. Ended up in level two instead of level ten where she belongs."

"Highly unlikely," the goblin said. "I am meticulous with my notes. Besides, monsters are no longer subject to torture."

"Anymore," Charlie said. "But she's not grandfathered into the dark lord's reprieve. A thousand years ago, she was a real piece of work, and she's been skating by in a much nicer pit than she deserves."

"Please, mister," I shouted, trying to pull away from him. "Don't make me go inside. I can be good, better than good."

"Doesn't seem that bad to me," the goblin said.

"You ever been tortured for a thousand years?" Charlie said. "It makes cowards out of the strongest among them."

"Do you have your papers?"

"Are you saying you don't believe me?" Charlie asked, his tone dangerously hostile. "I am a representative of Lucifer. To deny me is to deny him. Are you calling the Morningstar a liar?"

The goblin gulped loudly. Behind her, three demons appeared out of the putrid smoke and growled at her. They waited in the shadows for a soul to send to damnation and were none too happy the goblin was denying their prize. They were even less happy that she was arguing with one of Lucifer's minions, given she was only a goblin and thus inferior to demon and imp kind.

"No, of course not," the goblin said. "Please…don't even say a thing like that. Even the mere accusation could get me sent to the pits for eternity."

"I have bad news for you," I mumbled. "You're already in the pits, lady."

Charlie turned around and backhanded me across the face. "Shut up!"

He used as much force as he could muster, and though he would surely say it was an act, I felt the joy in his knuckles as they knocked against my cheek.

"Now," Charlie continued, "we have two options. Either you allow me to take this whelp to her torture, or I bring her to the Morningstar and tell him that you denied her entrance to the pits. Which will it be?"

The goblin turned toward the demons behind her, who inched forward slowly as she debated her options. "Fine, what do I care anyway? It's just another one to torture. The demons will love that." She read down her ledger. "There we go. There's space in unit twenty-three. I hope she enjoys being eaten alive by scorpions."

"I don't," I said.

This time Charlie didn't slap me. Instead, he punched me in the eye and knocked me into the ground. Even though he was small, he packed a mean punch.

"Leave some for the demons, please," the goblin said. "They demand all their souls be pristine upon torture."

"I'll get her fixed up before I take her to her final rest. Don't you worry about that."

"Very good," the goblin said as we disappeared into the bog. My body convulsed at the rotten stench of decaying hope.

*

The sound of human suffering rang in my ears as we descended deeper into the pit. All around me, a symphony of whips, chains, and iron maidens echoed against the pit walls. Bones cracked and skin ripped. Dis, the Brambles of Agony, any other place in Hell seemed pleasant compared to the unending suffering here.

"Now, what?" I asked as Charlie untied me. "We just walk around this pit until we go insane?"

"You might go insane, but I won't. I'm going to be just fine. The sound of torture soothes me. I hate walking, though, so I have a plan to find the dagger. Do you have anything that touched the goblin we're tracking?"

I looked down at the rope binding my hands. It was the same rope I used to bind runaway monsters. I'd used it on Yancy. "Only this rope that you bound me with and my bare hands."

Charlie grabbed the rope with both of his hands and closed his eyes. He hummed under his breath until his hands glowed blue around the rope. The light from his hands formed into an orb and rose above his body. Charlie opened his eyes, and the light descended into the abyss.

"That's a locator spell. If they can use it to find the dagger, then we can use it to find them."

I thought that the pit would be more frightening to the eyes, but the stench of hope draining off the tortured souls obscured everything around us. We were surrounded by fog in every direction, with nothing but the blue light of the locator spell for guidance. It led us like a beacon.

We listened for demons walking about, but they could have been six inches away, and we wouldn't have seen them. We descended all the way to the bottom of the pit, following the blinking blue light as we went. Eventually, the winding walkway dead-ended at a muddy embankment.

"Be very careful," Charlie said, stepping into the mud at the bottom of the pit. "This is the Bog of Bile. Those who have been tortured into nothingness come here to regenerate themselves. Their hopelessness gathers here, and it will quickly consume you if you let it."

"What does that mean?"

"You'll sink into the bog forever if you don't think happy thoughts."

"How do you think happy thoughts in Hell?"

"Well, I don't know about you, but thinking about you burning alive in a vat of acid does it for me."

"The bog affects you too?"

"It affects everything."

I felt myself deflating inwardly. The last of my hope was already draining from me. Hope was the only thing we had to hold on to in Hell. It was our one defiance to the dark lord. We could hold on to hope and the knowledge that it might get better in time, or we could fall into despair. Abandoning hope was the first step to accepting fate. Once hope was lost, then the true suffering could begin.

"Why are we even trying? It's useless." I trudged through the bog, my legs falling deeper into the sludge with each step.

"Think happy thoughts, Akta. Happy, happy thoughts." Charlie kept urging me. "Definitely don't ask stupid questions."

I closed my eyes and remembered Valhalla. I remembered my mother. I remembered walking through the fields of tulips outside the great castle. I often dreamed of Valhalla in my worst moments, and it always warmed my heart. One day, I would return to the great halls. One day, I would regain my freedom from the dark lord. One day, I would be free.

I felt slightly better. Better enough to open my eyes. A small smile returned to my face, but it soon washed away as the hopelessness returned. In my darkest moments, the glimmer of hope my mother gave me could keep me going for hours, maybe days, but here in the pits, it lasted mere moments.

"Watch yourself," Charlie said. "The glow is getting brighter. The demons must be close."

"Dig, you ignorant idiot!" a voice bellowed out from the fog near us. The voice was familiar. It was from the town. It was one of the demons. Tygil. Her voice pierced the air like a knife. It gave me hope.

"That's them," I said. "They must have found the dagger."

"Shhh!" Charlie said. "They'll hear you."

I opened my wings and fluttered into the air, my feet unsticking themselves from the bog. My head cleared almost immediately, even though I was mere inches higher than where I'd just stood.

"Wait!" Tygil shouted. "Did you hear that?"

"I don't hear nothin'," a demon shouted back to her.

"It's probably just a damned soul screaming out," one of the other demons replied. "It's like music to my ears."

A *thunk* reverberated through the air; the sound of a shovel hitting a wooden box. Yancy shouted up to them. "I found something."

"Pull it up!" Tygil said. "Pull it up!"

The demons grunted as they lifted the heavy box. Its metal sides crunched against the soggy ground as the bog molded around it. The demons clamored. "Say the thing. Say the thing!"

"Right!" Tygil replied.

We inched ourselves closer to the demons. We were right next to them now, so close I could feel their hot breath on my arm. The locator spell illuminated their shadows through the bog.

"*G'hyi'lu F'itu'lj M'yqeti!*" Tygil exclaimed.

A red glow filled the air as the box creaked open on its rusty hinges. The demons scuttled around it. Tygil reached into the box and lifted a glowing, red dagger into the air.

"The Dagger of Obsolescence!" they shouted. "Huzzah!"

"Let's get them, Charl—" I looked over at Charlie, but he wasn't there. Instead, I saw him reappear in a flash in front of the demons.

"Well done, boys!" Charlie was clapping his hands. "I'll be taking that."

"Charlie!" Tygil shouted. "I didn't expect to see you here. Where is the pixie?"

Charlie took in a great breath of air and blew it out. The fog parted, and there I saw them. Charlie, standing in front of the six demons, grinning at me. One of them was Tygil, and another one had one good eye. Yancy stood there, quaking in his boots as a shovel hung loosely by his side.

"I told you not to trust anybody, remember?"

Without saying another word, Charlie stabbed Yancy the goblin through the eye with the Dagger of Obsolescence. Instead of falling to the ground, Yancy's body glowed red for a moment and then fell apart as if it were made of dirt. A red streak of light broke apart from the dirt floating in the air and was sucked into the sinewy, curved dagger as if it had claimed the goblin's soul.

"Yes," Charlie said, eyeing the blade. "This will do nicely to take down the dark lord."

"Charlie," I shouted. "What are you doing?"

"You guys take care of her." Charlie pointed in my direction. "Make sure she doesn't get away. I'll take this to our assassin friend. There's no stopping us now."

The demons turned to me as Charlie snapped his fingers and vanished. I had been double-crossed by that slimy imp.

# CHAPTER 12

I pulled two throwing daggers from my belt and stood ready. I had never fought a full-grown demon and won. I had taken out imps and other monsters, but never a full-grown demon. In fact, every time I had ever gone up against one, I had nearly gotten myself eviscerated.

"I'm gonna rip you into a thousand pieces," Tygil said with a snarl. "And I'm going to enjoy it."

I dropped my feet to the ground to more power into my throw. When I landed, I flung both daggers. They embedded in Tygil's hide, but she did not even flinch. It was useless. I couldn't defeat a full-grown demon on my best day, let alone six of them.

I stepped backward through the bog. Immediately, what little hope I had left drained out of me. I would never leave these pits, not if the demons had anything to say about it. As my stomach sunk into my knees, I dropped into the bog below me. I saw other men and women in there with me, moaning despondently.

No.

I couldn't let myself disappear into hopelessness. I flapped my wings and looked upward, gripping two more daggers tightly in each hand. Thoughts of my mother filled my head again, and slowly my feet dislodged from the bog, and I floated back into the air.

One of the demons hurled a fireball, and I ducked to avoid it. I fired the four daggers in rapid succession. The demons were strong, but they were clumsy. Perhaps I could use that against them. Also, the bog was small and tight. I was made for flying in small spaces; they weren't. They couldn't open their wings.

"What are you going to do when Satan finds out about your betrayal?" I turned my face upward while I shouted so that my voice would carry.

"Nobody will ever find out about that!" Tygil snarled back.

"You are trying to use the Dagger of Obsolescence to kill the Devil, and you don't think anyone will find out?"

From above me, I heard a demon shout down into the Bog of Bile. "Did you hear that? Somebody is trying to kill the Devil!"

"That's right!" I screamed up through the pit. "These demons are trying to kill the Morningstar!"

"Shut up!" one of the demons with Tygil growled, throwing a fireball that I dodged easily. "SHUT UP!"

But I wouldn't shut up. I saw the fear spring into their faces as the demons above rushed toward them, closer and closer with each passing second. "I wonder what the other demons would say if they knew you were trying to USURP THE DEVIL! They wouldn't like it, would they?"

"Stop it," Tygil said, sniveling. "Don't you understand? Don't you understand we're just trying to help all of you?"

All around, her demon crew started to cry with her. They were shrinking into the bog. Soon enough, they were buried up to their waists.

"We just wanted to help," one of the demons whined.

"No," I replied. "You wanted to rule."

With the demons firmly embedded in the ground, I flapped my wings and flew away. I disappeared into the fog just as three torturer demons landed on the ground and stomped toward their new arrivals. I hoped they would be cruel to the demon traitors, but I didn't have time to find out. I had a Devil to save from assassination.

*

"Lucifer," I said as I flew high in the air above the pits. "If you can hear me. I need to speak with you now. I need to speak with you NOW."

I couldn't wait for a reply. Lucifer had told me he was having trouble hearing thoughts, that everything around this plot was fuzzy. I had to find him first.

I had no idea where the assassin would come from, but I knew the quickest way to Lucifer's castle was not through the Lake of Fire and up the stairs to the front entrance.

There was a back entrance carved into the cliffs beyond the Brambles of Agony. The purple door. On the other side of the cliffs was the lake of fire, but the door led travelers underneath the lake.

Very few people knew about the purple door. I'd learned about it centuries before, during Velaska's reign. The door led into a secret grotto beyond the Devil's personal dungeon. For countless millennia, the door had been guarded by my friend Quinn, a lizard monster who possessed a magic staff that could open the door. To my knowledge, it was the only item that could open it.

The staff was lost to me, though. Lucifer killed Quinn in the same battle he killed the fallen angel Zharaqiel. When Quinn died, her body fell into the Brambles of Agony, along with the staff that granted access to the purple door.

I had tried to retrieve the staff in the Brambles multiple times since then but to no avail. Now that the Brambles were on fire, though, perhaps I could find the staff in the embers of the dead vines.

The smoke was thick, and the fire was raging high into the air when I reached the Brambles. Their shrieks echoed for miles, the fire consuming every inch of their thorny visage. They flailed their vines high into the air as I neared them, begging for relief, but no relief would come. One thing Hell had in very small supply was water, and that's what the Brambles desperately needed to douse their flames.

The Brambles were thick with smoke as I flew over them, but they were also distracted by their pain, which meant I had a chance to look for the staff without being caught by their tangled vines. If I could find the staff, I could swoop down and retrieve it before the Brambles knew I existed.

Except, I didn't need to find the staff.

When I landed on the cliff, the purple door was ajar. Somebody had already opened it. Of course. Charon would never shepherd anybody across the lake who wished to harm the Devil, which meant the purple door was their only access point to the castle. They must have found the staff in the fire and were on their way to kill the Devil. I couldn't let that happen. I swallowed all my fear and disappeared inside into the black void.

This secret back entrance to the castle might let travelers bypass the lake of fire, but it also meant traversing this black valley where the Nothings lived. The Nothings were beings that filled you with dread; they moved through the semi-permeable membrane of Hell and Earth and fed on the living. They feasted on our loneliness and pain, swirling them around before they disappeared, leaving people feeling hollow inside in their wake. If I could survive the Nothings, I could make it quickly into Lucifer's castle.

The light from my wings barely glowed as I made my way through the dark void. I was heading toward a pinprick of light shining in the darkness. I took a deep breath and pushed thoughts of Hell out of my mind. Instead, I thought back to my time in Valhalla, of drinking with my warrior friends, of cavorting naked as often as I wanted, and of the total bliss which I have rarely felt since I left its walls. It was true that down in Hell I was able to hunt and use my talents, but up there, I didn't need any of that to feel happy. I was happy just existing. I was happy. I was happy. I was happy.

Just like the Bog of Bile, the Nothings fed on bad thoughts. It made them stronger, and the stronger they became, the more they manifested as your worst nightmares. But I wouldn't lose myself to the darkness. I would fight. I would beat my inner demons, just like I beat the ones in the Bog of Bile. I would save the day because that is what heroes did, and I was a hero. With those last thoughts, the light washed over me and spat me out into a garden grotto.

This little grove was once the prize of Velaska's castle, but it had fallen into disrepair under Lucifer's rule. No longer was the ground lush and beautiful. No longer did the brook babble or the waterfall cascade. It was sad to see the garden in such a state. Everything in it was dull, gray, and dead. Charon's great love, Yilir, who built the grotto as a respite from Hell's dark ugliness, would be upset if she knew what became of it. I had no time to dwell on its derelict nature, not while I had more important work to attend.

"Lucifer," I shouted. "Can you hear me?"

"Yes." His voice echoed loudly inside my own head. "Where are you?"

"I'm in your castle," I said. "I need to see you. Bring me to you now."

"How did you—"

"No time to explain," I insisted. "Just do it."

A snap rang through the grotto, and the blackness engulfed me. I rematerialized inside a study, adorned from floor to ceiling with leather-bound books. Lucifer was seated in a high-back leather chair in front of a roaring fire that lit half of the room. The other half was shrouded in darkness.

"What are you playing at?" Lucifer asked, placing down his book, "invading my castle without my permission?"

Two beady, yellow eyes peered at me from the darkened part of the room behind Lucifer. When the Devil stood to confront me, the Dagger of Obsolescence left the assassin's hand and flung through the room, end over end. A red flame consumed the air as the dagger hurtled toward Lucifer.

"Get down!" I shouted.

I pushed the Devil onto the floor. The dagger flew above our heads and embedded itself into the wall behind us. With one swift motion, I jumped up and pulled the dagger out of the wall, then flung it back across the room. It landed between the yellow eyes of Lucifer's would-be assassin. The yellow eyes in the darkness faded into the surrounding darkness. A moment later, a red flame swirled into the air, and the Dagger of Obsolescence captured the flame in its hilt.

"What was that?" Lucifer asked as I picked the dagger up off the floor.

"That," I said, holding the blade in the air to inspect it, "was an assassination attempt." The weapon was bigger than I imagined and heavier. It was forged with black metal and inlaid with runes from a dead language I didn't recognize. The handle was black and gnarled like the sinewy hilt, and the knobby handle bulged in my hand.

"The Dagger of Obsolescence," Lucifer breathed. "You found it."

"I think 'found' is a bit of an exaggeration, given the circumstances," I replied. "But yes. It is here."

"Give it to me," Lucifer said. "I will hide it at once."

"I'm afraid I can't do that, my liege."

"Of course you can!" Lucifer shouted. "I am the Devil! You will do as I say!"

I shook my head. "If I give this back to you, the Godless will stay underground until they are ready to strike again. There are more weapons in Hell that might kill the Devil than this dagger, and I may not be able to protect you from another attack. I have to lure your conspirators out of hiding so that I may stomp them out, and to do that, I'm going to need this dagger."

"It's a dangerous game you are playing," Lucifer grumbled. "But I cannot fault your logic."

"This is Hell, my lord. Everything is dangerous here."

# CHAPTER 13

I couldn't leave Lucifer alone while I tried to lure out the Godless from their hiding place. Then again, I couldn't trust just anybody with his protection detail either, which was why I called the only three people who never let me down: Ylfingur, his son Bjarngimur, and my brother Rasmus. They came when called and without question, at my behest.

"I don't need protection," Lucifer said, taking a seat on his throne of skulls. Bjarngimur, Ylfingur, and Rasmus knelt in front of him, their heads bowed low.

"Yes, you do," I said. "There's a group of murderers out to kill you, and they have the means to do it now."

"No." Lucifer pointed at the Dagger of Obsolescence clutched in my hands. "You have the means to do it. You're holding the only weapon that can kill me in your tiny hands."

"That's not true," I replied. "There are four more weapons that can kill you, and if we don't stop the Godless now, then they'll keep coming back. If they can get their hands on one weapon, then they can get their hands on the others, too."

"And we can deal with them when they do," Lucifer sneered. "Assuming that situation ever presents itself."

"Don't be stubborn, my friend. These are the bravest and most noble souls I have ever known. They will protect you with their lives."

Lucifer grumbled to himself. "Bravery and nobility mean little in the pits of Hell."

"Trust me," I replied. "I'll ferret out the Godless and make them pay for their crimes against you. Then, I will return swiftly. Meanwhile, my noble friends will protect you."

Lucifer looked up at me. "Don't let that dagger out of your sight."

"I won't." I stepped down the skull steps and toward my brother Rasmus. "Stand up, brother. You don't need to bow to me."

Rasmus pushed himself off the ground. "I know, but when in Rome, you know."

I grabbed him and hugged him tightly. "I'm sorry for dragging you away from your family. I will make it up to you."

Rasmus squeezed me. "You have nothing to apologize for, sister."

I let go of him and walked over to Ylfingur. "Where will you take the dagger?"

"I'm sorry, Ylfingur," I said. "It is not that I don't trust you or your judgment, but I believe it's better if I leave that a secret for now. When the time is right, I will tell you everything."

"You could hide it in the dungeon of this castle or throw it into the lake of fire, and nobody would ever be able to find it. Why take it away from here?"

"If I leave it here, then justice would not be done. The usurpers must be dealt with, Ylfingur, or they will come again. An example must be made."

"Perhaps you should let sleeping dogs lie," Bjarngimur said, walking over to us. "The Godless have failed, clearly."

"And now they will pay," I told him.

"As you wish," Ylfingur replied. "Rasmus, Bjarngimur! Take your positions."

I walked down the hallway away from Lucifer. I pitied him, having to rely on me for protection. Velaska had an army a thousand strong which fought for her, and Lucifer only had me. I squeezed the dagger tightly. I could not let him down.

*

After Charon dropped me off past the lake of fire, I flew to Aziolith's cavern. "Aziolith!" I shouted.

"Mmmmm," the dragon replied, his fire lighting the darkness. "The pixie, back again. Have you brought that which I have coveted for so long?"

"I have," I said, nodding. "But first, answer me this, do you wish to kill the Devil?"

Aziolith laughed. "If I wanted to kill the Devil, I would have done so already."

I took a step toward him. "And you swear that you have nothing to do with the Godless?"

"I swear on my oath as a dragon."

My eyes narrowed. "And the blood of your forebearers?"

"I swear on it, yes!" Aziolith hissed. "Why are you asking so many questions? I will not be accosted in my own home!"

I held up the dagger toward him. "I have brought it, then, for you to see."

Aziolith's head moved into the light of the bonfire crackling across the cave, and a smile spread across his broad face. "It is truly breathtaking. Give it to me!"

I pulled the dagger away. "That was not the deal."

"What? Of course, it was!"

"No," I replied. "I promised to bring it to you. I did not promise to leave it with you."

The earth quaked as Aziolith rose to his feet. "You dare play games with me, child! Give it here, or I will show you why every demon in Hell trembles at my presence!"

"Calm down!" I warned him. "I offer you a trade. A true trade."

Aziolith scoffed. "I would never trade with a deceiver such as yourself, not after what you have done."

"I offer it anyway. I will leave this dagger with you if you help me bring down the Godless."

"That is unfair and manipulative," Aziolith said, easing himself back down to the ground. "I thought better of you, Akta. Where is your honor?"

"I serve a higher purpose than my own honor, my friend. Saving the Morningstar is where my honor lies for the time being."

He shook his head. "I have no interest in the Morningstar. My interest lies with being left alone and escaping this infernal place."

His confession surprised me. "You wish to leave Hell?" I asked, confused.

"Of course, I wish to leave Hell. Don't you? I want nothing to do with this place. I long to return to the world of the living."

"I thought all dragons loved Hell."

"Nothing is absolute, my dear pixie. Most dragons would have burned you alive for your treachery by now. And yet, here you stand, unscathed."

"Does that mean you accept my offer?" I asked hopefully.

"It does," Aziolith grumbled. "What do you have in mind to catch the Godless heathens?"

"We're going to lay a trap."

"Hmmm," he replied. "Interesting."

"For this to work, I need to have faith that you will not break your vow and use this Dagger of Obsolescence against the Morningstar, nor will you allow any others to move on him."

"Why do you care for him so?" Aziolith asked.

I lowered my head. "He is my friend."

"Well, you and I are not friends, pixie, but you have something I want, and I am willing to play your game to receive it. If you need assurances, then I will give them to you. Hold out your arm."

"Why?" I asked.

"Trust me," the dragon growled.

I did as he asked and held out my arm. His hot breath fell upon me until it singed my flesh.

"Do not move," he said. "It is very important that you stand still."

Aziolith curled up his nose and spat a sharp line of fire from his mouth. The fire burned for a moment on my skin, but it did little more than sting my flesh. When he was done, a pentagram was burned into my arm.

"With this symbol, I vow to never use the dagger against the Devil, nor will I allow any others to do so. With this, we are bound together by our oaths to each other."

As he spoke the words, the burn marks receded from my arm until I could no longer see them. I rubbed my arm, and it was smooth to the touch.

"Thank you," I said to him.

"Do not thank me," Aziolith replied. "I still dislike you, but on this matter, we are aligned and bound for all time."

*

After leaving the dagger with Aziolith, my next stop was the central precinct to meet with B'rahg. Charlie and I had told him to get protection at the constable station, and, luckily, he listened to us. When I found him, he was sitting in a dark cell, shivering against the ground, as he stared up at the cracks in the ceiling.

"You look cold," I said when I walked up to him. "Quite cold, in fact."

"What do you want?" B'rahg snapped. "I have nothing to say to you."

"I need you to get a message to Charlie."

"That's nice, but I'm a little tied up at the moment."

I pulled the coin purse off my belt. "Five hundred Loo, if you do exactly as I say."

"It won't be worth it if I'm dead."

"So, you want to rot in this cell for the rest of your life? Cuz those are your options as I see them."

B'rahg thought for a moment. "If you want me to trust you, it'll cost ten times that. Five thousand Loo."

"One thousand."

"Four thousand."

"Two fifty. I'm being more than generous."

"Fine!" B'rahg said. "What do you want me to tell him?"

"Tell him that the assassination of Lucifer was a failure, that I took the Dagger, and that I've hidden it in Aziolith's cave. Do not tell him I fed you this information, or I will slit your throat, understand?"

"Yeah," he replied. "I got it."

I pulled a lockpick from my belt and fiddled with the lock. "Make sure he knows that Aziolith is gone from his cave, and it's completely empty, so he has to go now before the dragon returns, okay?"

"All right!" B'rahg replied.

The lock clicked, and the gate fell open. "If Charlie catches wind that I had something to do with this, I will take my money back out of your hide. I've learned many tricks in the pits of Hell, so don't test me."

B'rahg gulped. "Got it."

I placed my money purse in B'rahg's hands. "Do not fail me, or I will find you and dismember your body one bone at a time."

I turned and walked away. With any luck, Charlie would come to the cave with as many of the Godless scum he could muster to take down a dragon, and we would be ready for him.

*

The trap was set, and I returned to Aziolith's cave. Now, all we could do was wait for the conspirator to come to us. Charlie was careful and wouldn't want to show his face if he could avoid it, but I hoped that recovering the Dagger would be too much temptation for him to resist.

"Do you ever get tired of it?" Aziolith asked as he waited in front of the bonfire at the center of his cave. "Working for the Devil?"

"All the time," I replied, digging the Dagger of Obsolescence into the ground below me. "You know, I used to live in Valhalla."

"Yes, I've heard," Aziolith said. "How was it?"

"It was nice. Not a lot of action, though. Hell is all action all the time."

"Yes, and there is an odor in the air. Sulfur. I don't like it. I always preferred the crisp smell of the dewy mountain air."

"You would love Valhalla, then."

"It sounds nice and peaceful. My whole life has been a quest to find peace. This cave is the best I've done for myself up until now, but it can only offer so much sanctuary from the demons and monsters."

"What would you do if you found a way to leave Hell?" I asked him.

"Oh, I will find a way. It is only a matter of time."

"What makes you so confident?"

"There are many ways for me to leave Hell," Aziolith said. "It's just…most of them rely on other people to summon me. Rest assured, when the moment comes, I will be ready to vacate this place."

"And I will be there to stop you."

"Yes, you always were one to follow the rules."

"What is society without rules?"

"I suppose you have a point," Aziolith said, smirking. "I never much cared for society, though, so I'm happy to burn it all down."

I grinned. "You always were good at that."

"You made a joke, pixie," Aziolith said. "That was quite funny. Quite funny indeed."

From out of nowhere, Charlie appeared in front of us. Six of his demon minions followed behind him. They were new; I didn't recognize any of them. I hoped that meant the others, the ones I'd met, were rotting in the tenth pit of Hell.

"Find the dagger before the dragon gets—" Charlie looked up to see Aziolith breathing fire down upon him. "Oh, crap!"

"Charlie," I said with a smile. "It's been too long."

# CHAPTER 14

The demons surrounding Charlie were ready to attack, but we were prepared for them. Before they arrived, Aziolith and I had spent hours coming up with a plan to destroy them. First, Aziolith shot blue fire out of his nose, which surrounded the demons completely.

"Fire?" Charlie chuckled. "Do you really think fire will stop a demon?"

"No!" I replied, holding up the Dagger of Obsolescence. "I think this will."

"The dagger!" Charlie shouted, pointing at me. "Get it!"

Two demons jumped through the fire toward me, and I flew into the air to get some distance on them. The last time I used the dagger against a demon, it vanished with a single blow. I hoped I could vanquish these demons just as easily. If not, I would be torn apart before long.

One of the demons swung his ax at me, and I flew out of the way to dodge it, winding up with both arms and lodging the dagger into his skull. He was obliterated instantly, and I spun around to dig the dagger into the other demon's neck.

As the second demon broke into a million pieces, the remaining four demons jumped through the fire and ran toward me. I had never beaten a demon in battle before, but with the dagger, I could do so with ease.

I stabbed one of the demons in the stomach, and another in the side. They both exploded on impact, and the red fire from their ashes fell into the hilt of the dagger. The third demon swung her sword but missed. I rolled through her legs, digging the knife into her back when I rose up again. As the final demon charged me, I pulled back my arm and unleashed the dagger. It spun through the air and lodged into the demon's eye.

All around me, the ashes of defeated demons floated through the air. The dagger's hilt sucked the fire from the remaining demons before falling quiet. Behind me, in the center of the blue flame, Charlie snapped his fingers, trying to escape.

"Confused?" I said, floating into the air and landing in the center of the fire.

"Why won't it work!?" he bellowed.

I grabbed Charlie by the shoulders and lifted him into the air with one hand. With the other, I pressed the dagger against his ear.

"Aziolith made this fire special just for you. No creatures of Hell can teleport while they remain inside of it."

"That…that's impossible."

"And yet here we are," Aziolith said with a smile.

"Nothing is impossible, Charlie. You should know that, having been in Hell for so long." I pressed the dagger deeper into his cheek. "Now tell me, who is the leader of the Godless?"

He squirmed under the blade. "I don't know!"

"Soon, I will draw blood, and when I do, you will evaporate into a memory. Tell me who the leader is!"

"I can't!"

"Then you will die!" I yelled.

"FINE!" Charlie shouted, leaky tears of black tar spouting from his eyes. "Fine, I will tell you."

"Do it quickly, imp," I said. "I'm tired of this game!"

"It's…Ylfingur. He…he and his son…they lead the Godless."

"LIES!" I howled. "You will die for your deceit!"

"I ain't lying!" Charlie shouted. "It's true! It's all true! They've hated Hell from the first moment they got here. They especially hate the Devil. They worked against Velaska and went to war with Lucifer. You remember, right? They marched on Mount Olympus with him."

"I remember," I said.

"They were there on the Elysian Field. They were there that day when Lucifer begged for his life when he abandoned everything he stood for, when he abandoned them. Ylfingur and Bjarngimur never got over it. Never. You gotta believe it. It's them. I swear it's them."

I had to admit that Charlie's logic made sense. I didn't want it to make sense, but it did all the same. Ylfingur was always vocal about how much he hated Hell, even though he worked to maintain the status quo. He never liked his job as constable, and his son didn't like it either.

I shuddered. When I talked with him about the dagger, back at Lucifer's palace, he asked me to leave it with him. No. It couldn't be Ylfingur. I trusted him. I believed in him. I…left Lucifer in his care.

"I have to go!" I shouted to Aziolith, pointing a Charlie. "Do not let him leave!"

The dragon called after me. "What about the dagger?"

"You will get it when every member of the Godless is found and not a moment before!"

*

I flew as fast as I could across the barren wasteland of Hell and through the thick smoke pluming from the Brambles of Agony. I didn't have time for fear, or bad thoughts, which the Nothing would feed on. I sped through the purple door without slowing down. I kept my mind focused on the pinprick of light as I sped through the black void of the Nothings. In moments, I was engulfed by the light and appeared in the Devil's unkempt grotto.

"Lucifer!" I shouted. "Lucifer, can you hear me?"

I yelled, but there was no answer. I couldn't wait for him to respond. I bolted through the grotto and ripped open the door to the Devil's private dungeons. I flew down into the dungeon and passed the moans of the prisoners. I wondered for a moment if my adopted brother Odgeir still resided as a personal prisoner of the Devil, but I had no time to check on him. There would be time for that later if I was successful in my mission.

At the end of the dungeons was a set of stone stairs, winding up through one of the great towers. Finally, the stairwell let out at a long hallway, lined on either side with paintings of the great Devils of old.

I pushed on still, through the kitchen and the dining room until I'd reached the throne room. I slowed myself when I heard Ylfingur's voice.

"Did you really think you could abandon us all and not suffer the consequences?" he said. "We believed in you!" A punch landed on the Devil's cheek, and its echo reverberated through the hallway. I pushed open a door to the throne room and watched as Lucifer fell to the ground, his hands and mouth bound. Ylfingur was still yelling. "We trusted you! We would have died for you!"

"Enough!" I shouted, stomping through the door. In front of me, Ylfingur and Bjarngimur stood over Lucifer. Rasmus laid in the corner, unconscious. "Brother!" I called to him.

"He's fine!" Bjarngimur spat, pointing his great, spiked club at me. "He refused to join us."

"Thank the gods," I said.  I would not need to fight my brother this day, and he wasn't dead.

"The gods have nothing to do with us!" Ylfingur said. "And we have no use for them. I hoped to spare you this moment, Akta of the Forest, but you have forced our hand and discovered our true purpose."

"Let him go," I said, squeezing the Dagger of Obsolescence. "And I'll talk to him about sparing your life."

"Talk to him?" Ylfingur said. "This is the prince of all lies! There will be no redemption for him today."

"But there can be for you," Bjarngimur said. "Give us the dagger, join us, and live in a world free from the tyranny of the gods."

I gripped the dagger in my hand. "I think not. Lucifer may not be a perfect Devil, but he has done nothing to deserve death."

"And what have we done to deserve eternal servitude? He has done EVERYTHING to deserve death by working with the gods!" Ylfingur screamed. "We do not need them! Now, give the dagger!"

"If you want my dagger," I said, holding it up. "You can come claim it. In battle."

Bjarngimur looked at his father with his single, giant eye narrowed tightly in anger. With a nod from Ylfingur, he charged at me. I flew upward, stowing the dagger in my belt.

I pulled my bow off my back and fired three arrows into Bjarngimur's shoulder.

"Drop your weapon and yield!" I shouted. "No more blood needs be spilled today."

"If you are not with us, then your blood deserves to stain this ground as much as his," Bjarngimur growled, pulling the arrows out of his arm.

He charged again, and I let loose three more arrows into his chest, but they didn't slow him down. Bjarngimur swung his club, and I rolled to avoid it.

"I will not tell you again to stand down!"

Bjarngimur ran forward, one last charge. I could not avoid it anymore. I drew the Dagger of Obsolescence and slashed Bjarngimur across the eye with it. He didn't even have time to look back at his father before he fell apart in a puff of smoke and ash.

"Bjarngimur!" Ylfingur screamed, pulling a sword from his back and turning to me. "You will pay for that, pixie!"

"You have already lost a son today," I said. "Do not lose your own life as well."

"I will not live under an oppressive king for one more day. I fought for my freedom once, under your brother, and I will do so again, for as long as I am able."

Ylfingur charged, and I twirled away from his sword strike. He was strong and fast, but he was out of practice. His sword swings were wild and bold, and he left himself open for a quick counterattack.

"Don't make me do this," I said to him softly.

"I would rather die than serve." He spoke slowly, annunciating each syllable.

Pain seared my heart, but I knew what I had to do. Ylfingur rushed at me again. He raised his sword over his head, and I plunged my dagger into his eye. Tears ran down my face as Ylfingur fell to the floor and broke apart. His ashes floated through the air and combined with those of his son.

I dropped the dagger to the ground and ran over to Lucifer. I pulled the rag from around his mouth and unbound his hands. "Are you all right?"

"Fine," he said, rubbing his wrists. "I suppose I needed your help, after all."

"Don't give me too much credit. I'm the reason you're in this mess."

"Also true," Lucifer said, pushing up from the ground with a groan. He ambled over and picked up the dagger. He studied it a moment before speaking. "So much effort over so little a thing."

I nodded. "I will need it back. It is meant as a gift for Aziolith for all his help in saving you."

Lucifer gave me a blank look. "I cannot give it to you, little one."

"What do you mean? I made a promise."

"You should not have done so," Lucifer said, shaking his head. "You should never have offered what is not yours to give. The dagger is mine, and I will not yield it. I will stow it away where it will never be seen again."

"You will not be able to protect it forever. More will come. You have to trust me."

Lucifer looked down at the dagger. "I'm sorry, but I cannot part with it."

"I gave him my word," I said.

"You gave something you had no right to, and that is a burden you must carry."

"He will come for it," I said.

"And if he does, I will deal with him then."

I stepped forward and spoke through gritted teeth. "Don't make me regret killing my friends for you, Lucifer."

The Devil smiled. "Actually, I prefer 'my liege', come to think about it. You were right. Some formality is necessary in our relationship."

I growled at him. I should have expected nothing less from him. After all, he was the king of all lies.

"If you deny my request after I saved your life," I said, "I want nothing to do with you."

"You are in service to your lord until you are unbound," he replied with a smirk. "I will call on you at my leisure and you will jump when I call."

"There are other weapons which can kill you."

"And I will find them, too. I tire of this. Leave this place."

"You're making a big mistake."

"As Devil, it is mine to make."

Rasmus roused in the corner of the room, and I looked back at him. "Rasmus!"

"Go care for your brother," Lucifer replied. "You will get nowhere with me."

I ran over to Rasmus and placed my arm on his shoulder. "Take it easy, brother. You've had quite the day."

Rasmus rose to his feet, still woozy. "Where are Ylfingur and Bjarngimur?"

I looked over at Lucifer, who was standing there smiling and cocky, then back to Rasmus. "They are gone, my brother. Let's get you home, and I will tell you everything."

"Yes, Akta of the Forest. Go home and rest," Lucifer touched the tip of his blade. "You will be needed soon enough."

I could only glare at him. Centuries before, I had bound myself to the Devil. While I sometimes doubted my choice, I never doubted myself. I never wavered that I fought for justice, truth, and nobility. Now, I wasn't sure any of that was true. Not anymore.

I did not know what was going to happen, but I knew that I would not like it. Lucifer would see to that.

*

I tied my unicorn Winter to a large log at the base of the dragon cliffs in the far reaches of Hell and made my way up to Aziolith's cavern. My heart was heavy with the events of the last days, but I prided myself on being bound by honor, and Aziolith deserved the truth.

When I reached the ledge of his cliff, I saw the blue flame still encircling Charlie. Aziolith's face was lit with the soft glow.

"Akta," Aziolith said. "You have been away for a long time. I almost thought you were not going to honor our pact."

"She's not!" Charlie shouted from inside the blue flame. "Look at her. She can't even bear the thought of it. Oh man, this is good. This is real good."

"Quiet, imp!" Aziolith screamed before turning his attention back to me. "Is this true, pixie? Have you deceived me?"

I sighed deeply. "Not on purpose. I had every intention of giving you the dagger. The Devil refused to part with it. He told me it was not mine to give. I'm sorry."

The blue flame fell from around Charlie, and immediately he snapped himself away, vanishing from the cave as fast as he had come. I hoped I would never see him again, but I had the feeling our paths would cross again eventually.

"Leave this place," Aziolith said. "If I see you again, I will kill you."

"Aziolith, please listen to—"

"NO!" Aziolith shouted. "I have listened long enough. You have chosen your side, pixie, and I have seen your truth. Never bother me again, or you shall regret it."

I didn't say another word. He had every right to be angry at me. I was, too. I had always prided myself on being an honorable person, and now I questioned that with my every waking thought.

*

"That is a very troubling story," Gabriel said from atop the hill where we met. "I am glad you have protected the Morningstar, but part of me wonders if it would have been better to let him die."

I nodded. "It is my duty to protect him and any who carry the title Devil for as long as I serve them."

"Yes," Gabriel said. "I suppose it is. I will relay this information to Bacchus."

"And," I said with a sense of finality, "tell my mother I love her."

"Yes," Gabriel said with a smile. "About that. I have made special arrangements and…how about you tell her yourself?"

Out of the darkness, another image materialized. A dark-skinned woman with sharp, pointed ears smiled at me.

"Hello, sweetheart," my mother said.

The tears came immediately. I reached my hand to touch her, but there was nothing but air. My mother was as much a figment of the dancing lights as Gabriel. Still, I saw her, and I heard her. She was more real than she had been in three hundred years.

"Hi, Mom," I muttered through my tears. "It's good to see you."

"It's good to be seen, my love."

I stared up at her, and she stared back at me. I knew things were not going to be okay, not for a long time. There were more battles to fight. But at that moment, I felt the warmth of the heavens rain down on me; everything else washed away, and nothing else mattered. And I was happy. Even if just for a moment.

"I'm so proud of you," my mom said to me. "I want you to know how proud of you I am."

"I feel like I failed you," I replied.

She shook her head. "You did what you thought was right. I admire that about you. No matter what, you always stand up for what's right. I wish I had done more of that in my life. I often wonder if what I did made a difference, even now."

"It did."

"How do you know?"

"I found Rasmus, Mom," I said after a long silence. "He's down here with me."

My mother cupped her hands to her mouth. Tears streamed down her face. "And is he…"

I nodded. "He's fine. He married and had children, and those children had children. And they will have children, and those children will have their own children."

She pulled her hands from her face. "Then our line continues."

I nodded. "It does. We are a resilient people. Somehow, it will live on, in some way, far into the future."

"And will you protect them, too?" my mother asked.

"As long as I am able, in every way I can."

"Then, perhaps, in a strange way, this has all worked out for the best."

"I wouldn't go that far." I gave a wry smile. "However, I will strive to make the best of a bad situation."

"One day, we will be together again," Mom replied. "I love you very much."

"Until that day, I will do everything I can to make you proud."

"You already do, every day."

I wanted to reach out and hug her, but I couldn't. We were stuck, worlds apart, and yet, somehow, I felt closer to my mother than I ever had before.

*

If you loved this, check out *Ruin,* which features Julia Freeman, a descendent of Akta's, as she tries to navigate her life as a fairy starting in the 1970s.

Akta plays a big role in *Ruin,* and I'll hope you check it out. The book is three stories in one, following Julia and Akta through *Mystery Spot, Into Hell,* and *Last Stand.*

*

Now, here is a preview of *Ruin.*

# RUIN

*Book 8 of The Godsverse Chronicles*

By:
Russell Nohelty

Edited by:
Leah Lederman

Proofread by:
Katrina Roets & Toni Cox

Cover by:
Paramita Bhattacharjee

Planet chart and timeline design by:
Andrea Rosales

# CHAPTER 1

"I don't gotta do nothing no colored woman tells me to do," Duncan Lewis sneered at me. I planted my feet and gritted my teeth, trying desperately not to march over to his desk and scratch out his eyeballs.

The classroom "oohed" and "ahhed" as their eyes ping-ponged back and forth from the hulking brood at the other side of the room from me, the perturbed, black teacher standing at the front of it. Duncan was a behemoth of a man in a boy's body. He stood six foot three with buzzed, blond hair and bloodshot, brown eyes. His thick forearms folded across his chest, which swelled with pride at his racist statement.

"I'm not going to tell you again, Mr. Lewis," I said, trying my best to project authority when I had clearly lost any that I might have had. "Go to the principal."

"Make me, Ms. Freeman," he replied.

Any shred of respect the students held for me had dissolved five minutes ago when Duncan hurled a spitball into my long, straight, bleached white hair. It stuck in like glue, leading the whole room to burst into laughter. Still, I didn't back down. "I'm waiting," I said, glaring.

"I can see that, Julia," he replied, stoic. "You'll be waiting 'til the cows come home."

I fought the urge to leap across the desk and toss him through the window that backlit his broad shoulders. The way he sneered my first name like he knew me. I wanted desperately to fight, but that wasn't how I was taught. My mama taught me to capitulate to white folks because they will string up uppity negros as a lesson to others. I knew that truth all too well.

I combed my fingers through my hair one more time to pull out any spit left on it. My hair didn't used to be straight and bleached. I used to have a big, beautiful afro that would turn Pam Greer green with envy.

But that was back in Chicago. Back when I was in school before I moved home to take care of my mama in Chandler, Colorado. In this town, black folk lived on the other side of the tracks, where they wouldn't offend the sensibilities of good, Christian, white folk.

I dared to step across that track and apply for a job at the school all the white kids attended. Sure, segregation had been over for some years by 1974, but it's not like black folk could just move across town on a moment's notice, especially not to a house that cost double what they could afford, so they just stayed put and kept going to the same school just like they always had.

There wasn't really a black school and a white school anymore, not legally, but things hadn't changed so much since the 50s around here—no matter what the courts said.

The principal gave me a job teaching history, somehow, but nobody was happy about it. They called it affirmative action, and they called me a "token," but here at George Washington High, the pay was a lot better than across the tracks at William Howard Taft High, and I deserved that money. I worked hard for six years to get a Master's in history, but to get that money, I had to capitulate to make the white folks happy.

That meant I couldn't keep my afro. Now, my hair was "appropriate" for school and appropriate for Chandler; but that didn't matter. I still didn't get any respect.

"You are ruining your peers' education," I said.

"No more than you," Duncan replied to a room of chuckles. "I ain't the one tainting the classroom with my colored ideas."

I didn't know what to do. I couldn't back down, and I certainly couldn't take him on myself. I'd tried calling security into my classroom a dozen times before, and they were about as helpful as Duncan. Nobody wanted me here except for me.

It got deadly quiet in the classroom as we stared each other down. The air left the room, replaced with swirling eddies of tension.

Thankfully, the bell rang, breaking the spell. The students groaned under their breath as they collected their things. They wanted a fight. They might still get one, but not today. There would be plenty of time for fighting in the future, though. Tensions don't just fade away in Chandler; they built under the surface until something snapped.

"Alright, class," I said with a smile. "Since this distraction didn't give us any time to study, we'll have our quiz on chapters seven and eight next time without any preparation. Please study these chapters."

The class groaned again as they walked out of the classroom. They all wanted to be Duncan at that moment and stand up to me, but the truth is that Duncan was pathetic. He was the star football player, and he was dumb as a rock. Teachers passed him because he could hit people well and catch a ball. He would get to college on a scholarship if he managed not to blow out his knee, but eventually, he'd be back here working in a gas station, dreaming of his glory days for the rest of his life. Then again, I ended up back here too, so what does that say about me?

Duncan strolled up to the front of the room and cracked his knuckles on my desk. "I think I'm just gonna take the A and skip that test, Julia."

I laughed, looking him straight in the eye. "You don't have to come to class, but you will get an F."

"You don't know how this works, still, do you? You're the token hire, the joke. Nobody wants you here."

I leaned over the table. "Then we have something in common. Neither of us wants the other one here."

The loudspeaker creaked and crackled as it screeched through the room. "Ms. Freeman, please report to the principal's office."

Duncan pointed to the loudspeaker. "See?"

He strolled out as if he owned the place. He did, of course. In Chandler, he mattered more than me. That fact stung every day, but my mother beat it into my head enough. At least if you know the system, you can work around it.

*

"I don't know what to tell you, Julia," Principal Anderson said, shaking his shiny, bald head. His jowls slapped the sides of his face as he stammered. "The parents have complained, again."

It wasn't Principal Anderson's fault that the parents complained, but I couldn't help resenting him for it. "What is it this time? Way I chew my gum? Way I say hello? What could they possibly have to complain about now?"

Principal Anderson cleared his jowly throat. "Well, it's that hair, Miss Freeman. They…don't think it's appropriate."

I scoffed involuntarily. "I only have this hair because they told me they didn't like the cornrows, and I only had them because they didn't like the afro. I wake up at four am to straighten this goddamn hair."

I could tell my terse tone, and the fire in my eyes frightened him. That sort of thing, well…it scared white people, especially weak ones like Principal Anderson. They thought I was a wild animal, ready to strike at any time. Even the smallest hint of a temper sent them running for the door. Something about black people getting angry put white people on edge, even though they have all the power. Maybe it's because they have all the power, and they're worried we're gonna steal it back.

Principal Anderson scooted back in his chair, away from me. "I-I-I—"

"Speak up, Bob." I spat the words.

I had no patience for this back and forth. In the three months I'd been teaching, Principal Anderson and I had already held seven meetings about my appearance. Still, I wasn't supposed to be rude.

My mama taught me that—how to hold my tongue even when there was some nonsense taking place. She taught me to behave, to smile, to never raise my voice, and I didn't, for eighteen years. It's what got me out of this town alive when so many didn't, but after going to Chicago, and seeing a place where black people got along just fine, weren't looked at side-eyed when they walked into a restaurant and could puff out their chest with pride without fear of getting beaten, at least in the right neighborhoods, it was hard to act like a meek, obedient child again.

"I don't know what to tell you, Julia," Principal Anderson finally managed to say. "They don't like it. They think it should be shorter, more professional. They also have a problem with…"

His eyes tipped down to my clothes, a tasteful pantsuit that couldn't help but accentuate my curves. The parent-teacher association had a problem with me wearing slacks and a collared shirt now. Those bitties would say anything to get me fired.

"I am a curvy woman, Bob. I can't hide that."

Principal Anderson sighed. "The mothers would like it if you dressed more…matronly."

"I'm twenty-five years old. How matronly can you look at twenty-five? Do you want me to gain fifty pounds to keep this job? Cuz I'll do it, Bob. I'll do it."

He chuckled uncomfortably. "It wouldn't be the worst thing in the world."

I lowered my voice and dropped my eyes. "I need this job, Bob."

"I know, Julia. That's why I gave it to you. You're a damned good teacher, and your credentials are stellar. I want to keep you around, but it's only been three months, and you've gotten twenty complaints—"

"None of which are for my teaching."

Principal Anderson shook his head, disappointed. "And now I hear students are harassing you, too."

I took a deep breath and let it out slowly. "I'm losing their respect."

Principal Anderson placed his hand gently on the edge of the desk, expecting me to take it. "Don't take this the wrong way, Julia, but you never had it."

I was supposed to act like a meek teacher and tell him he was right, but I just couldn't. "It's always hard for all new teachers. I'm working on it, Bob. I'm getting through to some of them."

"Not enough, though, Julia. Not nearly enough."

I looked him in the eyes. "Are you firing me, Bob? Tell me straight."

He shook his head. "Of course not. Not yet, at least. I'm just saying you might be more comfortable at the…other school."

"You mean the black school across the tracks, right?" I said, pointing out the window behind him. "The one I came up through. The one no respectable white kid would attend even after everything that's happened in the last twenty years?"

Principal Anderson nodded, timidly. "There are a lot of good teachers over there."

"Then why ain't they over here, too?"

"Because they like it there," Principal Anderson said, smiling. "They're happy. They're respected. There is nothing wrong with that school, just because you say it's a black school."

"I didn't say there was anything wrong with it," I shouted. "That's not the point. Point is that I applied here, and I got hired here, not over there, and I should be able to work where I want as long as I'm doing my job right."

"I agree, but…that's just not how it is, and you know it. How are you going to feel when these kids get a lesser education, not because of anything you did, but because the other students don't respect you?"

I looked down at the ground. I couldn't deny that giving the children the best education was my top priority. "I would feel terrible."

"And how are you gonna feel when those really smart ones start to talk about you behind your back because you're a distraction to their education?"

"I'm gonna feel really bad about it," I replied. I could see him baiting me. Damn it, this wasn't on me. Not this time. "But how are you gonna feel, Bob, when I leave this school because those women wouldn't let me do my job? How will it feel when you let a bunch of old, white women convince you to fire a good teacher just because she's black? Are you gonna be able to look at yourself in the mirror and be okay with that?"

"I can look in the mirror fine, Julia. Just fine. My duty is to the students and make sure they get the best education possible. That is why I hired you because I thought you could provide that to them."

I stood up, seething. "I know why you hired me, Bob. We all know why you hired me. Thing is, I have more education than most of the teachers in this place. I got a Master's in history, Bob. How many of your teachers have Master's degrees?"

"Not many…"

"And how many have that Master's degree from Northwestern, huh? How many have them from one of the best schools in the country?"

"Not many."

"Not one of them do. Not one of them but me. I'll bet I'm the most qualified first-year teacher you've ever hired, and I'm gonna be the most qualified one that you've ever fired, too."

"I hope that's not true."

I headed toward the door. "You can tell those old bitties I'll start to wear my hair in a ponytail, and I'll wrap myself in a sweater whenever I'm in school. I promise you that, and if they ever want to talk to me—well, my door's open. Funny thing, though, Bob, I haven't ever heard from one of 'em."

"They won't talk to you except through me."

"I know they won't, Bob, and look. I know what you've done for me, giving me a chance to come back here and be with my mother. I know it's not easy for you."

Principal Anderson nodded. "Every day, it's something else. I'm trying, Julia. I'm really trying."

"And I appreciate that, Bob. I do, but I'm a human being with a goddamn Master's degree from Northwestern. I'm nobody's fool. I understand this game, and next year I might be right back over across the tracks where I came from, but until they kick me out of here, I am not going anywhere."

"I understand." He cleared his throat. "Uh, Julia, could you do me a favor?"

I stopped in the doorframe. "If I can, Bob."

"Don't tell anybody else you talked to me the way you did today, okay?"

"I was raised here, Bob. I know what's expected of me. Consider me the perfectly behaved teacher outside this office."

# CHAPTER 2

They used to play this show, *Leave It to Beaver,* when I was growing up, and it reminded me of Chandler. From the outside, Chandler didn't seem so bad. Hell, from the outside, it looked downright cheery, just like every other sleepy, little hamlet across this country, complete with smiling, happy people, clean streets, and perfectly painted houses. They could have shot *Leave it to Beaver* right down the street from school, that's how wholesome it was here.

But that's just a veneer.

Funny thing was, you didn't see a lot of black folks in that show. I'd love to see how Wally and the Beave reacted to a black teacher. Something tells me Ward and June wouldn't like it much. They might even complain to the school about their precious child being taught by a colored woman. It was hard being black in Chandler now, but it was harder when I was growing up.

Hell, if you were a white kid in Chandler, Colorado, in the 1950s, things were hunky-dory for you. Things came up aces again and again. Your parents had work. They had a house. You had friends. You had some money. Your future looked bright as can be.

But that was just one side of the train tracks. There was another side to Chandler, a darker side, and I mean that quite literally. It was the side the good, old white people of Chandler didn't talk about or visit, and they didn't want us visiting them, either. It was the side where black folks like me lived.

*

By the time I stepped out of George Washington High School, it was dark out. The dead of winter's crisp wind nipped at my nose. The cold never bothered me, but I didn't like the night. The streetlights lit up the streets, but I didn't trust it. Bad things happened in Chandler at night.

I stood at the top of the steps looking out at the quaint square that made up downtown Chandler. Restaurants and shops lined the square, and at its center was the park that made us famous, Mystery Spot Park.

Mystery Spot Park wasn't like any other park I'd ever seen. It wasn't even like any other park in Chandler. This park, well, it had something special. Right there, in the middle of the park, was a giant hole that led to nowhere. You could throw a penny down into the hole, and it would never hit bottom.

Before I left Chandler, they fed a rope down into that hole ten miles and still never found where it ended. It was one of the great mysteries of eastern Colorado, and people came from miles around in the summer to play with it, to feel the weird electromagnetic energy that made your hair stand on end. On a hot summer day, there was a line twice around the block to get a peek. This was the dead of winter, though, and nobody came to Chandler in the winter. The spot was special, but not that special.

I walked down the steps of the school toward Mystery Spot Park, clacking my heels faster with every step. I loved it there. One of the only joys left in returning to Chandler was my nightly walk through the park when the cold air drove everybody away, and it was quiet and peaceful.

I couldn't explain it, but the mystery spot seemed to draw me toward it like it had a magnetic charge I couldn't control. Of course, most people thought that, which is why they came from far and wide to see it and waited all day to stare into the abyss. There was something magical about that hole. Of course, that was crazy because magic doesn't exist.

Electrical charges crackled sparks through my hair as I danced along the edge of the spot, just like I had done so often in my youth. I closed my eyes and spun as fast as I could, until every hair on my head stood straight up into the air and twisted together in a ponytail.

"Hey!" A man's voice shouted at me. "Quit spinnin'. It's not safe to spin so close to the—"

I turned around to come face to face with a familiar face, Chuck Dixon, father of one of my most well-behaved students and nighttime security guard for the park. "I'm sorry, Mr. Dixon. I'm just strolling on the breeze and lost track of time."

"Oh. Sorry, Ms. Freeman. I didn't recognize you in the dark." He tipped his cap to me. "How is everything tonight?"

He was a handsome man, so I gave him my most flirtatious smile. I always knew how to smile right. "It's going just fine, and how is our lovely park tonight?"

He nodded. "Lovely as ever, my dear."

If I didn't know any better, I would think he was flirting back. The creases on the sides of his mouth turned up on the edges and I was pretty sure he winked when he caught my eyes. Mr. Dixon's wife passed away some years ago, and, like my poor mother, he had to raise his child all on his own.

The neon sign above Charlotte's Diner crept into my periphery and I remembered I was late to meet my mother for dinner. "I should be going, Mr. Dixon. Mama will be waiting for me."

"It's a pleasure, ma'am, and please, call me Chuck."

I strolled away from him, letting his eyes linger on me for a long moment as I walked. "I don't think I'll be doing that, Mr. Dixon, but thank you for the courtesy."

I always did know how to play the game.

# CHAPTER 3

Mama never liked to eat at home. Home was a cold, dark place on the outskirts of town that she only visited when she needed to sleep. It used to be a warm, welcoming place with a down to Earth charm to it when I was growing up, even in the worst times. But since I'd left for school, it turned into a place I barely recognized. The furniture was the same, but the soul had gone from it.

Mama raised me by herself, which meant she hustled and bustled my whole life. When I was a kid, she ran a daycare out of our backyard. She kept her rates low since our neighbors couldn't afford much, which made her very popular. Our house was always full of kids, laughing and playing. Mama loved kids, but the daycare was about more than that. It was about survival, and in my neighborhood, you did what you had to do to get from the beginning of the month to the end of the month without going belly up.

It ran her ragged, though. To eke out a living, she had to take on a lot of kids, and the more kids she took on, the more help she needed, but that meant paying people, and she couldn't afford to do that without eating up every dollar she made. So, she ended up with too many kids and too little help, which made her entire life…challenging.

When I got up in age, I tried to help after school, but Mama wouldn't hear of it. She worked extra hard to make sure I could study and focus on school. She wanted to make sure I could leave if I wanted, even if she didn't think I'd ever want to go somewhere else.

She was wrong about that. I'd wanted to leave Chandler from the moment I exited the womb. What I never wanted to do was come back, but that's all that Mama wanted for me. Sometimes, I think she got old just to spite me.

When I got back to Chandler, things were different for Mama. She treated herself to the finer things since the house was paid off, and she got a social security check every month. It didn't hurt that I had a decent salary and could pay for a few of life's niceties which passed mama by in her younger days. I didn't mind spoiling her a bit, either. After all, she raised me. Back when I was a kid, we could never eat out. Money was always tight, like ketchup on bread tight—and stale bread at that, so we didn't leave the house much.

Eating out these days was more than just luxury, though. Nothing tickled Mama more than having dinner at a restaurant that had refused to serve her when she was young. She took great pride in sitting at a lunch counter in a place she once couldn't even step into without getting arrested and munching on food that white people said she couldn't have until the government forced them to treat her like a human being.

Her favorite place to eat was called Charlotte's Diner, right across from the mystery spot. For years, they'd had a sign on their window that said, "No Coloreds Allowed," but the government forced them to take it down. Mama liked to sit right by the window, where that sign had mocked her for so long, and stare out at the park, where every resident of Chandler could get a good look at her.

She would sit in that diner, sometimes all day, while I worked, just staring at that the mystery spot, which is exactly what she was doing when I entered the diner to the jingling of bells over the door. Mama never told me where she was going, but Chandler's a small town, and there weren't that many options.

"Mama!" I called to her from the entrance. She sat at a booth looking out the front window of the place through the big lettering that plastered CHARLOTTE'S on the front sign. Mama didn't look up as I sat down across from her.

"Didn't you hear me?" I asked.

Finally, she turned to me. Her wrinkled face cracked on its edges into a warm smile. "I heard you, but I was deep in thought. I'm glad you found me, even if you are late."

"Of course, I found you, Mama. You're always here."

She chuckled. "I'm not always here, my love. I'm just mostly here. And if I wasn't here, you would find me somewhere else. I do very much like that Chinese place around the corner, too."

A kindly, old woman named Martha came up to us. She was dressed in the powder blue waitress outfit common among all the wait staff, but she was different in her spirit. Martha was the only one who treated us like customers whose money was just as good as anybody else's and not a nuisance. It took me months to realize it, but she was the only person who would ever come to our table.

Everybody inside Charlotte's turned up their noses at us when we entered the place. Waitresses turned their backs and refused our calls for service. Patrons asked to move away from our table. Under their breath, of course, but there would suddenly be a chorus of shuffling tables and scampering feet whenever we sat down. Whenever I passed by the diner and Mama wasn't there, nobody ever sat in Mama's booth, as if we were contaminated with the plague.

Then, there was Martha, who smiled brightly at us just like we were any two other humans. "Good evening, Julia! What can I get for you?"

"Coke and a burger, please. Medium. You know how I like it." I returned her smile. Behind her, a couple scowled at me, but I didn't break my grin. You couldn't let them see you break, ever. "Mama, what do you want?"

"Oh, I already ordered."

Martha jotted my order down in her notebook. "Yes, she did. I'll have both your orders up right away."

She scooted away as the other patrons went about their business. Charlotte's wasn't a big place, and I could hear the animosity oozing from every table. Luckily, I got very good at drowning it out, though, and replacing it with idle chatter. Mama taught me that.

"How was your day?" she asked.

I just sighed. I opened my mouth to speak, but I just…couldn't get out the words. All I could do was grunt. Luckily, Mama knew exactly what that meant after hearing it every day since I came back.

"That bad, huh?" Mama asked in her most comforting voice.

"As bad as yesterday," I said, shaking my head. "Better than tomorrow, I'll bet."

"I told you I could put in a good word at Taft. Good people over there at Taft."

"No money over there at Taft, Mama," I said, exasperated.

"We don't need money, dear. We got the house free and clear."

"You still gotta eat." I gestured at the room. "This place ain't free."

She stared out to the park. The school loomed beyond the mystery spot. "I don't gotta eat here, my love, just like you don't gotta work there."

"Then why do you?" I asked.

"Same reason you do it, my love," she replied, knowingly.

I knew why I did it, and I knew why she did it, too. It was because we could, and because we could, we were compelled to do it. The rush was exhilarating, making everybody else in town uncomfortable, just like we made them uncomfortable when Dad went missing. It had been sixteen years since sheriffs found him hung from an oak tree in Mystery Spot Park.

"You know it's his birthday next week," Mama said.

"I know," I replied. "How did you know I was thinking about him?"

"Thinking about him all the time these days, aren't you?"

She was right. I thought about him often. I thought about him every time I passed by the park where he was snatched, and every time I stood under the tree where they hung him for the whole town to see for the high crime of being a loud, black man in a town full of quiet, black men.

"It's not his birthday, though, Mama. Birthdays are for people who are alive."

Mama nodded. "That's true, but he was still born then, my love. Nobody can take that away from him."

"No. They could just take away his life."

The whole diner stopped at that moment as if the needle on a record player skipped a beat. Waitresses stopped their deliveries as the patrons stared at us.

"Hush yourself," Mama said. "That's not polite. There's a line, baby."

She was right. My dad being lynched wasn't something you talked about in polite company, especially not during dinner.

It wasn't decent to talk about men stringing up your father. It wasn't proper to talk about how they watched his face turn purple as he struggled for breath or to discuss them cutting his throat and watching him bleed out. That wasn't proper conversation in Chandler.

The act wasn't decent, either, but talking about it was taboo. If you were black, you didn't talk about justice unless you wanted to wind up on a tree yourself, and when you can't talk about something, you can't convict somebody of it, either. Not that a white jury was going to convict good ole boys of killing a black man. So, we just had to move on and swallow our pain.

They didn't even talk about it on our side of the tracks. My dad's death sent a message to the whole community. *Shut your damned fool mouth.* They didn't just string him up, they cut his throat across the voice box to remind us not to say a word.

When I was growing up, there was a lynching like that just about every six months, for over a decade. Like clockwork. White folks needed to send a message every once in a while whenever we forgot our place. It could have been any other black man on any other day, but that day it was my father. It wasn't some other little girl who lost her daddy. It was me.

That kind of act, it built up a lot of resentment between black and white folks. Even though there hadn't been a lynching in ten years, the animosity never went away.

I looked out at the diner and saw a dozen hostile eyes staring back at me. There was no shame; they didn't even avert their gaze. Worse, they were disgusted that we weren't ashamed at interrupting their dinner with our insistence on existing. In that chorus of ugly, beady eyes, I lost my appetite.

"Can we go, Mama?" I asked.

"No. I'm hungry," she said, unaffected by their gaze. "And I'm gonna eat, damn it. You don't gotta eat, but don't go spoiling my appetite. You gonna keep spoiling my appetite?"

I shook my head. I knew the code. Shut your damn fool mouth. "No, Mama."

Martha smiled when she brought us our food, and the eyes of the other diners eventually turned away from me. The chatter of the diner drowned out my thoughts. Mama and I ate in silence, her staring out at the mystery spot and me staring at her, both watching with wonder.

*

If you liked that, make sure to pick up *Ruin* today.